IN THE SHADE

OF

THE TEMBUSU TREE

JOY GREEDY

First published by Zeus Publications 2005
http://www.zeus-publications.com
P.O. Box 2554
Burleigh M.D.C.
QLD. 4220
Australia.

ISBN: 1921005793

National Library of Australia Listing:
Greedy, J.
In The Shade Of The Tembusu Tree

Acknowledgments

My deepest thanks to:

All the staff at Zeus publications for giving a voice to new authors, especially Bruce, Sandra, Kathy and Leanne
To my family for their patience and unconditional love
Diane Ahern, friend, quality controller and emotional barometer
Lea Greenaway, fellow writer and friend, for her guidance, vision and patient line-by-line editing
Jay Mckee for his expert advice, encouragement and first-hand experience in guiding me through the publishing maze
Stu Lloyd fellow hard-posting survivor, for his love of long lunches and red wine and his expert and often light-hearted approach to the 'joys of publishing'
Jayne Norris, friend and mentor, for her talent, exquisite taste and creative advice
Graham Byfield, well-renowned English watercolourist, for his delicate rendering of the tropical colonial houses of Singapore
Kerry Archer, Archer Communications, neighbour and friend
Jennifer and Poh Hong for expert proofreading of Singlish phrases and emergency supplier of disks and paper
Evelyn for her advice on Tagalog phrases and Filipino food.

Dedication

To my wonderful family: Mark, Joshua, Candice and three x four
paws.

The Tembusu Tree

Also known as the Singapore five-dollar note tree, is native to Singapore. Tembusu trees are impressive in size, hardy and adaptable. The Tembusu flowers are creamy white and especially fragrant at sunset. They are very popular with the birds that feast twice a year on the trees' red berries.

Two magnificent specimens thrive in the Singapore Botanical Gardens. Children can be seen sitting and playing in the Tembusu trees' low branches and they form a favourite backdrop for wedding photographs.

Chapter One
Esmirada
Makati Cemetery: The Philippines 1973

Boboy Espinosa sucked in his breath as he glanced at the fingernail moon, half hidden by a clouded sky. He revved the noisy bike and looked back toward the iron railing of the mausoleum. Without lights, his journey would be perilous, over rutted dirt roads littered with potholes and *lubak*. It was four kilometres to the midwife's shack.

Olina had given birth alone, stoically without a sound, while her two small sons slept on a tattered mat on the marble floor. Boboy cut the cord with his *bolo* and applied ash to seal it. The infant, a girl, was small but cried lustily. Olina laboured intensely, but despite Boboy's ceremonial leaf burning, the afterbirth would not come.

He reached the road bordered by broad-leafed banana plants and thatch-roofed huts. Tala's louvered shutters were firmly closed. He prayed fervently as he approached the midwife's house that she would be there.

Tala and Boboy arrived back as the light was starting to filter through the palms, to find the gravesite eerily quiet. Olina hunkered in the corner like a frightened animal. Under the most primitive conditions, Tala crossed herself, said a prayer and delivered the placenta. She gave Olina a bitter mixture of herbs and oil as she chanted an incantation, and then took the infant into her arms, checking it carefully. She cleaned the umbilical cord with a tincture and gave the baby to her mother to nurse. Olina was too exhausted to speak. She took Tala's hand and kissed it as a sign of respect for the older woman. The family could only afford a paltry donation. Tala assured her that she did not expect payment, but she took the small amount gratefully.

As the sun sliced through the palms, Boboy placed crossed sticks at the baby's head, to avert any harm that may come to the child while he was away. He then left for his job as a cigarette street vendor. His spirits were

1

high as the rusty bike spluttered along the roadside. Old men in broken-down beach chairs, smoking and drinking *tuba,* shouted "Hoy" as he passed. He rode on, over corrugated dirt roads, the hot wind cooling the sweat on the back of his neck. On his way he passed nippa grass and rippling green paddies. He waved at the laughing brown-eyed children and squabbling women. He grinned, pleased with himself; today he would buy Olina some Pop Rice and a Royal Orange. Today she would not have to clean the graves.

◆◆◆◆◆◆

Esmirada Espinosa was afraid of many things, but she was not afraid of the dead. She was born under a statue of Saint Maria in a stone mausoleum in a municipal cemetery. Her mother Olina, like all Filipinos, was highly superstitious; it was the woman's duty to keep evil spirits away from the home. Olina had dreamt the night before her birth, of a small silk-lined casket. Boboy, her husband, knew the dream could not be ignored, and was not surprised when he had to summon the midwife. This story, and many more, of how the two had met and grew up in the macabre surroundings, was told often to Esmirada and her two brothers, Manny and Ricardo.

As a child Boboy had moved to the cemetery after a typhoon destroyed the family's fishing hut on the island of Samar. His father had irregular work, while his mother was a market vendor.

They lived for a while under bridges, near railways in houses made from cardboard and scraps of corrugated iron. Olina's family had moved a decade ago from the countryside.

Esmirada loved her cemetery home; it was peaceful and carefree. She, Ricardo and Manny ran barefoot and wild with scores of other children who lived in the many village cemeteries in the area. They did not go to school but spent their days digging for valuable garbage in the nearby tip, or fishing for bottle tops and tin cans in the sewer. Secretly they would sit with the old men watching the *pula puti* and hanging about in the shade of the tattered tent awning of the *sari sari.* They listened with wide eyes to the stories, squabbles, *tsimsis* and idle gossip of the women. They would sit beside the road, and watch the rusting sugar-cane trucks roar down the highway, spewing diesel in a hazy band of pollution.

As Manny and Ricardo grew older, Boboy would take them along to sell cigarettes in the streets and later in the hotels. The exposure to many hazards: drunkenness, street fighting, drug dealing and prostitution, ate away at him, but Boboy had few choices in his life. Esmirada helped her mother clean the graves and mausoleums for a few pesos, and in the evening she sat on the cool marble floor sorting through the rice, picking out bits of grit and small pebbles. They ate salted fish by coconut-oil lamp, sitting on top of the crypt before finally lying down next to the entombed to sleep. On Sundays the family would wake before sunrise, pack, clean, and leave their home before the relatives of the dead came to visit.

Each October, the small family banded together and left the cemetery until after All Saints Day in November. Esmirada hated that time of the year. They would go to stay with their *Tiyo* in Tondo, a slum on the outskirts of Manila. Buboy lived with his wife Rosa and three small sons in a squalid plywood shack surrounded by even smaller hovels. Her *Lola* and *Lolo* lived nearby in a hut built from tin, scraps of wood and cardboard. Esmirada despised the ripe stench of garbage that lay festering in the heat, picked over by the slum children and flea-bitten dogs. The noise of the slums disturbed her after the peace of her mausoleum. *Tiyo's* dwelling was one room with a flimsy wall dividing it from the next family. You could hear everything: the curses, abusive taunts, wailing, miserable children and the strange animal grunting from the men and women late at night. They had to sleep in relays because of lack of space. A black cloud of mosquitoes would rise from the filthy ditches, and every time it rained cockroaches, trying to escape the deluge, would invade her makeshift bed.

Her saviour during these visits was *Lola;* she loved her small dark grandmother with her wizened face and teeth blackened from too much *betelnut.* The door to *Lola's* house was only four foot high, causing her to bend and stoop each time she entered. *Lola* was industrious, inventing a myriad of ways to make a few pesos. Her eyes had started to fail, forcing her to give up her sewing. Her latest venture was making kerosene lamps for the barrio. When Esmirada came to visit, she would help her search for jars at the dump. It was her job to scrape the filth and labels off in a bucket of cold water with her fingernails. *Lola* painted the lids and made wire handles and wicks, working from dawn to dusk in the small dirt courtyard of her hut.

Lola spoke English well but preferred a pot pourri of Tagalog and Spanish. She spoke to Esmirada in English, as she had done with Olina. As they worked, she regaled her granddaughter with superstitions, myths and folklore. Esmirada wasn't sure what they meant but she loved the intimacy brought about by the telling of the stories. Her favourite was of *Terengati*

3

the bird hunter. Her calloused hands would catch at her faded housedress and suddenly it became the winged-robe of the sky fairy.

Lolo, her grandfather, had had a stroke and spent his time lying on a woven pallet on the dirt floor. *Lola* resented the old man and the extra care he now required. Even when he had been able-bodied, he had been foolish and lazy. He had a drinking addiction, as *Lola* told it, and would whittle away the day lazing under the awning of the *sari sari,* drinking *tuba,* playing the guitar and singing endless Filipino love songs.

"He was *guwapo* when I first met him as a young girl. I was shy but he slowly won me over with his energetic smile."

Esmirada listened intently as the old woman expertly coiled the wire for the lamps.

"No matter how full the rooster may be, it will still peck grain when it is given."

She spat a gob of red-stained spit in the dirt and looked sideways at the old man. Esmirada had heard this proverb many times and had heard it applied to her *tiyo* Buboy as well.

Chapter Two
The Barrio
1983

When Esmirada was ten, the world she knew changed irrevocably. Her father, determined to leave the mausoleum for a better way of life, hit on a scheme with his brother Buboy, which was doomed to fail.

"It will be like winning the lottery!" was how he convinced Olina.

"Our ticket out of here!"

Buboy had been selling his blood for a paltry sum to a private hospital, when he came across a slum dweller called Enrique Orbeta who had sold his kidney to an Arab for 80,000 pesos. He had made money before that, testing for a potential donor, earning 300 pesos a day. With the windfall he had bought his wife and mistress jewellery, and built a cement house. This was all it took to convince Buboy he had nothing to lose. The look on his wife, Rosa's, and his mistress's face when he presented them with jewellery, would be reward enough. By becoming a broker, he could potentially earn 12,000 pesos per kidney.

Boboy was easily convinced. They moved to Tondo and the foul trade was carried out. Boboy lost his right kidney to a wealthy Chinese trader. Esmirada, Manny and Ricardo moved their meagre belongings into a two-roomed shack, packed between mazes of similar shacks. It had no running water but did have electricity. With the money he had made he proudly bought a small television set. Olina sold flowers and key rings at night near the hotels, and by day she took in washing. Boboy got a job at a nearby construction site.

The tin roof leaked when it rained, and banners of wet, rancid laundry filled their shack. Esmirada listened to the women and children crying themselves pitifully to sleep in the adjacent hovels. Wreathed by humanity day and night, she could not escape. Their yard was a series of rough planks that served as a common footpath. It was also the site of the communal sewer. Trains ran beside the shacks, barely clearing them. The children played, while the vendors sold their pitiful wares along the railway track. The shrill whistle alerted the crowd, causing them to scurry like rats to safety. At times lives were lost when they failed to move quickly enough to avoid the speeding locomotives. Conveniently, a coffin-making business resided nearby. Once the trains passed, life returned to normal. They would be back, squabbling, gossiping, setting up their stalls and getting on with the routine of living.

Lolo had died suddenly the year before, freeing *Lola* of her responsibility. She had now gone into the pig-raising business and shared her small courtyard with a sow and numerous of its offspring.

Esmirada, Manny and Ricardo would rise each day, wash under the common standpipe, and flee the slum before sun-up. The only interruption to the daily grind was when the worst typhoon to hit the Islands of the Philippines since the Second World War arrived with a vengeance.

Leaving one million homeless and five thousand dead, the disaster followed close on the heels of another typhoon earlier in the year. The families huddled together praying, waiting out the storm and then started the long road back to recovery, along with all the other slum dwellers, rebuilding their lives and hovels as best they could. Not long after the disaster, the Espinosa siblings started school. The boys rankled but Esmirada looked forward to the challenge, anything to get her away from the monotonous chore of wet laundry and her grandmother's pigs. At seven a.m. each morning the *NGO* bus would pull into the neighbourhood, loading up with children scrapping and fighting, laughing and crying, and take them to the old fortress. The children were divided by ages, sitting at tables and chairs in the bright sunshine. The smaller ones sat on the grass. There, they were taught rudimentary English and mathematics. At the end of each day, they proudly left with 1.5 kilograms of rice.

Esmirada was empowered by the school. Bringing home rice each day left her family money for books so she could continue her studies. Ricardo and Manny did not respond to the bribe, and after a week went back to running wild in the back alleys of the slums.

"God will help those that help themselves!" *Lolo* spat out.

Olina had heard it all before and wearily went on with her washing, too tired to worry about what her sons were up to. *Lola* soon roped them in; the streets were full of small, dirty creatures sniffing glue to dull the pain of their lives. She had more planned for her grandsons and would not allow them to spend their days in the company of thieves and cutthroats. She

6

inveigled a job for Ricardo, painting guardian angels onto caskets, and then delivering them by horse and cart to the homes of the deceased. Manny was more difficult. Handsome like his grandfather, he was already hanging around the *sari sari* eyeing the girls. He had a beautiful singing voice and had restrung an old guitar he found at the local tip.

"The monkey may be smart but he can still be fooled!" *Lola* quoted at his father Boboy.

Manny sold key chains with his mother from ten p.m. till five a.m. and helped look after *Lola's* pigs. He raised fighting cocks, and kept an old wooden baby pram in the courtyard, where he tried in vain to grow tomatoes. The tomatoes failed but the worms multiplied, so he sold them for bait to the fishermen at the port.

Esmirada proved to be bright and diligent. She worked hard. She made a good friend in Angelika De La Cruz and the two competed academically. Angelika was determined to finish her schooling and help the poor and needy and, maybe one day become a teacher. Esmirada was less positive. She received little encouragement from home. They were happy to have the extra rice and keen to keep her off the streets, but her mother complained bitterly about her workload and lack of help.

After almost five years in the brokering business, Buboy had done well! He had a small cement bungalow in the compound of the barrio and collected rent. He set up his own store for Rosa who was now pregnant with their fifth child. He sported large gold chains hidden within his hirsute chest and flashed a gold eyetooth every time he laughed; which was often. By contrast, Boboy, his younger brother, had not fared as well. He regretted his decision to give up his kidney. The brighter future he and Olina envisaged had disintegrated. He had lost his construction job because of ill health, and had to refrain from strenuous exercise and stick to a low salt diet; although he was glad his gift gave another a new lease of life. Olina sighed each time he made this remark, and carelessly threw more salt into the vegetable pot. *Lola* pitied her son-in-law, and despised Buboy even more.

"*Habang ang tao ay nasusugatan ito ay tumatapa!*" (Hardship makes people stronger!) she tried to console him. Olina rolled her eyes, having heard it all many times before, and had another fit of *tampo*.

On the eve of Esmirada's fifteenth birthday, the family gathered in the shack. Manny was now recklessly driving a speeding jeepney for a living, and Ricardo had a wife and small daughter. They occupied a shack further along the track: one room with a table in the corner, a mattress instead of a

7

woven mat and, his pride and joy, a karaoke machine. Her mother and grandmother had made *pancit* and fried pork rinds for her birthday treat. Eating the noodles on your birthday guaranteed a long life. Another brown-out forced them to eat by candlelight. Sitting on the floor all talking at once, their mouths full, her brother Manny smiled vigorously like a kid on a merry-go-round. He had a girlfriend called Pinkie now; Esmirada had seen him with her, hanging around the *carinderia*. She had a dubious reputation but it didn't seem to worry Manny.

After their meal Manny played the guitar and sang 'Danny Boy'. The ghetto suddenly became silent. The mosquitoes whined, and she could hear the chant of the garbage collectors as their cart rumbled along the wooden slatted walkway. She took out the buttons that she had been collecting since she was small. She sifted them through her fingers, marvelling at the different shapes, colours and sizes. Her mother came to sit beside her and Esmirada kissed her hand as a sign of respect, and to thank her for the special birthday treat.

Olina looked away, embarrassed, and said, "Today was your last at the school!"

Esmirada looked at her, stupefied.

Olina went on, "You can't stay there forever. You must have learnt all there is to know by now! *Lola* is getting old. She can't continue with such long hours. Your father has lost his job and *Tiya* will soon have another baby. She needs your help in the *sari sari*; she's willing to pay you well. You will marry soon and the money will be a start for your family. More than I ever had."

Esmirada stared open-mouthed. Was her mother mad? Marriage, family - what was she talking about? She was still a child. She saw that Olina was serious and meant every word.

She lowered her head to hide her tears and said, "*Opò nanay.*"

She could feel the eyes of her *Tatay* and Manny watching her. She took a deep breath and squared her shoulders; she didn't want their pity! The room, with its lingering smells of cooking mingled with wet washing, stifled her. She slid out of the door and sat next to the bleeding corrugated iron wall. She picked at the blistering paint with a fingernail. A movement in the darkness caught her eye and *Lola* hobbled out to sit with her. Esmirada's tears flowed unchecked; she laid her head in *Lola's* thin lap.

"I didn't even say goodbye to Angelika. What will she think when I don't come anymore?"

Her grandmother smoothed her long glossy hair.

"I wanted to be a nurse and help people. Am I ungrateful *Lola?* I have tried to be a good *babae.*" She wept silently, letting her tears fall damply onto her grandmother's thin cotton housedress. *Lola* sang softly to her the song of her childhood.

"*Pong pong cachile Pinanganak sa kabibe Sinong anak? Si Esmirada!*" She then began to tickle Esmirada's stomach, as she had done when she was only a small girl. Esmirada laughed and hugged her grandmother. Manny, still strumming and singing beyond the thin wall, heard her and laughed with his grandfather's smile.

Esmirada liked working at Rosa and Buboy's store. The interior was cool, the harsh light filtered through the tented awning. The *tienda* attached to Buboy's cement bungalow had a wrought-iron window that she would sit at and serve the customers. Outside the window there were rough bamboo benches, and a cascading bougainvillea blooming in the dirt yard. A bright red and white sign announced to all and sundry '*4 Rosa, Sari Sari Store.*' Underneath that a faded and bleeding San Miguel sign swung listlessly in the humidity. The awning extended out over the benches, providing a cool place to sit and eat snacks and drink soft drinks and *Tuba.*

Inside the floor was covered with lime green linoleum, which Esmirada would sweep twice a day and mop regularly. *Santa Nino* stood in the corner, forever watching and blessing the business. She took great pride in arranging the goods; above her head hung cellophane-wrapped packets of Pop Rice, shrimp and squid crackers, dried mango, noodles, mushrooms and hands of overripe bananas. To her left, within arm's reach, were stacks of rice, flour, lentils, nuts, salty sauces, *bagoong* and cooking oil. To her right, small pearly bubbles of shampoo, soap, baby powder, woven baskets and mosquito coils. Towards the back a small refrigerator hummed and thumped regularly throughout the day, working overtime to keep the Royal Orange, Pepsi, palm toddy, San Miguel and, her favourite vanilla ice cream cold. On the narrow counter Esmirada had arranged jars of sticky snacks, pork rinds, pickled vegetables and cigarettes; another sought-after commodity.

Esmirada was fast and efficient at making change and had no qualms about refusing credit. The *sari sari* never lacked a customer, from sun-up to sundown it was always busy. The little yard and benches beyond were a favourite place to hang out, especially in the late afternoon when the children returned from school and the adults from work.

The only irritant Esmirada encountered was Buboy and Rosa. Buboy was often not around; she knew his girlfriends, rent collecting and foul

9

trade in kidneys kept him away most of the time, but when he was there, to buy new stock or hang with his *kontrabidas* drinking palm toddy, she felt a mixture of unease, shame and fear at the way he slyly looked at her. Rosa was easier to deal with; she was lazy and spoilt and spent most of her waking hours demanding special treatment from those around her. Her four sons left the house early in the morning and did not return until dark. Buboy had them up to all sorts of tricks. She treated Esmirada like a common *bimay*, whining in her melodramatic way for sticky snacks and deserts. She was a hoarder and collected candles, plastic knives and spoons, badges and baseball caps. The house was full of items she wouldn't get rid of. She spent her days lying around, feigning exhaustion, playing bingo and reading gossip magazines with her sycophant friends, Peachy, Luz and Pepper. When Esmirada appeared, summoned for yet another errand, they would raise their eyebrows, pucker their lips and "psst" to each other as she left. They sent her to find the soya-milk vendor; drinking light drinks would ensure the coming baby would be light skinned. Rosa was fussy; she wouldn't drink coffee, as this would make the baby bitter; no crazy food, they caused birth defects! She couldn't be too hot or too cold, and she was not to be made angry or jealous. *Lola* encouraged these superstitions, making life more difficult for Esmirada.

Late one Wednesday afternoon, Rosa yowled from within the house for Esmirada.

"*Batang babae* go to the market I must have a pig's knuckle and buy me a lottery on the way back, I had a good dream last night!"

"*OpòTiya.*" She sighed, turned and left the compound, frowning at the heavy dark clouds that were gathering above the palm trees. She passed her barrio and saw bare-chested boys in dusty rubber slippers playing basketball. The basketball ring hung lopsidedly from the termite-infested backboard. She gazed again at the dark clouds through a maze of sagging electrical wiring. Scooting out of the way, a small, dark muscular boy almost knocked her down, as he flew for a pitted rubber ball.

She reached the market and passed the charcoal sellers in faded cotton dresses, braless with sagging breasts. The women sat on rusted oil tins with their legs sprawled. Their teeth were black from betelnut and their lined faces smeared with the filth from the charcoal. She didn't take another breath until she reached the aromatic herb-seller's stall and glanced at the mysterious unmarked bottles and jars. There were woven baskets full of fresh herbs and spices. The women sat on foldable chairs laughing, and waving to passers-by, they were clean in cut-off pants and T-shirts, their feet bare with shiny painted toenails. Again she held her breath while she bought the pig knuckle from the gap-toothed butcher, averting her eyes from the blood and gore on his overall. She hated the smell of fresh *baboy;* she passed him the money and fled. Coming around the corner, she stepped over a mother cat and her kittens down amongst the garbage, filth and rats, and came face to face with Buboy. He was just about to suck down a *balut sa puti*, like an oyster. He stopped and looked her up and down grinning, he flashed his gold fang, and waved the fertilised duck egg towards her face. She grimaced and bolted; she could hear his high-pitched laughter at her retreating back.

Just as the huge mercurial drops of rain splattered in the dirt, she ducked under the cloth awning. There was a crowd sheltering there and no sign of Rosa to serve the customers. She entered the back room and could smell the dampness of the cement, sensing something was wrong. A trail of straw-coloured liquid was splashed about the floor. Rosa moaned from a corner, her face ashen.

"Esme, get the midwife!"

Another moan left her dry lips, as Esmirada dropped the pork knuckle and ran from the bungalow. Rosa's baby was not expected for another two months. This was a bad sign.

Rachel the midwife lived past the barrio along a rutted dirt track. Esmirada had accompanied Rosa on many occasions to her monthly checks at the house. She enjoyed the visits and the relaxed atmosphere, feeling as though she was witness to a secret sect.

Rachel was examining a young woman about her age, when she barged through the beaded curtain.

"Rosa Espinosa has gone into labour," she blurted without taking a breath.

Rachel summoned Evelyn her sister, they grabbed a black bag and mounted a motor scooter that was carelessly leaning against the corrugated iron fence. By the time Esmirada had returned it was all over. Rosa lay pale and listless on a mattress in the corner, her beaded T-shirt covered in yellow vomit. The two midwives gathered around a small bundle, blocking Esmirada's view. *Lola* and Olina were there, having been summoned by one of Rosa's friends. Olina wiped Rosa's face and *Lola* stood looking over the midwives' shoulders wringing her hands. Rachel came to Rosa and spoke quietly to her. Rosa let out a guttural howl and buried her head in Olina's breast. *Lola* spoke to Esmirada.

"Go back to the store *anák na babae*." She took her gently by the shoulder and pushed her out of the way.

The following day the *sari sari* was closed. A yellow and black cloth hung in the window symbolising a death in the family. The lament of the mother for her dead baby girl went on for nine days. Esmirada helped the women prepare food for the mourners participating in the Novena. A small casket stood in the middle of the room. Esmirada had only looked once. The sunken face of the infant and its tiny scull covered in gauzy black wisps, melted into the crimson fabric lining. Finally after a simple service they all travelled by jeepney to the stone cemetery. Candles were lit and Manny played his guitar, Buboy struggled with a final prayer for his infant daughter as sombre clouds gathered above the dark outline of the distant hills.

◆◆◆◆◆◆

Esmirada felt her life had suddenly narrowed. She no longer helped *Lola* with the pigs; that detestable job had been undertaken by Ricardo's wife Perpetua. Her mother no longer sold key chains at night.

Manny took over the vending of the chains, flowers and cigarettes at Harrison Plaza at Manila bay. During the day he sped around in his motorised disco-cum-jeepney, with Pinkie's name spelt out on the back in bright colours.

Her father had become more incapacitated and rarely worked, he took to doing dirty deeds for Buboy's various ventures and spent most of his time with his comrades, lying about moribund, drinking palm toddy at the *carinderias*.

Olina continued to take in washing and the shack and alleyways were constantly wall-to-wall with mouldering laundry.

Esmirada had taken charge of the running of Buboy's household and store after the infant girl had died two years ago. Rosa never seemed to recover from the premature birth; she had become maudlin and depressed, overly superstitious, fat and demanding. She had no interest in her sons or Buboy.

Buboy was indiscreet with one of his mistresses creating a rare spark of life in Rosa, resulting in a screaming fit and bout of *tampo* that lasted for weeks. She soon reverted to her listless self again, eating sticky deserts and secretly drinking vast amounts of San Miguel.

She continued to spend her days sprawled within the bungalow, reading magazines and watching soap operas on the television. *Lola* and Olina had given up on her with disgust.

Lola quoting as usual, "What use is grass if the horse is already dead?"

Since turning seventeen Esmirada had felt restless. The barrio, the shack, everything around her seemed different; the colours much brighter! She was no longer aware of the garbage or small dirty creatures that slept under parked jeepneys to keep warm. Her family looked at her differently too; no longer a child. She had never really taken much notice of herself in a mirror before.

One Sunday when she went with Manny to Manila Bay, she stopped before the mirrored door of the hotel, and gazed in surprise at the woman she had become. She knew then why they looked at her in that way, longing and lascivious.

Buboy and Boboy had taken on the task of finding her a husband; they knew they had bargaining power. She was disturbed by their attempts, having nothing to do with the sordidness of it all. She would lie in her bed at night listening to the barrio as it shut down. Her thoughts were confused as she tried to silence her mind. She knew above all else from the teachings of *Lola*, that life as a girl with a strong sense of filial duty meant family, husband, marriage, children, and death!

She sighed wearily in the fug of humidity. A mosquito buzzed close to her ear and she rearranged her thoughts more honestly. What *Lola* had really taught her was: a good Filipina must be above all chaste, then if she is lucky there follows, marriage, pregnancy, childbirth, husband's infidelity, rites, beliefs and death! She rolled over and fell into a disturbed sleep.

◆◆◆◆◆◆

Esmirada knelt on the floor, weeping bitterly. *Lola* pulled her into the comfort of her lap, and soothed her as she had done as a child. Looking down she saw that her knees were bloody. Her blouse was torn, exposing her brassiere; her stained and crumpled sarong was pulled awry. She tried in vain to extract the hair from her face and rearrange the dense mass behind her neck. Her father looked on accusingly, his eyes bleary from too much *tuba*. Her mother could not meet her eye and wrung her chapped hands continuously.

13

"*Batà*, tell me what happened." *Lola* started to caress her hair and did not stop as Esmirada told them of her betrayal.

"I was mopping the floor of the *sari sari* as I always do, it was cool and quiet like the mausoleum of my childhood. I was humming '*Harana,' Ta-o po, may ba-hay,*" Esmirada turned her tear-stained face towards her grandmother pleadingly.

"You know how it goes *Lola*, you taught it to me!"

"Yes, yes child, tell *Lola* what happened."

"*Tiyo* came in. He smelt of *tuba* and he was leering at me in his usual way. I went about my work but he grabbed at my shoulders and grasped my wrist hard. I struggled with him."

A sob ripped from Esmirada's chest and she faced her grandmother as if the others were not present.

"He forced me to the ground and my hair came loose. Kneeling behind me, he picked it up and held it to his face. I tried at that moment to plead with him and make my escape, but he was too strong. He ripped my blouse and pulled roughly at my breast." She could hear the rapid breathing of her mother and saw her father fall to his knees.

"He grappled with my sarong and I tried to kick out at him. He pinned my legs apart and jabbed his fingers hard in between them. It hurt so much *Lola!*" Her grandmother rocked her back and forth, stroking the hair about her forehead.

"I was screaming and Rosa came to the door half dressed, carrying a bottle of beer. She saw what Buboy was trying to do to me and she hit him over the head with the bottle. She screamed at me to get out and not to come back! I never want to go back! Please *Lola*, never again!"

Lola removed Esmirada from her father's shack. There with the squealing of pigs in her ears and the stench of manure in her nostrils, she stayed with her grandmother until it was decided what was to be done with her! Boboy went to the cement bungalow of his brother. He was hurt and angry and wanted revenge, but on the way he fortified himself with palm toddy, so that when he arrived he was tearful and pathetic.

"Why, Buboy, why my *anák na babae*?" He blubbered and fell about the floor, blowing his nose into his hands and wiping them on his filthy pants. At first Buboy was sorry and remorseful but then he started to look for blame, and he found it in Esmirada.

"She's trouble, Boboy, the way she looks, that hair and body. She drives normal men mad, she is a temptress, she has no idea the power she has over

14

men!" Boboy knew only too well how the males looked at her in the barrio. "I couldn't help myself, no man could with those eyes."

Yes, yes the eyes; Esmirada had the most beautiful liquid brown eyes, spaced apart like a European and her nose, instead of like all Filipino's, like a baby, was long and slim. Her luscious mouth was as voluptuous as her body. Why was he cursed with a beautiful daughter? Buboy was right. It would only bring him shame and trouble; every Filipina knew it was her responsibility to guard her virginity! Buboy, however, had a plan, and as usual; Buboy's plans were flawless.

Chapter Three
Exile

Esmirada held her breath as she bought the grapes; the miasma of rotting vegetables in the heat was unbearable. She consulted her list; she had purchased the black-eye peas, oranges and cantaloupe. Today she was helping *Lola* prepare for the New Years Eve feast, her last before she left. Her fate had been decided without consulting her. Her father and Buboy were sending her away to work as a domestic maid in Singapore. The money, as Buboy pointed out, would be the only way they could survive, now he was unable to work. *Lola* was ageing and Olina was old before her time. At thirty-seven she was like a woman twice her age, in spirit as well as body.

Esmirada resigned herself to her fate; if she stayed she knew what would happen, her father would force her to marry some *promdi* and she would end up like Rosa and Olina. Or worse, Buboy would eventually have his way with her and she would be held responsible for her ruin. She was realistic enough to know her choices were limited; she was not about to become a nurse as she had hoped. This at least was a chance to escape. She could not stay and look the despicable Buboy in the eye; she had lost all faith in the weak protection of her father. Manny and Ricardo were angry but not angry enough to stand up to Buboy. They too saw the opportunity in her working in Singapore. All they could think about was the money she would be sending home. *Lola* was the only person she would miss.

At midnight the barrio erupted in a cacophony of noise, sounding as though they were at war. She opened the door and the one window to the shack, to let the good luck flow through the house and the evil spirits out. She ate peas for prosperity and wore a spotted blouse. The festivities were muted, the family eating in silence, a rift wedged between them. The day after New Year she went with Manny to Manila Bay to have her photograph taken for her passport. It was the first time. They shuffled

16

through the debris of firecrackers and roman candles that still lay on the street; she had woken up that morning with black soot in her nose. The photographer made a fuss over her picture,

"Very beautiful!" he shyly remarked.

He was hurt when she refused to look at it, but Manny ordered three copies. He treated her to a fried chicken lunch in Jollibee, another first, and then took her to the park to buy her a balloon from the vendor. The trees were thick and lushly green; she had never been to this part of the city before. The balloon seller was young, a friend of Manny's, he was grinning at her with very white teeth. She looked down at the bare and dusty ground, not able to meet his dark eyes. He was dressed in tight jeans, sneakers and a bright crazed-patterned waistcoat. Two women with black oiled hair and fashionable clothes accompanied him; they squatted on a blanket with a sleeping baby between them. Boldly he lifted her chin and smiled at her as he handed her the glossy red balloon. Manny laughed at the colour rising hotly to her face. He saw an *Amboy* sitting beneath the trees, his eyes following his sister as they moved on. Esmirada looked up shyly, meeting his gaze. His laconic grin made her feel light-headed. A sense of freedom washed over her as they walked away. Would leaving set her free from grinding poverty, superstition, marriage and a slow death? Or would it just be a trade-off for another kind of bondage! She turned and looked at the balloon vendor and his women. Feeling their sullen eyes on her, she suddenly let go of the string, sending the red balloon high above her head, sailing quickly out of sight.

At six the following morning, Manny took Esmirada to Ninoy Aquino International Airport in his jeepney. She carried with her a bag containing her meagre belongings and a small wad of borrowed pesos. After Esmirada left, *Lola* turned around the few tin plates she owned, in the hope that no accident or bad luck would befall the family left behind. Olina wept silently into her plastic pail of washing. Boboy went to Buboy's *sari sari* where they got drunk on a case of San Miguel.

Esmirada's passport, which she never saw, was handled by Fernando's Maid Agency. She took one last breath of polluted air and didn't look back. Beyond the sliding doors of the airport a family quarrel took place; the husband had been caught red-handed by his wife, returning with his girlfriend in tow. She pushed past the fracas and was met by the agent, a squat man of about sixty dressed in a bright red shirt and overalls. Around his bullish neck he wore heavy gold chains. She did not look into his face, or the frightened faces of the other girls. She sat alone, waiting for her flight to be called, and then, trembling in her back row seat, she watched the Chocolate Hills of the Philippines fall away below.

◆◆◆◆◆◆

At five in the morning Esmirada joined the others for a simple breakfast of cream crackers dipped in warm milk. She showered and followed the women into the yard of the semi-detached house in Singapore. The flight through the clouds and into the city had been like a dream. She had woken confused and unhinged. Unaccustomed to sleeping in a bed, her back was sore and tender. The airport was a huge city with a roof over it and the streets of Singapore were green and free from scavenging dogs and cats. Where were the street children rising up off the sidewalk to beg? There were no jeepneys, only modern buses and luxurious cars. She could not see any plywood and corrugated shacks down by the canals, only high-rise apartments and mansions everywhere.

Everything was strange to Esmirada, even small things like the light switches. She had never used a toilet with water inside a house before, all her life she had used a smelly communal latrine. The kitchen with its gleaming refrigerator, gas stove and sink was a wonder in itself; she had never used a sink and found to her surprise it cleaned quite nicely.

Esmirada's job was to sweep and mop the tiled floors, while some of the other girls washed and hung laundry. She watched carefully as one of the girls ironed the freshly laundered clothes. At midday she helped cook a simple meal of *bee hoon* steamed rice, salted fish and *sambal goreng*. She had more than enough to eat. Her first night in Singapore she sat with the others in the garden. In a far corner two of the girls were planting *kang kong* while the chickens scratched about the stubby yard.

At night in the room, the women spoke tearfully of homesickness. Esmirada was too overwhelmed discovering new things to miss anyone back in the Philippines. During her short stay in Garden Heights, she was to master the use of appliances and learn all she could about living in Singapore. They had lessons on laws and safety, most of which Esmirada accepted without question. Some of the other maids were troublesome and argued amongst themselves at night. Esmirada kept to herself as she had always done. She tried to make the most of her stay in the clean, safe house with running water and a private shower. It was liberating not to have to leave your clothes on to wash. She had a soft comfortable bed and all the good food she could eat. She compiled a letter home to *Lola* in her mind, telling her everything, as she lay silently listening to the other women talk of their loves, losses and superstitions. Sadly, a week later, Esmirada left Garden Heights. After a painful blood test and the indignity of a medical examination, her employer came to collect her.

Chapter Four
Lucinda
Singapore 1991

Her hand damp and hesitant, Lucy fumbled with the door of the taxi; she had been waiting in a queue in the soaring heat and humidity for over forty-five minutes. Her shoulders ached and her feet were sore. Sweat ran between her breasts and pooled in the waistband of her slacks. The fustiness of the vehicle overwhelmed her already assaulted olfactory nerves. A toothless driver with a large hairy mole stuck his face close to hers, as she tried to get in.

"*Cannot lah, I balik-ing oreddy.*" He slammed the door in her face, carelessly pulling back into the flow of heavy traffic.

She waited another fifteen minutes, her head feeling as if it was about to implode with the heat. Small, dark people pushed and shoved at her, willing her out of the way, back to her own country, or so it seemed. Was she invisible, did they not see her standing there? A twisted Chinese woman dressed in pyjamas, knocked her sharply in the shins with the bags she was carrying. She did not falter as she continued slap-slapping down the street, unaware she had committed an offence. All about her sweaty men tried to catch her eye, darting looks to their left and right, they asked, "Copy watch?"

Finally she managed to hail another taxi and slumped back, pushing her spine against the sticky vinyl seat. Tears of frustration welled in her eyes. She willed them away, so she could see if the driver was going in the right direction. She stared hard at the back of his bullet-shaped head. Why did he have coins shoved in his ears, she wondered? At least he had seemed to understand where she wanted to go. Tinny Cantonese music blared from the speakers and he drove like a madman, honking his horn and throwing up his hands in frustration. She was too timid to ask him to slow down. She emerged, almost falling from the back seat onto the pavement, into the shrine-like coolness of the hotel lobby.

A large turbaned Sikh relieved her of her packages. Bowing deeply, he said, "Welcome back, Mrs Leadbitter. This way if you please Mem." He propelled her firmly into the marble sanctuary of the Pacific Palm Hotel.

Holly and Cam would be back from school in half an hour. She decided she would sit in the lobby and wait for them with a stiff gin and tonic. A pretty Asian waitress dressed in a revealing Cheongsam came and knelt at her side; the slit in the uniform rode well up her thigh, displaying firm, honey-coloured flesh. She watched the faces of the Western men seated opposite, lust glittering in their eyes.

As she settled further into the yielding armchair, she took a sip of her drink, the wet glass slipping in her hands. She could feel the knots in her neck unravel, the dampness about her body and face cool. The alcohol coursed through her veins and she relaxed. With half-closed eyes she watched a family of five across from her. The children, overdressed in lace and frills, rushed about the marbled lobby, unchecked by their mother, who, legs splayed, was fanning herself on a leather banquette, next to an old man snoring loudly. They did not buy drinks, much to the displeasure of the hotel security who knew they had only come to enjoy the air-conditioning!

She relaxed deeper into the chair, letting her thoughts wander back to the night months before when Hallam had come home feverish with excitement. Brandishing a bottle of champagne, he had told her of their impending move to Asia. They had sat in front of the open fire of the over-furnished living room, sleeting rain slicing at the draped windows. He had rushed on like a schoolboy, bubbling with plans for a promotion and an overseas posting to Singapore. She had sat numb, lost for words, watching him as he threw back glass after glass in celebration.

"Singapore," she repeated dumbly, "we're moving to Asia?"

"Yes, my darling. Large houses, maids, private schools, exotic food and people, tropical weather, adventures to other Asian cities!" He kept on and on, listing the merits of Singapore, as though reading from a travel brochure.

"Did I mention the tropical weather?"

She managed an insipid laugh, and he took her in his arms. However her face, reflected in the mirror above the fireplace, conveyed her grave misgivings.

That night as she drew her cold feet into the warmth of their king-sized bed, she looked across at Hallam; he was already snoring softly. She sighed

21

and lay back discontentedly against her pillows, watching as his top lip vibrated with each breath. She had wanted to question him more on the so-called merits of this move. They had a good life in London; Lucy had worked hard at becoming the perfect English wife and mother. She had even lost her Australian twang to please Hallam, who grimaced every time she used an Australian euphemism.

She had grown up as an only child of a reserved countrywoman, so reserved her father left her when Lucy was eight for the local barmaid. She never saw him again and could not even remember what he looked like. Her mother, once he had left, had taken over a small post office on the outskirts of a rural town; she and Lucy lived on the premises. Once a week Lucy's mother would put on her best coat and hat and take a plate to the Country Women's Association. On Saturdays she played croquet on the manicured council lawns next to the tennis courts. She had a few good women friends with whom she played bridge once a week, but there were no men in her life. Early on a Sunday she would take an armful of flowers from the garden to decorate the Presbyterian Church, sing with the church choir and serve morning tea afterwards. Lucy attended Sunday school in the church ground annexe; later she joined the youth group where she experienced her first groping kiss. She taught Sunday school for a number of years, but eventually, during her late adolescence, she became cynical and disillusioned with the church and all it stood for.

Lucy went by bus, first to the local primary and then high school. Attractive enough with dark hair and wide blue eyes, she was a talented artist and good at sports. Sought after by the boys, she earned their respect as a friend. Not too pretty to be a threat, she found she was also popular with the girls. She fell in love in Year Twelve, only to have her heart broken during the summer holidays, when the object of her desire, Steve Hughes, left her for a blonde from the Catholic school. She drifted into teachers' college with ideas of becoming a primary school teacher, but dropped out after the first semester when she came home and found the vacuum cleaner, it's motor running, and her mother dead on the floor from a cerebral haemorrhage. She had left Lucy the little money she had and Lucy packed a backpack and took off for Europe.

It was in Majorca that Lucy fell in love. She fell in love with the balmy beaches and the blood-red sun that set high above the clumps of mountains. She stayed in a crumbling manor set in an olive grove, just outside of Valldemosa where the plump oranges and lemons were so abundant they literally fell off the trees at your feet. She spent her days exploring the old city of Palma, and painting rugged mountain scenes and sailboats on placid bays in watercolour.

She also fell in love with Liam, a Scottish university student, who was teaching English school children how to water-ski during their vacation. He was lovely, tall and golden with tawny hair and a cheeky smile. They had a wild and passionate affair that ended when Lucy came to the boathouse and found him glistening with sweat, a teenage girl wedged beneath him. She found solace in the arms of Liam's friend Hallam, who attended the same university. Hallam was broad and pale, unable to spend much time in the sun without turning puce; he had come for a week after Liam had promised him all sorts of attractions. He found Lucy instead. They spent a great deal of time laughing, eating, drinking too much Sangria and making love. The affair turned into a comfortable relationship, which led to a small garden wedding in Hallam's elderly mother's house in Bath.

Hallam went to work in the bank, and Lucy a small but chic art gallery, which was within walking distance of their London flat. They had two children, first a little blonde fairy who didn't resemble either of them and then a boy just like Hallam. She thought now of the wasted hours she had spent procuring the best schools for them.

The Leadbitters had a cosy circle of like-minded friends, who they travelled with to Spain each year on holidays, and with whom shared dinner and theatre regularly. She shopped in Kings Road, lunched with her girlfriends and sat on the board of directors for the annual flower show; she had won first prize last year for her botanical paintings. How could Hallam possibly expect her to give all that up, to ship off to a small god-dammed island in South East Asia? What about her art appreciation classes on Tuesday evening and her watercolour classes on Saturdays?

She watched Hallam's pale doughy cheeks puff with each breath. He snored loudly and she roughly cut off his air by pinching his nose. He snorted and rolled over, smelling of alcohol. She lay there on her back, brooding well into the early hours of the morning, listening to the comforting sounds of the wind and sleet against the windowpane. Finally, at about four, she slept.

A week later, she met her girlfriends at Browns for high tea and told them her news. She spared them any preamble and simply announced, as the tea was being poured,

"We're moving to Singapore. Hallam has been promoted. He leaves in two weeks! The children and I will pack the house and join him there in a month."

Emerald stopped pouring immediately and looked at her open-mouthed. Hilary, who had been ordering the service staff about, raised a beautifully manicured hand to her mouth. Livvy, who had anxiously made a start on the sandwiches, coughed and sprayed cucumber onto the linen tablecloth.

Emerald darted her over-bright eyes in Lucy's direction. "Darling, that's wonderful, how soon can I come and visit? Start compiling a list of eligible men for me the moment you get there!"

Emerald had recently gone through a very acrimonious divorce; they all suffered with her through the agonising details and division of assets. Lately she seemed to have bounced back, and despite losing a great deal of weight, was looking better than ever. Hilary dismissed the attention of the service staff with a flick of her slender wrist and leaned in closer.

"You will have to be ultra careful, sweetie, I hear those Asian women know all sorts of tricks to lure our men away, they can do strange things with their pelvises! They're so small and subservient, willing to accept the sort of treatment that we girls have fought hard to rise above. Of course though, you don't have to worry with Hallam, and think of all the wonderful parties, home help and travel you will get to do. I have heard tell it's the sort of place that whenever you stick out a limb, someone paints the end of it!"

Hilary frowned at Livvy as she took the opportunity to help herself to cake. She waved her sticky fingers in the direction of Lucy's rose embellished teacup.

"What will we do without you, Luce? Dull, grey old London won't be the same without our little Australian. I guess you will be closer to home."

Lucy tried to smile confidently between sips of Orange Pekoe.

Hallam had worked all week, convincing her of the soundness of the move, but she had woken this morning with clenched teeth and tightness in her throat that wouldn't go away. It did occur to her that she would be halfway to Australia, but it was not really a deciding factor. She looked about at the starched, spotless tables set beautifully with rose-patterned china and fine silver. Out on the street it was cold and grey but in the cosy room of Browns, it was warm and consoling. She leant back against the rich, dark-wood panelling and listened to the girls' gossip and make plans without her, it was as though she had left for Singapore already.

Chapter Five
The House

Startled Lucy looked up as a small, blonde girl in a candy-striped smock hurtled across the vast expanse of marble, with a tow-haired boy following close behind. They threw their backpacks at her and skidded to a stop at the foot of her chair. She clasped their sticky, hot bodies and breathed deeply the feral scent of their hair. They prattled on about their day at school, as she took them by the hands and steered them toward the lift. They both talked at once, anxious to tell her everything. She promised them a swim as they rode in the glass elevator, Cam clinging to her legs, afraid of heights, while Holly, nose pressed hard against the glass, watched as they rose into the clouds, high above the spouting fountain to their suite on the twentieth floor.

Cameron and Holly had settled immediately. The school, set in a verdant and lush tropical garden, was more than welcoming. Lots of little Australian, English and New Zealand clones rushed about excitedly that first day. Full of confidence and seemingly well travelled, they took Holly and Cam eagerly into their flock. The first week they both produced invitations to birthday parties. There had been no tears or trauma, only excitement and wonder at the new world they now found themselves thrust into.

Hallam as well was more than contented with his new position. He was C.E.O. of his office in the downtown business district and ruled his world with relish, in a glass tower that overlooked the milky river. His Eurasian secretary Elvira, gently but firmly oversaw Hallam's transition, and was now a formidable barrier to Lucy's incoming phone calls. Lucy had to admit that in the early days she had inundated the office with calls to Hal. She was the only one in the family who had not settled. With no home or job, she was not sure what she should do. The novelty of living in a hotel soon wore off, once the children had been ensconced in school. At first Hal

25

was sympathetic but after a couple of weeks he told her to, "Just get on with it."

The bank promised a house, but because of slow renovation work, the move would be delayed. She still had not seen it and had no idea what to expect. The mothers she met at the newcomers' morning all seemed to live in high-rise apartments or semi-detached housing. She had cringed on the first day when the taxi driver had pointed out the cement bunkers with highflying flags of laundry, a concrete jungle that flanked both sides of the bougainvillea-lined highway that was home to the locals. She watched the old men sitting with caged birds in the shade of the void deck and saw the children running and playing in a nearby playground. A vivid image of greenery abounded as the cab sped by.

Whilst waiting with trepidation for the house to be readied, Lucinda took to exploring the narrow alleys and palm lined streets close to the hotel. She discovered Arab Street with its array of hole-in-the-wall shops, full of exotic and dazzling fabrics, beads and tassels, sequins, ribbons and braids. The amber-skinned shopkeepers would beckon her, enticing her in to examine their wares.

Early one morning she followed the thronging crowd to the open-air markets. She climbed the narrow steps, following the jewel-coloured sari of a woman in front. Amongst the narrow rows between each stall, a myriad of smells overwhelmed Lucy. A toothless old man offered her coconut juice, which he had freshly husked, he held it out to her with dirty, cracked hands and she took it timidly, fishing in her leather purse for the right amount of coins. She examined the pickled vegetables and vats of bamboo; the floor was greasy with muck. She had realised too late she had worn the wrong kind of shoes, her white canvas espadrilles were already covered in filth. She examined the dry goods store; cellophane packs of wood-eared mushrooms gave off a musky scent. The loose barrels of rice were fragrant as were the cinnamon sticks, cloves, dried chillies and freshly ground turmeric. The dried fish, oysters and squid smelt vaguely of the sea. The vegetables were large and robust, unspotted, bruised or marked, unlike the Chernobyl mutations she had been obliged to buy in London.

A poor man with a dreadful deformity, resembling an angry red cow udder growing from the side of his face, offered her a rambutan that she took out of pity. She split the fruit with her thumbnail and took the translucent pod into her mouth; it was juicy and full of the delicious taste of summer. She gave him the thumbs-up and promised to come back for a bag on her way out. She took a deep breath and sighed over the luscious smells of the papaya, mangosteen, persimmons, lychees and green mangoes.

The auntie manning the store urged her to buy, *"Good lah you buy velly cheap!"*

Lucy fished for more coins and bought a bag of green grapes. She turned the corner and was accosted by a fellow with a toothpick hanging from his mouth; he had a large dirty plastic bucket full of fish on a trolley.

"Eskew me!" he shouted at her and waved her out of the way as he slapped past her, his trousers rolled up his hairy calves. He carelessly splashed her white slacks with stinking fish water, and turned and grinned at her cheekily. Withdrawing a large plastic comb from his back pocket, he paused, combing back his greasy hair. He moved the toothpick to the other corner of his mouth and resumed barrelling through the crowds.

The variety of the fish, live crabs, crustacean, prawns and octopus, amazed Lucy, but when the stall keeper offered her a live frog from the barrel, she swiftly rounded the corner and came upon the egg vendor. There were duck eggs, brown hens' eggs, speckled bantams' eggs, pickled eggs and tiny quails' eggs, not to mention black, mysterious one-hundred-thousand-year-old eggs. The only type of egg they did not have was your common white hens' egg, she later found out that white represented death, and so was not popular.

Whilst she decided that perhaps she would be brave enough to buy fruit, veggies, eggs, fish and spices from the market, the sight of the poultry and meat section would quickly convert her to vegetarianism. Ducks and chickens hung whole from hooks, their baleful eyes staring. Plastic dishes of innards lay amongst chicken feet. Two old women in pyjamas haggled over the price of a black chicken, the only one left; she knew the soup from these had powerful medicinal properties. Huge sides of strong-smelling mutton hung from the meat stall, still dripping blood. Offal, which ordinarily Lucy assumed would go into pet food, was on offer, with a queue of customers jostling to buy. The smell in the heat and thick air was fetid and she darted down another aisle to escape. She came across a beautiful Indian man with large white teeth, as he expertly ground fragrant spices with a wooden pestle. The tin plates were piled with pyramids of rich, ochre-yellow curries, as he carefully measured a deep desert-red powder. She bought a plastic drawstring bag of each and a bag of fresh coconut milk, and made her way out past the hawker stalls into the blazing sun and streets of Little India. Her artist's eye keenly noted the old shop houses with their faded pastels and ornate tiles; some were in desperate need of renovation. It was sad seeing these old beauties turn to dust.

During those early weeks she was lonely; Hallam was travelling, establishing his position in the region. The children were happy to wave her goodbye in the mornings as they boarded their little school bus. She would then sweat it out in the gym for an hour or two, swim and fill in time until the huge air-conditioned shopping malls opened later in the morning. Every other day she would explore her surroundings. Her dates with herself were interesting and an education, but by early afternoon she had had enough of culture shock. Retreating to the sanctuary of the hotel, she put herself into a self-induced coma until the children returned from school.

One Friday afternoon, she received a call to say their shipment had arrived and cleared customs. Nostalgia swept over her, thinking of all her precious things about her once more. Hallam phoned to tell her that the painting, retiling and renovation were finished. They could move in whenever they were ready. Lucy panicked. It had been so easy in the hotel: room service, laundry and housekeeping. The only responsibility she had, was saying 'no' to french fries with every meal the children ate. She put her fears behind her and drove with Hal and the kiddies the following morning to see their new home.

Lucy's excitement grew as they suddenly turned off the main highway into a shaded jungle road. Huge Tembusu trees with bird nest ferns draped and met in the middle, providing dappled shade. Her first glimpse of the house was a large, black iron gate, surrounded by handsome sealing wax palms, their scarlet stalks and stiff feather-like fronds waving gently in the breeze. Hal opened the gate and they drove up the curving gravel drive. Standing majestically on a slight rise, the house loomed above them. It had rained briefly that morning and a faint blue mist rose above the towering trees that bordered the two-storey bungalow. An ornate porch with crenulated columns projected below a first-floor veranda. The enclosed mock-Tudor verandas had chick blinds, painted in the traditional black and white of the Colonial houses.

They entered into the chengai-timber vestibule; the children ran noisily ahead eager to explore. Lucy took Hallam's hand and squeezed it with pleasure as they started to discover their new home. The lofty, beamed roof allowed the house cool breezes, which flowed through from the open verandas, stirred on by the overhead fans. The rooms were large and airy, closed off from the verandas by louvres.

"Mamma, come quick! We have a ballroom."

Holly was leaning over the balustrade of the wooden stairwell; her face, framed by her fairy-floss hair, was scarlet with excitement. They proceeded up the stairs to a huge living area on the second storey, open on three sides, the verandas giving access to the bedrooms.

"Well what do you think, do you like it, could you be happy living here?" Hal stood looking at her, knowing by the delighted look on her face, what her answer would be.

She threw her arms about his neck, reached up, and kissed him hard on the mouth. She looked around in earnest. "My only worry is that our furniture won't suit the colonial feel of the house." She frowned and started measuring with the palms of her hands and pacing out the width of the rooms.

Hallam laughed. "Well Luce, I guess that's your next project, to make this old mansion into a home fit for the Leadbitters!"

The following Monday Lucinda went back to the house alone, she wanted to explore further and have it all to herself for just one day. As she drove up the drive, the white stucco of the house was almost a luminous blue in the midday sun. She examined more closely the kitchen and all the funny little outhouses, wondering what their original use was. The back patio led down a sweeping lawn to a more recent addition: the pool and timber decking. At one end stood a cabana with an atap roof, shaded by clumps of bamboo and a mature travellers' palm at least eight foot high. She could hear the birds singing in a creeper-covered arbour. Moss-covered Balinese stone lanterns lined the path leading to the garden pool. Another broad expanse of lawn led down to the fence and the house next door. In one corner, beneath a trellis of wedding jasmine, stood a weather-beaten garden bench, surrounded by waxy ginger plants. She sat here now, taking in each detail and listening to the sounds of her tropical garden. She imagined another time, sunset cocktails and elegant women in rustling gowns, debonair men in Red Sea rig sipping stengahs, in the shade of the Tembusu.

Her reverie was interrupted by a shrill voice from behind.

"Halloo, anybody there?" A small grey face framed by wiry hair appeared between the clumps of bamboo.

"Hello dear, thought I saw someone prowling about, I'm the next door neighbour, Tuppy Devonshire."

Lucy stood and took the hand proffered through the fence. Tuppy's equine features smiled at her through the dappled light, she had enormous twisted brown teeth. She was wearing gardener's gloves and held a trowel in one hand.

"Won't keep you, dear, just thought I'd say hello, I'm just doing a bit of re-potting, my orchids are all pot bound."

Lucy laughed and pushed back a lock of damp hair from her forehead. "It's nice to meet you, Tuppy. I'm Lucy Leadbitter. We'll be moving in shortly, as soon as I can get the moving company organised, that is."

"Oh good luck, they do everything in their own sweet time here, my dear. I knew you were coming, Amber, on the other side, told me all about you at mah-jong last week. You must come and join us, we always have a few laughs, nothing too serious, must run before the afternoon downpour!" She walked away, saluting Lucy with her trowel as she went.

Lucy looked across at the other house curiously; she could see the tiled roof and the upper floor veranda, a fine wicker birdcage hung from the awning. The rest of the house was hidden by large clumps of bamboo and bougainvillea. The fact they knew about her already amused her. She wandered about, moving a few pot plants and scraping up still-wet paint that the workmen had carelessly dripped.

Above the spreading Tembusu the sky darkened, the breeze whipped at the palms and she heard the dull thud of a coconut in the lower garden. She took shelter on the back patio and watched as the storm gathered momentum. The noise was deafening as the deluge reduced the lower half of the garden to a small lake within twenty minutes. She stood welcoming the cool change it brought; she could smell the good earthy scent of the soil. As suddenly as it had started, it was over. The sun shone and the birds resumed their screeching high in the branches of a nearby Casuarina tree. She turned to see a slender figure coming up the drive.

"Hi there, I'm Amber and you must be Lucy." She shook Lucy's hand firmly.

"Welcome to Bukit Lalang!" Amber ducked her head to the side and smiled. The colour of the woman's eyes enchanted Lucy; they were a deep emerald green. Her hair gave her name away; it was thick and luxuriant, forming a rich halo around her oval shaped face. She held a hand up to shield her pale skin from the sun.

"It seems you know all about me already, I met Tuppy earlier."

Amber laughed, throwing her head back, displaying a creamy pink throat. "The Allens, who lived here before, worked for the same bank as your husband. They were transferred to Paris. Come over and have a drink with me. Have you eaten?"

She took hold of Lucy's elbow and steered her in the direction of a small gate hidden in the side fence. They carefully stepped over the storm water drain and entered Amber's lush garden.

Amber Van Engle's house was a mirror image of Lucy's. Now Lucy could see how her house needed to be furnished. The entrance foyer was simply decorated with a black lacquered cabinet on which sat a Chinese urn holding stalks of ginger. Suspended above was a brass and glass lantern.

Amber laughed when she saw Lucy admire the flowers. "I have been very naughty. I pilfered these from the bottom of your garden. I can't for the life of me get them to grow. I hope you don't mind."

Guarding the stairs on both sides were two meditative wooden statues from India. Tropical paintings from Bali decorated the stairwell. Lucy took a deep breath as she entered the upstairs sitting room, three voluminous sofas in vibrant cobalt blue and lemon sat upon a magnificent Persian carpet, reflecting the same blue. An enormous low Thai coffee table held Amber's treasured pieces of English silver. In a corner stood an antique red lacquer wedding cabinet, in the opposite corner a Burmese temple angel rested serenely on her wooden pedestal.

Lucy begged to see the bedrooms and Amber proudly led the way. The master bedroom was in blue and white with an English printed bedspread and matching wallpaper frieze.

"I sponged the walls myself. Hell of a job, but looks effective, don't you think?"

Lucy sighed appreciatively. "Oh, it's just perfect. I would love to do something similar, could you show me where to get the paint?"

Amber took Lucy's elbow and continued the tour. "Of course, sweetie, I'll take you there myself!"

Amber confessed to having two children as they moved into what was obviously first a boy's room and then girl's. This was great news for both of them, as they attended the same school and would travel on the bus together.

"Andrea and Tom will be thrilled. The Allens didn't have any children, only two small noisy dogs."

They passed through the dining room, decorated in forest green. A rattan glass top table and chairs gave it a casual feel. A large oil painting covered one wall. Amber had an eclectic collection of birdcages that she had amassed from around Asia. They entered the kitchen and a small brown woman, whom Amber introduced as Honeyko, was preparing a tray.

"Hello, ma'am," she smiled and hopped from one small bare foot to the other.

They went out into the cool, shaded patio beneath the house. Amber seated Lucy at a round table covered in Indonesian batik. A sandstone Balinese goddess with a pink frangipani behind her ear sat observing them. Hanging above was a fine wooden birdcage, which Amber told her she had found in Lombok.

"Amber, everything is so exotic and the colours you have used are just lovely, I'm afraid my old English furniture will look boring and very ordinary, the house deserves so much more!"

Amber patted her hand as she poured them both a glass of white wine. "We'll start tomorrow, I'll take you to the paint shop and the upholsterer, after that we can comb the antique shops. It takes a while to get a collection together. After all, I have been here for a long time and in Thailand and Hong Kong before that. You'll get there!"

Honeyko crept up on them silently, placing sandwiches, cheese and salmon mousse on the table before them. Deftly she refilled their water glasses and then quietly padded away.

"Have you got a maid sorted out yet?" Amber asked.

"I haven't given it much thought. Hal said when we move in I should go and see an agency, but I'm a bit doubtful about having another woman living in the house."

Amber laughed, showing her small, white, even teeth. "We all feel like that in the beginning, but believe me, once you start mopping those floors and washing and ironing each day, you just might change your mind! Besides, in Singapore with all the parties, dinners and balls you will have to attend, you'll need a baby sitter. Honeyko has a little friend whose employer is about to be transferred, I can make some enquiries, if you like. I've met the girl and she seems sweet."

On cue Honeyko slipped out with a piece of paper with her friend's name and phone number and slid it in under Lucy's plate. Amber's beautifully shaped brows shot up and Lucy laughed. The lunch wore on into the afternoon with Amber and Lucy exchanging as much information as time would allow. She left to pick up the children from school, having discovered that besides weekly mah-jong, Amber also held painting classes on her patio. She felt pleased with herself as she stopped at a traffic light. She had achieved a lot today. She could hardly wait to tell Hallam; forgetting he had left for New York last night and would not be back for weeks.

Lucy had to put her shopping adventure with Amber on hold when the movers arrived with the furniture. It didn't take long. Seven small men swarmed like ants all over the house. Despite their size they heaved and lifted and had the well-loved possessions she had chosen to bring in place by nightfall. As she suspected, it all looked rather small and dull in the vast rooms. Their voices and footsteps echoed as she and the children dragged the appropriately marked boxes to their right places. She could have done with Hal's help at this stage, but had a feeling he was not going to be around much in Singapore.

The children bade a sad farewell to their suite on the twentieth floor and left the comfort of the Pacific Palm Hotel; secretly Lucy was pleased to be going. Two days before Hal was due home, he called, saying he would have to stay longer. She was disappointed, but at the same time it gave her more time to shop with Amber. She wanted to have the house in order by the time he arrived back.

Amber took her to Kampsey Road where they rattled about the dusty pavilions, full of antiques, sideboards, room dividers, beds, chairs, chests, curios and rats. They deliberated over Persian carpets, durries and kilims. Together they found a reclining budda and a rotund laughing one that would look wonderful in her foyer. She bought lamps from Burma, side tables from Korea and teak from Indonesia. Amber was an expert haggler and won the shopkeepers over with her sense of humour as well as her beauty.

A week before Hal's return she had painted the children's bedrooms in ultramarine blue, and had sponged theirs in antique gold and almond. She had, on Amber's advice, scanned the classifieds at the 'Fresh To You' or FTY supermarket as it was known locally, and picked up a rattan bar and table and chairs for a bargain. She discovered a derelict, heavy, old German piano for Holly to practise on, and Hallam to belt out his favourite show tunes.

She hired one of the painters to spray paint the bar, tables and chairs in colours to match her Persian carpet and durries. Her newly upholstered chintz lounges were in the palest of lemon in an Asian print. She filled the house with white orchids in large urns in readiness for Hal's return.

"Dad's home! Mamma, Dad's home!" She could hear Cam shrieking from the pool as a car crunched on the gravel of the driveway. A wet and squirming Holly was already in his arms.

"What did you buy us?" Cam called as he jumped at his father, wrapping his skinny legs about him.

33

Lucy stood back and watched the scene. "Hey, do I get a kiss?" She threw her arms about Hal's neck and said, "What did you buy me?" Lucy took him by the hand while the children flapped about his legs, leading him up the stairs and into the newly decorated house.

"Oh Lucy, you have done wonders! Is all this ours?" He looked about incredulously; he slipped his arm about her waist as she led him from room to room. He was amazed at what she had achieved in the six weeks he had been away.

"You haven't blown the budget I hope!"

She looked up at him to see if he was serious. He laughed and slapped her on the rump.

"How about a drink? I'm stuffed after that long flight home!"

They sat outside on the patio listening to the night sounds. The children were playing with a game that Hal had bought them in the States. Lucy mixed them a gin and tonic and they clinked glasses, toasting his return.

"I still can't believe what you have done. The house looks wonderful, and it feels as though we have been here forever."

The overhead fan cut through the thick air noisily. A nightjar called mournfully from the casuarina tree. Transparent geckos stalked the walls looking for mosquitos, as Lucy sluiced her drink down and relaxed.

Taking a deep frangipani scented breath, she said, " I love it here, Hal. I didn't realise how much I had missed alfresco living after I left Australia. I don't miss the grey of London at all, and the kids haven't given it a thought. I hope we'll stay awhile."

Hal picked up her hand. "So do I, Luce. I really like my job and even the travel is not that bad." He swivelled his eyes toward her. "You don't mind me travelling every now and again, do you?"

"I don't love it. I know it's part of your job. It seems all the men have to travel in this part of the world."

He sighed and took a long pull of his drink. "Yeah, ain't that the truth."

"Daddy, look! The Rod Stewart birds!" Holly was jumping up and down and pointing to the sloping lawn beyond the pool. A band of brown and white birds with an unruly crest of white feathers on top of their heads, hopped along like a child's wind up toy.

Lucy laughed. "They do have Rod's hairstyle, I must admit! I'll get us a book on birds so we can find out what they're called."

Hallam took his small daughter onto his lap. "I think from here on, no matter what, they will always be the Rod Stewart birds for me."

Lucy looked at him in the fading light. He was different somehow: leaner, his hair was longer and his face tanned, and he had lost that pasty, bloated look.

She told him all about Amber, the upcoming classes and her interview with the maid. She suspected he was only half listening. Maybe it was jet lag or the pressure of his job; she dismissed it and went inside to fumble about in her new kitchen, preparing the evening meal.

Chapter Six
Esmirada, Madam and the Boy
1991

Madam Wei ling Leng was a robust woman with tightly permed hair and enormous eyes behind her thick glasses. She ran a travel agency and had hired Esmirada after her Indonesian maid 'did not work out' and was sent back home. She was a widow with a ten-year-old son and an aging father to care for.

As she sped through the morning traffic in her shiny new car to her flat in Toa Payoh, she set down her rules to Esmirada in no uncertain terms. Esme listened without interruption. Madam abruptly came to a stop in front of 'A' block and parked the car. Esme was disappointed. The cement building had few trees and scattered about the base of the stairwell was rubbish and cats eating leftover hawker food. The small patch of grass in front of the building was littered with sun-dried cat turds. It wasn't as nice as Garden Heights. They walked up the flight of stairs, smelling vaguely of human waste, to the fifth floor and entered the small three-bedroom flat. Madam Wei Ling Leng showed her the room, which she would share with the ten-year-old boy. He was a shorter version of his mother, with the same thick glasses and frightening stare. He ignored Esmirada and concentrated on a small flickering screen in front of him, only moving when his mother swatted him about the head, urging him to do his homework.

"Boy, still playing computer game ah! Tomollow you taking test, sure get geelo one!"

Madam Wei Ling Leng bustled about the narrow rooms, picking up clothes and briskly throwing them into drawers. Esmirada followed close behind, taking in every detail. Madam had already explained that she would take two days to train her, after that she would be on her own. She pushed Esme forward into the old man's room and roused him out of bed. He was

36

digging in his nose with his good hand and stood unsteadily when they entered; he gave Esmirada a drooling grin.

"*Wha so swee!*" Madam swatted at the old man.

"*Aiyah, you siao liao, is it? She good ger, you all the time tok kok!*"

The old man stood leering at Esme in his dirty pyjamas, as his daughter shoved him toward the toilet.

Together they prepared lunch. Madam Wei Ling Leng showed her how to cut up the vegetables, small and even, tossing them into a hot kuali with a little oil and garlic and salted soya beans. Esmirada steamed the rice in the rice cooker, marvelling at how easy it was to prepare. Madam Wei Ling Leng was pleased; she found she only had to show Esmirada something once.

Esmirada grew to like the small short-sighted woman; she was always fair with Esmirada, whom she called Esme from the first day. Madam Wei Ling Leng in turn congratulated herself on choosing such a smart girl to leave in charge; she enjoyed having another female's company. Each evening during the national news she would invite Esme to watch the television in the cluttered sitting room. The soft night air would flow through the open grill of the common corridor. The old man remained in his room and the strange myopic boy at the even stranger apparition he called a computer. The open grill was an observation post for Madam Wei Ling Leng. As tenants passed by, she would call out and engage them in a bit of gossip. She was friendly and seemed to be well liked by her neighbours.

At five each morning Esme left her bed to wash and dress and prepare the rice gruel for the savoury porridge. She then got Uncle out of bed, and headed him in the right direction for the bathroom. He had had a series of small strokes, but could still manage to make himself understood and walk in a faltering gait. Esmirada tried hard to attend to him as quickly as possible. The old man made a habit of grabbing at her, but mostly she was too fast for him. He would ramble on in Hokkien, which she couldn't understand, but by the leer on his lopsided face she knew what he was wanting. She became adept at scooting quickly away from his grasping bony-fingered hands.

Madame Wei Ling Leng and the boy would leave together each morning, returning early in the afternoon. Once they left, she soaked the laundry in a big plastic bucket and then took the uncle downstairs to the void deck. Madam Wei Ling Leng lived on the fifth floor, she proudly told Esme that soon the building would be modernised and have lifts installed.

Esme had never been in a lift and was just as happy to use the stairs. She would install the old man with his equally senile friends in the shade of the void deck, and leave them to listen to their caged birds or play checkers. For the next hour she escaped to the Toa Payoh Central markets, where she quickly bought her supplies of bean curd, bamboo shoots, chillies, sausage, coriander, fresh kway teow noodles and coconut milk. As a special treat for Uncle she would buy a brown, wrapped packet of chicken rice for his midday meal, and then hurry back to the block to do the washing. Washing by hand, she hung the laundry to dry on bamboo poles from the kitchen window. She then cleaned the flat, swept and mopped the floors, washed the windows and watered the plants. At midday, she took Uncle's *makan* to him and walked him after lunch to give him some exercise. With his arm held firmly so he could not grab, she would do a round of the common area. She encountered many old uncles and aunties, some more lucid than others. Teenagers playing prohibited ball games would stare at her openly and make comments like,

"*Wow she dam jude man!*" They would then purse their lips and make a loud wet sucking noise at her. At other times they were more aggressive, "Want to *sio-sio*, not?" Pumping their skinny hips in her direction in an obscene manner.

Tossing her head in the air, she ignored them like the cockroaches beneath her feet. The old man chuckled and muttered under his breath before she dragged him, complaining, back up the stairs to his room for an afternoon rest.

Esmirada only had one Sunday off a month. On that day she went to the church in Thomas Road; she had no interest in going to Orchard or Prosperity Plaza. The maids who hung about the void decks told stories of Sundays spent at Orchard. She went there once and found hordes of women laughing and taking photographs of each other, running about like adolescent children. They were waiting for the dancing to begin; she couldn't believe it, rows of Filipino maids in pointy boots, line dancing in the vast mall to Country and Western songs.

The first church she attended was Catholic; it had a strong congregation of Filipino maids yammering through Mass, as though they were at a rock concert. The choir, full of pimply teenagers, sang out of tune with the organ. During the morning there was a market and coffee served on the void deck. She stopped attending after a while, preferring to spend her Sunday instead having *makan* at the Toa Payoh Hawker centre, or Kentucky with Madam Wei Ling Leng and the sulky boy. Eventually she discovered an independent church in Chinatown through Madam Wei Ling Leng's son. They had attended a Wednesday night meeting of Boys' Brigade, and Esmirada saw that the following Sunday there was a service in Tagalog.

Silently she entered the large hall, and looked timidly about. A Sister dressed in a navy blue suit and white blouse immediately stood to welcome her. The sun fell evenly on the polished wood floor, as she listened intently to the words of the visiting Archbishop. The service was without guilt, unlike those she had attended before. Esmirada's heart was filled with faith, as though God had touched her personally. She was dignified by the pastor's sermon. Even though she was a lowly maid, she knew God loved her; his words were good news to Esmirada.

Her life of domesticity continued unchanged in the small H.D.B. flat underneath the Toa Payoh flyover. She continued to thwart the unwanted attentions of the old man, and learned to roll over and go back to sleep when she found the myopic boy silently leaning over her in the middle of the night. He salvaged his strange behaviour by allowing her to listen to Rejoice Radio; they would drift off to sleep with the blessings of the dulcet tones of the pastor.

During the seventh lunar month of the Hungry Ghost, Uncle had a stroke and died. Because there was no eldest son, Esmirada and Madam Wei Ling Leng took on the ceremonial duty of washing the body. Madam Wei Ling Leng instructed Esme on the custom of dressing the deceased in four suits, as well as other bits of odd clothing for his long journey home. Madam's friends helped carry the old man down the stairs to the void deck, where he was laid out behind a screen. Esme placed his favourite possessions on a chair. His daughter lit two candles, which Esmirada had to promise would remain burning, to allow the sprit of the old man to see his friends. Madam Wei Ling Leng spoke to him as though he were still alive, as she burned joss sticks, announcing each mourner as they arrived. While they played mah-jong, Esmirada arranged food and soft drinks for the visitors. Together with the boy and his mother, she kept vigil over the corpse, keeping rats and the huge population of stray cats around the building from disturbing him.

The sound of weeping and wailing and loud music hung in the sultry night air, trying to ward off the evil spirits that lurked about, hoping to claim the soul of the deceased. On the last day, everyone came together for one final meal. The last rites were performed and then the coffin was carefully removed, to be loaded onto the flower-decked truck. Esmirada stood in the sweltering sun and watched as the bright paper rustled in a small dusty gust of wind; she heard Madam Wei Ling Leng's sharp intake of breath as the heavy wooden coffin slipped, bumping hollowly on the side of the truck. Esmirada knew this was a sign of bad luck!

The bad luck came on the seventh day after the old man's death, as the boy and his mother burned elaborate paper offerings and money; everything Uncle could possibly need in the afterlife. After the ritual burning, Madam Wei Ling Leng drove them back through the heavy traffic to the now empty flat.

She sat Esme down in the living room and in a small voice said, "Sure got big bill this month. *Jia lat,* funeral costs, but how to pay? Without Uncle, how can keep you? You good *ger, I hepch* you with good transfer *lah.*"

Esmirada fixed her eyes on the small patch of mourning cloth on Madam's sleeve. What could she say? She had no choice in the matter. That night she lay listening to the words of hope on the Rejoice Radio, a cold stone of fear lying next to her heart.

Chapter Seven
Yolo

Lucinda rushed home from the F.T.Y to find Yolanda or Yolo, as she liked to be called, waiting with Holly on the back patio. Holly was showing Yolo her vast collection of Barbie dolls; Yolanda was patiently dressing them and placing them carefully in the Barbie town house. She seemed very young but perhaps Amber was right, youth was sometimes a good thing, you could train them in your own way.

She greeted Lucy, shyly looking down at her bare feet.

"Hello, Yolanda. Holly, go and start on your homework and don't forget French lessons at five."

Holly wanted to protest, but one look at her mother's face convinced her otherwise. Lucy examined the young Filipino girl as she continued to stare at her feet. She was short and stocky, only coming up to Lucy's shoulder. Her legs and arms were thick and muscular, her back broad. She had a pleasant face, not pretty, but alert.

"What duties have you been performing for your current family?"

Yolo screwed up her face in what would become a familiar expression when asked a question.

She scrubbed at her forehead and then said, "Cleaning, washing and ironing, looking after the children, the dog, and washing the car."

"What about cooking, Yolo, can you cook anything?"

"Yes, ma'am. I learnt to do spaghetti bolognaise, chicken curry and Thai food, that was my sir's favourite. I went to a class with other maids to learn."

She seemed proud of her achievements. Lucinda had never had to interview anyone before and knew she was probably omitting the most revealing questions. She read the references Yolo proffered from her current employer; she had been working in Singapore for six years.

41

Holly and Cam came down to have a swim and Holly boldly took hold of Yolanda's hand.

"Can I show her the garden, Mum?" Yolo giggled.

"Off you go then." Lucy watched, full of doubt; did she really need a maid? Apart from the baby-sitting, they managed well enough. Although she had fallen behind with Hallam's shirts and had taken them to the cleaners. She saw Cameron, her shy retiring one, reach out and take Yolo's hand. They looked happy and natural together, laughing and teasing one another. As she watched them in the garden, her doubt began to dissolve slowly. Perhaps she would give it a go and see what happened. By the time they came back, she was ready to call Yolo's employer and organise the transfer.

Amber walked her through the paperwork, and within a month Yolanda had moved into one of the small rooms connected by a covered walkway to the back of the house. Lucy had bought a new bed, mirror, chair and rug to make it cosy. It wasn't air-conditioned but it was shaded beneath the old tree. Yolo said she preferred a fan anyway, so Lucy had one installed. She had a squat toilet and a shower in an adjoining room. Once she moved in, she seemed content with the arrangement.

Hal rarely noticed Yolo's presence; as long as the house was running smoothly and his shirts were starched and ironed, he was happy. He didn't really notice Lucy either. He reached for her at night only on the odd occasion, and when he did it was perfunctory and unsatisfying. Lucy convinced herself it was the long hours he spent at work and travelling. She knew she dared not complain, life was going well for the Leadbitters. The children were happy at school, had friends and parties to go to and many extra curricula activities. The weeks flew by, taken up with French lessons Monday, gym Tuesday, Cub Scouts and Brownies Wednesday, friends over to play Thursday and swimming lessons at the Expat club on Fridays. Lucinda was never home. Mondays she played tennis at the Expat club, Tuesdays she had watercolours on Amber's patio, Wednesdays she played mah-jong, Thursdays mixed medium classes and Fridays she did a trolley round at the Mount Napier Hospital. Besides her heavy social life, they were also in demand for parties, dinners, balls, openings, lunches and charity events. She had employed, through Amber, a tiny Chinese woman as a dressmaker who came to the house regularly for fittings; she was wonderful at copying designs from *Vogue* and charged next to nothing for her services. Lucinda also had in her employ a pool cleaner twice a week and a family of Indian gardeners who pedalled up on their bikes, balancing brooms, parangs and a lawn mower between them.

Her classes on Amber's patio proved to be a source of valuable information, not just the enrichment of the art, but the stories that flew around the table from the other expat wives. Lucy excelled; she knew she was the most talented in the class. Thursday classes she soaked up like a thirsty sponge. She had never attempted oils, acrylics or pastels before. She hung on the teacher's every word. While the others were happy to dabble, eat and gossip, Lucinda was steadily learning and she enjoyed every minute of the lesson.

The mah-jong sessions were a different story. At first, not being a card player, Lucy found the rules confusing. Even the history of the game was lengthy and puzzling. She loved the cool feel of the ivory tiles beneath her fingers and the clicking sound they made as they were moved swiftly over the green baize mat. Too long she studied the depictions of bamboo, Chinese characters and dragons, faltering on her turn. They tended to play the American and Japanese versions but some of the players, who were old hands at the oriental game, were dissatisfied with the variation in the scoring. And of course, the small matter of not playing for money.

Each week they would go to a different house, the hostess providing refreshments. The first week she played they all went to Tuppy's house. Her quaint colonial was full of dusty treasures she had accumulated in her thirty years in Singapore. She and her retired army general husband spent their days playing tennis, golf and holding up the bar in 'Red Lips Corner' at the Expat club. Tuppy's aging Indonesian maid served stale cracker biscuits with unidentified dip, or dry curled Spam sandwiches. The tea was likened to drain water and the coffee so bitter it was left to go cold as walls were formed, tiles discarded and sets made.

The following week at Angel's apartment, high in the sky with panoramic views of Singapore, they sat wrapped in pastel tones of salmon and apricot. Angel served strawberry daiquiris and paper-thin Vietnamese prawn rolls. The game was punctuated with shrieks of laughter and miscalculation of scores. Lucy got her chows, pungs and kongs completely confused.

Maids and their foibles were often the topic of conversation, along with extramarital affairs and other people's husband's infidelities! Ellie, an Australian, regaled the group with Juta, her maid's, latest folly.

"Last week the wretched girl used bleach instead of fabric softener in the washing machine. I'm just hoping tie dye fashions come back in soon!"

Amber roared with laughter and choked on her prawn roll.

"Well you'll never guess what Cora did," said Jean, a girl from South Africa. "I went to a 'Parent and Teacher' meeting and had dinner in Holland Village on the way home. When I got back I thought the apartment was on fire. It was full of smoke. She had papered the kitchen walls with newspaper and was cooking a fish on the stovetop. It was completely black and the paper was on fire when I got there! Cora panicked and ran out of the apartment. I found her later, hiding out with another group of maids near the children's playground!"

Lucy usually didn't bring Yolo into the discussion. She was a harmless little thing, but the daiquiris had loosened her tongue.

"Last week I nearly died when I came home from tennis. I came in through the kitchen looking for her and there hanging on the line was three of Hallam's suits, dripping wet from the wash. They had shrunk to a size that would fit a small boy. Cameron will have a nice little set of business suits in a year or two!" They all doubled over with laughter, and Angel poured another round of daiquiris.

Instead of going straight home after mah-jong, Lucy decided she needed coffee. She and Amber sat with their feet up on Amber's back patio, looking out at the flourishing garden. Lucy slid her eyes toward Amber. "Do you think there is any truth in the stories about the men visiting Bangkok?"

Amber bit the side of her sultry lip. "Angel is always on about it, and it's a real thing with her. She caught her husband red-handed. She knows he visits the massage parlours and prostitutes when he is there. He maintains it's part of his job to entertain his visiting bosses. He told Angel that they expect him to participate. He tells her he goes for 'relief massages' but Brian told me it's all bullshit. These guys talk when they get a few beers into them. Angel knows relief is not all he goes for!" She took a sip of scalding coffee.

"Does Brian go to massage parlours when he's away?"

Amber sighed and looked out at the garden. "Probably. They all seem to. It's part of living in Asia. If it's handed to them on a platter, they won't say no. Angel's pretty bitter, but says nothing. Each time Peter gets caught out, she flashes another diamond!"

Andrea and Tom burst through the kitchen from school, starving, demanding Amber's attention.

"I'd best go. My two will be screaming at the bottom of the stairs looking for me. Thanks for the coffee, sweetie."

Amber squeezed Lucy's hand and walked with her to the hidden gate.

"Amber, how did you get such magnificent green eyes?"

Amber laughed. "Oh, you silly girl. They're contact lenses. My real eye colour is hazel, but don't you go telling anyone at mah-jong!"

That night Lucy really looked closely at herself in the mirror, she was still slim with good legs and since she had been playing regular tennis she had a nice tan. Her hair was straight and dark, cut in a neat bob with no sign of grey; she had known since primary school that she wasn't a beauty. Her small heart-shaped face was smooth and lightly tanned, accentuating her wide blue eyes. She kept herself fit and knew that she had a certain sex appeal; in the early days, Hallam could not keep his hands off her. She wondered what had changed.

The following week everything was thrown into chaos. Holly came home from school with the chicken pox. The poor child was covered all over in fierce red macules. Even the inside of her mouth had not been spared. She was miserable. Lucy spent her days bathing her in bicarbonate of soda and applying calamine lotion, reading and playing games with her to distract her from her irritating misery. She knew Cameron would be next. Luckily Amber's children, who they played with regularly, had already had them. Alarmed, she wondered if Yolo had had them in her childhood. She pictured herself nursing the whole household!

Hal was away but due back that night. The phone rang late in the afternoon; Lucy was expecting a call from him. She hadn't heard from him in days. He didn't know of Holly's suffering. She heard a loud crash on the landing of the stairs, and went out to find a painting had fallen; the glass had splintered into a thousand pieces. She looked up and saw Yolo's stricken face; in her hand she clenched the phone.

"Don't look so worried, Yolo, we'll have it reframed, and it's not the end of the world."

The woman started to sob, dropping the phone. She flung herself into Lucy's arms, babbling incoherently. "It's a sign, *aswang*, my *batà* my Naty she is gone, *patáy*."

Yolo continued to sob hysterically; Lucy untangled herself and called Amber. She asked her to send Honeyko over, to try to make some sense of what had happened. Yolo lay on the timber floor of the foyer, curled in a foetal position. Honeyko rushed in and knelt at her side. They spoke in rapid Tagalog. Honeyko fell back onto her haunches with tears running down her cheeks. Lucy stood helplessly, holding Holly, who was also crying. Amber arrived with her hair wrapped in a white towel from the shower.

"Tell me what's happened!"

Honeyko, visibly shaking, told her that Yolo's mother had called. "Yolo's six-year-old daughter Naty was run over by a government bus and killed on her way to school this morning!" Honeyko went to Yolo and held her as she continued to sob on the floor.

Amber raised her eyes to Lucy. "She will have to go home as soon as possible, Lucy. I'll make the arrangements, and you look after Yolo with Honeyko."

They carried Yolo to her room and put her on her bed. Lucy gave her a sedative; it calmed Yolo's hysterics, leaving her crying quietly into her pillow. Honeyko stayed with her throughout the night. As Lucy closed the double doors to the kitchen, she could hear the doleful weeping of a mother for her child. Lucy hated herself for doing so, but she locked the door. She had no way of knowing what the woman would do in her state of mind, maybe her own children would be at risk. Depressed, she went to bed after checking on Cameron and Holly. Placing a damp cloth on her little girl's feverish brow, she thought of another child lying dead in a province somewhere in the Philippines.

Hallam did not return that evening; by the time he came home, Lucy had taken a haggard Yolo to the airport. She carried four large jars of coffee in her small bag. "For the wake," she told Lucy.

Honeyko had told Lucy how much a simple funeral would cost, and she gave Yolo more than was required. Yolo took it gratefully. Lucy watched as the diminished figure of the grief-stricken woman went quietly through customs. Until that phone call, Lucy didn't even know Yolo had a child. She was a mother, like herself. She felt ashamed at having taken so little interest in the woman with whom she shared a house and her own children. She went home to her bungalow on the edge of the jungle, not knowing how she would cope without Yolo. She realised how much she had come to depend on her. Her stomach contracted and tightened at the thought of the weeks ahead without her.

Chapter Eight
The Way of the Apostles

Madam Wei Ling Leng, as good as her word, had efficiently organised a transfer for Esme, complete with glowing references. She was sorry to let the girl go and would miss her company.

Esme had been regularly remitting money each month to her family in the Philippines, after paying off the agent fees for six months. She learnt through the occasional poorly written and misspelt letter from Manny that her father was ill and had lost his room in the slum. Olina and he were living in Lola's shack. Esmirada's money was going toward medicine and keeping the three alive, as Lola was no longer able to work. Ricardo now had three small mouths to feed and the eldest one was attending school thanks to Esmirada's earnings. She also found out that Buboy, after visiting a prostitute late one night, had been stabbed and robbed. He was left to die alone on an unlit road, in a puddle of foamy, dark blood.

Esmirada stood quietly in the kitchen of Madam Yi Feng as she and Madam Wei Ling Leng discussed her in Mandarin. She surreptitiously stole glances at her new ma'am and her surroundings. Similar homes in the quiet, leafy street surrounded the semi-detached two-storeyed house. She could hear birds singing and Madam Yi Feng's twin daughters laughing as they played on the swings in the garden, a small white fluffy dog nipped at their heels as they tore about. The young mother was sleek and polished, her shining ebony hair hung to her shoulders and moved fluidly as she turned her head to openly examine Esme. Her dark eyes flashed as she coldly appraised her. She tapped her blood-red talons impatiently on the marbled bench top as Madam Wei Ling Leng dutifully listed Esmirada's achievements. The interview came to an abrupt end, and Esmirada watched sadly as the rotund figure of her previous employer disappeared beyond a bank of bougainvillea.

Madam Yi Feng wasted no time in putting Esmirada to work. She instructed her about her duties in perfect English, and told her how she wanted the work to be executed.

"I am a very busy woman, I am involved in charity work and have many civic duties to perform, as well as running my boutique in Oceanic Plaza. My husband is a very important businessman in Singapore and we entertain diplomats, bankers and high-powered foreigners. I will not tolerate disobedience, sluttish behaviour or dishonesty. The minute I hear of any indiscretion, you will be sent home immediately!"

She glared coldly at Esme, her deep, red lipstick leaving a stain on her slightly protruding teeth. "Do you fully understand?" She spat out in Esme's direction, one hand placed provocatively on her hip.

"Yes, ma'am," Esme replied, her eyes lowered, carefully studying the pristine marble flooring.

By the end of the first week Esme was so tired she could not even summon the strength to cry. She crawled into the tiny bolthole off the pantry that was her room. It was so small it couldn't fit a proper bed, so she slept on a pallet on the floor. She missed the comforting words of Rejoice Radio to send her to sleep. The dog, Jilly, received better treatment, sleeping in a cushion-lined basket in the kitchen.

During those first few weeks Madam Yi Feng squeezed every bit of time and energy out of Esmirada, and in return showed her nothing but contempt. Esme was instructed not to take food from the refrigerator without permission. All she had to eat was a tawdry amount of bread for breakfast, instant noodles for her midday meal, and fish and rice late at night, after she had cleaned the leftover bones and debris the family spat onto the table during their gluttony.

Each meal was a banquet: double-boiled soups, roast duck and chicken, noodles and rice, all cooked by Esmirada to Madam's precise instructions. The little girls were fat, bad mannered and spoilt, taken by car to preschool, piano lessons, mandarin lessons and tutoring for gifted children.

Esmirada's day started at five with breakfast preparations, and did not end until well after midnight. Whilst her ma'am went about her daily routine of tennis, hair and spa appointments, mah jong with her *tai tai* friends and occasionally visits to her boutique. The handsome *towkay* was rarely home. On the rare occasion when she was forced to address him, he ignored her, acting as though she didn't exist. Although, when her madam was out, he would engage her in cheeky conversation, making Esme uncomfortable. He forced her to scurry away like some animal to the sanctuary of her hole in the wall. She tried to befriend the little girls, Pearl and Ruby, but they treated her in the same manner as their mother, telling her she smelt bad and slamming the door in her face when she approached the television room.

For the first month Esme was not permitted a day off. Instead she was allowed to accompany the family to Sunday brunch at the lofty Riva Hotel down by the Singapore River. While her ma'am and sir guzzled champagne and entertained their guests, Esme sat at the children's table, taking care of the twins and two horribly obese boys, who spent the entire morning stuffing their faces with food. The children were rude and boisterous, disturbing other families around them, spilling drinks and fighting with one another. Despite the beginning of a throbbing pain in her temple, Esme was happy to be there. She had never been anywhere as lovely as this room and hotel. The lobby was grand with a vast expanse of dazzling white marble. A staircase carpeted in rich colours swept majestically up and spiralled out of sight to another mysterious level. The buffet hall where they were seated was light and airy, overlooking the yellow river. Slender, pale women and foreign men with large noses laughed and ate as the sun spilt across the wooden floor and velvet seating. Esme was examining the beauty of the timber flooring when her small charge made a disgusting heaving noise, and promptly sprayed an arc of multi-coloured vomit across the room. Madam Yi Feng shot a menacing look toward Esme and motioned her to remove the child immediately. Esme half-carried, half-dragged the dead weight of the boy to the women's lavatory and did her best to clean the vile mess. Madam Yi Feng entered in a cloud of expensive perfume.

Seething, she spoke between clenched teeth. "What did the boy eat? Didn't you watch how much he had! You were greedily stuffing your own mouth and not supervising the poor child!"

Esme was stupefied. "No, ma'am. I didn't eat anything, only water to drink."

Madam Yi Feng rose from her crouched position and took the boy by his hand. She stood and faced Esme, grabbing her wrist hard, twisting the skin of her arm painfully. "I said no dishonesty. Don't lie to me, you have made me lose face in front of my friends and the whole restaurant!"

Esme stood, tears pricking at her eyes. The smell of the boy's vomit hung heavy in the closed space of the cubicle.

The door flew open and the mother of the child rushed in, full of concern. She swept up the boy and cooed, "My little prince, are you better now? Something must have disagreed with you. Come, boy, come to Mummy."

They swept out of the room without another word, leaving Esme standing alone, the boy's disgusting stain seeping into her one good dress.

During Madam's weekly mah-jong sessions, Esmirada was required to serve the refreshments. Running back and forward to the kitchen, she served freshly made *bubur cha cha* and *popiah,* refilled water glasses and kept the jasmine tea hot. The noise of the clicking tiles and the woman's high-pitched chatter was like being in a birdcage. She couldn't help but overhear snippets of their conversation.

"She's small, won't eat much *lah*, but pretty, you should have got an ugly one! Did your husband pick her?" Shrill laughter and more click clicking of the tiles.

"She's right *lah*, the uglier the less problems you will have! And I say never give them a day off, pay them extra or take them out for a meal, but no days off!" A buzz of agreement fell over the felt-covered table.

"If you do let them go off, they talk and get big ideas and start answering back!"

Not all of Madam's friends were unkind, she found the expats who came to play thanked her when she poured their tea and looked her in the eye, not pretending she was invisible. They often helped her by bringing the dirty plates and cups to the kitchen and placing them by the sink, sometimes engaging her in conversation about her country and family. Madam Yi Feng always had a way of bringing her down and reminding her of her lowly status within the house. Madam often won at mah-jong. When she did, she was fawned upon and congratulated by the other players, smugly collecting her winnings and looking down her nose at Esme as she cleared the table.

"Well, unless you're a winner, you're nothing. Isn't that right, Esmirada?"

All Esme could do was mutely walk away, humiliated once again.

Living in Changi was very different to Toa Payoh; Esmirada never left the house to go to the markets as she had once done. Instead, each morning at eight the phone rang and she would read Madam's carefully compiled list to Annie Bee Grocers. At midday the cocky Malaysian uncle delivered the goods, leaving them on the kitchen bench, after vainly flirting with her.

She enjoyed the quiet solitude of the house when the family had gone for the day. She gathered and sorted the dirty clothes and put them into the washing machine, which she had easily mastered. Instead of bamboo poles, the clothes were strung in the back airing room to dry while Esmirada attended the rest of the house. She padded silently about the girls' rooms, where the wooden shutters admitted spangled sunshine onto the white bed covers. Plumping the batik cushions and placing a plush teddy bear in a cane chair, she hummed softly to herself the songs of her childhood. Carefully she dusted the collection of delicate jade pieces beside the rosewood furniture, and admired the delicate inlay of marble that no one ever sat on. She avoided looking at the stern portrait of the ancestors from China, feeling their eyes upon her as she moved about the room. In the cool interior of the master bedroom she had been instructed to clean and dust but touch nothing, she could feel the flinty eyes of Madam Yi Feng boring into her back from her formal wedding portrait above the bed.

No matter how sophisticated, gracious or Western Madam Yi Feng tried to behave, Esme knew she stood on the toilet to pee, left her soiled underwear on the floor, and hawked phlegm into the bathroom sink every morning like a dirty old man. She always finished as quickly as possible in this room and retreated to the garden to feed banana to the parrots and hornbills, which visited each day. In the marble entrance foyer was a black slate pool with red and gold carp, Sir's pride and joy. Sir was the only one allowed to service the carp and the pond, but Esmirada liked to stop during the day and admire the deep black pool, with the plump, colourful fish darting from end to end.

Her peaceful reverie ended at midday, when Ruby and Pearl returned from preschool with their mother. She gave them their lunch of chicken, vegetable and rice or dumpling soup while Madam changed her tennis outfit, and had a nap. The twins would watch television and then go on to their afternoon lessons, leaving Esme to iron the clothes and prepare the evening meal. Most evenings Sir and ma'am would have a function to go to, Esme had to fix Madam's hair and fasten her jewels. Often there would be grand balls and formal occasions; Esme sighed at the magnificent gowns and jewellery her ma'am wore. The jewellery was kept in a safety deposit box at the bank. Sir thought it unnecessary and a nuisance, since he would have to retrieve it whenever she wanted something special to wear.

She overheard Madam telling him, "I will not take any chances with that girl in the house!"

Ruby and Pearl took advantage of their parents' absence to wilfully misbehave, refusing to go to bed and fighting with each other. They ate forbidden food and sweets, threatening to tell their mother that Esme had in fact eaten the food. This had happened more than once, and the mother

51

always took the children's side, scolding Esme in front of them as they smirked behind her back. She would pinch Esme's arm, her eyes glinting maliciously, until she cried out in pain. After that, the twins took to scolding Esme, kicking and pinching her when she tried to put them to bed. At times, it was too much and she went to her hole in the wall in tears, praying to God for a release.

A frequent visitor to the house in Changi was Joel, Madam Yi Feng's Filipino dance instructor. He arrived dressed in a see-through nylon T-shirt and black fitting trousers that flared out over his sharp-toed boots. He greeted Madam Yi Feng with air kisses and hugs. He taught her the cha-cha and Latin American dances late into the afternoon. Esmirada glimpsed the enraptured look on her madam's smooth little face, as he dipped and twirled her leopard-printed clad body about the living room. Joel accompanied her to the balls and mid-week dances, when Sir was out of town. Esmirada knew of these dance instructors. They were legendary in the Philippines, swivelling elderly woman about the dance floors. Manny at one time had great ambitions of becoming an instructor, but he had two left feet. Most were just toy-boys for the *tai tais*. Joel did not come cheap. Esmirada knew her madam paid up to three hundred dollars for a night of dancing.

Joel was in the habit of stashing his small leather clutch bag in the kitchen. Esmirada moved it once, spilling the contents of mouthwash, cologne, mints and condoms all over the floor. Often he dashed in to have a quick spray, before lavishing more attention on the demanding Madam Yi Feng. When he took a break, he went to Esmirada's toilet to smoke, gargling furiously with mouthwash before he went back to his partner. When Madam went to her room, Joel came to talk to Esmirada, trying to convince her of his genuine intentions. What he didn't know was Esmirada heard every noise in the house, and late at night when Sir was out-station, she heard Madam's tiny dog-like yips and Joel's huffing and panting.

He stood in his tight trousers sipping on mineral water, waving his manicured hands about, jangling his fake gold bracelets. "I'm well known in the Philippines you know! I'm lavished with cars, clothes and holidays! One of my clients, an eighty-year-old *Lola,* gave me a house! There's no hanky-panky with my clients; I keep a distance when I am dancing. I have the respect of their husbands. I may be only a dance instructor, but once on the dance floor, I am in command. I make all the moves and make them look good!"

Madam's whining voice came from the living room, and Joel minced away, reeking of cologne, anxious to satisfy her every need.

The family greedily embraced all of Singapore's cultural and traditional holidays. They celebrated Christmas, as well as Chinese New Year. During Christmas the house was transformed with green and red garlands. In the front foyer a real fir tree imported from America stood festooned with coloured lights and baubles. Friends and family were entertained over dinner with roasted turkey and goose, delivered in boxes from the Riva Hotel kitchen; numerous bottles of X.O. brandy would disappear during the course of the evening. Christmas Day was spent recovering from the excesses of the night before.

On Christmas Eve, Esme took a deep breath and timidly asked, "Please ma'am, may I attend Midnight Mass?"

Madam Yi Feng looked away contemptuously, but relented when she saw the dark look on her husband's face. "After dinner is finished and everything is cleared, then you can go!"

By the time Esme reached the welcoming place of worship she was weary and flagging, but the service and singing the praises of the Lord gave her a renewed energy and once more filled her heart.

The Pastor spoke to them as one. *"But the angel said to them. 'Do not be afraid. I bring you good news of great joy that will be for all the people. Today in the town of David a Saviour has been born to you; He is Christ the Lord." Luke 2: 10-11*

"I wish you all a most blessed Christmas this year. May the light of the lord Jesus flow through you into the darkness of the world to bring peace and joy to many, and may the year to come be for you the 'Year of the Lord's Favour.'"

◆◆◆◆◆◆

By Chinese New Year the mental and physical cruelty dealt out by Madam Yi Feng and her daughters had become routine. During the fifteen days of the festival, Madam was in a happy mood and chose to ignore Esme. She shopped constantly, bringing new clothes and shoes into the house, for herself and her daughters. Esme was exhausted with the constant cleaning, scrubbing and cooking sweets and *nian gao* and preparing raw fish salad. Faltering, she stood unsteadily on a ladder, decorating all the doorways with red banners inscribed in gold. Pussy willow and cherry blossom was placed in urns in the foyer and the twins decorated the display with numerous red packets. The Kitchen God was reverently hung and waxed; duck, melon seeds, groundnuts, sausages and mandarin oranges were ordered from the grocer.

On New Year's Eve the candles were lit and guests and family arrived for the grand reunion dinner. Madam was resplendent in a red cheongsam. She gaily flew about, respecting her elders and venerating her ancestors. The house was a picture of filial piety and family togetherness. At eleven p.m. sharp, the children brought tea to their parents and grandparents. In return, they were showered with *hongbao*. There was no red packet for Esme; feeling left out, she hovered in the background, clearing and cleaning. At midnight she threw open the many windows and doors, as she had been instructed, allowing the benevolent spirits to enter and bring endless good luck to the family. Her head rang with the banging of pots and pans by the children, warding off evil spirits. She finally crawled to bed with the sound of drunken *gongxi facai* ringing in the year of the monkey. The following day the family departed to gamble in Genting Highlands, leaving her and Jilly the dog alone and in peace for a week.

On Sunday Esmirada decided she would take half a day and go to church. Ma'am and Sir would not be back until Tuesday, and there was no way of their knowing of her absence. She caught the bus into Chinatown and walked the short distance to the House of Worship on the corner. Halfway there she was caught in a torrential downpour, without so much as an umbrella. She arrived dripping like a stray dog and sat as close to the back of the church as she could. She had a few friends with whom she was on nodding terms, but none that she knew well. Since starting her new job at Changi, she had only attended service once - on Christmas Eve. There was a quiet American, an elder of the church. He always smiled and nodded in her direction, but had never spoken to her. Esme liked his face; it was luminous and round, his eyes crinkled up when he smiled. He looked very kind, but was rather large and overweight, prosperous, as they say. Today he conducted the sermon, and spoke of the women and men who were working far from home to provide for their families. He stood at the front of the church; the sun suddenly shone through the stained glass window and lit the back of his head like a halo. Esmirada hung on his every word.

"Behold what manner of love the Father has bestowed on us, that we should be called children of God." 1John 3:1. Timothy paused for effect and looked out over the congregation.

"How Christian are you? God is unfailing in his love for each and everyone; we are all sons and daughters of God. I thank God for all our

54

foreign workers and pray for all Singaporeans to support them in their loneliness." He smiled and motioned the congregation to stand.

"Let us pray, be strong and of good courage, do not fear nor be afraid of them; for the Lord your God, He is the one who goes with you. He will not leave you nor forsake you." Deuteronomy 31.6.

Esmirada felt that he spoke only to her. She was serene and confident as she ducked out the side door at the finish of the service; she failed to see the large American watching her go.

Rounding the corner of her street, her confidence and serenity failed. Parked in the driveway was a strange car, and on trying the front door, she found it unlocked. The house was quiet, save for the soft hum of the air-conditioner and overhead fans. She saw that Jilly was no longer in the kitchen where she had left her, and was busy sniffing in the garden. She heard a noise from the guest room in the far corner of the house - no more than a soft sigh. She looked around urgently for a weapon and saw a ceremonial Japanese sword out of the corner of her eye. She carefully removed it and trod steadily toward the closed door. There again she heard another sigh. She threw the door open before she could lose her nerve. Her hands went to her mouth, and she dropped the unsheathed sword with a clatter on the marble floor. A naked woman screamed and made a grab for the sheets. Peering from beneath her was the damp, smug face of her boss.

"Oh come now, Esme. You're not going to use that on us, are you? A good Christian girl like you?" He laughed and the woman fell back, sighing with relief.

Esme closed the door, the heat rising in her face and spreading to the roots of her hair. She busied herself in the garden for a while, and then escaped to her room off the pantry. An hour later, she heard a car door slam and the gravel spray up in the driveway.

He came to her door, holding a fifty-dollar note, as if he was offering a dog a bone. "Esme, I want to talk to you."

She came to the door, holding onto the handle for support. He put the fifty where she could see it on the counter top, and started to fix a drink. She stood examining her feet, feeling the warm, soapy tiles beneath them. Jilly came and lay down, offering her belly to be scratched. Sir took his time, stirring the whisky slowly and taking a long pull. He approached her, and boldly traced the outline of her jaw with his cold fingers.

"So lovely, but so God-fearing! Will you find it in your virtuous heart to forgive Sir his sins, Esme?"

She pulled away from his hand as it sent a shock through her body. She stumbled on her words; she was not as eloquent as he was. "It is not up to me to forgive you, sir. It is nothing to do with me."

He took another long pull and swirled the liquid around his tongue before he spoke. "So ma'am will be told nothing of this afternoon! And from next Sunday you will have each one off to go to church and pray for my heathen soul!" He laughed and languidly took his drink to sit in the garden with Jilly.

Esmirada felt empowered, what if Sir knew of Joel's late night tuition? She was tempted but knew she would never tell. To do so would be wrong in the eyes of God.

The following Sunday Madam Yi Feng came to her. "So now you have become a favourite?" She took hold of Esmirada's chin and jerked it painfully. "What have you done behind my back to deserve special privileges? I told you I won't put up with sluts in my house!"

Esmirada looked away disgustedly.

"He tells me you deserve Sunday's off, but that is all you will get, no wage rise and only Sunday mornings, you are to be back here by midday!"

Esmirada watched her as she walked away, a sickness mounting in her gut as her eyes fell upon a large new diamond, sparkling on Madam's finger. The gambling must have paid off; Esme took the fifty-dollar note her Sir had left, and deposited it in the collection tray at church that morning.

Esme became adept at avoiding crossing paths with Madam Yi Feng. She did her work diligently with the knowledge that, come Sunday, she could be alone with her thoughts and prayers for a few precious hours. Madam's taunts and little acts of cruelty continued, but Esme had gained strength from her beliefs and no longer cried at night. The American had struck up a friendship with her at church, and would search her out each Sunday; this wonderful man had suddenly come into her life, and was teaching her the way of the Apostles.

Madam Yi Feng contrived to go for a spa weekend in Bintan with her *tai tai* girlfriends. She needed Esme to take on the twins, and so she was unusually cordial. The week before Madam was to leave, Esme attended her chores as usual; she carefully dusted the jade, and the antique ceramic lady with the bird. She arranged a bouquet of lilies and pink orchids on the glass table in the foyer, and went to receive the groceries for that night's dinner party. Ruby and Pearl arrived from school and were hot, sweaty and quarrelsome. She fixed their lunch and gave them a cool drink while their mother went to rest.

Esme spent the afternoon preparing food for the special dinner. Sir's bank colleagues, and the new American diplomat would be in attendance. Madam Yi Feng was fussing over name cards, deciding who would have the pleasure of sitting next to her. She looked down and to her horror saw the severed body of the priceless antique, lying on the floor besides the Bonsai tree. She screamed for Esme to come at once! Esme wiped her hands on the tea towel as she meekly entered the room. Her ma'am stood cradling the fractured statue in her pale, slender hands. Pearl and Ruby stood at the door to the television room, looking nervously at their mother.

"What happened to my statue?" she spat at Esme.

Esme saw the look exchanged between the twins. "I don't know, ma'am. I dusted it this morning and it was all in one piece."

Pearl spoke up, "Esme broke it and said she would blame Ruby." Ruby nodded, her ebony hair reflecting dark blue lights.

Esme could not believe what she was hearing. "No, ma'am, she lies. The statue was in one piece, I swear!"

The veins in Madam Yi Feng's neck stood out darkly. "My daughter does not lie, you stinking whore!"

Esme saw a flash of scarlet claw as Madam picked up a rosewood chair and hit her full in the face. She could taste blood in her mouth, and hear screaming in her ears. It was not her screams, but those of the twins. Their mother had laid into them with flailing hands, trying to shut up their terrified shrieks. She felt strong arms lift, and place her carefully on soft bedding; something cold was pressed against her eyes and nose. Gradually the roaring in her ears receded, and she tried to sit, but she was pushed back down. She lay helpless, listening to them.

"You have gone too far this time, you stupid bitch! If she goes to the Embassy you'll be charged."

She could hear the fear in Madam's voice as she spoke. "She won't go to the Embassy. I'll deny everything; say she fell. You and the girls will back me up!" Her voice was near hysteria.

"Pull yourself together, this dinner has to go ahead!"

She heard the door close; she struggled to her feet and went back to the kitchen. Nothing was said, it was as though nothing had happened; she went to the bathroom and examined her face. A dark bruise spread across her cheekbone and there was blood between her teeth. One of her eyes had started to swell; she put some cold water on it and rinsed her mouth.

That night the dinner party went ahead as planned. They kept Esme in the kitchen, but when she did appear she avoided the eyes of the guests. She overheard Madame Yi Feng explaining away her bruises superficially.

"Stupid girl fell over a broom she left lying around. These maids are in another world most of the time!"

Esme felt humiliated, confused and alone. She did not know what to do. She didn't want to be sent back home, but she couldn't stand this treatment any longer. She went to bed that night and prayed to God to show her the way.

Over the next few days the twins were sullen and quiet; they obeyed their mother without question. The backs of their legs had angry red welts from the beating they had received out of guilt from their mother. She went to church on Sunday and hid her face at the back of the room. The American, whose name was Timothy, came to find her at the end of the service.

He was horrified when he saw the livid bruising. "Who did this to you," he demanded.

She started to tell him the manufactured excuse she had almost come to believe, but found it impossible to lie to him. Her suffering at the hands of her employer poured forth, all the cruelty, humiliation and despair flowed from her like a fountain. Afterward she felt absolved and cleansed.

He took Esmirada back to the house and waited for the family to return. She hid in her room as they went behind closed doors. Timothy came back to the kitchen with a sobbing Madam Yi Feng at his heels. He asked Esme to pack her belongings; he was taking her to Sister Mary's shelter, until she decided what she wanted to do. Esme stood docilely at the door with her few possessions. Madam Yi Feng stood with her husband, defiantly staring Esme down.

Timothy spoke, his anger barely contained. "This woman is helpless. A maid sells her services, not her soul! You have exploited her dependence on you; she is nothing more than a vulnerable, lonely overworked woman. I will pray to God to forgive you for your cruelty, but the law may not be so lenient!" He turned abruptly on his heel, leaving Madam Yi Feng pale and quaking in his wake.

Sister Mary's terrace house in China Point was a haven for Esme. Sister Mary sat patiently while she told her sad story; she advised Esmirada of her options and left her in peace while she decided which course to take. In the meantime, Sister Mary visited Madam Yi Feng only to have the door slammed in her face. The second visit with Madam's husband was more lucrative.

Esme had decided not to press charges; she couldn't return home, they were all dependent on her salary. The situation there was even worse than what she faced here. Madam Yi Feng had agreed graciously to a transfer, with references, and all the money owed Esme, including her repatriation fare home. In the meantime, Sister Mary helped Esme return to school, at a volunteer organisation in Emerald Hill that ran courses for Filipino maids.

Esme was suddenly spending all her free time learning to type in the morning and practising basic nursing skills and first aid in the afternoon, encouraged by Timothy, who boosted her confidence by telling her, "You don't want to be a maid all your life!"

Nevertheless after two weeks, Esme found herself back at the agency in Garden Heights, but this time she was much wiser and more confident, and she had Timothy on her side.

Chapter Nine
Aminta

The weeks following Yolo's return to the Philippines were chaotic in the Leadbitter household. Cam had the chicken pox, though not as severe as Holly. Once he recovered, Lucy tried to maintain her social activities and those of the children, but the ironing had started to pile up. She shared Honeyko when she could for baby-sitting, but it was too much strain on the girl to expect her to wash and iron for both families.

Yolo travelled over an hour from her province on the back of a truck, to make a brief phone call to Lucy in Singapore. She would not be coming back!

The crunch came when Hallam, leaving for a trip to India, could not find enough clean shirts to pack. His shouting rent the tree-lined street of Bukit Lalang.

"By the time I get back, I want a new maid installed. Otherwise, Lucy, you will have to give up your precious painting and mah-jong and stay at home and get the housework done!"

His eyes bulged and Lucy thought he was going to have a heart attack; she knew how overworked he was. She promised him, as he took a cab to the airport, that she would hire a new maid as soon as possible.

Reluctantly Lucy missed her weekly game of mah-jong, and went with trepidation to Prosperity Plaza. There were numerous agencies to choose from. They all looked the same, sparsely furnished with cheap chairs and carpet, without as much as a painting on the wall to make them a little more cheerful. She rode up the escalator twice before deciding on 'Samfu Maid Agency.'

A young Muslim woman in a traditional *tudung* and *buju kurung*, handed her a book containing photographs and bios of the young women available. Lucy chose one of the torn plastic chairs with the foam innards spilling out, and sat in the corner closest to the air-conditioner. She wished

Amber were there to help, especially when the agency owner, who peered over her shoulder making comments, decided to join her. He was short and squat, with a grimy white shirt that had salty crescents under the armpits. His black hair was greasy and flecked with dandruff; he had one gold tooth and long dirty fingernails on his pinkies. Lucy fidgeted as he pointed with the fingernail; she noticed he had a large sapphire ring and chunky gold Rolex.

"Good job you come to me *lah*. We have the best of the crop. You see this one tiny, won't eat much and this one ugly, won't cause any trouble *lah*!"

Lucy sat shocked, perspiration prickling at the back of her neck as he proudly pointed out the sombre gallery of faces.

"We have shorthaired and fair skin, no dark skin! All guaranteed docile and obedient! You pick, I give you good price."

He walked away, picking the inside of his ear with his dirty fingernail, smelling the harvested contents and then flicking it in the direction of the floor.

A diminutive woman entered with a brisk Singaporean. The Muslim receptionist took the girl's papers, and asked her if she had money for lunch. She nodded without speaking. The receptionist explained to Lucy that she was being sent home, and had to remain at the agency, while her employer cancelled her work permit.

"Either it's here or the police station!" she said, shrugging her small shoulders.

Lucy looked at the young maid who was intently examining the stained carpet and wondered what she had done to warrant such treatment. Lucy chose ten girls to interview the following Sunday, deliberately picking the more attractive.

Out on the elegant Avenue of Orchard Road she watched the chic Singaporeans and the trendy expats go about their lives, secure in the fact foreigners were looking after their homes and children. She knew the maids' lot was a bleak contrast to their daily lives, but she brightened up after a café latte and went shopping for shoes.

The following Sunday she woke early, had a swim with the children, and breakfast in the shaded pool cabana. She prepared lime, sprinkled tropical fruit and plump segments of pink grapefruit. Slowly she sipped her coffee, watching Holly and Cam throw breadcrumbs to the mynah birds that hopped about the ginger plants. She shooed them off hurriedly to collect their swimmers and towels, to spend the day at the Expat club, with Amber, Andrea and Tom.

Lucy carefully prepared herself for the maid agency interviews. She tried to look businesslike in a white, crisp blouse and neat skirt and pumps; she even carried a pencil and notebook. Amber, this time, had prepped her with all the right questions. The interviews started out well. Lucy was relieved when the receptionist told her the owner was off on Sundays. The first few girls were neat and clean with good references, and valid reasons for leaving their current employer. One was transferring because her madam's children had grown, and she no longer needed a maid. Another girl told of how her boss had lost his job, and couldn't afford to keep her. From then on the interviews and candidates began to deteriorate. The next girl, a little older, burst into tears, and told her the old man in her care would not leave her alone.

"He wants to fondle my boobies all the time, and even comes to my room at night!"

Lucy felt terribly sorry for the woman, but was it her place to rescue her?

Another girl told a story of humiliation and abuse at the hands of her employer's teenage children.

"They kick me and spit at me and call me disgusting names."

Lucy was horrified when the maid told her who her employer was. It happened to be a woman with whom Lucy played mah-jong. She couldn't wait to tell Amber!

Others had sad stories of children back in the Philippines, and philandering and absent husbands. Aging, sick parents, and whole families to support. The women seemed as though the life had been sucked out of them, their eyes vacant and posture defeated.

One girl told Lucy, "I can't complain about the family I live with. They give me enough to eat and don't beat me, but I haven't had a day off in two years! Those kitchen walls can get pretty boring after a while."

Finally she came to the last, hoping to end on a high note, but this girl was just as pathetic. "Half a day off for church on Sundays, but not enough to eat, just instant noodles, eggs and rice day after day."

Lucy had heard enough. She was shocked. She didn't have the heart to interview any more girls. She wanted to make up her mind quickly. She was angry that Hal was not there to help her. It was his decision as well. Lately everything was left to her. She decided on a short list of the first three girls, and was glad she was spared the look on the faces of those that were let go. One girl stood out from the rest. She was well spoken and confident with good references. Lucy also noted she had nursing, as well as secretarial skills. Perhaps just a little too confident, maybe too good to be true, but Lucy was tired, her instincts befuddled. At least Hal would be impressed, so she went ahead and signed the papers, handing over her credit card and passport. She had had enough for one day and quickly left, happy to be out on the street again.

She met Amber for drinks and dinner at the club and they sat companionably on the terrace, while the children swam and jumped off the diving board, with swarms of other kids. Brian was in Bangkok and Hal still in India, She ordered gin and tonics and Lucy told her all about the interviews.

"God, Amber. You wouldn't believe the stories I have heard today!"

"Oh honey, try me. I bet I have heard them all."

The club was full; maid's day off, no one wanted to cook! The balmy night closed in softly about them, as they ordered more drinks. Friends passed by their table and stopped for a chat. The children returned and they sent them for showers. Lucy was now completely relaxed. Today had been stressful, but in two weeks she would be free again. She would be able to get on with her life of painting, tennis and mah-jong with no worries about babysitting, meals or washing and ironing.

She raised her glass and made a toast. "Here's to Expat life and long may it last."

"I'll drink to that!" said Amber, throwing back her head and laughing.

The children joined in, clinking their glasses of Shirley Temples, contented and tired after a carefree day in paradise.

◆◆◆◆◆◆

When Lucy's new maid Aminta arrived, she brought with her a fierce electrical storm, which lasted for three days. If Lucy had been superstitious, it would have been a prophetic warning of things to come. The storm brought down ancient trees, power lines and cut off the phones. The vast canals of the city overflowed, flooding the streets, gardens and houses. All manner of debris swept through Lucy's garden, bringing with it pythons, cobras and an army of insects all trying to escape the rising waters.

Cameron found a spitting cobra sheltering on the back patio. He tried to approach it quietly, but it reared up angrily, splaying out its magnificent hood. Lucy didn't know what to do, so as usual she called Amber. Amber arrived wearing sunglasses, armed with a spade and a can of insect repellent. Under Amber's hissed instructions, Lucy stood on the table and sprayed the snake in the face with the insecticide. Amber hit it from behind with the shovel at least five times before it lay down and died. It's serrated body continued to weave about the patio long after the reptile was dead. They had to have a gin and tonic after the killing, even though it was still early in the morning. The floodwater finally halted at the top step of the patio, and receded within hours, leaving in its wake a city rinsed clean.

A woman claiming to be the new maid Aminta arrived later that afternoon. Lucy stood watching her as she ambled up the drive, in no way resembling the girl she had interviewed two Sundays ago. Amber raised her eyebrows above her coffee cup, as she watched her sashay across the lawn. She carried a fake Louis Vuitton bag and was dressed in black lace and tight cut-off pants. Lucy took her to her room and threw open the door cautiously, waiting for Aminta' s appraisal.

"It's small, but I like the idea of being separate from the house."

Lucy took a deep breath and said sarcastically, "Well, that's a relief! You look different, did you do something to your hair?"

Aminta placed her bag on the bed and started to unpack personal items. "My friend cut it and permed it for me. More fashionable this way, don't you think?"

When Lucy interviewed Aminta at the agency, she was wearing a modest white blouse, slacks and running shoes. She was also wearing glasses, and had her hair tied back in a simple ponytail. This new Aminta had a short fluffy bob, no glasses, painted fingernails and high-heeled wedges.

Despite the transformation, her work was as described in her references. Within days, Aminta had the house running efficiently. Her cleaning was fast and thorough, as was her washing and ironing. She cooked superb meals, both Asian and Western and related well to the children. She had her own routine and resented any interference from Lucy.

"She is as I thought, overqualified! I feel totally superfluous in my own home!" Lucy complained to Amber over drinks at the Expat 'Pub and Grub' night.

"Listen, honey, I don't know what you have to complain about, just sit back, read a magazine and let her get on with it, enjoy it while you can, and don't for goodness' sake complain to Hal!"

Lucy felt ungrateful; she hated whinging expat wives, and besides, Hallam was thrilled with Lucy's choice. His shirts were impeccable and the meals delicious, the house was running like clockwork, the kids were happy, and he enjoyed Aminta's chirpy little presence about the place. In fact, around Hallam, Aminta actually glowed. If Lucy didn't know better, she would have thought that she was flirting.

Aminta was firmly ensconced in the house. Every afternoon as she ironed, loud rock music blasted from her room. Following the evening meal, she disappeared behind her closed door and the music would start up again, well into the night.

Hallam just laughed. "Let her have a bit of fun. It's her free time, after all, and she's not hurting anybody."

He was right; Lucy was just edgy waiting for something to go wrong. She started to concentrate on her daily activities, especially her painting. Her tennis and mah-jong improved noticeably once she left the running of the house fully in Aminta's capable hands.

The phone calls started about a month after Aminta's arrival. Short calls at first, but then they became longer. Aminta disappeared out the back with the remote, and talked all afternoon while she was ironing. Occasionally there would be a call for Lucy, but the majority were for Aminta. Lucy started to feel like Aminta's secretary. She confided in Hal one night after he had returned from a long trip to the States.

He sighed impatiently and said, "For God's sake, Luce, what's wrong with you? Surely, you're not going to deny the poor girl a chat with her friends. She does everything around here as it is, and she's in the house six days a week. You know how social Filipinos are. You're starting to sound like a spoilt bitch."

Lucy's timing was way off. Would she never learn? Hallam and she were growing apart with all the travelling he did; their lovemaking was sporadic and without passion, the last thing she wanted to do was alienate him further with her petty problems.

With nothing to worry about except her social pursuits, Lucy concentrated more and more on her painting. She enjoyed the lessons, but realised they were really just a gossip session for the other women. She started to make field trips on her own, sketching the more interesting colonial buildings, and what was left of Chinatown and Little India. Hidden amongst the towering skyscrapers were the legacies of Colonial rule. Parliament house, City Hall, Empress Place, Victoria Concert Hall and the Cricket Club, bordered by an oasis of green, these buildings were once caressed by the sea. Spending hours in the hot sun, her head shielded by a large sun hat, Lucy compiled a sketchbook. She attracted passers-by, who stood curiously watching the strange expatriate woman. Once a week early in the mornings while the children were at school, she would escape. As well as serving as an inspirational and creative exercise, it got her out of the house and away from the prying eyes of Aminta.

Whenever she walked into the kitchen, Aminta would suddenly appear. She dogged her every move, and questioned what she was doing there. Lucy started to sneak about her own house, just to make a snack or a cup of tea. She would pad into the kitchen, open the cupboards soundlessly, and then sneak out again. On Sundays she oiled the hinges, so that she could open and close doors without Aminta suddenly appearing, her black eyes flashing at Lucy as though she was violating her domain. Even the plants and flower arrangements became a source of resentment between the two. Lucy would place a planter in one spot only to come home and find Aminta had placed it elsewhere. Lucy spent hours arranging the flowers, only to find Aminta in her absence had rearranged them, and moved them to a more aesthetic location.

Amber told her she was becoming paranoid; it was just a power struggle. "Show her who's boss. Don't be so timid. She's too good a maid to fall out with. You'll be sorry if you do."

So, on Amber's advice, Lucy tried to regain some control over their lives. Instead of leaving everything up to Aminta, she planned the menus and did the grocery shopping. When she held a dinner party, Lucy insisted on doing most of the cooking, but all her efforts backfired. The children complained that Aminta's spaghetti bolognaise was better than hers, and Hal complained about the quality of the meat and fish, claiming Aminta's purchases were superior. After cooking for the dinner parties, Lucy was too tired to eat, and ended up drinking too much and becoming belligerent. Hal turned his back on her after one such episode, and climbed the stairs to bed in stony silence. All the time Aminta would be standing in the background, a satisfied smile on her dark face, witness to Lucy's humiliation and frustration. Lucy badly wanted to slap that face, but instead gave up and went back to the only pursuit that gave her confidence and satisfaction - painting.

Once she had completed the sketchbook of Government buildings, she started on the ornate, pastel terraces in Emerald Hill and Boat Quay. She tried to imagine the days of traders and godowns and the frenzied loading and unloading of cargo. She would take a deep breath of that peculiar Asian smell: soy, exotic spices and open drains. In her imagination she could see the jostling for space of the wise-eyed boats, along the overcrowded river.

It was all gone now, the godowns were restored as restaurants and bars, and the river now boasted fish life, the junks had long since disappeared, with only the odd one ferrying tourists along the waterways.

After one long session sketching black and white bungalows in Cornwall Park, Lucy was caught in a storm and forced to wait huddled under an awning for the downpour to end. The children had gone to the club with Amber, for swimming lessons and dinner. Hal was still in Thailand. She had promised to join them at the club later but now she was soaked through to her underwear and would have to go home first. Lucy felt pleased and happy that she had now completed her final sketchbook. As soon as she had time, she would anxiously start to transpose them onto watercolour sheets. She drove home, dripping, singing to the local radio. Not even the devilish motorbike riders or the maddening taxi drivers could dampen her spirits.

She bounded up the patio steps two at a time, and entered the cool interior of the bungalow. She heard trilling laughter coming from the dining room. Candlelight flickered in the draught of the overhead fan, illuminating the kitten-faced Aminta. She sat next to a sheepish Hal, enjoying an intimate dinner for two.

Hallam stood nervously, dropping one of Lucy's best linen napkins to the floor. "Luce! Surprise, I came home early, only to find my family missing in action! I was lonely, rattling about this old dining room by myself, so I asked Aminta to join me."

Lucy's stomach contracted violently, and the tips of her fingertips went cold. "Well, it all looks so cosy, I won't stay. I'm off to the club for dinner with Amber and the kids."

She turned and ran upstairs, locking the bedroom door. Her body trembled as she changed her clothes. Her hands shook so much she could barely do up her buttons. She swallowed profusely and propelled herself down the stairs two at a time into the car, sending up loose gravel, as she gunned it out of the drive and headlong into the evening traffic.

Her face burned as she took deep swigs of her double gin and tonic, trying to control her shaking hands. Amber took the children to the games room so she could compose herself, and then she blurted out the little domestic scene she had just witnessed.

"The bitch! That's going too far. What the hell does Hal think he is playing at?" said Amber, the heat rising in her pale face.

Lucy didn't want the children to overhear. Holly, especially, had big ears, so she let the humiliating subject drop. Besides, she wasn't sure that

Amber wouldn't tell the others at mah-jong next time around. They sat and ate large platters of *nasi goreng* and *prawn mee*, all except Lucy, who had no appetite. She drowned her sorrows in gin and had to be driven home by Amber, leaving the car at the club to be collected the following day.

She rose quietly at dawn and walked in the misty garden, listening to the birds peppering the Tembusu tree. A dull pain above her left eye radiated down and lodged beneath her jaw. She was nauseous, compounded by vertigo; all she could manage was a cup of mint tea and two aspirin. Feeling cowardly, she couldn't face the black eyes of Aminta, or the bovine look of concern from Hal. She dressed haphazardly while the house slept, and took her paints, collected the car and went to the nature reserve. There she sat, brooding and painting landscapes for the better part of the day, until she could summon the courage to confront Aminta. She knew Hallam would be lost trying to cope with the children and their activities. Cam had soccer on the oval at Lisbon Road and Holly had ballet in the opposite direction at East Coast. Let him sort it all out for once. Maybe he would appreciate her a little more when he realised all she managed to do in one day.

She arrived back to rock music cutting through the peaceful afternoon. Aminta was chopping vegetables into small pieces with a sharp-bladed knife. The implement flashed expertly in her hands as Lucy entered and abruptly switched off the radio. Aminta ignored her and continued chopping. Lucy put a hand onto Aminta's skinny brown one, and a carrot flew off the bench and skittered across the floor.

Aminta turned her flashing eyes toward her. "What is it, ma'am?"

Lucy fought to control her rapid breathing and said, "I think you know, Aminta! I think it is extremely inappropriate for you to have dinner alone with my husband. In fact I think it is inappropriate for you to eat with the family at all. You are a maid here, not a guest!"

Aminta started to protest, but Lucy held her hand up, silencing her. "I don't care if Sir asked you to join him. You know what is acceptable behaviour; I will not tolerate you overstepping your position in this house. You are the maid and I expect you to behave like one. Do we understand each other?"

Aminta sniffed and wiped her nose with the back of her hand. "Yes, ma'am."

As Lucy left the kitchen, she could feel Aminta's cold eyes and the sharp blade of the knife aimed at her spine, which shortened involuntarily.

She hurried away, panting heavily up the stairs to the sanctuary of her room.

Hal came home with the children, exhausted, angry at Lucy's sudden disappearance. He was perplexed at her outlandish behaviour the night before, and thought she was making a 'mountain out of a molehill' over Aminta having dinner with him. The evening meal was sullen, with pregnant pauses between courses. Aminta sulkily and slovenly slammed down the food and then vented her rage in the kitchen, finally retiring to her room to play her rock music at an ear splitting level. The children watched a video and went to bed, tired from the day's activities, oblivious to the heavy atmosphere that pervaded the house.

Sunday morning Lucy watched Aminta from the balcony window, as she left to meet her friends in Orchard Road. Her cheap perfume hung heavily in the early morning air. She minced along the driveway in platform boots, her skin-tight jeans tucked into them. She wore a red bra that was visible through her black lace top. How could she have chosen Aminta? The woman had duped her, and now she could do nothing but live with her mistake.

Lucy climbed back into bed with Hal, her heart heavy. She knew there was only one way to make things right between them. She reached for him and he turned over, holding her tenderly. To her joy and anticipation, he kissed her deeply, making love to her urgently, over and over again.

Chapter Ten
On the Game

In November, Singapore was transformed. The city suddenly resembled downtown Europe. Fairy lights festooned the trees lining Orchard Road. Hotels and malls experienced a severe 'snowstorm'. Lights like diamond pendants were strung from one side of Orchard Road to the other, and the overly ambitious air-conditioners in the department stores added to the wintry atmosphere. Lucy took Cameron and Holly to see the snowmaking machine at Robertson's, and they had their photographs taken with an oriental Santa in front of a styrofoam winter wonderland.

At school the children performed in the annual Christmas play. Lucy hauled out her old sewing machine to somehow miraculously make an elf, a fairy and a camel's outfit. For a change Hallam was in town. With Christmas fast approaching, business travel had slowed to a trickle. They all went to the ornate Victoria Concert Hall to see 'The Amateur Players Club' perform a traditional English Pantomime with an Asian twist. Amber, Brian and the children joined them and they had a heavy Italian lunch with lots of red wine beforehand. Post lunch, Hal snored loudly in the front row. The Dame took advantage of him, flaunting his pendulous breasts in his face, but Hal continued to sleep, totally oblivious to what was happening around him. The children were hysterical with laughter, and it was one of the happiest afternoons they had had as a family for some time.

The invitations for Christmas parties and drinks arrived daily; Millie, the diminutive dressmaker, was kept busy sewing dresses for Amber and Lucy to attend all the festivities.

Lucy frenetically ploughed through the crowds, from one department store to the next, in search of the perfect Christmas gift. The traditional Christmas carols with their scenes of snowmen, chestnuts roasting on open fires and glowing faces of children, contrasted ridiculously with the heat, humidity and sudden tropical rainstorms of an equatorial Christmas.

70

Strangely enough for Lucy, it brought with it a sweet nostalgia for the Christmastime of her childhood, spent visiting friends in the fire-ravaged bush or holidaying with her mother on the balmy coast of Queensland; sweet memories long forgotten, after years spent in England.

Lucy, Cam and Holly spent hours in the kitchen, preparing Christmas goodies; they excluded Aminta from these preparations and she went to her room, sulking. The children helped Lucy make Granny's fruitcake, densely packed with glazed fruits and nuts. They each had a stir of the pudding and made a wish. Then they stamped out Christmas tree cookies, and decorated them with hundreds and thousands.

"I don't think we should put them on the tree, Mum, because the geckos will eat them," Cam said in a very serious voice.

"You're right, sweetie, I don't think these will last long anyway, with you lot."

Holly carefully piped out meringue snowmen and Cam decorated their faces. Hallam came home unexpectedly later that afternoon; he was in a sentimental mood and played their favourite carols from their days in England. He rounded up the children and together they made a nativity scene, with paper mache, Cam's farm animals and an angel hovering over baby Jesus.

He wrapped his arms around Lucy's waist. "Tell me we don't have a party to go to tonight, please."

She turned and smiled up at his generous face. "Tonight, a special dinner at home, with just me and the kids, okay?"

"Perfect, how about a G&T?"

She watched him go, hoping nothing would spoil this Christmas. Everything seemed back to normal.

That evening Lucy made scallops and mussels in a pink peppercorn sauce, and Aminta made lasagne for the children. They ate outside under a sky filled with stars. The nightjar sang and the fan lazily cut through the ropey air. They finished a mellow bottle of red, and Hallam opened another. The children went upstairs to finish off their Christmas lists and Aminta went to her room.

"Remember last Christmas at the Dorchester? Seems a million light years from here!"

Lucy laughed, remembering how all twenty of their friends and children shared a table in the hotel. It was a snowy Christmas Eve, with the crystal voices of the cathedral choir ringing in the icy air. The food, wine and atmosphere were magical. They had all stood in front of a huge, perfectly

71

shaped tree, decorated in antique baubles and real candles, and exchanged gifts. At midnight, they listened to the bells of the city, calling them all to Mass. This year she knew would be different, but still special. She would try hard to make it so. They finished the last of the wine and headed to bed. In passing, Hallam mentioned that his secretary Elvira was leaving him for another company. Lucy was not sure why, but that was the best news she had had for quite a while. Once in bed, he turned to her and they slowly made love.

The following morning she heard the phone ring as she slid into the driver's seat. She ignored it, knowing it would be for Aminta. The calls had not ceased. Sometimes at night, when Lucy answered, the call abruptly ended, and Lucy jumped to the conclusion that it was a male. She had planned, once Christmas was over, to look into having the calls traced, but that could wait. Right now, she and the children were going to buy a Christmas tree. They drove to Thompson Plant Plaza, the sunroof open and singing 'Santa Clause is coming to town' at the top of their voices.

They moved slowly between the sun-washed rows of trees. The heat brought out the rich scent of the imported Douglas and Noble firs. An old man trundled along close behind, hoping to get a sale. Lucy left the decisions up to the children, while she picked out pots of deep, red and pale lemon poinsettias, looking closely through the rows for the most vibrant and healthy of the bunch. She also bought a cedar wreath to go over the kitchen door. When she returned, Holly had chosen a rather spindly Douglas fir; the old man was doing his best to persuade her otherwise.

"*Not nice lah, aiyah too skinny branches*! But if you want, *hup ply*. Want or not?"

"No, I think perhaps that one over there would look better. What do you kids think?" Lucy steered them towards a beautifully shaped tree with fuller branches. It gave off a heady aroma of fresh pine.

"This one is bigger, Cam! We'll take this one, Uncle," said Holly, taking over the negotiations.

"You *wait awhile ah.*" He scurried away to get the necessary paperwork.

"This will look lovely in the foyer. Just the right size and shape. You kids chose well!" Lucy kissed the tops of their heads.

The uncle came scurrying back with his order pad. "This one *solid siah, shiok! Will fetch tomollow* to your place, *can lah.* Where you stay?"

Lucy patiently gave the address.

"Sorry ah, can say again?" He licked the tip of his pencil without waiting for her to finish.

She repeated the address twice, eventually taking the pad and writing it out herself. They paid and bid the old man, "Merry Christmas."

He patted the children's heads. *" Ger vely chio, boy vely yan dao!"*

On Christmas Eve Amber organised one of her famous parties, a profusion of food and champagne for the adults, and a visit from Santa for the children. Smugly, queen of her kitchen once more, Lucy helped by preparing her favourites: smoked salmon, haddock and asparagus tartlets, mince pies and Stolen. The turkey and stuffing were ready for the oven the following day, as was the glazed ham and Christmas pudding. After tonight's party, the family would go to a midnight service at the small Methodist Church near the children's school. Aminta had been more than agreeable all week, and approached Lucy late that afternoon, as she was wrapping Christmas gifts and placing them under the tree.

"Ma'am, I wanted to let you know I will be going to church tonight, for Midnight Mass."

It was a statement rather than a request; one Lucy could not refuse. It was Christmas, after all.

Guests spilled out of Amber's bungalow onto the patio and into the garden. Amber had employed the services of the waiters from the club, and they were doing their best to keep the glasses refilled. Vast quantities of food, champagne and mulled wine were consumed, which Honeyko was busy replenishing; Lucy had offered the help of Aminta but Honeyko preferred to work alone. Lucy knew that Honeyko didn't like Aminta!

Santa distributed gifts to the children. Dancing to old favourites, Hal threw Holly into the air, catching her and swinging her to the beat. Cameron and the boys were in the television room, playing with their toys. Lucy's tennis coach, Ramley, had her cornered in the kitchen as she poured more wine; his big dark hands began to rove. Diplomatically she tried to extricate herself from under him. Later she noticed Angel pinned beneath him, but she didn't seem to mind. He was extremely handsome with his flashing smile. She watched amused as Angel pressed her arms together, trying to make the most of her cleavage; she had been dieting over the festive season and had lost weight. Tuppy hovered close to the buffet table, piling up her plate and enjoying the spread, whilst the Major General had moved no more that a few inches from the bar.

Brian was a congenial host. He kept the drink supply coming, and the ice bucket filled. Mioko, the petite Japanese girl who played mah-jong with

73

them, was sitting on Angel's husband's lap. She was nodding vigorously, her eyes glassy, hanging on his every word. Lucy knew Mioko spoke very little English, but that didn't seem to worry Peter. She heard Amber's gutsy laugh coming from the garden. Lucy saw her throw back her head and take a long pull of her champagne, surrounded by a group of admiring men.

By eleven-thirty Lucy knew she would have great difficulty convincing her family to go to church; they were having too good a time. Finally, with much complaining, she rounded up Hal and the children and they boozily went off to the midnight service. The church had standing room only; families, dressed in their best clothes, were wishing each other, 'all the very best for the season'.

The sweet voices of the choir resounded up to the wooden beams and spilled out onto the moonlit lawn, where small children ran about, their eyes bright with anticipation. Listening intently to the Christmas message, she could feel Hallam swaying beside her, smelling strongly of mulled wine.

"Christmas is a time to rethink all that stands in the way of God's Love. This Christmas may Jesus fill your hearts with his peace!"

"You will show me the path of life, in your presence is fullness of joy, at your right hand are pleasures forevermore." Psalm 16; 11

The congregation, talking as one, spilled out into the warm, frangipani scented air. They wished each other, "Merry Christmas and Happy New Year," as they scooped up tired, overexcited children to go home to Father Christmas. Lucy felt the expatriate community tried harder to make the celebrations special, sharing their joy and good wishes with each other, in the absence of their extended families.

Filled with goodwill, she drove home, Hal nodding beside her, asleep. Holly and Cameron, too, gave in and slept the moment the car was in motion. She listened to Nat King Cole sing her favourite Christmas carols as she drove through the dark streets. Hal woke and carried their sleeping children upstairs. With no fireplace, they hung their stockings on the ends of their beds. Hallam was tired but poured another glass of wine, while Lucy dutifully filled stockings and placed gifts under the tree. She found him passed out, snoring loudly, and fully clothed on their bed. Gingerly she changed, slid between the sheets and without waking him wished him a "Merry Christmas."

She had forgotten the foyer lights and padded silently downstairs. The clock in the hallway struck four. Moonlight spilt evenly across the lawn, and illuminated a small figure creeping slowly up the drive, shoes in hand.

74

She watched Aminta, her luminous face darting about her cautiously, as she found her way to her room. Lucinda sighed, turned off the light and went to bed, rolling Hal onto his side to ease his laborious snoring.

Nudged from a deep sleep, Lucy opened her gluey eyes and found Hallam grinning down at her, brandishing champagne and orange juice and a beautifully wrapped gift. The children's delighted shrieks echoed through the lofty rooms of the house. She rolled over, looked at the time, and realised she had only slept for two and a bit hours. Cameron and Holly romped on their bed like warm puppies, displaying their spoils amidst laughter and wonder at how Santa knew exactly what to bring them.

Hallam kissed her temple and said, "You did good, Mamma. How about my specialty breakfast, and then I get to play Father Christmas!"

Holly let out a deep belly laugh and bounded off the bed then downstairs to supervise in the kitchen. Thankfully it was too early for Aminta. Hallam had always been a good cook, creative and inventive but messy. He and Holly set about making smoked salmon omelettes with dill sauce. Cameron made the Bucks fizz using lots of bubbly and little juice, so that by the time it came to gift giving, they were all falling about giggling stupidly. Aminta came through the kitchen door, sheepishly, to find them still dressed in pyjamas, sitting amongst reams of wrapping paper, pulling Christmas crackers and telling jokes. Holly ran and gave her a small gift, Lucy fished beneath the tree and handed her a prettily wrapped hamper, with lots of delicious goodies from Marks and Spencers. Aminta took her gifts back to her room, saying nothing and giving nothing in return.

Late that morning, Hal snoozed while the children swam in the pool. Aminta and Lucy tackled the turkey and ham. The Van Engles were joining them for a late Christmas lunch; Lucy planned to eat at about two in the afternoon. Aminta silently prepared the brussel sprouts, and broccoli for the puree, and the pumpkin and potatoes for the baking tray. Lucy stuffed the turkey with the chestnut stuffing and struggled with it to the oven. The honey-glazed ham, which she had prepared the day before, was resting on the sideboard, covered in foil. She prepared a starter of smoked trout parfait, and put it in the refrigerator to set. All that was left to do was the dessert Hallam had promised to prepare.

Lucy tidied the wrapping paper and finally opened Hal's gift. In the privacy of her room, she opened it slowly, peeling away each delicate layer of paper. Hallam was in the kitchen with Aminta, preparing his brandy butter and meringue and chestnut pie. The box contained a silvery confection of underwear and a black velvet pouch with a delicate gold and diamond bracelet. It was lovely; she fastened it hastily and flew downstairs to the kitchen to thank him. She could hear Aminta's tinny laughter. Lucy couldn't imagine what the sanguine Hal could say that would cause such mirth; she'd never found him to be that funny. Aminta averted her dark eyes when she entered.

"Hal, it's just lovely!" She held up her slender wrist for him to see. He wiped his hands and held her wrist in his huge paw, admiring the trinket, as though it was the first time he had seen it.

"Suits you, Luce. Looks lovely on you." He went back to beating his meringue, Aminta slyly hovering about his elbow.

She walked slowly upstairs to dress, Aminta's laughter following her. The effects of the champagne were wearing off and leaving her a little melancholy. She would wear the new underwear he had given her and surprise him tonight when they undressed. Unfortunately when she tried them on, she found he had bought them with a much smaller woman in mind. Disappointed, she wrapped them and placed them in the box. They would go into her bottom drawer along with all the other gifts Hal had bought her over the years that were not quite right.

She set the dining room table with her finest Christmas dinner service and silver flatware. Holly, her tongue clenched firmly between her teeth in concentration, put Christmas crackers and nametags at each setting. Lucy hung mistletoe above the door and put a silver urn full of fresh red berries and white orchids in the centre of the table. She stood back in admiration; the table looked lovely.

When the Van Engles arrived, the house was fragrant with the delicious smell of roasting turkey. They brought with them a coldbox full of wine and champagne, a basket of Christmas goodies with a handwritten note that said, "From my kitchen to yours at Christmas," and an armful of colourfully wrapped gifts.

The bungalow on the edge of the jungle in Bukit Lalang rang with laughter, singing and merrymaking and the sound of children playing Marco Polo in the pool. The Indian gardeners, happy to have a day off, peered over the fence and shook their heads in bewilderment at the strange antics of the foreigners, as they walked along the road to the bus stop.

At dusk, when the Rod Stewart birds appeared, a second round of guests arrived. Lucy brought out more food and opened another crate of champagne. Hallam pounded away on the piano and the crowd gathered around to sing Christmas carols, which by early morning had deteriorated into bawdy ballads. The party was still in full swing as Aminta, who had left after dinner, came sneaking back through the gates and made her way unnoticed to her room.

Hung over and irritable, Lucy hastily packed the following morning for the family to leave for Bali on the afternoon flight, leaving Aminta to look after the house until their return on New Year's Eve.

◆◆◆◆◆◆

In Bali, Lucinda concentrated on her painting, while Hal spent most of his time on the phone. She started a Bali sketchbook. Bali and its mystical spirit and customs were an inspiration to Lucinda. She had heard so much about the island and seen so many photographs and paintings. Visiting for the first time and looking, not with a tourist's eye, but that of an artist, helped her to produce an abundance of creative material.

Cam and Holly swam every day and went to the kiddies' club each afternoon to paint, make kites, carve fruit and play games. Hallam worked; Lucy slept, swam and painted. She started with their hotel. The Oberoi was a mysterious old lady, with individual compounds in magnificent gardens by the sea. She painted the split gates and temples, lotus ponds with their statues of gods and frogs, floating pavilions and the garden bathrooms.

In the evenings they walked along the rutted roadway, passing *Warungs,* where the locals gathered to chat and drink coffee and beer. They watched the family pass by, flashing their white teeth, smiling by way of greeting. Motorbikes whizzed past, only inches from where they walked. Lucy tried to peer over the decorative walls to the compounds beyond, to catch a glimpse of the local houses. They sat by the sea with the smell of burning incense heady in the warm night air, and ordered cocktails and spicy Indonesian food, *nasi goreng*, fish with pickles, *satay* and chicken curry. The children ran and played hide-and-seek barefoot in the sand, while Lucy and Hal sat in the warm night air, holding hands.

One stormy day she walked along the beach with Cam and Holly. The sky was navy with sombre, low-lying clouds, and the sea a dirty yellow. Mangy dogs ran up to them, looking for food, and hawkers, having had a slow day, pestered them to buy. In the distance, they saw a colourful procession. One of the young men selling kites explained to them it was a funeral procession and cremation. Lucy was fascinated and from a distance, while the children played in the sand, she furtively sketched the ceremony. The procession reached the beach, carrying a highly decorative cremation tower, a sarcophagus in the shape of an animal encasing the bones of the dead. Lucy watched mesmerised as the entire tower burnt.

The boy told her with the smiling teeth, "The Balinese believe that the body is returned to the elements, and the soul to heaven."

She bought kites for the children without haggling. His grin widened when she offered him a few dollars extra.

They walked back by way of the ocean and stopped under a Banyan tree. The branches had grown down and re-rooted in the earth. They watched a ritual cockfight, but Lucy thought it was cruel, and dragged the reluctant children away.

It was raining again the following day and over breakfast in their pavilion Hal suggested a trip to Ubud.

"Listen, brats, stop that noise." The children were in the pool, playing their favourite game; as usual it had developed into an argument, with Cam accusing Holly of cheating.

"Let's all go and have a look at some rice fields. I don't have to work today. We'll have lunch in the mountains overlooking the river."

Hallam rented a jeep and they climbed in eagerly, looking for a bit of adventure. The small rattling jeep took them into the mountains, past floating shrines, stilted barns and terraced rice fields. They watched the procession of beautiful women, balancing colourful offerings on their heads, making their way to the temples. Lucy sketched constantly. The jeep passed over an ornate Dutch bridge, and monkeys scuttled from the edges of the roadway into the protecting jungle.

All along the way, villagers rested in stilted, thatched-roofed pavilions. The thatch was oily and black, made from the fibre of sago palm. They visited Ubud's main palace and watched a performance by a local dance troupe with interest. The beautiful dark-haired maiden enticed Hallam to dance, but when she approached Cam, he hid behind Lucy shyly and refused to go. Holly, however, brazenly picked up the steps and hand movements immediately.

They lunched in a hotel high above the terraces and fast-flowing river. The wide windows opened out onto the misty, blue mountains. A myriad of butterflies wafted on the cool breeze, as the family watched the white water rafters on the boiling river below.

A hazy red sun shone high above them on their final day. Hallam worked and sent faxes, while Lucy painted the flowers in the gardens. Cameron and Holly swam and ordered their favourite *satay* for lunch. Lucy phoned Bukit Lalang, but there was no answer.

She called Amber. "Hi, honey, how's everything going? Did you get the tickets for New Year's Eve?"

Amber answered breathlessly, "Sorry, Luce, just ran in from the pool, we have a few people over for a barbecue lunch. I have the tickets; we're all set; I rented a video for the littlies so they'll be happy. You should see the great dress Millie ran up for me, that woman is a genius! We won't tell any of the girls at mah-jong or she'll put up her prices."

Lucy could hear the laughter coming from the pool in the garden below.

"Listen, sweetie, how's Bali, I'm dying to hear all about it, have you bought much?" Amber was a shop-till-you-drop type, whereas Lucy spent most of her time painting, although she had managed to buy a few souvenirs.

"I'll show you when I get home. I'm worried, Amber. I just called the house and didn't get an answer. Have you seen Aminta about?"

Amber had been bracing herself, hoping Lucy wouldn't ask. She and Honeyko knew that Aminta had not been home since the family had left. Late one evening, she had seen Aminta returning with some local in tow. She had taken it upon herself to investigate, knocking on Aminta's door, only to find her alone. She suspected the guy had jumped out of the side window when he heard her.

"Well I was going to wait until you returned to tell you this, but our little Aminta is leading a double life. She's been away from the house and entertaining at night. I think you might have to confront her, Lucy, or risk losing your five thousand dollar bond. Sorry to spoil your last day."

Lucy felt ill. She hated confrontation, but she couldn't let this go. She wouldn't tell Hallam. He always stuck up for Aminta, finding reasons for her recalcitrant behaviour. God, this was all so sordid. She had to think of Cameron and Holly, and she would not allow this behaviour in her own home. God knows who the woman had been bringing into her house while she had been away. She felt violated and shrunk at the thought of what lay ahead. Aminta might be a good maid, but the late-night phone calls, the clothes, the porcelain fingernails and now the men, was too much. She had to get rid of her.

Her jaw clenched tightly, Lucy sat in the small seat of the plane. A baby in the bulkhead cried persistently throughout the flight, wrestling in the small and inexperienced arms of its mother. Lucy fidgeted, wanting to take the child and calm it. Hallam and the children were plugged into the entertainment system and didn't seem to notice. She constantly rehearsed the scene she envisaged with Aminta; she would be firm and strong.

As it was, it turned out to be a complete anti-climax. When they arrived home, crumpled and grumpy from the flight, the house was locked and Aminta missing. Hallam thought nothing of it until later in the evening when it came time to press his dinner suit.

"Did you give her time off?" he asked accusingly.

Lucy went to see Amber and found her luxuriating in a hot tub, having been to the hairdresser and manicurist, in preparation for New Year's Eve. Lucy felt cheated; she had had no time for such preparations. Amber poured them champagne, and listened sympathetically to Lucy as she raged. Finally she calmed down and Amber organised her.

"Bath the kids and bring them over. Honeyko has got a special treat for dinner. We've ordered 'Rockie's' pizza and she made a huge pitcher of Shirley Temples. I have a stack of videos for them. They'll have a ball! Grab Hal's shirt and dinner suit and I'll get Honeyko to press them for you. Now sit down on the edge of the bath and I'll give you a manicure and pedicure and put your hair in hot rollers."

Lucy did as she was told. She didn't have the energy to argue. She had to conserve it for the battle ahead. Amber salvaged the evening and they all left by taxicab for the club at eight. The four children were happily ensconced in front of the television, stuffing pepperoni pizza into their mouths and drinking Shirley Temples from champagne glasses.

The Expat Club was heaving with beautifully gowned woman dripping with jewels, and men in dinner jackets and black tie. The dance floor had been given an extra coat of beeswax, and the tables were elegantly dressed, awaiting the guests. The tree and Christmas décor sparkled beneath the crystal chandelier in the lobby, as members kissed and hugged enthusiastically, wishing each other 'Happy New Year.'

Lucy, her polished, sun-kissed shoulders bare in her turquoise gown, looked almost Grecian with her hair swept into a chignon, which Amber had expertly wound for her. They moved elegantly across the gleaming expanse of floor, Amber in figure-hugging, black silk, to find their table. They claimed a space, reserving it with their evening bags. Hallam secured glasses of champagne and the men were already in party mode, popping streamers and wearing ridiculous hats. Lucy put all thoughts of Aminta from her mind, as she quaffed her bubbly a little too quickly. They had a noisy table of ten. Angel, dressed in an oyster-coloured silk gown, was drunk before the entrée was served. Her husband Peter was sliding his hands over the pert, velvet-clad bottom of Mioko, whose towering English husband was talking shop at the wet bar. Tuppy wasted no time tucking

80

into the food. She was talking to Hallam, her mouth full, spittle flying in all directions. Hallam tried to look interested, but was only half listening. Amber signalled Lucy to rescue her from the foul breath and boring conversation of the Major General.

The revellers happily ploughed into a meal of carp, roast venison and baked pear pancakes, washed down with copious amounts of red and white wine, topped with champagne. Throughout the dinner, streamers shot off randomly, everyone wore hats, and the noise of whistles and paper horns was deafening. Lucy tried to eat her venison but multi-coloured streamers filled her plate, the dye from which ran into her champagne, turning it a rosy pink. A three-piece orchestra played during dinner and then the more informal entertainment of "Rough and Ready", dressed in sixties gear, brandishing guitars and wicked grins, took to the stage. The table abandoned their food and flocked to the dance floor. The room filled quickly to capacity with writhing, rocking and gyrating bodies. Lucy knew that most of them, including her, would regret such strenuous antics come the dawn of New Year's Day. By midnight, she was well on the way to being not just tipsy, but staggering drunk, but then just about everyone else in the club was in much the same state.

The pendulum clock, high above the trophy cabinet in the foyer, struck midnight with a resounding peel of bells. Silver balloons rained from the raftered ceiling, showering the revellers with silver glitter that filled their hair, eyes and mouths as they kissed, and clasped hands and bodies in a tribal dance of goodwill. The Royal Ghurkha band, resplendent in their Blackwatch tartan, piped in the New Year to inebriated cries. The dancers formed a circle and threw their legs and arms high in a drunken Highland Fling. Amber grabbed Lucy by the hand. They took off their high-heeled sandals and ran to join the queue of dishevelled women waiting to jump off the bar into the arms of the burly rugby team. The Men's Bar was the sacred and exclusive domain of the male members of the club. The only night of the year it was violated by the presence of females was on the Eve of the New Year. Lucy didn't see Hallam hidden near the squash courts, making a lengthy, animated phone call on his bulky mobile; and he didn't see her throw herself with joyful abandon into the strong arms of the rugby players.

◆◆◆◆◆◆

Splashing water and laughter filtered into Lucy's sodden brain. She opened one crusty eye cautiously, and saw a blurry, crumpled, turquoise mass that she recognised as the remains of her ball gown, in the corner. Strewn across the floor were the remnants of debauchery, party hats, streamers, noisemakers and a street sign.

Oh, my God. She sat up with a jolt and a sickening pain shot through her body. Her brain sloshed about like egg-yolk and she gingerly lay back on the pillows. Where did they get that street sign? She knew where, because she recognised the name. The street that housed the Expat club, but how did it come to be in her bedroom? It was illegal, she was sure. She remembered the boy who had been caned for vandalism. All this thinking made her brain ache and her stomach lurch. The smell of cooking drifted up the stairs and permeated the room. It sent her lurching to the bathroom; she clutched the toilet bowl as though it were a life preserver and wretched her heart out.

Falling back against the rumpled, damp bed sheets, she slept for what seemed like hours, but was only minutes. Hallam entered, disgustingly cheerful, carrying a tray laden with Bucks Fizz, eggs Benedict, bagels and freshly percolated coffee.

"Happy New Year, darling! What a night! Kids are in the pool, Aminta has gone off for the day, and all's right with the world! Sit up, my girl, a hair-of-the-dog is what you need. This will fix you right up!"

The only thing that registered in Lucy's spongy brain was the name Aminta. She tried to speak, but found her tongue too thick. The coffee he offered burnt the foulness from her mouth and she felt slightly better.

"What do you mean, Aminta's gone off? Where was she yesterday, and how the hell did we get that street sign?"

He forced her to have a sip of champagne, but it turned her stomach, and she pushed it away roughly.

"I was in the kitchen, cooking, and the little dark maiden pounced on me, scaring the shit out of me. Apparently she had stayed with a friend who was being sent back to the Philippines. She helped her pack her boxes and went with her to the airport to see her off. She came home just after we left for the club. I didn't think you'd want her hanging around here all day, so I gave her the day off. It is a public holiday, after all."

He crossed the room, chuckling. "Looks like someone was in a hurry to get me into the sack!" He picked up Lucy's underwear, sandals and dress and laid them reverently across the back of the armchair.

"Well, look what we have here." He picked up the accusing street sign as though it were some sort of trophy. "Never knew old Brian had it in him. I dared him to do it, and I guess he was drunk enough to do anything. Well, just about anything." He laughed at his little joke.

"Hallam, you and Brian will have to take it back. It's stealing."

He threw the sign aside and came and lay down next to her. "It will make a great souvenir. Stop worrying, no one saw us, and it was five in the morning! How about a New Year kiss?"

Lucy did not come downstairs until noon. Hallam had cooked a barbecue and set lunch in the pool cabana. The aspirin started to take effect and she felt marginally human. Holly called out to her to join them in the pool. She swam for a while and then lay quietly in the shade, listening to the sounds of the children's play and thinking with mild disgust about her overindulgent behaviour the evening before. Hallam slept, spreadeagled in the hot sun. Lucy pushed her feet into her sandals, and went into the house to retrieve the spare key to Aminta's room. She had had the key cut just before Christmas. Aminta didn't know of its existence.

The key slipped easily into the lock. She turned it cautiously, calling the girl's name, just in case. Her eyes took a moment to adjust to the dim interior; a musty sweetness made her nostrils twitch. The room was chaotic, clothes thrown everywhere, stale and rotting food, unmade bed and accumulated grime. A dusting of cheap face powder spilt across the dressing table and onto the floor. Lucy picked up a jar of cream with a missing lid, and read with interest, "Bust Developing Cream".

On the table next to the bed was an overflowing ashtray and packet of cigarettes. A carafe of Californian wine lay half-finished next to a pair of discarded, strappy high heels. A calendar hanging on the end of the wardrobe had been marked off with black crosses. She picked up a Singapore Airlines diary and flipped through it; it contained names and places written in Tagalog. She recognised bags, shoes, children's clothes and things of Hallam's that she'd discarded. Aminta had retrieved and saved everything.

A familiar yellow envelope, lying carelessly on the bedside table, caught her eye. She closed the door behind her and sat down against it while she inspected the photographs. There were numerous shots of the dining room, the table set with her best linen and china. Seated about the table were complete strangers. Confused, she spilt the rest of the photographs onto the floor, sorting them roughly with both hands. More pictures of her dining room, this time with Aminta sitting on the lap of one of the men. He had his head thrown back, laughing, and his hand resting comfortably inside her dress on her small breast. There were numerous pictures Aminta and other girls in similar poses. In each photograph Aminta was with a different man. She recognised the dress the maid was wearing. Frantically she searched Aminta's wardrobe and found it. It was one she had never worn, and then she saw, lying in a dusty corner, the underwear Hal had given her for Christmas, soiled with dark, crusty menstrual blood. She reeled back with shock, the smell of the room sickening her. Unsteadily she lurched out into the blinding daylight, but not before she saw the half-hidden framed photograph of a small, sad-eyed boy, a gaping hole where his smile should have been. She rushed upstairs to douse her feverish face with cold water. Thirstily she put her mouth to the tap and drank.

The phone rang and she jumped. It was Amber. "Hi kid, how are you feeling? Happy New Year! What a night, best New Year's Eve I have ever had."

Lucy let Amber ramble on without interrupting, until finally her supply of gossip had run dry. Only then did Lucy tell her what she had found in Aminta's room.

"My God, she's on the game!"

"You mean prostitution?"

Amber sighed at Lucy's naivety. "Of course prostitution, she's certainly not playing at Girl Scouts. Listen, Lucy, this is what you'll have to do. You have to cancel her work permit immediately, but say nothing to her because I think she might bolt and you'll lose your bond. There's no telling what she might do, so you have to play it close to your chest. Put your silver and jewellery away. You'd better check and see if anything is missing. Once you get the paperwork done, tell her she's going home and to pack her bags, then take her straight to the airport."

Lucy felt exhausted; she pressed her cold hand to her aching forehead. "Amber, I don't know if I can do this."

"Don't you worry, leave it up to me. It's probably best if we get the agency involved. I'll be with you. Say nothing tonight and we'll go first thing in the morning, send the kids over here for the day."

Lucy followed Amber's instructions, avoiding Aminta when she returned. Hallam had made dip-in-egg with toast soldiers and they were in bed by eight. She watched Hal through half-closed eyes as he packed his overnight bag for Malaysia, whistling cheerfully as he carefully zipped it closed. She couldn't sleep. Instead she lay awake, biting the inside of her lip, thinking of the small boy in the photograph with the tragic harelip.

The following morning Cameron and Holly were brittle and uncooperative. Uncharacteristically, she yelled at them, and they went, teary and sniffling, to Amber's house. She hated Aminta for putting her and her family through this. She dressed hastily and slipped her feet into a pair of comfortable shoes. Amber called her from the hallway, and she squared her shoulders, took a deep breath and went to confront Aminta. Amber, in total control; stood in the doorway, calmly sipping a cup of coffee.

"The game's up, honey! We know what you're up to, pack you bags you're going home."

They had Aminta cornered in the kitchen like a rat. Amber held the envelope of photographs in her manicured hand, and threw them across the counter top at Aminta. Smirking, Aminta shrugged her shoulders, and tossed the tea towel she had been holding to the floor.

"Let me make a phone call." She ignored Lucy, speaking directly to Amber, sensing she was in charge.

"Nope, no boyfriends or should I say, pimps, involved. Just pack your bags, and make sure it's only what you arrived with."

Lucy's stomach tightened and she held onto the kitchen bench for support. Aminta shoved past her, flashing her dark eyes in her direction. Amber stood at the door, while the maid quickly threw her pitiful belongings into her fake designer bag. Lucy locked the house and had the car running. Aminta shambled out and shoved the bag roughly at Lucy.

"Don't you want to check what I'm taking?" she sneered.

"No more games, Aminta, I've had enough. Have you stolen anything from me?"

Aminta wiped her nose with the back of her hand and said, "No." She slid into the back seat with Amber, and Lucy locked the doors.

At the agency, they were cool and unconcerned; this sort of thing was a daily occurrence. Aminta was put into a room and asked if she had lunch money. She just shrugged her shoulders and picked up a magazine to read. Amber left with Lucy to go to Foreign Assist to complete the necessary paperwork. First stop: Philippine Airlines, where they bought the cheapest one-way ticket they could on the afternoon flight. At Foreign Assist, they took a number and sat in the rigid bucket seats and waited. It was a slow day and they didn't have to wait long. No questions were asked, the passport and work permit were cancelled and the fees paid, all very matter-of-factly. Lucy walked out of there feeling as though she had been released from jail. Sighing with relief, she went to collect Aminta.

Silently they drove along the bougainvillea-lined expressway. Aminta's confident swaggering had disappeared and she now slumped inconsolably in the corner of the car, her forehead pressed hard against the window. They parked and alighted, Aminta sandwiched between them. When they reached the departure hall and approached immigration, Aminta made her break, and ran, heading for the automatic doors and the street. Lucy screamed, adrenalin surged through her stressed body; she threw down the bag, ticket and passport and sprinted after her prey. Lucy's tennis coaching came in handy, the muscles in her legs pumped and she easily outran her quarry, grabbing her by her flying hair and wrestling her to the ground, much to the amazement of the stunned, open-mouthed businessmen and tourists. Amber caught up with them, along with a fat and perspiring security guard, who took Aminta into custody and escorted her through security. Only then did she look back, her black eyes flashing. Her final comment to Lucy caused her legs to go weak.

"You're a fool! You don't know what's going on under your nose. You'd better keep a close eye on your husband." Aminta turned, shrugged off the hand of the security guard and disappeared through customs. Lucy crumpled into the car next to Amber.

"Come on, let's go down to the club for lunch. We'll sit and watch the tennis, and lust after the yummy Ramley." Amber squeezed Lucy's leg and took off at great speed into the midday traffic.

Chapter Eleven
A Kind Employer

Lucy's problems didn't end with Aminta's departure. The late-night phone calls continued. Hal was travelling more than ever and for longer periods, leaving Lucy to deal with the calls, which became increasingly abusive. The callers, all men, didn't believe Lucy when she told them that Aminta had gone. Finally she informed them she was having the calls traced, but not before one of Aminta's customers turned up at the house looking for her.

Lucy was alone with the children, when a florid, meaty-faced Chinese man peered through the louvred window. Her heart lurched painfully, while Holly screamed and became hysterical. Lucy called the police, but by the time they reached the house, the intruder was long gone. The two extremely young police officers advised her to get a dog or have a burglar alarm installed. She decided the latter would be less trouble.

Hallam had promised Lucy a trip to India during Chinese New Year, but with no maid to look after the children, he went alone. Instead, she decorated the house with pussy willow, and hung red fire crackers around the doorframe. She and Amber took the children to Chinatown to trawl through the outdoor stalls, resplendent in red and gold. They bought novelty items to make hats for Angel's Chinese New Year party. They ate noodles at a nearby food court, under a flashing string of lights and saw a rat the size of a small cat disappear down a nearby drain.

On every corner there was a lion dance. The hypnotic drumbeat and the mystical dragons wove through the thronging crowds, ducking, weaving and performing acrobatic tricks. The following day they went to the Chingay Parade in Orchard Road. The sun beat down, frying their brains as they stood three deep in the crowd, craning their necks to try to see the performance. The sky darkened and they made a run for it along with everyone else, all surging forward at once. They found refuge in Denny's and treated themselves to chocolate Sundaes, while waiting out the storm.

Lucy had tacked the invitation to Angel's Chinese New Year party to the notice board weeks ago. At first she had declined because Hal was away, but Angel insisted.

"If you said 'no' to every invitation just because your husband's away, you would never go anywhere; besides there will be others on their own. It's always more fun that way, darling. You'd better be there!"

As a result of that conversation, Lucy now sat crossed-legged on the floor with Holly, designing a hat to wear. She had got as far as turning on the glue gun, but needed inspiration. She flipped through a few local magazines and illustrated cookbooks, but they only made her hungry.

Holly was keen to help. "Maybe you could do a hat with chopsticks and noodles."

Lucy looked at her daughter lovingly and kissed the top of her head. "Brilliant child! Come on, Hollyhocks, let's get to work."

They glued red and gold stamped fabric onto a conical straw hat Lucy had bought in Bali. Holly fetched a Chinese bowl and they filled it with cream-coloured wool, representing the noodles. She then stuck a pair of lacquered chopsticks into the bowl, and a couple of dried chillies to complete the illusion.

At the party the following Saturday, Lucy's hat was a great success. She stood on Angel's breezy terrace, looking out over the lights of the city, with a lychee martini in one hand and holding onto her hat with the other. Angel's maid, Rani, barefoot but dressed in a pale blue-striped uniform and white, starched apron, ducked in and out, handing around Chinese dim sum.

She smiled shyly at Lucy and whispered at her elbow. "Ma'am, I have a friend who wants a kind employer. She's very nice." The girl looked hopefully at Lucy.

"I'll see, Rani, I'm not sure just yet what I am going to do."

"But, ma'am, you can't look after the house and children all by yourself, you need my friend Esme to help you!"

Angel signalled Rani back to the kitchen, ending the conversation. Lucy's confidence had taken a battering after Aminta's betrayal, but she knew that eventually she would have to find someone else.

Later in the marbled dining room, Angel caught up with her. She was wearing a coolie's hat and had tied a beautiful batik sarong about her lithe body.

"Rani told me she spoke to you about Esme. Listen, Lucy, this girl is good, cooks and cleans like a dream and is highly religious to boot. No trouble like the other one! If I wasn't so happy with Rani, I would take her myself. She's had a rough time, poor kid. I personally know the Chinese bitch that employed her. I play mah-jong with her and she is a real cheat. I don't blame the husband for playing around; he's loaded so she turns a blind eye. She took all her frustrations out on Esme. God, I wanted to hit that cow myself, after I saw what she did to the poor girl, but Esme didn't press charges. Like most of them, she couldn't afford to go home. Think about it, Luce, that house is far too big for you to manage and why should you."

Lucy promised Angel to give it serious thought and went to find the loo upstairs; she stopped to admire a black and gold calligraphy piece on the stairwell, which Angel had recently commissioned. She stood for a while outside the locked door of the bathroom, but grew impatient, deciding to use Angel's en suite. She quietly entered the bedroom and there, entwined on the apricot chaise longue, was Mioko and Peter. Mioko's silk dress had ridden up above her waist and Peter's hand was buried in her slickly parted flesh. Intent on their game, they failed to notice her. Flustered and feverish, she hastily made for the foyer; she couldn't meet Angel's eyes as she pleaded exhaustion, and one-too-many lychee martinis. Promising to interview the maid Esme, she got out from under Angel's scrutiny, before she said too much.

Chapter Twelve
The Quiet American

When Timothy Waldon first saw Esmirada Espinosa at a prayer meeting, he was so mesmerized by her unspoilt beauty that he forgot to pray. Timothy had come to Singapore to teach English to a group of conscientious, bright primary school pupils. He lived in a humble two-bedroom apartment above a cane shop. Although he enjoyed teaching, at times he felt dismayed by the lack of emotion the children portrayed. They were extremely efficient at regurgitating facts, but watching their blank faces day after day as they dutifully opened their textbooks, saddened his soul. Whilst they were well trained academically, their social skills were poor. Pushed aside by over-ambitious parents, and forced from one private tutor to the next, left them little time for socialising.

How different his own childhood had been, growing up on the windswept beaches of Martha's Vineyard. His father was a Methodist Minister in Boston, but had died when Timothy was only five. He and his mother moved to the vineyards where she procured a job in real estate. They lived in the family's ginger bread house, as they were known in Oak Bluffs.

Timothy's father holidayed with his family as a small boy at Oak Bluffs Methodist camp. Along with many other devotees and their families, they attended services in the huge iron tabernacle in the town centre. After years of enduring leaking tents, Timothy's grandfather built a humble cottage with fancy wooden scrollwork, which stood to this day.

Timothy loved the close-knit, caring spirit of the small town. As a boy he remembered the flying carousel, and Illumination night in late August, when the trees were garlanded with Japanese lanterns. As a teenager, during the summer, he worked at one of the hotels looking after the island's holidaymakers. He supplemented his mother's meagre income by delivering milk and eggs on bicycle for a local farmer. During those long hot summers, he longed to be out surfing on Stonewall beach or sailing a catboat around Chappy Island with all the other teenagers.

During the seventies when he was in Boston at College, the bottom dropped out of the real estate business when the indigenous Indians claimed back their tribal lands. His mother happily retired to the ginger bread cottage, and spent her days cheating at croquet. Each university break, Timothy dutifully returned. They picnicked on the island and wandered down beach paths lined with colourful rugosa roses to the ocean beyond. He cooked corn and lobster over open coals and ritually attended church on Sundays. As the weather closed in and the holidaymakers disappeared, they would lunch at the inn, sitting close to the open fire at a table set with crisp white linen and fresh flowers.

His mother died early one autumn when the leaves had turned to russet; he returned to bury her in the small cemetery called Lambert's Cove, next to the father he couldn't remember. He left the island for the last time as a solemn formation of geese passed overhead.

Timothy had been lonely when he first came to Singapore to teach. He met another Singaporean teacher who gave him a list of churches, but offered to introduce him to his own place of worship. Harold Seng Loh and his wife Joyner helped cultivate Timothy's sense of belonging in Singapore. He participated wholeheartedly in the small church in Chinatown Point, becoming a church elder and Boys' Brigade volunteer. Through Sister Mary he was awakened to the plight of foreign workers. Helping to make them a part of the church, no longer strangers, fulfilled Timothy's need to belong to the community. He was appalled by the cruelty he read on a daily basis in the national newspaper, and did all he could to support Sister Mary and her refuge in Emerald Hill. It had been his idea to start the school, rallying businesspeople, expats and ambassadors to give generously. Volunteers had help set up courses ranging from business, counselling, cooking, hairdressing and dressmaking. He had further plans to develop the grounds for recreational use.

The Sen Loh's had become his family. He spent Christmas and Chinese New Year in their home. On Sundays after church they went to the hawker stalls to eat stingray and chilli crab, sitting amongst the plastic buckets of soupy water where the stall workers half-heartedly washed their dishes. He drank warm beer and sugar cane juice, and listened to the shouts of the hawkers; it gave him a feeling of contentment. He loved the heat and humidity, sharp smells and warm rain. He knew God had a plan for him and he was happy for it to unfold in Singapore.

Timothy had always been shy with the opposite sex; he'd watched Esmirada closely before he summoned God to help him find the right words to say to her. He knew there was a time for everything but once he had finally spoken, he was impatient for the relationship to grow. He read everything he could about the strict social codes and Filipino etiquette on courtship. The more he read the more confused he became. He realised, compared to the West, how claustrophobic those codes could be. Just holding hands with a man could have serious complications.

Esmirada hadn't encouraged nor discouraged his clumsy attempts to get to know her. She merely smiled politely, with her eyes lowered beneath her luxurious lashes. When she came to church with her face hideously bruised, he felt so protective of her. He was full of hatred for the person who had inflicted that injury, but knew that wasn't very Christian. After the confrontation with Esmirada's employer, he was frustrated that Esme would do nothing, until, after speaking with Sister Mary, he understood her situation. He realised how easily he could have lost her, if she had gone back to the Philippines. God moves in mysterious ways. Their friendship and trust had grown, and now he treasured the few hours each Sunday they had together. Only last Sunday he heard her laugh for the first time. He told her all about his hometown in Martha's Vineyard and in all innocence she had said, "Who was Martha?"

When he told her that Martha was the name of the discoverer's mother-in-law, she bubbled over with laughter, displaying her small white teeth. When Esmirada started working for a new family, he held his breath and prayed that she would continue to attend church. His heart overflowed with gratitude when he saw her shining face smile up at him from the congregation. She stayed for the entire service and afterwards for discussion group. Later when he went to the hawker stall with Harold and Joyner, he saw her having lunch with Sister Mary and some of the girls from Mary's refuge. She was talking animatedly and laughing; he couldn't keep his eyes off her.

◆ ◆ ◆ ◆ ◆ ◆

At first Lucinda was very watchful with Esme. After Aminta she was highly suspicious, but couldn't find any fault with her. Her work was meticulous; she was polite, discreet and painfully shy, especially when Hal was around. She was more relaxed with Holly and Cameron. Lucinda often walked in to find them talking away playfully, but Esme shied away in her presence. She knew from the agency and Angel that her former employer had abused Esme. She kept that in mind when dealing with the girl.

Hal returned from India bearing gifts as well as a mysterious stomach bug. Lucy was exhausted nursing him. She breathed a sigh of relief when he finally recovered and went to New Zealand for a conference. He was distant, as usual, but had promised them a trip to Australia during the children's summer holidays. Lucy had started painting again, and her group had decided to hold an exhibition of their work at the club, with proceeds raised going to a children's charity. She had set up a small studio for herself at the far corner of the connecting veranda; it was cool and shaded by the chick blinds and trees beyond. She spent many contented hours in her small haven, listening to the birds and the sounds of the children playing in the pool. Esme slapped calmly around in her bare feet, cleaning and dusting, all the while whistling a childish little tune. Lucy found her presence comforting. She often came home from tennis or afternoon tea with the girls to find Esme and Holly cooking. She would creep up on them and startle them.

"What are you two doing?"

Holly would let out a belly laugh but Esme's eyes were like a frightened rabbits, so she stopped trying to surprise them. Esme could cook wonderful Asian food, her vegetables were a work of art, but at Holly's insistence, she had learnt to cook all the family favourites.

One night at dinner, as Lucinda prepared to leave for a trivia night at the club, Holly announced proudly, "Esme's spag-boll is better than Aminta's, Mum, and heaps better than yours!"

She saw the quick smile on Esme's face and the appreciation in Cam's as he took another serving.

"Esme is low maintenance," she told Amber over lunch at the Marco Polo Hotel. "She cooks all her own food, prefers to eat alone, her room is like a shrine compared to what it was like in Aminta's day. She is truly an angel. Goes to church every Sunday and is home by five in time to cook the children's dinner and do the dishes. She is a gift, Amber!"

Amber took another sip of her spritzer. "You deserve her, after what you've been through, honey!"

Lucy painted furiously as the exhibition approached. She was hoping for big things to come out of having her paintings on public view. After returning from mah-jong one Wednesday, she heard a ruckus in the upstairs rooms. She found Esme brandishing a broom in the direction of two monkeys, who had accessed the veranda via the Tembusu tree. They had made a mess of her paints and easel. A red paint tube had been bitten in two, smeared about the floor, and mixed with monkey urine. One had perched on her easel and defecated onto an unfinished painting of Raffles. Lucy was furious and picked up a broom and hurled it in the monkey's direction. It screeched loudly and bounded onto the window ledge, where it sat calmly playing with its meaty genitals while it peed. After its mate scurried off, he too finally left, bounding from tree to tree and ending up in Amber's garden, where the dog gave chase. She and Esme cleaned up the mess.

Esme started to laugh, covering her mouth with her hand. "I don't think the monkey liked your painting very much, ma'am."

Lucy looked at the ruined watercolour and laughed as well. Cameron and Holly came home and eagerly ran off to Amber's to see if they could see the monkeys.

After the monkey incident, Esme and Lucinda were more comfortable with each other. They talked in the kitchen, planning meals, and often after dinner on the patio. If Hal was away, she would sit for a while and tell her about church and her home in the Philippines. Nothing personal, just little nostalgic things, like how she missed the soya-bean man who delivered fresh soya milk mixed with caramel. Or the way the sky would change when a storm or cyclone blew through. She never mentioned her family, but Lucy knew she sent all of her money home.

Hal came home for a week and worked long hours at the office, and then flew out again to Frankfurt and New York, missing the final week of school and the children's open day and fete. She attended and had a wonderful day, winning the mothers' sprint race. The following Monday was the exhibition. Lucy invited the children and Esme but then realised, because it was held in the Expat club; the rules stated no maids. Lucy was exhibiting a number of paintings. She had been very prolific in the last two weeks, painting until late at night in poor light to finish. Her work received a lot of interest; by the end of the second day, most of her paintings had a red, 'sold' sticker next to them. The children came briefly, had a quick look and then dashed off to the pool. Amber sold one painting, Tuppy none, Mioko's calligraphy sold, as did Jean's brush paintings. The American Women's Association approached Ellie, wanting to reproduce her flower paintings onto greeting cards. On Sunday evening, the women sat on the terrace drinking wine, and toasting the success of the exhibition. Lucy was pleased, but was surprised at how remorseful she felt when she watched her paintings leaving with their new owners. The cheques in her handbag made up for it. She ordered another bottle of wine and some of the club's delicious spring rolls. They toasted their success once more, Amber grinning at Lucy as they touched their glasses.

♦ ♦ ♦ ♦ ♦ ♦

Timothy found Esme quite talkative at church on Sunday. She told him all about the monkey incident, her madam's paintings and all the new dishes she had learnt to cook with little Holly at her elbow. During the discussion group, she was more involved than usual, giving her opinions and sharing her experiences. Timothy watched her blossoming before his eyes. She was more beautiful and lit from within than he had ever seen her before. After lunch with the group, she went to the markets to buy her weekly supply of provisions. This time she allowed him to accompany her. He watched as she made her selections, noting the concentration on her lovely face and film of sweat above her lip. He saw too the admiration from the men around her. Esme seemed not to notice and went about her business quietly and confidently unconcerned. He walked her to the bus stop and as he handed her bags to her, his hand brushed briefly against hers. She looked away and he could see the colour rise in her face. He wanted so badly to fold her to him, but knew it was too soon. He could wait. He had no choice. He had to be patient and win her love with kindness and understanding. He watched as she made her way up the aisle to take her place at the back of the bus. As it pulled away from the curb, she turned to him and smiled a secret half-smile, and then quickly looked away.

Esme alighted from the bus two stops before Bukit Lalang. It was late afternoon and the heat of the day had dissipated. A warm breeze lifted the wisps of hair that had escaped her bun and cooled her damp neck. She liked to walk along this street under the filigreed canopy of rain trees. She peered over gates to flowing lawns beyond, often seeing the children playing in the garden or pool, and families gathered with cool drinks after the heat of the day. The other maids, returning from their day off, greeted her as they passed, laughing, in groups of twos and threes. She thought about the service today and of course about Timothy. He was such a good man; he made her feel special. She thought too about her ma'am and the children. She liked them. They made her laugh and were very kind and good to her. She did not think much about her sir, he was never there and when he was, he said little. He didn't always treat her ma'am well, and late at night when the family were sleeping she would hear him talking quietly on the phone.

95

She knew he had something to hide, but then most men did. That is, most men except Timothy.

♦ ♦ ♦ ♦ ♦

Hallam arrived home early from New York via Frankfurt, during a torrential downpour. Lucy heard a car door slam. It was still dark out. She hadn't been expecting him home for at least another week. He came and went at will. Part of the intrigue for him, she suspected, was keeping her in suspense. He entered the room dressed in a heavy winter suit; he slung his cashmere overcoat over the nearest chair and sat down to untie his shoes. She wasn't sure why, but she pretended she was in a deep sleep. She could smell the dry, asphyxiated smell of the plane on his clothes. The brick-like mobile phone that was never far from his side buzzed and he silenced it immediately, going to the bathroom to take the call. She could hear the low murmur of his voice; she couldn't make out his words, but the tone sounded intimate.

He came to bed and slipped in silently, keeping to his side, trying not to disturb her. She listened as his breathing slowed and deepened, until finally he was snoring. Over time, she had become used to sleeping alone. Sometimes she found his presence intrusive. She dozed, listening to rain peter out, and then quietly got out of bed. She showered and dressed for her trolley round at the hospital. Afterwards she was going for yum cha with the girls. It was Amber and Ellie's birthday. The children were staying with friends before they left for Australia the following week.

She sipped her tea on the patio, watching the mist evaporate from the sodden deck. A squirrel rushed up the bougainvillea and the mynah birds hopped about the wet grass. She was irritated that she would have to change her plans for the weekend now Hallam was home. Amber was taking her and the children to the dragon boat races at the Quay and then to Pongol for seafood. Tonight was pub night at the club, and Saturday night they had Gluttons and Gourmets. This month they were going to a Middle Eastern restaurant, with an authentic belly dancer from Turkey. Reluctantly she decided to ring and see if they could seat one more.

Esme whistled quietly to herself as she swept the patio. "Good morning, ma'am, heavy rain last night."

Lucy looked carefully at the girl as she continued her rhythmic sweeping; she was stunning, but seemed unaware of her beauty. In the mornings there was a dewy freshness about her that Lucinda envied.

"Morning, Esme. Sir came home early this morning. Perhaps you should let him sleep for as long as he needs today. He'll be jet-lagged after his flight."

Esme put her broom down and took up a mop. "Yes, ma'am. I heard him come in this morning. I'll be quiet around the house."

Lucy left the garden and went to fetch her handbag. Hallam's briefcase was sitting beside the front door, and she resisted the temptation to open it. Too many of her friends spent their time feverishly going through pockets and wallets; she didn't want to live that way.

The trolley round went by quickly that morning; she was working with a tall girl from New Zealand, called Linda. They chatted and traded information, as they handed out magazines, replaced water in flower vases, and fetched toiletries for those in need from the hospital kiosk. Lunch with the girls turned into a boisterous session, lasting until late afternoon. The restaurant was full of noisy patrons squabbling over their selections as the old ladies trundled by with their laden trolleys. They ordered wine and jasmine tea, as Amber expertly whisked spring rolls, pork dumplings, and prawn filled noodles from the passing trolley. At the end of the meal, Ellie and Amber were given gifts. Lucy was embarrassed when Amber opened Angel's gift: a pair of skimpy G-string panties, with 'Grand Opening' written on the front. An old uncle at the next table put his hands over his eyes and looked away shyly. His wife slapped his arm and glared at Amber for being so bold. As the staff were setting the tables for dinner, they unsteadily made their exit into the tropical heat of the late afternoon.

Lucy went first to pick up Holly from Livvie's house. Livvie was Norwegian and her mother was a tall, voluptuous blonde, who wore little in the way of clothing. She found the girls playing dress-up in the garden, while Livvie's mother Hette sunned herself topless by the pool. Lucy felt overdressed when she invited her for a glass of lime and soda. Hette tied a sarong lazily about her hips and languidly sipped her drink. Her magnificent breasts pouted at Lucinda. Holly was bubbling over with excitement as they drove through the heavy traffic to pick up Cameron from Pim's house. The boys were playing soccer in the garden; Pim's mother was from Thailand, and ran a business from home. She was busily engaged on the phone when they arrived, so Lucy dispensed with any chitchat. Pim got his moon-shaped face from his father, who was a brusque German, but his honey-coloured skin and eyes were from his mother. He was a pretty boy.

Lucy arrived back at the house to find Hallam still asleep. She flipped through the mail while the kiddies went to have a swim. Mostly bills, but a sweet-smelling, violet envelope caught her eye. Hurriedly she tore it open and skimmed the contents; it was from Emerald. After filtering through the gossip and current news, Emerald finally informed her that she would be arriving for a two-week visit at the end of the month. She had booked a hotel just in case, but would love to come and stay at Bukit Lalang, if possible. Lucy let the letter drift to the sideboard and went to fix herself a gin and tonic. Lucy wasn't quite sure if she, or Singapore, was ready for Emerald. She was part of another life; one Lucy had left behind. Sitting in the garden under the jasmine bower, she took a deep, richly scented breath and a long swig of her drink. She watched the children playing in the pool, their smooth brown skin glistening in the late afternoon sun. She looked up at the veranda as the shutters abruptly flew open.

Hallam stuck out his tousled head. "There you are, Lucy. God, what bloody time of the day is it? I'd love a drink. I'll have a quick shower and be down."

Lucy resented his sudden appearance, spoiling her peaceful moment alone, but dutifully went to get him a drink. The children clambered about with wet, slippery bodies, as he scooped them toward him. Asking no questions, Lucy decided it would be easier to accept things as they were. Smiling, he lowered the children to the ground; and came and kissed her briefly on the forehead, leaving a dampness there that she was eager to wipe away. She cancelled pub night with Amber and Esme and cooked a stir-fry for dinner. Sipping casually on his whisky and soda, Hallam sat and discussed their planned trip to Australia. The children had never visited her homeland, and she was anxious to show them everything. Hallam gladly went along with all her requests. She studied him closely. Each time he returned from a trip, he seemed to have changed. Tonight she noticed he was more precisely groomed, stylish, even healthier, much more vibrant and happier than she had ever seen him. She knew she wasn't responsible for these changes; she wondered who was.

In a flurry of excess baggage and lists of forgotten items, the Leadbitters finally left for the airport. With the family gone, Esmirada wandered from room to room through the silent house, picking up discarded clothing and stripping beds. She threw the louvred windows wide and silenced the noisy air-conditioners. The warm, damp air pervaded the cool house; she left small footprints in the moisture of the polished wood as she moved from room to room. The silence was peaceful; she hummed contentedly the songs of her childhood as she went about her work. Her ma'am had left her a long list of instructions, which she had stuck to the refrigerator with a magnet. The jobs, Esme knew, were designed to keep her busy throughout the next four weeks, but scanning them now she calculated she would have them completed in two days. Hugging her arms to her chest, a fission of pleasure ran through her at the thought of being alone in this peaceful house.

Esmirada planned to do some gardening. Honeyko had given her seeds to sow and cuttings from various plants and herbs to cultivate. She would start this very afternoon planting the bergamot, coriander and parsley. The oregano she had given her last month was flourishing amongst the potted orchids next to the garage. She also had a cutting of passionfruit that she was going to plant behind her room. After lunch, she would start immediately on a bamboo frame, on which to grow the vine.

◆◆◆◆◆◆

Lucinda gratefully accepted yet another glass of champagne from the slender hostess. She was a nervous flyer and the champagne helped to settle her. The children were quiet and absorbed in their books, games and movies. Hallam drank whisky and worked, scribbling away on sheafs of yellow legal pads. He was comfortable and confident; after all, he spent more time in the air than on the ground. He was such a frequent flyer the Singapore girls knew him by name, and upgraded them to first class. The hostesses were all beautifully presented and gracious. She saw how Hallam flirted and accepted their hospitality so naturally. His familiarity irritated her. She was tired and in a bad mood. The effects of the alcohol began to wear off. She looked at her feet. They seemed large. In fact she felt gauche and cumbersome next to the lithe, petite Asian women. She read her *Vogue,* ignoring the advertisements and flicked through until she found her horoscope; it was disappointing. She checked on the children, went to the toilet and slept for the rest of the flight.

The family arrived in Sydney on a clear, warm evening. It was dusk and although it was the start of winter, the weather was particularly mild.

A grinning taxi driver greeted them. "How youse going? Good flight?"

His knobbly knees were hairless above his long socks; he threw their baggage effortlessly into the boot of the mini bus and took off at great speed. He talked non-stop throughout the short journey, asking questions and giving a running commentary on the state of affairs of the local government.

Hallam had rented a serviced apartment in Circular Quay; it was spacious and decorated in bright tropical prints and colours. It had an indoor swimming pool that boasted a perspex bottom. After a light supper, the children threw on their swimming trunks and Hallam took them to the pool. Lucy busied herself with the unpacking of suitcases and plans for the following day. She had decided to take them to the Taronga Park Zoo, the Opera House and the Botanical Gardens. Hallam had a few meetings and would join them for dinner.

They slept well that night and left early the next morning for the ferry ride across to Taronga. The quay area was crowded with commuters, tourists and buskers. Lucy held the children's hands tightly as they negotiated the crowd toward the ferry terminal. The briny smell of the glassy-green water brought back childhood memories for Lucinda as it lapped against the docks. The ferries, painted in cream and dark green, were unchanged since her childhood. She watched as they back-pedalled furiously, churning up a frothy spray.

They boarded and hustled for a seat up front. The ocean breeze was crisp but not cold, and the light was clear and crystalline. They sat with the wind in their hair as Lucy pointed out the grotesquely painted face of Luna Park, Fort Dennison and the Heads of the harbour. Cameron took numerous pictures of the dazzling sails of the Opera House with his new camera. The sun glistened on the gelatinous water; they waved to people having breakfast and early morning coffee in the restaurants along the quay. The huge coat hanger bridge with its looming stone piers shut out the sun momentarily as the ferry chugged by. Rosellas and gulls wheeled and darted in and out of the great grey scaffolding. Small craft scudded out to sea in the brisk breeze and pleasure boats and ketches loaded with holidaymakers waved as they passed. The ferry Matilda unloaded her cargo of passengers quickly and efficiently. The threesome made their way up the hill to the zoo beyond.

Once again Lucinda was flooded with nostalgia. There had been some renovation but many of the enclosures were of the same dark cave-like stone of her girlhood. The giraffe and elephant enclosure hadn't changed, but the aquarium was new and modern. She remembered her mother taking her to see the sharks when she was Cameron's age. Hammerheads, grey nurses and tigers swam in a tank, housed in a fine Victorian building. The children skipped hand in hand through the bright borders of flowers and glossy banks of foliage, rounding corners to discover new and exciting animals. They lunched in a small kiosk with other families on freshly battered fish and thick crunchy chips dipped in tomato sauce. The pigeons and bush turkeys plundered the leftovers, much to Cameron's delight as he took more photographs. Later in the afternoon the vast windows of the Opera House gave them an opalescent view of the harbour as they joined a tour of elderly Americans, lumbering along the plush carpet.

Footsore, they made their way back to the hotel as the last rays of sun bounced off the opera house sails. Lucy filled the spa bath with bubbles and Cam and Holly jumped in, sending soapy suds up the white tiled bathroom walls.

"Thanks for a great day, Mumsy!" Cameron said as he was making a sudsy beard for himself. She could hear squeals of laughter as she retreated to sit and watch the dying light of the harbour.

"Look, Cam, I have a soap-suds bikini." Holly's belly laugh echoed down the hallway.

"G'day, mate."

She could hear Cameron mimicking repeatedly, until Holly shut him up by pushing his head under water. Hallam arrived and joined her, but their conversation seemed fragile.

"How was your day?"

"Fine thanks, did you get to meet the people you needed to?"

"Yes it was very productive, sorry I couldn't join you guys, sounds like you had a lot of fun."

"That's okay. How about tomorrow? We're planning a trip to the Botanical Gardens and the Museum."

He looked at her sheepishly. "Sorry, Luce, I've set up some important meetings. I have to fit in with the client's plans and make myself available when they are."

Lucy shrugged and turned away; she wouldn't let him see her disappointment. She left him nursing a drink while she went to get the children out of the bath.

They had dinner in a small pizza restaurant at the Rocks, it was busy and the tables were cheek to jowl with tourists of all nationalities. The pizza toppings were simple and abundantly piled onto fresh crisp bases. They drank house red from glass tumblers, the salads were old fashioned, with iceberg lettuce, wheels of oranges and chunks of red tomatoes. The service was fast and they were in and out within an hour.

The streets of the Rocks were packed. Revellers spilt out of the Victorian pubs where they stood drinking their schooners in a glowing yellow light, discussing the day's work and calling good-naturedly across the street. "How yah going, mate?"

She could hear the thump and rattle of a bush band coming from the bar on the corner, and longed to join the thronging crowd, but Hallam steered them back toward the hotel. He had calls to make. They stopped briefly at the Quay to watch the street performers, an old battler wielding his bow across a scarred violin, and a couple of half-caste aboriginal boys playing the didgeridoo. Lucinda slept well again that night, listening to the ferries blast their horns as they back-pedalled, turning around in the harbour. She had dozed in front of the television; the sounds of the familiar, flat accent lulling her to sleep, whilst Hallam, in the adjoining room, made feverish phone calls to Asia.

Soft salt air caught at the fine wisps of Holly's hair, as they crossed the green sward of the Domain. Lucinda could see the chemical blue of the ocean through the elephantine Morton Bay figs. She took a deep, sharp, tangy breath, as she watched the children roll down the lush green hill into the Royal Botanical Gardens. The garden was as she remembered, a Victorian artefact and site of the first convict farms of Australia. White cockatoos perched decoratively on a pine tree, sent down a screeching racket as they passed beneath. They approached the pond and Holly read excitedly from the information board.

"Hey, look here!" she shouted. "The pond has eels living in it. They eat the ducks!"

Holly sat expectantly on the bank, hoping for a glimpse of an eel devouring a duck, while Cam walked amongst the birds, warning them of their fate. After hot chocolate and coffee in the kiosk, they walked up the hill toward the Conservatorium of Music and the Museum. On the way, they passed trees hung with rubbery, black fruit bats. The smell alerted them to their presence long before they saw them, filling the air with their peculiar stench. The museum was even better than she remembered; they spent hours trawling the exhibits before going to the Hyde Park Barracks for lunch. Lucy sat on the deep shady veranda, with boronia creeper cascading over the wooden railing. She leant back against the cool sandstone walls, sipping her glass of chardonnay, while the children ate their first Australian meat pie with dollops of rich tomato sauce and the inevitable fat hand-cut chips.

In the late afternoon while they were visiting the aquarium in Darling Harbour, the sky darkened and a southerly blew in. Lucinda looked from the windows of the Maritime Museum and saw the sea had turned navy; the waves were choppy and spewed white foam against the sandstone steps of the harbour.

She hailed a cab back to the hotel and the cabbie entertained the children.

"I'm as mad as a scorpion in a sock. Just when I thought I could knock off, the weather turns wet enough to bog a duck!"

Holly couldn't stop giggling and all Cameron could do was stare up at this wondrous creature, not knowing what on earth he was talking about. All evening Cam went on with his newfound Aussie slang. He kept Holly and Hallam entertained throughout dinner at Doyle's on Watson's Bay, while Lucy watched the flickering harbour lights of the luxury cruisers and ketches, full of champagne-guzzling and beer-drinking locals.

In the limpid light of the early morning, they made their way to the airport, and boarded a domestic flight to Brisbane. Cameron and Holly made a list of the places they wanted to see, Lucinda leafed through The Woman's Weekly and Hallam slept. He had the ability to fall asleep as soon as the plane started to taxi down the runway, and would not wake until the seat belt sign was turned off. The flight was brief and before they knew it they were waiting on the footpath with the baggage, while Hallam negotiated a rental car. First stop: Gold Coast. They would stay overnight and try to fit in as many of the sights possible. A highly excitable Cameron sat in the back seat, reeling them off to his father as he tried to find the freeway exit.

"Oh Dad, we have to go to Dream World, Sea World and Movie World. I want to see the big Banana, the big Pelican, the big Prawn and the big Shell!"

Holly butted in, "Don't forget, Cam: Aussie World, Ettamogah Pub and Nostalgia town." She looked at her brother, smiling smugly.

Lucinda could see Hallam was getting exasperated. "Okay, kids, let Daddy concentrate on his driving. We'll try and do as much as we can, but try to remember that we want to have a holiday by the sea as well. Daddy needs a rest."

Hallam ignored them and focused his steely gaze on the road ahead.

The following day they did manage to go to Sea World and Movie World, but the temperature rose rapidly and there was very little breeze. When the soles of Hallam's heavy shoes began to stick to the asphalt, he decided they'd had enough. Cameron started to whinge, but quietened down when she placated them with large Cokes and ice creams, and they continued on to Noosa, where a rented house on the beach awaited them.

The house turned out to be perfect for their needs, three levels falling away to a white meniscus of sand. To the side of the house was a silvery wooden deck with a small plunge pool and barbecue facilities. The deck ran the length of the house with a table for alfresco dining and lots of room for lolling about on sun lounges. She took a deep breath of sea air, and looked to the distant, blue-tinged mountains. She was full of inspiration to paint; she couldn't wait to get started. They were within walking distance of Hastings Street, the centre of Noosa, and on the other side a short walk to the National Park.

The kids changed and ran screaming towards the incredible blue ocean; Hallam fixed a drink and headed out toward one of the banana chairs, to lie like a pale frog in the afternoon sun. Lucy took a walk along the squeaky sand, glistening with silica. She watched her slanting shadow as she had done as a child; she threw off her sarong and joined the children in the warm, sensual sea. In the evening they sat after a dinner of sweet prawns and salad, drinking vast quantities of summery tasting wine. In the golden flicker of candlelight, listening to the roar of the ocean, Lucy felt that at last she was home.

Before Hallam was even awake, the children were swimming. Their skin was soft and fuzzy from the salt as Lucinda towelled them off for a walk in the National Park. The narrow path wound up the hill with the ocean on one side and banks of acacias and pandanus palms on the other. They saw pods of dolphins swimming in the clear water of the rock-strewn beaches. Cameron pointed out a koala and her baby and, on rounding the bend, they came across a joey stuffing its furry little face full of gum leaves. They returned, sun-flushed and tired, to meet Hallam in town at noon. He had booked a table at Sails, where they sat watching the locals in their crisp white designer separates. The tourists lying in the warm sand got up lazily from time to time for a ritual bathe in the ocean.

"We've finished, Mamma. Can we go and swim?" Holly jumped from one foot to the other as Lucy applied sunscreen and hats before she let them go. She settled into her rattan chair and Hallam announced, "I've invited a friend to dinner tonight."

Lucy spluttered on her daiquiri. "I didn't know you knew anyone here."

Hallam pushed back a lock of her hair with his plump white hand. "He's an old friend of mine. We went to school together. From memory, he was older by a few years. He moved here some time ago to paint. Apparently he's a rather celebrated artist in these parts. He was a bit of an eccentric at the old public boys'. He made a lot of money through a gallery he ran in London, and then he disappeared, only to turn up in this part of the world all these years later."

Lucy was intrigued. "Is he gay?"

"No. In actual fact he was married for a long time, but his wife died of some sort of cancer just after they moved out here."

Lucy turned her thoughts to more practical matters, wondering what to have for dinner. She had seen some lovely pieces of tuna at the fish markets earlier today. She would get Hallam to put them on the barbecue and on the way home she would get some more wine. Suddenly she felt quite excited about meeting this mysterious artist. Her eyes were overbright as she finished lunch and walked back to the house, while Hallam took the children for ice cream.

Alex Erindale proved to be a very entertaining dinner guest. He delighted the children with outback tales of the bush and his pets at his rain forest home in the hinterland. He told them about his rosella and kookaburra and a goanna named Joanna, who visited each day for a morsel of chicken that he specially prepared. He even had a carpet snake he called Diamond Jim, which kept the mice population down in his studio.

He and Lucy dominated the conversation with art and she showed him her portfolio, which seemed to impress him. He painted mostly oils but also loved to dabble in pastel. The subjects he chose were wide and varied: portraits, landscapes and seascapes, and of course he painted from life and ran a workshop out of his studio on Tuesday evenings. Lucinda was fascinated. She tried to guess his age, but found it difficult. He had a full head of dark, wavy hair, greying at the temples, which he wore tied in a low ponytail at the nape of his neck. He was tanned, but his face was unlined. She guessed he was in his late forties.

"Did you know that an old friend of yours and Hallam's visited me last summer?"

Hallam looked at Alex from the corner of his eye, as he poured more wine.

"Oh, who? I didn't think I knew many of Hallam's old friends." Lucy looked eagerly at Alex.

"Well, you've let the cat out of the bag, old boy; I wasn't going to tell Lucy. I think she harbours bitter memories of our friend Liam."

Lucy's eyes opened wide and a grin spread across her face. She clapped her hands together. "Liam Ormond! Oh, my God. I haven't seen him since the wedding! He was a bit of a naughty boy, but that was all so long ago! He was so sweet, I could never think ill of Liam; we were only kids, after all! Alex, you must tell me all about him. Did he ever marry?"

Alex laughed; Hallam seemed uncomfortable the way the conversation was going. "I think he married a few times but he's not anymore. In fact he has a cute little Filipina he travels around with called, appropriately enough, Spanky."

Lucy roared with laughter. "I'm glad to see some things never change. More red, Alex?" Lucy watched him as he sluiced down his drink, and poured him another.

Alex had arrived in a mud splattered Range Rover with a bicycle attached to the back. Everything about him was sensuous and passionate; he ate, with great gusto, all that was put before him. He quaffed vast quantities of wine and laughed from deep within. He hung on Cameron's and Holly's every word, encouraging them and bringing out Cameron's shy talents. Holly didn't need any encouragement. She and Alex made a great dinner party team. He was genuinely interested in Lucy's art, especially the subject matter, and spoke after dinner about marketing her work, if that was what she wanted. Hallam was the only one who was subdued; he watched Alex through half-closed eyes, questioning him in a desultory manner from time to time. Over coffee and cognac, he left the table and went to make a phone call to Asia.

"I don't know what you guys have planned tomorrow, but how would you like a trip to Fraser Island?" Alex sat grinning at her, as the children jumped up and down, pumping his huge hands.

"Do I have any choice in the matter? I think by the electricity these two are generating, the answer is yes!"

Hallam returned, empty drink in hand. "Yes to what? You have to be careful what you agree to with this old goat."

"How about it, old boy? A day trip to Fraser tomorrow?" Alex inclined his head to the side, smiling at Hallam.

"Sorry, old chum. Count me out. I have work to do and calls to make, but by all means take the family."

No one seemed particularly disappointed that Hallam would not be joining them. They lingered over cognac, making plans for the trip to the island.

Hallam sat for a long time after everyone had gone to bed, watching the path of moon on the ocean. He smoked a cigar, sucking the acrid smoke deep into his lungs. The ocean roared in his ears as it crashed on the rocks below. Seeing Alex again had ignited long-buried memories of Liam, his old nemesis, so smug, handsome and rich. Good at everything, creative as well as sporting, just like Lucy, so fucking perfect it made him sick. It was a pleasure to win her away from him, a small sweet victory. Thinking of the wretched boarding school made his clammy skin cool in the brisk breeze off the ocean. He had been bullied unmercifully for years. He didn't have the money to buy them off like Liam and Alex. His thoughts turned to his own son; thank God he will never suffer the humiliation of ragging and initiation. He took a swig of whisky and inhaled deeply. The alcohol and cigar combined to make him deliciously light-headed, helping to ease his guilt and complicity.

In the yellow early morning light, Alex arrived to collect Lucinda and the children. They were still half asleep and Alex said little. Lucy began to think that perhaps the excursion had been a mistake, but by the time they reached the ebb tide at Noosa River, they were fully awake and animated. Alex drove the next thirty-five miles, pointing out interesting landmarks. Passing a sanctuary where camels lay about in bowls of dust, Alex slowed to allow Cam time for a photographic opportunity.

"Dirty smelly things!" He winked at Holly and looked across at Lucy cheekily.

They arrived at the ferry and waited on the grassy verge, where they formed a convoy with the other four-wheel drives. Cameron spotted a large roo with a joey peeping from her bulging pouch. Not far downriver was her mate. They twitched their ears at each other and bounded off before Cam could take out his camera. Once on the ferry, the children began asking questions. Alex pointed out his bull bar, snorkel and survival gear.

"Do you think we'll need it?" Cameron asked fearfully.

Alex laughed, his eyes disappearing into sunburnt creases; he playfully ruffled the boy's hair in reassurance.

Alex expertly drove off the ferry, taking a dusty side road; they were suddenly on a broad, oceanside beach, stretching for seventy straight miles. Tearing off at great speed, he ignored the fifty-mile-per-hour limit.

Careening over sand hills, he sent them flying in the air, jarring their spines in the process.

"Keep an eye on the tides, Cam!"

Cameron did as instructed and kept a vigil at the open window.

They came to a skidding halt below towering red and yellow sand hills. Lucy fell from the vehicle with a numbed spine. Cam found an empty coke bottle and layered it with the colourful sand.

Back in the Land Rover, Alex began to sing melodically, enunciating each operatic word beautifully. Next stop was the rust-bubbled hull of an abandoned cargo ship. Lucy noted from the dates of the graffiti that it had been there some time. They clambered around and took photographs; Lucy and Alex sat back in the sand, watching them.

"They're great kids, Lucy. You and Hallam are very lucky."

"I think they're pretty special. How about you? Do you have any of you own?"

He looked toward the great rusting hulk. "No my wife and I were never blessed in that way. I married late. I was a virgin when I married Inke. I've only ever known one woman. She died four years ago."

He was so candid, Lucy couldn't think of a sincere thing to say. She brushed the hair from her face and sat in uncomfortable silence, trying to compose herself. He turned to her and took her hand.

"I'm sorry, I'm making you feel uncomfortable. I have a terrible habit of wearing my heart on my sleeve. I should learn to be more discreet!"

Holly came back, screeching to a halt at their knees, showering them with damp sand. "I'm starving. When do we eat?"

They piled back into the Rover and drove to the great Cape, where they stopped for the lunch Lucy had packed. After eating they walked the huge sand hills, where the children rolled down the other side to the sea beyond. Alex took hold of Lucy's hand and they ploughed down the hill, laughing, the wind in their hair and sand flying up behind them.

By the time they reached the ferry, it was dusk and the mosquitoes had started to whine. They stopped for a simple dinner of fresh oysters, prawns and bread and butter at the Noosa River Café. While the children went to look at the live fish tank, Alex talked about his art.

"I'm planning another exhibition at the end of the year, that's if I get enough material together; I tend to sell my work faster than I can paint. I really love your work, Lucy. You have talent. The Asian theme is so fresh, would you be interested in a joint exhibition?"

Again he took her by surprise. "I might. I'll have to think about it. I'm afraid I am not as prolific as you. My social and family commitments don't leave me much time."

"It's all about discipline, Lucy!"

She laughed, but she could see he was serious. "Oh really. And how do you discipline yourself, Alex?"

He moved in closer and looked around conspiratorially. "I paint in the nude, wearing only my favourite hat!"

Lucy threw back her head and laughed. People turned to look at them and smiled.

"No, really. It's true. In the nude at first light until lunch time, and then I cycle to meet my friends at the surf club or my favourite restaurant, and spend the rest of the day gathering inspiration!"

Holly came and laid her head on Lucy's lap and started to drift off to sleep. They shared one more glass of wine because Alex was driving, and then drove home in silence. They found Hallam sitting on the deck with a nightcap. He tried to cajole Alex to stay, but he pleaded exhaustion. He had to be up early the next morning to finish a portrait.

Lucy saw him to his car and impulsively kissed his cheek. Alex suddenly turned to her as he opened the door. Pulling her toward him, he kissed her long and hard on the mouth. He smiled wickedly and jumped into the car, leaving Lucy gasping for breath.

Lucy didn't see Alex again until their last day, but she thought about him constantly. The night after their trip to Fraser Island, she lay feverish, with his face branded on the back of her eyelids. Hallam had little interest in the trip and asked few questions. He was preoccupied with work and the calls he received at all hours of the night. Lucy spent her days hoping to catch just a glimpse of Alex, but by their final week she gave up, thinking she would never see him again. She spent all her time with the children and her painting and was now reluctant to leave.

As they put the final cases into the boot, a familiar car pulled up and Lucy's heart lurched.

Grinning broadly, Alex stepped out. Fresh and crisp in white cotton, he flashed a smile and threw his ponytail over his shoulder. "Hello, family. Couldn't let you leave without saying goodbye!"

Lucy tried to lean casually against the minivan as the children gathered around him.

"I've something for you, Lucy!"

He came over and stood near her. She breathed in his clean smell. He handed her a cylinder and she flipped off the top and carefully extracted the rolled paper. Hallam helped her unroll it and placed it on the bonnet of the car. It was a beautiful pastel of the children playing in the white surf on the beach. The colours were magnificent; he had captured their likeness and the ethereal quality of the Australian light: milky blues and silvery mauves with touches of yellow ochre. Lucy stood with tears pricking her eyes, poring over every detail.

Hallam let out a low whistle. "You have real talent, old chum, and an original like this will be worth some money in years to come."

Alex grinned. "Most artists are only valuable once they're dead. You may have to hang onto it for some time!"

Lucy took Alex's hand. "Thank you so much. We'll treasure this. It is so much like them, did you do it from a photograph?" Lucy lifted Holly and Cameron up to look.

"Hey cool, you're really good, Alex. Nearly as good as our mum!"

"Oh, no. I have a long way to go to be as good as your mum." He winked at Lucy. "To answer your question, Lucy, I took a couple of snaps of them and then chose the one I liked the best. I'm quite pleased with how it's turned out. I did another composition for myself. When you come back, I'll show it to you."

Shyly she kissed his cheek, remembering another more recent kiss.

"Guess I'd better let you all go or you'll miss your flight. Have a safe journey, and see you next time."

The children waved madly as the car pulled away, Lucy watched him in the rear view mirror until he was out of sight. By the time they boarded the Singapore Airlines flight home, she was more unsettled than ever. She was determined to go back and further her painting. She had an exhibition to work towards.

Chapter Thirteen
Misadventure

Esmirada watched as the huge prehistoric lizard stalked the garden, looking for cats. She had spent the day digging and planting, and had a satisfied ache in her bones. Her cuttings were coming along and she hoped her ma'am would be pleased. She knew they would be back in two days' time and looked forward to the house being full once again. She had enjoyed her solitude, but found after Sunday at church that the start of the week was very lonely.

After the service last Sunday, she and Timothy had shared lunch, and he walked her to the markets and the bus. She enjoyed the stories of his early childhood and college days, and he seemed eager to hear about her life. She knew he wanted more from her, but she wasn't free to do so. Her stomach roiled when she remembered how he had tried to kiss her at the bus stop. She had turned her head away, and too late had seen the hurt and confusion in his eyes.

The phone rang and she threw down her shovel, rushing into the cool interior. Picking up the receiver, she heard Sister Mary's voice on the line. She spoke in rapid Tagalog.

"Hello, Esme. It was lovely seeing you at the counselling session on Sunday. You have a real gift, you know dear. I'll get right to the point and won't keep you; do you remember Laani, the sad girl with all the problems?"

Esme did remember; she had thought about her throughout the week. "Yes, Sister, of course. Is she alright?"

"She's very depressed and I want to go and see her, but I think she would respond more if you came along as well. Could you come early tomorrow? I won't keep you long; I know your madam's away, would she mind do you think?"

Esme thought about it for a while. She knew she wasn't supposed to leave the house, but felt that this one time it would be all right. "I'll meet you at the church, Sister, and you can take me to her."

The sister rang off and Esme went to close up the house for the night, thinking of what she could possibly say to Laani that would make a difference to her miserable situation.

The bus to Yishun wasn't air-conditioned and was overcrowded. Esme and Sister Mary had to stand all the way, only managing to get a seat two blocks from Laani's H.D.B. By the time they got off they were damp with sweat so they stopped at a Seven Eleven and bought iced tea. The uncle behind the counter poured the tea into plastic bags and inserted a straw, pulling the drawstring tight so it wouldn't spill. Gratefully they sipped the tea as they walked the few blocks to Laani's.

Sister Mary broke the silence. "The employer works throughout the day, so we can speak to Laani in peace. I've tried talking to Madam Lim, but she denies any misdoings and now refuses to see me."

They reached the block; there were maids milling about the playground with small children in their care. The building had been recently renovated and smelt of fresh paint. The two women took the elevator to the eleventh story. Esme was still unsure about elevators, and stood with her back hard against the wall, while Sister Mary pressed the buttons. They walked along the void deck and peered through the open grating.

Sister Mary called out to Laani. She appeared timidly at the door. "Can we come in and talk, dear?"

"No, the door is locked. My ma'am locks me in when she goes to work."

Mary looked at Esme with dismay. "How have you been, Laani? Are you coming to church on Sunday?"

"My ma'am will not allow me to have days off anymore. She said I have been spreading lies about her. She beat me with the clothes pole and scolded me. I wasn't allowed to eat my noodles and went to bed hungry." The young girl started to cry. "I want to go home to my family, but she won't let me go. I asked her if I could go to the agency, but she locked the door. You must go, the neighbours will tell her I talked to you!" She started to weep.

An Indian woman in a drab sari came to her door and scowled at them. She stood staring for a while and then got bored and went away. Laani sat on her haunches on the floor behind the locked screen, sniffling and wiping

112

her nose on her sleeve. Another neighbour looked out down the corridor, giving them a disapproving stare.

Esme put her hand through the bars and Laani grasped it. "I'll pray for you, Laani, God won't let you suffer any longer."

"I've been praying, but he seems to have forgotten me." She sobbed.

Sister Mary put her hand on the girl's shoulder, patting her like a child. An old man pushed by them, snarling at them as he shuffled slowly along the void deck. "This will only make matters worse. We had best go."

They walked back the way they had come, and dejectedly rode back to the church in silence, where Esme left the sister to catch two more buses back to Bukit Lalang.

A heavy storm woke Esme that night; she looked out and saw the garden already awash. She hoped her cuttings would survive. She awoke to a sombre sky; the rain lay in murky ditches about the garden. The gardeners would have a big job ahead cleaning up broken branches and fallen bougainvillaea. The only casualties were her banana plants; one plant was bent in two and the other had fallen in the dirt. She busied herself before breakfast tying them to bamboo stakes, and then went in to open up the house. She spent the morning making the beds with fresh linen and opening the shutters to allow the rooms to air. She mopped and dusted, and cleaned the blades of the overhead fans. She took out the air-conditioning filters and held them under a running tap next to the garage.

After her lunch of rice and steamed fish, she left for the markets. She bought fresh fruit and vegetables, fish, chicken, rice and a large bunch of white orchids. She allowed herself the luxury of a taxi ride home because she had such a load. She ignored the unwanted attention of the taxi driver when he said, "You pretty girl, you got boy? Girl like you should have boy, what perfume you wear *lah*?"

She refused to answer him and he drove off in a huff, only giving her just enough time to get her packages out of the trunk of the car.

When she walked up the sweeping drive she saw Sister Mary squatting in the shade of the patio. The sister's face was closed and dark. Esme could see immediately that something was wrong. They sat in her small room and Sister Mary unfolded the tragedy that had happened that morning.

"After Madam Lim left for work, Laani fell from the kitchen window - eleven storeys to her death. Madam Lim told the police it must have been an accident while she was hanging out the laundry."

Esme looked at her hands. She felt very angry. She looked at Sister Mary and her eyes filled, but she didn't cry. "I think Madam Lim is right. Laani was unhappy, but she knew to take her own life would be a sin in the eyes of God. It must have been an accident."

"Yes," echoed Sister Mary. "Another sad accident."

With the family home and Sir leaving for the States, Esmirada had only time to think of Laani in her prayers. Deep down her anger and resentment grew; in the national newspaper, in the home section on page five, there were two brief columns devoted to Laani's story.

'A Filipino maid fell eleven floors to her death on Wednesday, after losing her balance while hanging out the laundry. Laani Rosita Reyes, who was eighteen and 1.45 metres tall, had stood on a stool in the kitchen, apparently in order to hang laundry on the bamboo poles outside her employer's flat in Yishun Central. The maid's employer, Madam Lim, was not present at the time, having left for work an hour earlier. Madam Lim's neighbours did not see anything. One elderly man heard the sound of bamboo poles breaking, and looked over the void deck to see Ms Reyes's body lying in the car park. Laani was taken by ambulance to the National Hospital, but died on the way from multiple injuries. Madam Lim described the incident as "unfortunate". The Government had in the past expressed concern over high risks taken by employees in hanging clothes on bamboo poles, in particular those that required chairs to do so. It was noted that in the last few years at least twenty maids have been injured or killed while hanging out clothes to dry from their employer's high-rise flats.'

◆◆◆◆◆◆

Esmirada had a letter from home. She hadn't heard the postman. Bukit Lalang, with its long, winding drive, was quiet during the day and she could usually hear the squeaking of his brakes as he stopped at each house. Her ma'am came, flourishing a thin airmail letter; she seemed to expect her to be happy at receiving it, but Esme knew it would not be good news. Carefully she opened the flimsy envelope. It was from Manny. Boboy's health had deteriorated further, and there would be need of more medication. Pinkie was pregnant. Her family were threatening to kill Manny, or at least castrate him like a pig. He had gone into hiding for a while. When things settled down, he and Pinkie would disappear and get married. Pinkie wasn't happy with this idea either, but he didn't know what

114

else to do. Rosa had remarried and left the barrio. Olina had taken over the running of the *sari sari* and she, *Lola* and Boboy had moved into the tiny room off the back of the shop. Perpetua and Ricardo had finally had a boy; they called him Enrique, a handsome little son. Manny hoped Pinkie too would have a son, less trouble than a girl. The letter ended with requests for money, and as usual asked nothing of her life or how she was.

◆◆◆◆◆◆

Timothy Waldon was deeply troubled. That week he had spent many restless nights. He had been grumpy and preoccupied with the children in his class, and now the poor girl's death hung over him like an evil black cloud. He had been foolish, so foolish with Esmirada; he had beaten himself up wondering what could have prompted him to act in such a loutish way with her, just when he was gaining her trust and admiration. He knew why he wanted to kiss her; he had been deeply in love with the woman from the first moment he set eyes upon her. He should have known better. After all, he had read many books, trying to get some insight and understanding of the way she may think and behave. He had read that the Filipino culture was steeped in tradition and superstition, and that virginity was revered, if not sacred. He had put her in a compromising position and hated himself for it. How was he going to regain her trust and respect?

She didn't meet his eye; she sat in the back of the church, the sun shining on her silky hair. They all prayed for their lost sister and for those that had been lost in misadventure before her. The service was solemn and without its usual vibrancy. He didn't expect her to stay for counselling, but she surprised him by pulling up a chair and joining the circle. He and Sister Mary had spoken at length during the week; it had been his suggestion that Esmirada accompany her to see Laani. He felt, and still did, that a female understood the emotional and psychological make-up of another woman, especially in her culture. He had gathered the church elders that morning. Joyner and Harold had brought in people from the Foreign Assist Ministry as well as some Grass Root Leaders.

He addressed the group, introducing Sister Mary who was to play an integral part in the plan he was about to unveil. Sister Mary's refuge and school was regarded highly amongst the elders but now they were going to go one step further. Timothy had formed a civil society group that aimed to improve the lives of domestic workers.

"Our poor brothers and sisters have no rights of protection! They have been used as a cheap commodity. Up until now we have worked with Filipino maids only, but now we are helping Indonesian maids who have been abused and exploited. Sister Mary and I will be working closely with the government to bring about new rules of protection and to try to change the attitude of the community. At present, the attitude is that they are inferior; we desperately need to instil respect for their services and culture. These people are powerless. How can any of us possibly reject these helpless souls?"

Timothy looked at Esmirada and saw the look in her eyes; it overwhelmed him and filled him with hope. He could see respect and admiration shining from her, and he sent up a silent prayer to God.

Chapter Fourteen
Artist by Commission

Holly and Cameron were keen to get back to school, they had had six weeks' holiday and Lucy was quietly pleased to put them once more on the school bus. They were progressing well, both in the top grades. Their round of activities exhausted Lucy but she could see how the children, especially Cam, had responded. He had become a prolific reader, well beyond his years; she found it hard to keep up with his reading list. They had a full social life of parties, sleepovers and camps and seemed happy and well adjusted. Hallam was travelling again and privately Lucy was glad he had gone. He tended to bring an atmosphere of tension into the house and the bedroom.

The house and garden had flourished under Esme's care; Lucy went back to tennis and mah-jong happily, catching up on all the changes since home leave. However, reluctantly after all this time, she gave up her painting lessons; Lucy decided the lessons were a waste of valuable time. New girls came and the program regressed to include the beginners. Those that had been there the longest grew bored, and sat drinking copious amounts of coffee, and gossiping.

She received a call from a German woman who wanted to commission Lucinda to do a pastel of her shop house; she was very impressed by Lucy's work at the recent exhibit. Two days later an English woman commissioned her to do a portrait of her black and white Colonial, with her two Labradors lounging about the garden. And so Lucinda's business was born, she sought Hal's advice and applied for a permit and registration. She had thick white cards edged in gold printed with: *Houses have their own ways of dying, falling as variously as the generations of men, some with tragic roar, some quietly, while from others the spirit slips before the body perishes. Howard's End, E.M.Forster, 1910 Lucinda Leadbitter, artist by commission.*

On the edge she added her own leitmotif: a black cat, which she had included somewhere in every one of her paintings. She was chuffed with her commissions and was thrilled each time she handed out one of her handsome cards. She would love to write to Alex, and tell him of her achievements.

She cast her eye over her studio on the veranda and decided she needed more professional equipment. She invested in a larger easel, photographic material and a larger workspace, and so claimed for herself part of Hallam's gym area. She did this while he was in Jakarta; he didn't use the area anyway and had grown soft and lazy of late. She worked on her commissions by day when the light was at its best and while the children were at school. She reluctantly dragged her attention away from her art for a few days to prepare for Emerald's visit at the end of the month, which, frankly, she resented. In fact any interruption to her work lately made her feel resentful.

She and Esme overhauled the guest room, giving the rattan furniture a fresh coat of white paint. She added new curtains and a Persian carpet, which she planned to pay for out of her first cheque, if Hallam complained. The day before she arrived, she went to the flower markets and bought a huge bunch of white tulips and roses for the room. Emerald would be here ten days and during that time, Lucinda had planned plenty of social activities to keep her busy. There would be a 'Welcome Back Party' for the club members, a fashion parade, a murder mystery night at Angels, and she had sent out invitations for a stand-up cocktail in the garden. Hal should be back by then from his trip to Turkey. She would need his help, so hoped he would not be delayed like he usually was.

Lucy stood with an expectant crowd, waiting for the British Airways flight from Heathrow. She could easily see over their heads so hung to the back. She spotted Emerald immediately, overdressed in a ribbed-wool suit with a fur coat slung casually over her arm. Emerald waved enthusiastically, her numerous gold bangles bouncing on her slender wrist. She looked even thinner that when Lucy had last seen her in England. Emerald kept turning and blowing kisses and waving while she waited for her luggage.

Lucy, feeling foolish, mouthed through the glass, "How are you, how was the flight?"

Emerald carried on the pantomime, miming back at her. Lucy had no idea what she was saying. She collected what seemed to be an enormous amount of luggage for ten days, and made her way, tottering on her stilettos, to the glass sliding doors. She threw herself into Lucinda's arms.

"Darling, you look wonderful, so tanned and toned. I can see this life is doing only good things for you."

Next to Emerald, Lucy was very casual in her white capri pants and sleeveless top and sandals. Emerald was all tawny hair and red lipstick; she was even wearing panty hose.

"Did you manage to get any rest on the flight?"

"Oh, sweetie, I sat next to the most delicious man who told me his whole life story, champagne and laughs all the way, I am exhausted, didn't sleep a wink, too excited!"

Lucy steered her to the glass doors and out onto the street. As the doors parted, the heat and humidity rushed in, hitting Emerald in the face like a wet rag. She reeled back in shock, teetering on her high heels.

"Oh my God, Lucy, how do you stand it? I never thought it would be this hot, I hope my room is air-conditioned!"

Lucy had forgotten how difficult Emerald could be. This will be an interesting ten days, she thought, as she threw the heavy luggage into the trunk. Emerald sat fanning herself in the cool air of the car; she had thrown her fur and jacket onto the back seat and was struggling in vain, trying to remove her damp panty hose in the confines of the car.

Lucy drove her to Bukit Lalang as quickly as the traffic would allow. Emerald lay back, exhausted, not interested in the sights of the city. When they turned into the tree-lined drive, she sat up and looked about her.

"Lucy! This is like a film set, it's so tropical!"

As Lucy negotiated the drive, the house in all its glory rose before them. Emerald got out of the car, barefoot and speechless. Lucy led her through the double glass doors and into the covered portico. She stood, mouth open, looking about her. Esme ran down the stairs to greet the guest.

"Hello, ma'am. Welcome to the house," she said, scurrying to the car to bring in the luggage.

"My God, Lucy, a little brown maiden, such a lovely little thing! "

Lucy watched Emerald as she slowly climbed the stairs, her limp hand trailing the banister. Esme and Lucy followed, hauling Emerald's bags awkwardly up the stairs.

Emerald, after a long sleep that lasted the better part of a day and a half, took on the role of guest as though to the manor born. She made good use of Esme, demanding her attention at all times of the day and night, as though she was her personal maid. She lounged by the pool, helped herself to cocktails and eagerly dressed for whatever activity Lucy had arranged. She loved the lunches with the girls, played tennis like a pro and even caught on to mah-jong. She talked loudly throughout the fashion parade, and afterwards bought most of what had been on show. Amber and Angel were fascinated with her. Tuppy steered clear of her and the others tolerated her politely. Having discarded her heavy London clothes, she trawled Orchard Road for the latest fashions.

Hallam returned from Indonesia in time for the club's 'Welcome Back Party.' He was more than happy to escort Emerald. She swept down the stairs to greet him with a vast amount of bronzed skin showing, her tawny hair piled high on her well-shaped head. Lucy, preferring a more casual look, wore a simple black sheath. She couldn't help a stab of jealously when she saw how attentive Hallam was toward Emerald.

Emerald shone. Her green eyes flashed as she danced seductively with one obliging husband after another.

Amber stood on the fringe of the dance floor, watching her from the corner of her eye. She took a long pull of her drink. "She's certainly enjoying herself."

Lucy watched as Emerald wrapped her slender arms about Brian's neck. "She had a real shit of a husband, she deserves a little fun after what she's been through."

The waiter refilled their wine glasses.

"I guess she's making up for lost time, you'll never get rid of her, Lucy. The men love a bit of new blood." They watched as Emerald changed from one partner to the next.

"Uh oh, now she's with Peter, he doesn't miss a trick." Amber raised one eyebrow, following the couple on the dance floor.

"Where's Mioko?" said Lucy, looking about the room.

"She's still in Japan, but hubby is holding up 'Red Lips Corner'."

Lucy looked toward the bar and saw the lanky frame of Mioko's husband, talking to Hallam and a few other members.

At two in the morning they managed to half-carry, half-drag Emerald to the car. She fell asleep in the back seat, snoring loudly. Hallam had to carry her up the stairs to her bed. Lucy was not impressed and went to her own room, slamming the door behind her. Hallam left for Turkey two days later, leaving Emerald's ongoing entertainment to Lucy.

Saturday night was Angel's murder mystery night; they each received invitations detailing their individual characters. Set in the fifties at an American high school, Lucy's was a cheerleader. Emerald was disappointed her character was a fusty old librarian. So she set about needling Lucy into swapping. Lucy didn't really care one way or the other, anything to keep Emerald happy; she only had five more days to go.

Angel had gone to a lot of trouble to make the night a success. The dining room was decorated like a fifties prom, with streamers, football banners and pom poms. The day before, Emerald and Lucy had combed the shops and the haberdashery looking for costumes and props. Emerald was dressed in a hot pink, short, flared skirt that she had found in a teenage boutique. She wore a pink, spotted halter neck top; long blonde wig tied with a chiffon scarf, white boots and pom poms. She looked fabulous, all of eighteen. Lucy wore her old woollen pencil skirt, a twin set, pearls, glasses and her hair tied in a scarf. She carried a load of books tied with a leather strap. Esme smiled shyly when they came downstairs, and took photographs of them before they left. Lucy looked back toward the house. Holly and Cam sat illuminated by the television, contentedly eating fish fingers.

Dinner was typical American high school cafeteria: hot dogs, hamburgers, fries and rum and cokes. Seated next to Lucy was Giles, Mioko's husband; he was dressed as a professor. Angel looked fabulous as the queen of the prom. She was sitting next to an interesting guy named Rupert, whom Lucy guessed was Emerald's date. Peter tried to look like James Dean, in his leather motorcycle jacket and rolled up jeans, but with his middle-aged paunch didn't quite pull it off. During dinner they played out their parts convincingly. Everyone remained sober enough to guess the murderer – Rupert!

Once the play-acting was over, Angel led them onto the patio for more drinks. It was a lovely night, there had been the usual afternoon thunderstorm leaving the city rinsed and fresh. Emerald had dispensed with the wig. She was in the corner talking to Rupert, her tawny hair clinging to her face. Angel came over with a glass of red wine.

"I thought you were supposed to be the cheerleader, Lucy?"

Lucy shook her head, freeing her hair from the scarf. "Don't ask, Angel, let's just say it was easier to give in than argue. Who's Rupert? He seems nice."

"He's a doll, friend of Peter's from Kuala Lumpur, works for the same company. His wife hated Malaysia and went home. She's since found someone new. Poor guy, he really is a honey. I'd love to fix him up with someone special."

Lucy looked toward the couple. "Perhaps Emerald is not our girl."

Angel took a sip of her wine. "I think you may be right, we'll save him for someone really special!"

By early morning they were still dancing and drinking. Amber had an argument with Brian, who left abruptly. Peter and Emerald were slow dancing seductively, and Angel was cozying up to Rupert. Giles could hardly stand and held onto the bar for support. Lucy was driving, and so was now only drinking soda water. She was bored and bloated and wanted to go home, but Emerald was having too good a time and wouldn't leave. Peter could see how restless Lucy was getting; he stumbled drunkenly toward her.

"I'll bring Emerald home later, Luce, or failing that, she could spend the night!"

He winked blearily in her direction and made his way unsteadily back to the bar. Emerald thought it was a brilliant idea and gave Lucy a wet kiss. Lucy said goodbye and left, full of misgiving.

Esme was up early having breakfast with Holly before she went to church. Cam was still hunkered down in his bed clutching his baby pillow he had had since his birth. Lucy sat by the pool in her swimmers and sarong with a strong coffee as Esme left to catch her bus. Cam, who had just woken, came to sit by her, watching Holly feed the birds. A taxi drew up and a very hung over, dishevelled Emerald stumbled from the car.

"Lucy, pay him, I don't have any God-dammed money on me!"

Lucy fetched her purse and paid the driver. Upstairs she found Emerald spreadeagled on the bed, her make-up grotesquely smeared. She pulled off her boots and pulled the covers over her and went back to join the children. Only four more days to go and counting!

Amber edged through the garden gate and slumped into the nearest chair. She was hung over and belligerent. "Bloody Brian slept in his office; I can't for the bloody life of me remember what the argument was about!"

Lucy poured more coffee. "What time did you leave?"

Amber squinted into the sun painfully as she gingerly sipped her coffee.

"Oh I guess about four, Emerald was slow dancing with Peter, Rupert had left and Angel had gone to bed. I think we went a bit overboard, Emerald certainly knows how to have a good time!"

"That's what I was afraid of. I'll call Angel later and apologise for my guest's behaviour!"

Lucy took all four children to the movies that afternoon while Amber and Emerald slept. Later they went ten-pin bowling and had dinner at Denny's.

They got back home around six. Emerald was out by the pool with a gin and tonic, looking much better. Lucy mixed herself a drink and topped up Emerald's.

"I really tied one on last night, can't remember a darn thing after you left, I hope everyone realises it's been a long time between drinks for me, with the divorce and all."

Emerald's tone convinced Lucy she really should call Angel.

Peter answered and sounded dreadful; he had only just woken up. Angel picked up the phone in her bedroom.

"Hi, sweetie, just wanted to say thank you for a great night. Everyone sure seemed to enjoy themselves. Glad I left when I did though, by the look of Emerald this morning."

She could hear Angel sigh. "Lucy, you were great, but I must say your choice in friends leaves a little to be desired. I know we were all drunk, but I had to throw her out of our bedroom at six this morning! Peter was paralytic, the worst I've seen him for a long time. Anyway I'm sorry, love, but she really is a bit of a slut! I won't come to your cocktail party, Lucy. I hope you understand. I don't want to face her again. Peter can make up his own fucking mind!"

"Oh, Angel. I'm so sorry. She was always a bit wild. I guess because she is so far from home she thinks she can get away with anything." She apologised profusely to Angel and then went to read to the children before putting them to bed. Seething with anger, she calmed down enough to confront Emerald, but found she had disappeared, this time to her own bed.

Hallam didn't make it home in time for the cocktail party. As usual Lucy carried on without him. She hired a few of the waiters from the club and had them cater the food. It was midweek and guests came and went as they pleased. At nine-thirty she had about eighty people by the pool. Emerald, slightly more subdued, was in her element, wafting about the garden in a leopard print dress, her tawny hair standing out with the humidity. Peter came without Angel, had a few drinks and mingled with his male friends. Mioko, who had just returned from Japan, demurely entered with Giles at her heels. Peter signalled to her from across the expanse of lawn, spiriting her away to a far corner of the garden to talk in private. Lucy could see them close together, silhouetted against the roots of the banyan tree. Giles must be either blind, or stupid, or both; she thought. The party was over early, by twelve she had seen out the last of the stragglers. Amber stayed to help clear up, while Emerald, pleading exhaustion, went to bed.

123

The following morning Lucy woke to loud shrieks coming from Emerald's room. She pushed open the door to find the woman jumping up and down on her bed, clutching a towel to her body. Esme was circling the room with a baseball bat held high above her head, ready to strike. Suddenly Lucy saw a movement in the corner and a large sleek rat appeared. Esme lunged and hit it cleanly, killing it instantly. Emerald ran screaming into the bathroom. Esme ignored her, grabbed a garbage bag and scooped the dead rodent into it neatly. She picked up the bat and the bag and quietly padded out of the room. Emerald returned, her complexion a turgid green, her brow beaded with sweat.

"I feel ill! Did you see what she did with that bat? She's a savage! God, Lucy, I don't know how you can live in this place!"

Lucy left her to finish packing and went downstairs; the children were examining the rat in the bag with great interest before Esme deposited it in the garbage bin. Lucy couldn't help but smile. Emerald's visit had reminded her how much her life had changed since leaving England.

◆◆◆◆◆◆

Lucy finished her commissions and was paid handsomely. The house on the edge of the jungle once again returned to normal. She held a sale of her works at the upmarket fair at the Pacific Palms Hotel, and found her paintings to be in big demand. She had decided to do a calendar of her watercolours for Christmas, and prints of some of her smaller works. A week after the fair the developer of a boutique hotel on the riverfront approached her. He wanted to buy a series of her shop house prints for the guest rooms. Lucinda was ecstatic. Her hard work was paying off and with two more commissions under her belt, her work was starting to be noticed.

She hurried home that afternoon to find the garden had been invaded by thieving monkeys. The children and Esme were diligently guarding the passionfruit and banana trees with brooms, baseball bats and tennis racquets. Each new day she wondered how she had ever survived before Esme came along. Coming home to her was like coming home to a wonderful wife!

As Lucy's paintings evolved into a full-time business, filling her days and fulfilling her creativity, she thought less about the problems of her marriage. It was easy for her to brush aside Hallam's long absences and lack of communication. She knew the trips away were not all business. Nightly he was entertained and wooed by clients. She knew only too well

124

what was available for men alone in Asia. She even managed to subconsciously ignore that now they rarely made love, and if they did it was usually after a boozy night and they were both drunk. She suspected that Hallam had someone else, but she said nothing, preferring instead to hope for the best.

Amber told her, "All men go through phases."

They'd been married a long time. Marriages cool off after so many years. He paid the bills and took them on holidays. She and the children wanted for nothing.

Lucy first started writing to Alex to tell him of her success, and then later to speak to him of her fears regarding Hal. She convinced herself she wasn't doing anything wrong. Only later, when the letters became more intimate, did she start to experience *frissons* of guilt, but with Hallam's lack of interest and absence, it was easy to justify her confiding in another man.

In late September she was having lunch with Amber; they sat in the coffee shop of the Marco Polo hotel. Amber picked at her salad; she was on yet another diet, and watched as Lucy ate her *laksa* with great gusto. Lucy talked between slurps of spicy coconut gravy. She had just seen the final prints of her shop houses for the hotel, and she was thrilled with the results. Amber pushed her salad away.

"Do you think you have time to spare for an old friend, and have dinner this week?"

Amber was slightly jealous of Lucy's success. The sarcasm in her voice did not go unnoticed by Lucy. She thought about the week ahead, it was tight, but she nodded, "Yes," between mouthfuls.

"I'm worried about Angel, Lucy; she hasn't been coming to painting or tennis. She came to mah-jong briefly and then left before morning tea. When was the last time you saw her?"

Lucy reluctantly pushed the large bowl away and took a sip of iced tea. "At the fair last month, she came to my stall and bought some prints."

"How did she seem to you?"

Lucy took another sip of her drink. "Just the same. She was her usual self, worried by how much money she had spent. We promised to have coffee soon, but I guess I've been a bit preoccupied lately; we didn't get around to it. Do you think this thing with Peter and Mioko has got out of hand?"

Amber sighed and signalled the waitress. "I've had it with not drinking, I need a glass of wine! How about you, Luce?"

Lucy shook her head and ordered another iced tea.

"I saw Mioko at the parent and teacher night. We were on our own as usual, so she came home with me for a drink and supper. Over wine she broke down, and in her faltering English she told me Giles had found out she had been sleeping with Peter. He's left her and the children, she doesn't know where he is."

Lucy signalled for a glass of wine. "Oh shit, does Angel know what's going on?"

"She knows they've had an affair, but Peter told her it was only a fling, and it was all over before it really got started. That's not the story Mioko told me. She says Peter's leaving Angel, but that's not all, it gets worse. Mioko's pregnant to Peter!"

Lucy's hands flew to her face. "Oh no! This will destroy Angel!"

Lucy and Amber knew Angel couldn't have children and it had been the biggest tragedy of her life. She wanted to adopt, but Peter wouldn't agree, so they remained childless.

"I think we should go and see her! Maybe Mioko is imagining all of this. Who knows? Half the time I can't understand a word she says."

"Actually, Lucy, I felt pretty sorry for the girl. She has no idea what to do, I think that's why she went home to Japan, to try to sort herself out, but she's more confused than ever. She's much younger than any of us you know. Giles is about fifteen years older than her, and so is Peter!"

"God, men are bastards! Right now it's Angel I feel sorry for. At least Mioko has the children. Angel doesn't have anyone. Oh hell, look at the time, I have to pick Cameron up from cubs. Come over, I'll be back by about half six. I promised the kids moon cakes, and lanterns in the garden tonight, for the festival."

Lucy threw down a fifty, grabbed her bag and ran for the door.

Amber called around at seven. She wound down the car window and shouted, "Come on, Lucy, Angel is waiting."

Lucy kissed the children and instructed Esme on what to give them for dinner. "I won't be gone long. I'll be home in time to light the lanterns. Be good!"

They found Angel in a state of drunkenness. She was barefoot, dressed in a black nightie; her hair was loose and fell about her face in a dirty sheaf. Her usually beautifully made up face was raw, her eyes bleary and swollen. She looked twenty years older. Lucy was shocked by her appearance. Rani the maid wasn't in the apartment; Angel couldn't remember where she'd gone. She leant against the bar, slopping red wine and chain smoking. She lit one, put it down, forgot and lit another. She sat on a stool at Amber's

126

insistence. Amber smoothed her hair and went to her room to fetch her robe.

"He's gone you know Lucy. He's left me, left me for a fucking Jap, with a house full of brats! He never wanted children. I was the one who wanted them, he never did!"

She lit another cigarette and slopped more wine into her glass. She started to sob, her head falling forward. "What am I going to do? Where am I going to go? I've lived here for twenty years. This is my home; I don't know anywhere else. I was born in India. Apart from boarding school, I've lived all my life in Asia."

Amber and Lucy sat listening to her life history, until she was too drunk to talk. Then they gently washed her, changed her nightclothes and put her to bed. Lucy heard the front door click and found Rani creeping across the marbled foyer. She seemed relieved to see them.

"Hello, ma'am Lucy." She was embarrassed and looked at her feet. "How's my ma'am? Yesterday she and Sir had a big fight. He went away. Ma'am yelled at me and told me to leave, so I went to stay at my friend's."

"It's good you're back, Rani, we need you, she was upset yesterday. She won't yell at you again."

Rani set about clearing the debris: wine bottles, broken glasses and clothes strewn about Angel's usually immaculate living room.

"I am going to stay, Lucy. Could you get Honeyko to fetch my overnight bag and a change of clothes? I don't think she should be alone."

"Do you want me to stay with you?"

"No, you go home to the kids. I'll feel better knowing you're next door if something happens."

Amber stayed with Angel, and the following day they talked for hours, drinking black coffee and going over and over Angel's options. After lunch she left her with Rani.

Lucy was painting on her veranda when she quietly slipped up behind her. She'd framed Alex's pastel of the children and it was hanging in the stairwell. It was the first time Amber had seen it.

"Oh, Lucy, this man has talent, the children's likeness and the colours are exquisite, it's a beautiful pastel!"

Amber stood for a long time admiring Alex's work. She approached Lucy's easel and examined the watercolour she was completing.

"Come and have a coffee. How's Angel?"

Amber sighed. Lucy could see how tired she was.

They sat overlooking the garden. The sky had darkened and the birds flew about, agitated. Another storm was brewing. Esme brought them coffee and carrot cake that she and Holly had baked that afternoon.

Amber laughed. "Lucy, I'm supposed to be on a diet!"

Lucy cut them both a small slice and placed it in front of Amber.

"Angel's not good; I'm really worried about her. Mioko's translation was right, Giles has left her; he moved into a small flat off Orchard Road and has asked for a move back to head office. Peter wants Angel to leave the apartment; it's in his company's name. He told her he's going to marry Mioko, and yes, she is pregnant, supposedly with his child. He's staying with Rupert in Malaysia until things settle down. I took Angel today to see my doctor, he gave her some sedatives, she is emotionally and physically exhausted!" Amber massaged her temples with the pads of her fingers.

"What will she do, where can she go?"

"She has friends all over the world but she doesn't want to burden them, she's got a sister who lives in Sri Lanka, they didn't always get on but she has asked her to come and stay. She's going to sort out a few things and go for a visit later. Peter is already pushing for a divorce, apparently the marriage soured years ago but they hung in there out of habit. Can't see him and Mioko lasting, but who knows? Maybe this is what Peter has wanted all along, a family! Or a least a child of his own."

Hallam returned from his latest trip, and over dinner in the garden she told him about Angel, Peter and Mioko. To her surprise he already knew. Apparently Peter had confided in him months before.

His only comment: "Peter was bloody unhappy in that marriage, no children and he hated the thought of adoption. Anyway, half the time Angel was pissed and hanging off some bloke in a corner at some party. The marriage was dead long ago!"

Lucy looked at him, shocked. "Is that what's going to happen to us? Will our marriage die a slow death?"

He looked at her, his eyes guarded. "What are you talking about? It's entirely up to you. It all depends on your happiness, doesn't it Lucy? Isn't that the way? If the wife's happy, everyone's happy. Besides, we have children to think about!"

She was shocked at the aggressive nature of his reply. She wanted to challenge him, ask him what he meant exactly, but Cameron and Holly came jumping into their father's outspread arms, ending the conversation.

It was easy for Lucinda to write to Alex secretly. She had a post office box for her company and she received his letters there. Now and again she was filled with guilt and decide not to reply, but then Hallam would leave and her guilt would dissipate. In her letters to him she perceived herself as a very different woman. She told Alex things Hallam would never want to hear. She let her inner child rule; her life was suddenly filled with an unexpected gift of intimacy.

Angel left to visit her sister in October; she stayed a few weeks and then returned to the apartment. Peter had started divorce proceedings. Mioko took the children and went back to Japan, initiating a divorce from Giles. She planned to wait there until Peter summoned her.

Late on Friday evening in mid-October, Peter went to the apartment to have Angel sign the papers. He found the front door unlocked and no sign of Rani. He searched the silent apartment for Angel and found her floating in the jacuzzi in a rose-coloured foam of her own blood.

Lucy had just put the final brush stroke on a watercolour when the call came. Brian was with Peter and Amber, who were too distraught to speak. He asked her to come over as soon as she could. He didn't give any details, except to say Angel had been taken to hospital.

When Lucy arrived, an ambulance was pulling slowly out of the ornate gates of the condominium. There was no siren and no haste. A police car was parked in the "No Parking Zone" at the entrance to the foyer. Her hands shook and her stomach contracted, shrinking against her spine, as she rode the elevator to the penthouse. Amber came to her as she entered, her face contorted with pain. Her body trembled violently as she bent her head close to Lucy.

"She's gone, Lucy, she took her own life, we tried to revive her but it was too late."

Blood pounded in Lucy's ears and she sat on the floor heavily, Amber holding her arm awkwardly. Brian came to her with a tumbler of brandy but a bitter bile rose in her throat, and she vomited all over Angel's peach-coloured carpet. She could see Peter, his face grey and lined, sitting in the office with two policemen; he looked at her with concern and then buried his head in his hands and wept.

In the early hours of the morning, Lucy tried to call Hallam in Bangkok, but he wasn't in his room. She left an urgent message for him to call home but he never did. Desperate to speak to someone, she automatically called Alex. At first she sobbed, sitting helpless with the phone slipping out of her damp hands. She gained control of her breathing and poured forth the details of Angel's death. He listened without interruption, soothing and comforting her. As the pale light of morning crept between the shuttered windows, she felt cleansed and renewed. Without Alex, she would never have got through the night. Finally, she slept.

Esme sensed the sadness within the house. Her ma'am had not painted for days. She overheard the hushed phone calls and saw ma'am Amber's tears. Rani called Esme. She was frantic with guilt. She had been sent away that day. Had she stayed maybe things would have been different. Esme soothed her and talked to her like a little sister. All Esme could do to help was counsel the distraught maid, run the house efficiently and take the children away from the unhappiness. She and Holly cooked endless batches of biscuits and cakes, and Cameron helped her plant a new vegetable garden behind the garage. The passionfruit vine was bearing fruit, as were the banana and lime trees. Lucy was grateful to Esme for taking the children aside, giving her time to come to terms with Angel's death. The house was polished and the smell of good food filled the rooms.

Esme left a small prayer on her ma'am's pillow, which Timothy had given to her when Laani died. She wanted to share her pain. Lucinda found the prayer two days after Angel's death.

"Deep Peace of the running wave to you, Deep peace of the flowing air to you, Deep peace of the quiet earth to you, Deep peace of the shining stars to you, Deep peace of the Son of Peace to you." Gaelic Blessing.

◆◆◆◆◆◆

News of Angel's death did not appear in the papers. A private cremation took place two days after she died, attended only by Peter and her sister, who had flown in from Sri Lanka. A week later a memorial was held in the Methodist church. Hallam returned, remorseful at having missed her call. He was full of excuses, maintaining they had put her through to the wrong room or they must have misheard the name. She listened quietly, telling him it was too late and didn't matter anymore.

The small brick church blossomed with bougainvillea, spilling in an arc above the entrance. The interior was filled to capacity; the front of the church was a riot of flower arrangements, filling the air with a cloying, mawkish scent, which turned Lucy's stomach. A large studio photograph of Angel stood at the pew, it had been taken with a soft lens, giving her the look of a fifties' film star. Lucy knew she had had it taken at Hidden Beauty Studio as a gift for Peter, and was disappointed with the finished result. Amber and Brian stood next to Peter and Angel's sister, who looked eerily like Angel from behind. Tuppy, wearing a straw hat that looked as though she had sat upon it, wept loudly. Lucy knew Angel would have laughed with her, as she smiled secretly to herself. Hallam was solicitous and had been tender and loving since his return. All it did was make her feel as though she needed air.

Angel's sister Ruth read the eulogy. She told the congregation of their happy childhood together, growing up in India, of how Angel got her name because she was an unexpected gift. As a little girl she was angelic and a joy to both their parents. She had a lovely singing voice and sang with the church choir. They had many servants and a cook. As a child, they all loved her; she was the spoilt baby.

"When as a young woman I left to go to Paris after university in England, my big romantic adventure, my parents wrote and asked if the teenage Angel could join me. She had grown tired of finishing school in Switzerland and wanted to travel. I was incensed at the intrusion but, in reality, having Angel with me gave me the courage and strength to do things I would never have done on my own. She was a rebel, with a flair for enjoying the finer things in life. She loved good food, wine and friends and was a joy to be with. She was always welcoming, throwing open her home to guests. She made sure your every need was taken care off, she was generous, a wonderful cook and hostess, her parties were always superb. I know Angel's biggest regret was not having children, she would have been a wonderful mother."

She broke down and Peter wept openly, cradling her in his arms. The congregation was silent as Ruth composed herself once more, and read the first verse of a poem that was one of Angel's favourites. Tuppy, in her gravelly voice, read a faltering piece from the bible, and then the congregation sung two hymns chosen by Peter. The minister read a short prayer, and then it was over.

Hallam clutched Lucy's elbow as she faltered. The congregation mingled, kissing and wiping away each other's tears. They spilled onto the lawn in the harsh, slanting afternoon sun, the unmistakable beat of the 'Rolling Stones' belting out 'Honky Tonk Woman' rent the air. It was Angel's favourite. The minute she heard it, she would be up dancing. They laughed and cried, remembering her as she was, and as she would have wanted to be.

131

Chapter Fifteen
Alex

Alex originally wanted to meet Lucy Leadbitter out of curiosity. He had known Hallam as a boy at school and then again later for a brief period in Spain one summer. He didn't like him. He found him patronising with an acerbic sense of humour. Hallam wasn't much of a sportsman, being slightly effeminate and clumsy. Alex's most disturbing memory was Hallam as a senior, dishing out the brutal and often humiliating practice of ragging new students. He remembered that he always excelled at maths and was good on the debating team, but he was never part of Alex's group.

Liam Ormond was a friend of Alex's sister, a very good friend! Alex had found them in a contorted naked embrace in front of the open fire one Sunday afternoon. The following summer Liam had invited everybody to Majorca where he was teaching water skiing. Alex went for a week, surprised to see Hallam there; he didn't appear to be the type for a beach resort. Alex enjoyed his time on the island but found the whole place too crowded and full of English tourists. He and another friend took off for Amsterdam where they smoked a lot of weed and drank a lot of booze. He had discovered an art gallery near Dam Square that had the most ethereal sculpture; he was captivated by the sensual curves of the design. He noted the artist and went to track her down. She was working by day as a waitress in a coffee shop and Alex fell in love at first sight. That girl was Inke.

Alex's mate went back to Uni at the start of semester but Alex stayed on. Inke was more worldly and sophisticated than he was and had a boyfriend, but Alex was tenacious. To eke out his savings a little longer he got a job at Fat Cat City handing out pamphlets to prospective customers, but as fate would have it, his mother got sick and he had a telegram from his father, telling him to come home immediately and get back to University.

He was surprised when he received an invitation to Hallam's wedding the following summer, and broken hearted to hear that Inke had married her boyfriend. He avoided both the wedding and Inke when she came back to London the following year.

Alex remained in contact with Liam Ormond, who one summer came to visit. He had in tow a cute little Filipino called Spanky who was a constant source of amusement for Alex.

Most of the time Spanky wore very little clothing, but she always wore platform shoes with every outfit. Alex knew the reason; she was only four foot five inches tall. She was masterful at eating and talking at the same time, rarely to him, only to Liam. Liam would amuse himself by promising her things and then withdrawing that promise, as if to a child. That would provoke Spanky into a brow-raising, lip-puckering sulk, which could last for days. She snacked constantly on sticky bits, which stuck to the floors, attracting ants. When Alex pointed this out to her, she shrugged her honey-brown shoulders and said, "Many black ants, you'll be rich!"

While painting her long talon-like toenails and reading trashy gossip magazines, she ate squid crackers that smelt like day-old prawn heads.

Alex wasn't sure why Liam had brought her with him. She didn't swim or walk or attempt any activity whatsoever. They left her behind each day when Liam went off surfing and Alex painted. She seemed content with this arrangement as long as Liam took her to buy a lottery ticket, and play bingo at the local pensioners' centre. She was obsessively superstitious, she believed in *aswang*, some kind of vampire that steals body parts, she told Alex. When she first entered the house, she counted the number of steps.

"*Oro* gold the best, *plata* silver, next best." She did a quick calculation in her head and drew in her breath. "*Wah, mata*, death."

Liam ignored it all, kissing her on the top of her head, and asking her to give him a massage. When she was happy with him she called him Honey, when she was sulking she called him Joe. Each day for lunch she would blacken a fish on top of the stove, then she poured sticky, dark sauce over the whole thing, and took it to her room to eat.

In the evening while Liam and Alex sat chatting over a vodka tonic or wine, Spanky would drink asti spumanti until she grew bored. She would then ask Liam in a little-girl voice if he would like the "comfort". If he didn't, she would pout and sulk. If he did, she would purr like a kitten and take him off to their room. Alex was left listening to the squealing, thumping and banging, leaving him without any doubt what was going on in there.

During this enlightening visit, Liam told Alex all about Lucy. He told him of their days romping in and out of bed in Spain and how, when she caught him in *flagrante delicto*, she ran straight into the ample arms of the undeserving Hallam. He gave Alex a letter Hallam had sent him, not long after they moved to Singapore.

My dearest, most deserving friend,

Well here I am and all I can say is: I never want to leave! Paradise found, my friend. Forget the boring old tart London.

Excellent club with all the G&T I can drink. Family all taken care of, nice looking little Filipina to keep the wife happy! The women in the office can't keep their hands to themselves and luckily don't know the meaning of sexual harassment. In fact they fight over a little bit of extra attention, if you know what I mean! They really go for the Angmohs here and the meatier the better.

To get away from the stress of it all, I take a quick flight to Bangkok to buy silk shirts and tailored suits. The Thai women are beautiful and creative with their hands. You don't know what you're missing, my friend! Just a bit of advice if you are thinking of a hardship posting: come alone. You'll enjoy yourself much more!

The letter went on, but Alex got the gist of what attracted Hallam to living in Asia. It seemed that Hallam had not changed much. Alex's curiosity was whetted. After seeing Hallam again and meeting Lucy, he was not disappointed. He agreed with Liam: Lucy was indeed wasted on the likes of Hallam.

The letters had started innocently enough, news of the children, her painting success and her business, but they had grown more intimate on both accounts. He wrote of his years alone, how little time he had had for women when he was working hard to build up the gallery. Of meeting Inke again at one of his gallery openings, her standing there alone in a cream wool coat and boots up to her thighs, a lacy cap covering her long dark hair. How badly Inke's husband had hurt her, his drug addiction and that Inke too in time had become addicted. She had years of nightmare abuse, until she picked herself up and finally left him. By the time Alex found her again, she was clean, drug free and sculpting.

They married the following spring and lived in a small but elegant flat above Alex's gallery. Over the next few years the gallery, Alex's art, and Inke's sculpture became a great success. It all fell apart when Inke was diagnosed with lung cancer. She had part of her lung removed and chemotherapy, but the specialists maintained there was little they could do for her. Alex had read of a pioneering doctor, who was experimenting in removal of arterial blood, mixing it with pure oxygen and then reinstating it into the body. He was located across the other side of the world in Queensland, Australia. They were both convinced to try it, after yet another wet, cold winter that left Inke almost dead. They had nothing to lose.

He sold all they owned and moved to Noosa. They bought a home in the hinterland with a studio where they both could work. Inke loved it from the moment the plane touched down. It took them all of two days to find the house of their dreams. Inke had had one treatment and the chance to enjoy her new home for three months before she died.

It had taken a lot out of Alex to write of Inke to Lucy, but he felt good after doing so. He had hardly spoken of her since her death. The morning Lucy phoned him, he had almost decided the letters must stop, but hearing her voice again brought all the passion from that first kiss rushing back. He had planned that kiss. He had thought about it all day when they were on the island. Lucy had all of the talent and a lot of the spirit that Inke possessed. She was the first woman who stirred his feelings, but she was married with children. He decided to leave things alone for a while and see what fate had in store for him; he couldn't stand losing another woman at this time in his life.

Chapter Sixteen
Christmas of Redemption

After Angel's death, Lucinda withdrew socially; she no longer went to mah-jong and frequented the club less. She and Amber still had lunch, but just the two of them, excluding the others. It was painful for her to hear the gossipmongers shredding details about Angel. Peter left Singapore and went to work in Malaysia. The relationship with Mioko ended and she stayed in Japan to have her baby alone.

The letters between Alex and Lucy dwindled, at first they became less intimate and then less frequent, perhaps they had burnt themselves out after Lucy's frantic phone call. On the other hand, maybe it had been a mistake, but she knew in her heart that final kiss from Alex was no mistake.

In November, Lucinda was invited to the opening of the boutique River Hotel, which featured her work. A nonchalant Hallam accompanied her; they were treated to a champagne reception in the glossy marble foyer. The darkly handsome Italian who ran the hotel made a theatrical fuss of her, taking her by the elbow and steering her from one dignitary to another. They stood and ate delicate canapés out of Chinese spoons and had their photographs taken by the society magazine, *Tatler*.

From the publicity generated from the article, she had more commissions than ever, and toward the lead up to Christmas she was painting full time. She held her Christmas Fair along with other stallholders in the vast ballroom of the Gilmore Hotel. The calendars sold extremely well, as did her prints; by the end of the second day, she had sold out and had a book full of potential clients for the New Year.

Hallam toasted her briefly during a business dinner. Lucinda rarely attended these dinners but this one was a special Christmas get-together. It was the first time she had met Hallam's business associates and knew she was under scrutiny. She wore a dark suit and piled her hair into a chignon.

136

When she glanced at her reflection in the bathroom mirror, she was pleased with her appearance.

The dinner was a Cantonese banquet, held in the private Jade room of a revolving restaurant. Hallam was extremely gregarious throughout the dinner. The women were all young and beautiful, except for Linda, Hallam's elderly, short-sighted secretary. They laughed at all his silly jokes, fawning over him, taking his coat, vying for the seat next to him, and even ordering the food on his behalf. Some of the young men from the office were included, but they were shy and socially awkward, seeming much younger than the women. Lucy decided the compulsory two years National Service, which took them out of the community, contributed to their gauche behaviour. They seemed to find Lucy extremely funny, and giggled like girls each time she tried to engage them in small talk.

It was the first time she had met Elvira, and she was puzzled as to why she had been invited. She had left Hallam's office over a year ago. Her appearance unnerved Lucy; she had only ever spoken to the woman on the phone. Her voice was cool and elegant, well educated with a slight American accent; she had a throaty laugh that made everyone look her way. She regularly threw back her head and laughed at Hallam, giving him a sidelong glance from beneath her lashes. Her small, golden hands dripped with blood red, tapered nails. Lucy watched as she slid them along the table to lay claim to Hallam's arm every time she made a point or wanted to gain his interest.

As the meal progressed, Lucy became more anxious. She felt clumsy, and her chopsticks were like wooden stakes in her hands. She dropped her prawns and splattered sauce on the snowy tablecloth. Hallam caught her eye in annoyance. Elvira summoned the waiter with a fillip of her fingers, and procured a fork and spoon for Lucinda. She was humiliated, as the others all tittered behind their small bony hands, and Linda looked on sympathetically behind her thick glasses. She wanted to drive the chopsticks through Elvira's heart. She tried to calm her nerves with wine but that made things worse. Her tongue became thick in her mouth and she couldn't think of anything worthwhile to say, so she continued drinking and dropping food.

At one point, she slipped out to the ladies' room, only to find her elegant hairstyle had come undone, and her suit had a soy sauce stain down the front. She repaired the damage as best she could and looked up to find the elegant Elvira watching her like a snake in the mirror.

Hallam drove home in stony silence. He was already in bed by the time she came out of the bathroom. The wine, the baneful dinner, and her humiliation put her in a dangerous mood. She wanted an argument!

"I didn't know the sensational Elvira was Indian!" She spat the last word out at Hallam's ponderous back.

"What does it matter what race she is? Actually, if you must know, she has an Indian mother and a Dutch father. I didn't know you were such a racist, I guess you live and learn. Your social skills were appalling tonight, perhaps you should drink less!"

Lucy was enraged. She struck out at him, pulling the covers from his body and forcing him to face her.

"They treated you like some kind of royalty and me like I was some decrepit old aunty. What's with all the sucking up, anyway? Surely they get paid enough without having to fawn all over you!"

Lucy was sitting up in bed, her face twisted and her hair matted about her head. Hallam turned his back on her and feigned sleep.

"Elvira looked like some cheap whore in her mini skirt and skimpy blouse, showing off all that she wished she possessed!"

Hallam turned and lunged toward Lucinda, slapping her hard across the face, sending her reeling from the bed to the floor. He panted like a wild animal, looking at her with blazing eyes. She stumbled to her feet, pulled the string of her nightie back onto her shoulder, and fled to the bathroom where she locked the door and collapsed weeping onto the tiled floor.

The savage argument was not mentioned again that weekend. Lucy painted and took the children to various birthday parties and activities; she was remorseful and full of blame. She asked herself why she was so abusive when she drank; she made a vow to give it up.

Hallam left for London on Sunday night for a month, one last trip before Christmas. He was cautiously tender with her and indulgent toward the children, promising to bring back all manner of gifts from Harrods. Before he left he cornered Lucy in the bedroom.

"I want you to try and make this a happy Christmas. To do that, we need to get out of Singapore. I've booked us a flight to San Francisco in the States and then on to Yosemite Valley for Christmas. It's time the children saw some snow again."

She could see how hard he was trying. Amber would be disappointed that they wouldn't spend Christmas together. They had sat over latte's only last week at Holland Village, planning the perfect day to make up for all the sadness, but Hallam's wishes came first.

◆◆◆◆◆◆

Timothy Waldon continued to spend his only afternoon off searching the library for anything he could get his hands on regarding the Filipino culture. He read reams of history books about the Spanish invaders, martyrs and heroes; how the Philippines were referred to as the Pearl of the Orient, the national bird was the Philippine eagle; the milkfish the national fish and the sampaguita was the national flower. He really wanted to learn about the people; he read about their traditions, superstitions, fiestas and food, but, he finally realised, lying one night in his lonely bed, that the only way he would ever understand them was to go there and see for himself.

His courtship of Esmirada had reached a stalemate since the bungled kiss. He shared his religious knowledge with her and tried to draw her out on her background. She seemed happy to hear about his former life over lunch at the hawker stall, but told him very little of her own. Sister Mary tried to explain that perhaps she wasn't as proud of her own history, and that he should give her time to get to know him more.

He could see how happy she was; he thanked God for the good family that she worked for. They appeared very generous and Esmirada spoke in glowing terms of the children and her ma'am, 'a famous artist in Singapore'. She spoke of the beautiful mansion in the vast gardens where she lived, and all the lovely treasures the family owned. Esme was especially animated when she told him about the food she cooked, and how loving and good they were to her. Timothy couldn't help but think she was more appreciative of him when she was unhappy. He knew his thoughts were unchristian and berated himself for his selfishness. All he could do was wait and continue to hope God was on his side, he knew He had a plan for him, he just prayed that Esmirada was part of that plan.

In the meantime he continued to live a righteous life, his work with the school and refuge was going well. Donations had been steadily coming in, and the Singapore and Philippine Governments had been generous and forthcoming in their support. There had been less abuse reported in the papers, and since the safety campaign had been highlighted, less accidental deaths. Sister Mary had been working with Foreign Assist to produce a small booklet on safety in the home for foreign workers, which would be available in the New Year. He just had to learn humility and patience and look forward to each Sunday, when he could gaze at Esmirada and hear her voice once again.

◆◆◆◆◆◆

As Lucy expected, Amber was very disappointed that they had decided to go away for Christmas. The two women sat side by side at the Ladies' Christmas Lunch at the club, eating yet another turkey dinner with still twelve days to go until Christmas. Amber whispered to Lucy from behind her hand.

"I can't believe you're going to leave me at the mercy of Tuppy and the Major. Have a heart! How will I get through the day?"

Lucy sniggered. "It'll be fine. You'll have a great time and we'll be back in time for New Year. We don't leave until the twenty-third so it's virtually only a week."

Frivolity had quickly returned to the group of expats with a never-ending round of Christmas parties and drinks. Angel was mentioned and a few tears shed, but life went on. Lucy went to Angel's apartment block for the first time since her death, to attend a tennis lunch. She saw a moving van at the entrance; a new family had rented the penthouse. She left the lunch early, feeling jaded and sad, not in the Christmas spirit at all.

◆◆◆◆◆◆

Toward the end of December all Cameron and Holly could talk about was snow. They were looking forward to a white Christmas. It had rained continually for five days in Singapore. Everything, from clothes and furniture to food, was damp, soggy and mouldy. On the eve of their departure a mini cyclone blew through and delayed their flight by four hours. When they finally boarded they were so tired they slept immediately, landing in Hong Kong for a stopover and then on to the States.

They gained time and arrived on the same day they left. Hallam had booked a hotel for two nights so they could see the sights of San Francisco, before heading by car to Yosemite.

The children were tired and brittle at first. Lucy did her best to jolly them along. Hallam had little patience with them when they were cantankerous. After a light supper and walk around town to see the Christmas lights, they sat in the hotel in front of the open fire, drinking mulled wine before bed.

The following day they were fresh and ready to explore. They sandwiched into a cable car and rode up the hill and down to Fisherman's wharf.

Hallam dug Lucy in the ribs. "Look, Robin Williams!"

The actor was hanging onto the rail at the door, wind in his hair and a look of pure joy on his face. Hallam behaved like a small boy amongst the hoard of tourists, browsing about the carnival atmosphere of the wharf. A cold wind blew across the bay and they pulled their winter coats closer. Lucy held on to Cameron as he climbed onto the railings to look at the sea lions, lying in the tepid sun on pallets in the bay. As the wind changed direction, the stench hit them in the face and made their eyes water.

"Oh boy, they sure do stink!" he said as they retreated further along the deck to have a look at Alcatraz through the coin-operated binoculars.

Cameron wanted to go to the Island but Hallam had other plans. Lucy stopped Cam's whingeing by buying him a cannoli pastry. Hallam's plan was to explore the cannery and then go to Washington Square. They picked up tickets for a cable car tour, which took them via the Golden Gate Bridge. From there Cam could get a good look at the prison and Lucy bought him a book on its history. Coming back they passed through Chinatown and on a small patch of green in front of the church, elderly Chinese were performing a silent ritual of *t'ai chi*.

They rode up and down narrow streets admiring the old terraces, or Mansard Ladies, as they were known locally. Lucy felt as though she were on a film set; everywhere she recognised streets from the movies or television programs. Late in the afternoon, they took a helicopter ride over the city and the bay. The sun was just going down and washed the Golden Gate Bridge in a honey-coloured glow. From their vantage point Cam got a good view of Alcatraz. They saw the magnificent sweep of the beaches, and homes of the rich and famous, tucked away in the velvety green hills.

The wind died down as evening approached and they promenaded past the Italian restaurants, looking for a good place to eat. They found a busy place with an open wood oven; Hallam ordered antipasto and pizza. The food was good and the restaurant cosy. Jet lag kicked in and Cam fell asleep on Hallam's lap. They finished and Hal carried him back to the hotel on his shoulders, while Lucy piggybacked a sleepy Holly.

The morning of Christmas Eve, Lucy woke to find Hallam missing. He left a note saying he couldn't sleep so had gone to get the rental car. Lucy showered in the cold bathroom with the taste of steam in her mouth. She packed the cases and ordered breakfast before she woke the children. They ate in a desultory manner, half asleep; by the time Hallam returned, they were more lively and ready to explore by road.

It was relatively easy to manoeuvre out of the city. The freeways were well marked and the traffic was still light at that time of day. Hallam made good time. By lunch they were almost to the Valley; the family stopped at a quaint Indian outpost, where good, home cooked food was served in large portions. Although the wind was crisp, the day was clear and bright, and there was certainly no sign of snow, but by the time they drove into the valley, the wind had picked up and the temperature dropped.

Hallam pulled the car up at a popular lookout before descending. There was a line of vehicles parked at angles; the drivers and their passengers had disembarked, taking turns to have photographs in front of the famous El Capitan. The children, who had been asleep, scrambled out of the car to take in the breathtaking view. Cameron, the keen photographer, was snapping away.

"Hey, buddy, save some film until we get there!"

Yosemite Valley stood magnificently before them, backlit in a ruddy glow of late afternoon light. The fissured granite of Half Dome and Glacier Point rose above them, the waterfalls cascading in a pearly halo. The wind whipped thin flags of snow on the peaks above the canopy of ponderosa pines. The kids sat glued to the window as they entered the busy village, glowing with fairy lights, as they drove on to the lodge.

Ahwahnee Lodge loomed above them, stone grey in the fading light. The family made their way through slushy snow into the welcoming warmth of the cavernous entrance. A huge, overly decorated pine stood in the lobby, groaning with gifts. From the dining room Lucy could hear carol singers and the clink of glasses and cutlery, as guests enjoyed an early dinner. Lucy and the children read the 'Bear Aware' posters by the huge fireplace, while Hallam checked in. Their assigned room was at the end of a long corridor, decorated with Indian carpets and artefacts. The old polished floorboards creaked as the children rushed ahead.

The room was spacious with a huge king size bed, that looked out onto The Royal Arches and Glacier Point, now dark against the soft glow of sky. There was an adjoining room for the children and a balcony with a small table and chairs.

The dining room was the size of an elegant barn; it had lofty, vaulted ceilings and row upon row of glistening chandeliers. The room had donned

142

its traditional Christmas mantle of green and red, and candlelight flickered at each table. A dapper gentleman, dressed in an immaculate dinner suit, sat at an ebony baby grand. Behind him, resplendent in scarlet and white, the choir stood ready to perform. Lucy looked at the bank of windows reflecting the scene, and at the dark, looming, snow covered peaks beyond; it was perfect.

Lucy caught Hallam watching her over the top of the wine list, and took his hand across the table. The waiter appeared and informed them of the chef's recommendations. Hallam ordered a bottle of red from the Napa Valley.

"Very good choice, sir. In fact Robert Redford ordered the same bottle just last night!"

Lucy's eyes lit up and Hallam laughed. "Well, as you can see by my wife's face, she's impressed."

The waiter winked at Holly.

"Where was Mr Redford sitting?"

"Why, right where you are now, madam."

Lucy rolled her eyes heavenwards and hugged Holly impulsively. They began to order their food, but then requested a further five minutes in family discussion, because Holly wanted spring rolls and Cameron tom yum soup, neither of which were on the menu. They settled for grain fed chicken instead.

The cold, fresh mountain air and good food settled the children to sleep almost the minute their heads touched their pillows, but not before they had hung their stockings at the end of their beds. Lucy explained that part of Santa's gift to them was this holiday but she still had two suitcases full of gifts hidden in the wardrobe.

She set up a small fir tree, which they decorated, and then she took the gifts and placed them under the tree. Hallam and Lucy braved the chill and sat for a while on the balcony, watching the dark clouds drift past the moon above the mountaintops.

"Merry Christmas, Hal. It's so beautiful here, a Christmas to remember."

He was gentle and tender in his lovemaking, taking time to please her; afterward she remained in his arms, drifting into a deep and dreamless sleep.

Cameron was up at sunrise; he woke Holly and together they plundered their stockings and were waiting to open the gifts about the tree. Hallam made them wait while he opened a bottle of champagne. Holly and Cam sat in the big double bed, laughing, and throwing gift-wrapping all over the room.

Afterward they dressed and followed the snow covered trail to Mirror Lake. Hallam pointed out droppings, which probably belonged to a coyote. They quietly rounded a copse of black oak and beside a rocky outcrop, nibbling on exposed sedge, was a Mule deer with a magnificent rack of velvety antlers. Cameron was quick enough to manage one photograph before the deer sensed their presence and darted off into the forest of oak. Holly scraped up enough snow, which was only thin on the ground, to make a snowball, and they had a snow fight before hiking back to the lodge for Christmas lunch.

Lunch ended at four that afternoon. They had made friends with a few other families, who challenged them to a game of Trivial Pursuit beside the fire in the library. The Leadbitters came second, but that was because Hal fell asleep halfway through, and they had to battle on without him. Late in the afternoon, the winning family led them all on an expedition into the village for a tour of the Ansel Adams Gallery, and a pizza at the family Pizza Hut.

They were asleep in bed by nine o'clock having had, "The best Christmases ever!" according to Holly.

Lucy agreed, and smiled across at her husband, as she swept them into her arms and carried them to bed.

For another four days the family hiked along the banks of the icy rivers, took picnics to eat beneath waterfalls, and discovered an ancient Indian village. They combed through a settlers' cemetery, examining the headstones and exclaiming at the young age at which they had died.

Reluctantly they left the valley to make the long drive back to San Francisco, and to board the flight that would take them home to Singapore.

Once in flight in the capable hands of the Sarong Kabaya clad hostess, Lucy turned to Hallam and thanked him for a wonderful Christmas. He had redeemed himself; he was attentive and fun with the children, and loving and caring with her. He left his business behind, rarely using the phone. The marriage was as it had been before they came to Asia, he was the Hallam of old, laughing, teasing and making love with great skill and tenderness. She sighed and Hallam took her hand in his. Her only hope was that it would last.

144

Chapter Seventeen
A Very Good Sign

Esmirada missed having the family home for Christmas. The house was damp and eerily quiet without the children. The inclement weather had continued, making it the wettest Christmas on record. But just as suddenly as it had started, it stopped, and the hot sun burnt off the haze. Her garden flourished before her eyes. She harvested all week long, taking limes, passionfruit, bananas, avocado and papaya with her to church. Timothy received a gift basket of home grown produce trimmed with red and green ribbon.

On Christmas Day, they held a well-attended service with a visiting pastor from Baguio City in the Philippines. Afterward Harold Seng Loh and his wife Joyner asked Sister Mary, Esmirada, Timothy, Sister Amelia and Nora to Christmas lunch in their home. Esme hesitated when they issued the invitation, she always had lunch with them following church, but this was a very special family day. Joyner pointed out that the church was the only family she and Harold had, so she shyly accepted.

Harold and Joyner had a small semi-detached house in Bukit Batok; it was sparsely furnished but very clean. The front entrance was completely tiled in beige, which continued through the house to a small back patio. There was no garden, not even a blade of grass, Esme sadly noted. A sea of shoes decorated the entrance; Esme removed hers and neatly placed them on the bamboo shelving. Esme had baked Christmas cookies and a fruit cake to give to Mary to share at the refuge, but once the invitation was issued, she held on to them tightly, to contribute to Joyner and Harold's Christmas lunch.

Timothy had been quiet all morning, but seemed pleased with the gift she had given him. He now stood towering in the doorway, blocking out the bright sunlight, while Harold rearranged the little furniture they had, to make way for borrowed tables from the Muslim family next door. Timothy helped carry them into the room, and Esme set about finding cloths, napkins and tableware to dress them. She then hid herself in the kitchen with Joyner, preparing the festive lunch.

Joyner had prepared a roast chicken rubbed with honey and garlic. Esme set the oven and got it started. She then turned her attention to the mixed salad and mutton chops with deep fried potatoes. Joyner didn't seem very experienced in the kitchen, and was relieved and grateful for Esme's help. The food was different from what her ma'am served at Christmas, but Esme decided it looked delicious. She finished off the buttered rice and placed her Christmas cake and cookies in the centre of table for a nice effect. Joyner didn't have a tree or any trimmings, but she did have some fairy lights above the entrance to the house, which Harold now proudly switched on.

Timothy blessed the meal and said grace, thanking Joyner and Harold for their generosity. The laughter from the small house spilt onto the quiet tree-lined street, as they enjoyed their Christmas meal. There was no wine or champagne as there would have been in Bukit Lalang, but Timothy and Harold had a cold beer while the women had fruit cordial. Esme helped clear and wash the dishes, resetting them for the cake and cookies.

Timothy stood to make a toast and to wish everyone, "A Merry Christmas and Happy and blessed New Year."

Esme's face glowed with satisfaction and humidity from the kitchen when they congratulated her on her fine cake and cookies. Timothy waited for the inevitable spread of colour from her neck to the roots of her hair that he had grown to love.

The party ended at four. Esme stood to leave, thanking Joyner and Harold profusely. She said goodbye to Mary and the other Sisters and walked to the end of the street with Timothy to catch the bus home. They sat in the shade of the deserted bus stop. It was the first time all day Timothy had had a chance to talk to her alone.

"Esme, thank you so much for the wonderful gift basket. It is even more precious knowing you grew and nurtured them yourself! I haven't given you my gift yet."

Esme turned her face to him with pleading eyes. "Oh no, Timothy, you don't have to give me anything, my gift was so small."

He took her damp hand in his and she didn't pull away. A breeze ruffled the top of her hair and a thin line of sweat formed on her upper lip.

Timothy took a deep breath and cleared his throat. In a hoarse voice he said, "I want to marry you!"

Esme took a great gulp of air and bit her bottom lip between her small even teeth. She pulled her hands from him and raked them through her hair. She could feel her heart beating a tattoo against her chest. He could see the fear and confusion in her eyes. He was afraid she was going to run away. He took both her hands and held her there.

"You don't have to give me an answer right away. We're still getting to know each other, but I want to let you know how I feel and what my intentions are."

Esme said nothing; she looked into his eyes and gently kissed the palm of his hand and held it to the curve of her cheek. She stood on wooden legs as the bus approached, let his hand drop and without looking back, climbed the stairs to the bus.

Timothy watched until it was out of sight; he was confused. He slumped against the wooden seat, remembering the warmth of her face, and the moist kiss she had planted on the palm of his hand. He saw this as a good sign. Yes! It had to be a good sign; he sent up a silent prayer to God and walked slowly back to his flat.

Esme rode home with a smile upon her lips. Warmth and generosity surged through her entire body. Finally she settled back against the sun-warmed seat, and thanked God for this wonderful day and for bringing Timothy into her life.

Chapter Eighteen
Hey Joe

Lucinda was on library duty at the children's school. She returned the borrowed books to the shelves; and had an empty half hour, before Year Three began their session. She liked being a library mum; it gave her a chance to observe the school and the children at close hand. Cam and Holly were chuffed that she was a library monitor. On those days she would sit with them under the sprawling banyan trees and eat lunch, watching them play and interact with the other children. Cameron had lost his awkwardness, and had stopped biting his nails. He was a precocious reader and had moved on from infants' into primary school level in less than a year. He was a competitive swimmer and held the 'tadpole' breaststroke record at the club. Holly was more confident than ever: class captain, leader of her brownie pack, and heavily into dramatic arts both on and off the stage.

Lucy's duties at the school gave her a break from her business. She'd come back after Christmas to a full book of commissions and had now graduated to portraits. Last week she finished a pastel of a small girl, as a gift for her father's birthday and she was currently working on a watercolour of an American family with their dog.

She watched Nurse Sally walk briskly from her office along the corridor. When she saw her she waved and came quickly across the lawn to where Lucy was sitting.

"Hi, Mrs. Leadbitter, I've been flat out all morning checking heads for lice. You had a call from your maid at about eleven. I'm sorry I didn't get to you sooner. She wants you to call her at home. You can walk back with me and use the office phone if you like."

Sally tossed her brown curls away from her face and they walked back together, discussing the never-ending problem of head lice.

Esme answered immediately, she calmly told Lucy that her brother had called informing her of her father's death. She needed to go home. Lucy's heart sank. She relied heavily on Esme, and she remembered what had happened when Yolo had left after the death of her daughter. What would she do if Esme didn't return?

When she got back to the house, Esme was cooking a selection of dishes. She had them cooling on the kitchen bench, ready to be sealed in plastic containers and frozen. Lucy was overwhelmed by her efficiency.

"Esme, you don't have to worry, I still know how to cook."

Esme was quiet and unemotional; Lucy watched her carefully and said little, other than how sorry she was over her father's death. The maid thanked her politely and went about her preparation for her departure. Lucy booked her on the afternoon flight the following day; she noticed that Esme only packed one small overnight bag. Lucy decided it would be best if Esme took her home leave early, and have a month with her family, as long as she promised to return.

Before Esme left, Holly gave her a bunch of flowers she had picked from Amber's garden and Esme gave Lucy a small note with the name, Timothy Waldon, and the church phone number written on it. She asked Lucy to call him and explain what had happened, and that she would not be able to attend church or counselling for a month. Lucy took her to the airport and watched as the small woman disappeared through customs. She sighed heavily and wearily turned to go home, facing a month of washing, ironing, cooking and cleaning. It was not until the Monday that she realised she had forgotten to call the church.

♦♦♦♦♦♦

Timothy Waldon was the happiest he had been for a long time. He and Esme had an understanding. The week after his hasty proposal, they had lunch and he nervously coaxed an answer from her. Although she didn't give an outright 'yes' she did say, once they got to know each other a little better, and she was free from her financial commitments to her family, they would consider the future.

That was good enough for Timothy. He was walking on air until the following Sunday, when Esmirada didn't come to church. All sorts of horrific scenarios went through his tired brain. Had she changed her mind, had something dreadful happened to her, or was she merely required to work that day for some reason? All Sunday night he tortured himself with doubt. He decided he had to call the Leadbitters when he returned from school on Monday afternoon.

On Monday morning Lucy found Esmirada's forgotten note and called the church. She spoke to a Sister Mary who promised to pass on the message. Later that day Mary called Timothy at school and told him what had happened. Timothy was filled with relief when she told him of Esme's father's death, then with guilt for being so selfish. He approached the headmaster and asked for a week's compassionate leave.

He decided, right or wrong, he had to be with Esme. He wasn't sure what sort of a reception he would receive, but he was willing to take the chance of rejection. Sister Mary wasn't convinced of the soundness of Timothy's plan, but she could see how genuinely in love he was. The girl needed a push, so she played matchmaker and gave Timothy the details of where in Manila he could find her.

◆◆◆◆◆◆

Esme felt the aircraft gather speed, she closed her eyes and pushed further back into the seat. The vibration went through her body as they became airborne. She looked at the drops of water splaying outward on the small window. She wedged herself against it and watched the lush greenery of Singapore fall away.

She thought of Manny's brief call. Boboy had haemorrhaged and died early in the morning, before *Lola* and Olina had risen. Her father had been a weak man, but she loved him. She thought about her early childhood in Makati and how happy and carefree they had been. She remembered Boboy sitting under a coconut palm, drinking *tuba* and sharing out Pop Rice, telling stories of his own childhood on the island of Samar and the typhoon that literally blew the family away. She remembered how he would take them to sit and watch the cockfights with the old men of the village, her father always losing on the outcome. It was always their secret, kept at all costs from Olina. No matter what had passed, Esmirada knew she only had one family, and now she must return to bury her father with dignity.

Walking out of the airport she was greeted by the familiar raw smell. Nothing had changed. She joined a snaking queue of returning maids carrying boxes and bags, bursting at the seams with cheap gifts for their families. Esme had brought nothing but the money to pay for the funeral.

150

She looked over a sea of babbling relatives and friends and saw Manny, his handsome profile haloed in a plume of cigarette smoke. He lay back lazily against his gaudy jeepney. She could see the name of his son, Carlo, below Pinkie's. She walked to meet him with her eyes downcast.

"*Mabuhay.*" Manny took both her hands in his and held her from him. "Well, look at you, little sister, all grown up!"

Manny was wearing a black armband out of respect for his father. She looked away quickly before he could see her tears. His jeepney had become more highly decorated since she left; he had added coloured plastic streamers, a metal horse to the hood, and flashing coloured lights. He still drove recklessly, swerving around a corner and narrowly missing a horse-drawn carriage. There was a political rally milling about near the church, and the traffic suddenly came to a standstill. The beggars and hawkers rose from the gutters and started to swarm like flies; she suddenly missed the clean streets of Singapore. They tried to talk above the din. She asked him about his son and Pinkie, and of her mother and *Lola,* trying hard not to utter Boboy's name.

Esmirada's face was moist with humidity as they arrived at the *sari sari.* The black and yellow banner of mourning hung in the barred window of the small shop, the banner they had hung years before after the death of the infant girl Ariel. The rusty '*4 Rosa*' sign hung in the courtyard; the San Miguel sign had fallen and lay in the dust next to a pair of worn out *tsinelas* that had been discarded beside the path.

Lola squatted on the packed earth of the courtyard. Beside her a tin bowl rested on a remnant of cement. She was preparing the evening meal, dipping her work-worn hands into a woven basket and an orange bucket full of dirty water. The courtyard was as she remembered, bamboo slatted and swept clean. *Lola's* wiry arms moved slowly about her task. A yellow mongrel dog began to whine. She squinted through rheumy eyes, and held up a hand to shield them from the late afternoon sun. Hiding her face in her gnarled hands, she wept. Esmirada went to her and lifted her frail body from the ground; she took her hands and kissed them. Olina waited at the door, swallowing hard, unable to speak. Wringing her raw hands together, she held them out to Esmirada. She came to her mother and clasped her to her breast; she could feel her thin shoulder blades through the faded cotton dress. Her hair was now completely grey and pulled back severely. Her appearance saddened Esmirada. Her once handsome face was thin and shrunken. Her teeth blackened and lymph nodes swollen, her mother had aged considerably since Esmirada had left.

The poor deceased was laid out in the front room of the cement house. Esme had sent money for a proper embalming and funeral service. Now that she was home, the wake could begin.

Rosa was there with her four adult sons; she had grown fat and slovenly, but greeted Esmirada warmly. Her sons were very like Buboy in appearance, and just as prosperous, judging by the amount of jewellery they wore. Rosa had come back to live in the two-storey cement bungalow attached to the compound with her new husband, Corky. He now collected seven hundred pesos a day for each of the rooms within the compound. Olina and *Lola* looked after the *sari sari*, and for fifty pesos a day Olina cleaned and swept her landlord's bungalows.

Esmirada asked for a moment alone with her father. She stood close to the casket, careful not to cry. She didn't want to prevent his soul from resting in peace. He was cold and waxen; his eyes bruised and tightly closed. His hair had gone grey and was thinly plastered to his skull; she reached out and touched his rigid chest. Her hand recoiled; quickly she took her rosary from the pocket of her black dress, cutting it with a knife, breaking the cycle of death. She then placed it beside him, praying quietly for his soul. Manny came and lifted the confused children one by one over the deceased, to ensure their long life.

The women of the barrio had spent the previous evening and day preparing food. Manny arrived with Pinkie and his newborn son; he sat and played his guitar mournfully in the courtyard. Ricardo produced a pack of cards, he was followed closely by a weeping Perpetua and three small girls, Gigi, Mandy, and Rose. Enrique, his son, toddled about, scattering scrawny chickens in his path. Buboy's four sons, Joey, Rodolfo, Jose and Torre, sat at the dusty tables under the ragged awning, drinking *tuba* and singing along with Manny's guitar.

Boboy's wake was well attended. The mood was anything but solemn. All the slum dwellers and tenants came to say prayers, eat, drink and play cards, remembering the good times with Boboy.

Esmirada and her family ate *pancit bichon* and chicken *adobo* by candlelight, fondly talking about him as the children ran wild in the courtyard. For Esmirada it was a reunion of sorts. With her uncle Buboy gone and forgotten, another unsolved murder in the slums, and her poor father dead, she finally found it in her heart that night to forgive them for sending her away.

◆◆◆◆◆◆

Timothy contemplated the back of the headrest in front of him. The flight was monotonous, his long legs cramped in the narrow confines of the seat. At times, the turbulence was welcome, breaking the tedious journey. He talked at length to a Filipino sitting beside him. The man was a seafarer, and over the years had been hired by many shipping companies. He was skilled and proficient in English but had lost his job to cheaper Chinese labour. The deployment of not only him but many more Filipino seamen from tankers, bulk carriers and glitzy cruise lines meant the Philippines was no longer the leading provider of crew to shipping companies.

"My whole life has gone down the drain, man! I don't know what I am going to do back in the Philippines. My wife left me and my only skills are as a sailor. I'm going back to see my family and then try for a position on one of the luxury liners."

The young Filipino fortified himself with whisky and then slept for the rest of the journey. Timothy knew an increase in the unemployed was the last thing the government needed. For a while it took his mind off finding Esmirada. Perhaps he should have warned her of his arrival but he had no way of knowing how to do that. There certainly wasn't any phone contact. Which led him to believe her circumstances were pretty poor. He decided to check into a hotel and then go about searching for her.

He wasn't prepared for the chaos at the airport! Timothy stood towering over the raving, hustling crowd. Manoeuvring himself to the customs area, he was met with indifference and a cursory glance as his passport was promptly thrown back across the scarred counter. He could feel slum children plucking at his sleeves and trouser legs, but he refused to look down. His only goal at that moment was to retrieve his bag and procure some sort of transport to the hotel he had booked.

The taxi driver was friendly and espoused all manner of advice as he journeyed through the clogged traffic to the Manila Seaview Hotel. He lectured Timothy sternly about safety, and told him to remember that the women of the Philippines must not be defiled. Timothy stared at the bleak drab streets; they passed a wooden cart where a pair of gangrenous feet, ravaged with putrid sores, protruded from the end. Each time they stopped at a traffic light, ragged bodies pressed against the windows, with hands outstretched and pleading, large brown eyes. He looked up and saw a billboard with a peeling poster of the Lord; and below the message: *Jesus Saves!* Timothy studied his hands helplessly, and prayed for the journey to end.

The Manila Seaview Hotel didn't actually have a view of the sea; however, it was within walking distance of the foul beach and tainted water of Manila Bay. There was a faltering waterfall in the marbled lobby and overzealous security. The room was clean and adequately air-conditioned. An all-night bar and restaurant were at street level and a swimming pool, should, 'Sir require one,' on the third level.

It was late afternoon when he arrived; he had already decided that he wouldn't begin his search for Esmirada until tomorrow. He walked the two blocks to the sea wall, passing the humble street dwellers gathered in their masses to beg. He walked through the filth and excrement that the poor lived in, sleeping beneath jeepneys and pieces of cardboard, their only shelter. The profound poverty was distressing. A few times he was tempted to reach into his pocket, but knew in his heart it would be a paltry drop in a sea of suffering.

Ragged women languidly flayed their washing in the murky waters of Manila Bay as he sat on the crumbling wall. It was sunset and the rusted hulls of the fishing boats reflected the last of the rays, while the children splashed about happily, oblivious to their surroundings. A young girl, no more than sixteen, walked slowly up the rubbish-strewn beach.

"Hey Joe!"

She sidled up and fingered the camera he had slung about his neck. Her worn hands roved over his shoulders and arms, catching on the fabric of his shirt, and came to rest on his thigh. Her voice was submissive as she tried to negotiate the cost of a blowjob. Timothy removed her hand from his leg.

"You want a virgin, Joe?" Her eyes became desperate as he stood to leave. In a hollow voice she said, "I'm still a virgin, Joe. No shit!"

He looked back in the fading light to see her leaning against the sea wall, still waiting for a customer, listlessly throwing stones at a stray dog too emaciated to move.

He made his way back toward the sanctuary of the hotel, stopping on the way at a restaurant where he ordered a beer and noodles. The beer was cold and the food warm and comforting. An aging woman sat opposite, wearily watching him eat. She lost interest when a drunk lurched through the doors. Quickly pulling him aside, she roved her hands over his chest, pleading and pressing her body against his, steering him to a booth in the back. Timothy paid the bill and left. As he passed another bar, a similar scene played out. An enigmatic sign hung lopsidedly in the dirty window: *'Deposit your guns*

154

at the door'. He thought of Singapore, where you deposited your umbrellas at the door, how much more civilised it was.

He slept in fits and starts, listening to the strange street sounds and the wheeze of the air-conditioner, which sometime during the night seized and stopped abruptly, along with the power. He showered, avoiding the edges of the shower stall that were black with mould. His trousers felt velvety and damp with humidity. As he shook them, mosquitos flew from the folds.

He had a full American breakfast in the hotel coffee shop and then caught a taxi to the outskirts of Tondo. The streets were even shabbier in the bright sunlight; the only splash of colour was the huge garish billboards advertising up and coming attractions. For whom? he wondered.

The taxi took him past what looked like a walled city, but on closer inspection was a cemetery with palatial and monumental tombs stacked closely together. Looking to the corrugated tin hovels in the shantytown beyond its walls, Timothy realised the dead had better accommodation than the living. Consulting his map, he discovered it was the Chinese Cemetery and that the small store that Esme's mother ran was not far away.

The driver let him out on a dusty street, where boys in tattered T-shirts and worn rubber thongs played a game of basketball. Timothy sheltered from the sun under a rotten fabric awning, and asked one of the boys where the *'4 Rosa sari sari'* was. The child, no more than eight, smiled at him, showing the decayed stumps of his teeth. He took Timothy's hand and led the way. As they walked, other groups broke away and joined them. By the time they reached the compound, he was surrounded by a band of small, chattering children. They found the store closed for the day.

One child, a wizened girl, spoke, "It's closed for the family burial!"

Timothy paid the children for their kindness with candy that he had brought, and followed the stunted girl through a series of maze-like alleys and putrid ditches until they came upon a wide street. There he saw the funeral procession rounding the corner. An ancient flat-top truck held the simple coffin, whilst a decorated jeepney followed. On foot, a large crowd had gathered, playing guitars and singing mournful songs. Timothy joined the thronging crowd taking up the rear. They came to a simple stone cemetery on the outskirts of the city. There prayers were said under a relentless sun in an incredibly clear sky. More guitar playing and a final prayer and then the crowd dispersed, leaving the grieving family to make their way home.

Timothy waited by the jeepney, his heart pounding, until Esmirada appeared. She was holding two frail women close to her side, as they picked their way through the rubble. Esme was wearing a simple black dress and looked serenely beautiful in the bright sunshine. The men all wore black armbands and even the children had a piece of black cloth pinned to their chests. When Esme looked up and saw Timothy, she stumbled. He rushed to help her. The two old women stood stupefied, looking at him accusingly. Esme at first was shocked but then she held out her hand to him and smiled.

Back at the *sari sari*, the women had prepared more food for the mourners. Esme introduced Timothy and took her grandmother and mother aside to explain who he was and why he was there. He became the object of much curiosity. Manny, Ricardo and her cousins questioned him closely. He was humbled by how simply her family lived. He had brought gifts for her mother and grandmother but was disappointed that they put them to one side without opening them. The children, however, enjoyed the candies he showered upon them.

He wasn't able to speak to Esme alone until just on dusk, when the last of the funeral guests left to go back to the village. Her mother and grandmother were exhausted, but would not leave her without a chaperone. They sat a short distance away on a straw pallet, while he and Esme sat under the palm fronds in the courtyard of the *sari sari*.

"I hope I haven't compromised you by coming here. I just wanted to be with you at this time, and I wanted to ask your mother if I could marry you. I wish I could have asked your father. I'm sorry it was too late."

Esme put her hand on his. "I'm glad you're here, Timothy. You now know where I come from. It worried me that you expected more. My brothers like you. They can see you are a decent man. You must go now back to the hotel, you can come again tomorrow."

Manny was waiting to drive him back in his jeepney. On the way he questioned him closely about his intentions toward his sister. He seemed satisfied with Timothy's answers; he dropped him at the hotel, swerving casually into the curb.

"See you, Joe!" he called, as he did a tight U-turn back into the manic flow of traffic.

As Timothy settled for the night, a thousand images flooded his brain, the immense wealth of the city existing side by side with profound poverty. He felt guilty having escaped the tormented souls that were now roaming the city, begging, stealing or selling their bodies for the cost of a drink or glue to sniff. The smiling faces of the children, the elderly with their fixed but friendly gaze, and the beauty and mystery surrounding the funeral custom. The mastery of languages amazed him. Esmirada spoke Spanish, English and Tagalog, a legacy, he knew, from colonial rule. Once again, her courage and beauty humbled him, how lucky he was to have found her, this woman who must have seen so many hardships and horror in her short lifetime.

The following week Timothy saw Esmirada every day, always in the company of her brother, mother and grandmother. He took the whole family to *Jollibee* for a lunch of fried chicken that cost him very little. They walked in the city and parks, always mobbed by curious locals wanting to see what the American would say or do. Esmirada held an umbrella above his head, sheltering him from the furious sun. He protested at first, but then saw it was her way of looking after him.

On the final day, they sat in the courtyard with her elderly grandmother. She hadn't said much to him during the week, but today she was talkative. She asked him what his church believed.

"We believe in one god, three people: God the Father, Son and Holy Spirit. We pray to the deity of Jesus, we believe in his virgin birth, his sinless humanity, his bodily resurrection and his ascension to heaven. We believe we are the one true church; we welcome all believers, regardless of race, colour or standing."

She seemed satisfied with his answer and took his hand in her gnarled one. "You're a good man; you will make our Esmirada happy. You must say *Gusto kong makapiling ka habang buhay. Pakasalan mo ako, Mahal"*

Esmirada smiled and held out her hand to *Lola*. "She's telling you how to make a proposal in the Philippines."

Lola then told Timothy a myth. "When *Kabunyan* or God was making man, the first one was so raw, he threw it away. This was white man. The second was overdone and burnt. This was black man, but the third come out just right: golden brown, the Filipino! You are lucky; your children will be very beautiful like our Esmirada. You go now, Timothy Waldon, and come back soon to marry our girl."

Timothy knew this was the blessing he had been waiting for. Esmirada walked him to the street. She rose up and kissed him lightly on the cheek.

"Goodbye, Timothy. Safe journey, I'll see you on Sunday in three weeks."

157

Chapter Nineteen
Incriminating Evidence

With Hallam and Esmirada away, Lucinda neglected the housework so she could complete her commissions. Word had spread and her portraits of children and animals were in demand. The local *Sunday Times* interviewed her. She looked confident and pretty in the photograph taken on her veranda studio with her framed works in the background. Hallam, when he returned from the States, gave it a cursory glance before throwing it down to go and have a game of squash with Brian. She kept the article to send to Alex.

The Expat club had commissioned her to do a watercolour of their exterior, which she had just completed. Amber organised a cocktail party in the foyer for the unveiling, and once again, Lucinda appeared in the national paper. Hallam was not present, begging off at the last minute because of a meeting. Lucinda knew jealousy was a large part of the reason he failed to acknowledge her sudden success. All the intimacy and passion they had experienced at Christmas had evaporated when they returned to Singapore. Hallam's work demanded all his time. He was either travelling, at the office or entertaining clients. While she was immersed in her painting, she was secretly relieved he didn't seek her company, but when Esme finally returned at Chinese New Year, Lucy stood back and realised her marriage was miserable.

At lunch at the Marco Polo one Tuesday, she confided in Amber. "Since Christmas he hasn't come near me, we don't seem to have anything in common anymore, other than the children. He's either away or working; he's not in the least bit interested in my painting. He has neglected the kids; Cameron was so hurt when he missed his soccer final and Cub Scout camp. It was such a shame, all the other fathers were there with their sons, and I was the only mother! Cam was so embarrassed. I know Holly was upset when he missed her ballet recital but she's more resilient than Cam, she gets over things quickly." Lucy toyed with her food and ordered another spritzer from the waiter.

Amber reached out a hand and gave her a squeeze. "These guys work their guts out here, Lucy. Try not to be too hard on him. Brian's the same, although I must admit he wouldn't dare miss the kids' activities. He does try to organise his travel around everything that they're involved in."

Lucy sipped her drink.

Amber looked at her from the corner of her eye. "Are you still writing to Alex?"

She bit at her bottom lip. "Every now and then, but I sense he has tired of the communication. I think I scared him off when I called him when Angel died. I was so needy. Poor guy didn't know what to say, and I guess it brought back the pain of his wife's death."

Amber pushed back her salad nicoise. "I hope you've hidden those letters from Hal. What would he do if he found them?"

"They are not incriminating, Amber, but just the same I keep them in my safety deposit box out of harm's way." Lucy wanted to change the subject. She had given too much away about her marriage and Alex to Amber.

"I have an idea for Hal's birthday next month. I want to take him on a surprise trip to Bangkok on the E and O train. He always loved trains as a boy and he mentioned he would like to do it sometime. Maybe just what we need! To get away for a while without the children. Would you and Brian like to come? It's only for four days."

"Sounds great, but wouldn't you prefer just the two of you? It would give you time to work a few things out."

"I'd love you to come; Hal's more relaxed with you guys around. It keeps him off the phone to the office. I'll give you the dates, run it by Brian and see what he thinks."

"Having sex on a train would be so erotic! Lucy you are a clever girl!"

They finished and signalled for the cheque. Lucy grabbed it. "This lunch is on me. You paid for the last one, and besides, I've been a dreary companion, unloading all my woes on you, you poor thing."

Amber laughed, throwing her luxuriant hair back. "That's what friends are for, honey, I keep telling you that!"

They left to pick up the boys from school and take them to soccer practice.

As they walked out Amber asked, "How's Esme since she's been back?"

"She seems fine, she wears a small piece of black fabric each day, and doesn't hum when she goes about her work like she used to, but she seems to have accepted what's happened. I guess the poor girl doesn't have much choice. I know her family depend on her entirely. She paid for all the funeral costs, you know. I offered to help, but she refused."

"You're lucky to have her, Lucy, she's a great kid. I think it's time for Honeyko to have a little holiday. She has suddenly gone off the boil. It happens. Can't say I blame her, housework is bloody monotonous!" She rolled her eyes dramatically as she gave the car jockey five dollars to retrieve her car.

♦♦♦♦♦♦

Timothy spent three miserable weeks waiting for Esmirada to come home. He kept praying to God to bring her back to him. He made her promise on the last night in the courtyard that she would return. He had many doubts. Despite her father's death and the appalling conditions in which they lived, Esmirada seemed happy and at peace amongst her people. After touring the slums, he realised the Espinosa's were a lot better off than most, only because of Esmirada's sacrifice, and the money she earned in Singapore as a domestic servant. When he married her, he promised she would no longer be a maid. He intended to take over the care of her entire family if need be, but he was determined that the only person she would continue to serve would be God.

When he was in the Philippines, he found a book on wedding etiquette and superstitions, and spent the weeks, while waiting, educating himself. What he read was both illuminating as well as confusing. Every facet of Filipino life is related to superstition and folk beliefs. He looked forward to discussing them with her the following Sunday, but right then he had a sermon to write.

♦♦♦♦♦♦

It wasn't difficult for Esmirada to leave home once more; she had done what she came to do; give her father a decent burial. She had no wish to stay in the barrio amongst the thieves and glue sniffers. She worried that the next time she saw *Lola* would be in a coffin, but *Lola* was strong, and now more determined than ever to see her wed to Timothy. Her mother was less enthusiastic but then her mother had lost her enthusiasm for living a long time ago.

She was contented to be back in the mansion on the edge of the jungle, although she sensed troubled times ahead, Sir was just like the men in the Philippines, never satisfied with what they had.

As *Lola* would say, "No matter how full the rooster, it will still peck grain!"

Timothy sat watching the doors. It was getting late and most of the congregation had taken their seats. The back row where Esmirada usually sat, half-hidden, was already filled. He felt a hand at the small of his back and he turned to look into her lovely upturned face. He laughed and took a gulp of air, settling himself enough to speak.

"You're back! Praise be to God for bringing you home safely. It's wonderful to have you amongst us again, Esmirada." He resisted the urge to crush her to him, led her to a seat in the front row, and began the morning's worship.

Timothy spoke of 'The meaning of life'. With soft eyes, Esmirada watched his every movement, the inclination of his well-shaped head, his expressive hands, and the way his eyes flashed with energy when he spoke of God.

"The Bible says, *'Life is a trust, a loan from God for a short period of time.' Job 1:21 'All life comes from God (1 John 5:20)'* Life is a gift, there is no bargaining with it. So easily, it is here today and gone tomorrow."

In conclusion, Timothy said, "Dear God, we give to you our lives so you may save us from our sins, let your mercy, Oh Lord, be upon us."

The congregation stood and joined hands. Their voices becoming one, they sang out clear and true, *Psalm 89:47. Remember how short my time is.* Esmirada's voice rose with the other worshippers, and reverberated out into the lush green space where the children sat in the shade, listening to their Sunday school teacher telling them how much Jesus loved them.

Mary, Joyner and Harold were sitting at a table under a mango tree in a quiet corner of the hawker centre. As they walked in, a bow-legged hawker with missing bottom teeth waved a stained menu in Timothy's face.

"*Eh Ang moh*, this one *tok kong one!*" The hawker, his grubby vest pulled up to cool his protruding belly, grinned at Esmirada. He stood in her way until Timothy stepped in, moving him along.

When they arrived at the table, the group stood and Harold produced a bottle of sparkling wine from a tin bucket of ice. Mary brought out five blue plastic glasses. Timothy took the dark green bottle, frosty from its bed of ice and ceremonially popped the cork. Esmirada laughed and covered her mouth with her hand. Harold poured and made a toast to the happy couple. Timothy watched as she surreptitiously took her first sip of alcohol. The bubbles went up her nose and fizzed on her tongue, leaving a fruity taste. She couldn't stop smiling! Timothy ordered dishes she had never tried: chilli crab, seafood *char kway teow* and her favourite chicken rice. It was a feast finished off with sweet, creamy mango pudding. She couldn't drink all her wine, so Mary finished it for her.

"When is the big day, is it to be a long engagement?" asked Harold.

Timothy looked quizzically at Esme.

"We haven't set a date. I'd marry her tomorrow, but Esme has to decide."

She looked at him gratefully. "This is something Timothy and I must discuss first. There is a lot to take into consideration."

Her answer disappointed him. When they were in the Philippines, Esme's grandmother had told him they couldn't possibly marry this year; 'bad luck' was all she said. Esme later explained the superstition surrounding siblings marrying in the same year. She said she didn't believe in *pamahiin*, but Manny had to marry Pinkie as soon as possible, now there was a baby. Pinkie's relatives had threatened to kill him otherwise.

They stayed longer than usual. The lunch crowd began to thin and an old woman in yellow rubber boots started to hose around the table, splashing their ankles with dirty water. Esme watched the mynahs hop about, looking for scraps; she looked at Timothy's strong profile and followed his hands with her eyes as he made a point. It hadn't been love at first sight, as in the romance novels; more admiration to begin with, but now, when she looked at him, she felt desire weakening her bones, quickening her heart and causing the blood to rise in her face, and remain there until after they had parted.

Joyner and Harold left to shop at the markets and Mary went to catch her bus. Timothy picked up the glasses and placed them in a plastic bag. He picked up the cork, took out his pen, and wrote upon it. 'Esmirada and Timothy's engagement lunch,' followed by the date.

"This is just the first of many celebrations to come. This isn't quite the romantic setting I had in mind, but at least it's memorable."

He took from his pocket a small red-velvet box; he could hear her sharp intake of breath as he placed it in the palm of her hand. Esme's hands shook as she flipped the lid; a heart shaped diamond with a simple gold band, blinding in its brilliance, nestled on a satin bed. She had never seen anything quite so beautiful or so perfect. Timothy took her small hand and placed the ring on her finger, and she started to cry. Her hands shook and her nose ran. He took his handkerchief from his pocket and wiped it for her, giving it to her to keep.

It was all too much for Esmirada. She didn't deserve this man. She looked at the ring on her finger, and the world about her suddenly turned shabby in comparison to its beauty. She sniffed and looked at Timothy. His eyes were glistening. She traced the outline of his open face, and reached up and kissed him gently on the mouth. She didn't care who saw. No one else existed.

She carefully took the ring from her finger and tenderly placed it in the velvet box, snapping it shut. "Will you take care of it for me until we are free to marry?"

The old aunty in the rubber boots came back with her hose, carelessly spraying them once again, and Esmirada bubbled with laughter. Reluctantly, they left to walk the short distance to the bus stop; he watched and waited, as he always did, until she was out of sight.

◆ ◆ ◆ ◆ ◆ ◆

Lucy was out on location the following Friday, sketching and taking photographs of a row of shop houses for her new calendar. When she returned home, Esme came to her with a red shirt.

"This shirt looks new, ma'am. I think it should be sent to the drycleaners. The label says dry-clean only."

Lucy looked at the shirt without recognition. It was expensive, Ralph Lauren. Hallam must have bought it when he was last in Bangkok. She knew for sure it was the real thing - one hundred percent silk - certainly no copy.

"Thanks, Esme, I'll drop it off with some of my things on Monday.

On Monday Lucy went to see her doctor about the persistent rash on her hands. It had become worse since Christmas and was now keeping her awake at night. Small, bespectacled Doctor Lim put it down to an allergy caused from her paints. He gave her some cream and cotton gloves to wear while she worked.

On the way home she stopped in at the Eastern Orient Express office to book the surprise trip to Thailand. The young Chinese girl behind the counter took her details and they worked out a suitable date.

When she consulted her computer to confirm the booking, she looked up from the small screen and beamed. "Oh, so you are a repeat guest, Mrs Leadbitter. I see you and Mr. Leadbitter did the same trip same time last year!" She swivelled the screen toward Lucy so she could read the details. "Is your address still Bukit Lalang?"

Lucy stared at the screen and the small black print that jumped out at her, thinking that surely there must be some mistake. Hallam's full name accompanied by Mrs Leadbitter, followed by details of their address. In brackets a special request for a chocolate anniversary cake. She looked at the date, last Chinese New Year when Hallam was supposedly in India.

The girl kept smiling, watching Lucinda, waiting for her to speak, but the words stuck in Lucinda's throat. Her hands began to itch. Absentmindedly she tore at them, causing them to bleed. The girl's smile faded as she continued to wait patiently. Finally Lucinda stammered something about checking dates before she proceeded. She made her way to the automatic doors, lurching out into the unbearable heat of the day.

Lucinda brooded for two days. Looking back through her diary, she checked dates, when and where Hallam was supposed to have been. She found many discrepancies. She was wretched and her hands were raw by the time she called Amber to ask her to lunch. Amber sat and stoically listened as she told her of her fears.

"I've known all along there was someone else. If he's not having sex with me, he must be having it with someone!" She was on the verge of tears, she had not eaten in the last few days and she sat now, ignoring her food and concentrating on her wine.

"Have you spoken to him? There may be an explanation of some sort."

Lucy sniffed. "I called him Monday, but as usual he was not in his room and didn't return my call. For all I know, he is not even in Jakarta. He could be anywhere. We don't talk, he never tells me anything; he has never stayed in contact while he was travelling. I always thought if something happened to one of the kids I would never know where to find him!" Lucinda raked at her hands and Amber placed her hand on top of hers, to stop her tormenting the raw flesh. "What am I going to do, Amber?" Lucinda held her head in her hands.

"You have to confront him and talk. It may not be too late. Maybe he has gone off the rails; all men do at some stage. But you really must talk before you do anything."

On the way home Lucinda picked up the dry-cleaning. The red shirt mocked her. Who had given him that? she wondered.

That evening once the children had gone to bed, she feverishly rifled through the belongings in his wardrobe and drawers, looking for evidence of his infidelity. She stood looking at the growing pile of gifts, Visa receipts for flowers, underwear, jewellery, and resorts that she had never heard of, let alone visited. She shoved it all into a box with the red shirt and went to the garden with the gin bottle.

Hallam was due home on Saturday.

On Friday, she cancelled her trolley round at the hospital and went to his office. She knew when Hallam was away they closed for lunch, spending an hour and a half at the food centre across the road. He often complained how everything stopped for lunch, no matter how much work there was. She greeted the security guard breezily as though she had every right to be there. He was picking at his teeth with a matchstick, reading the daily paper, and barely acknowledged her. She nervously rummaged in her bag for the keys she had found in Hallam's drawer. She knew they were the right set because she had delivered them to the courier when Hallam last went to the office on the weekend, forgetting to take them with him.

The key was stiff and Lucy had to twist and turn it before it eventually unlocked the door. The office was silent except for the sound of a drill coming from another floor. She looked in Linda's room. It was empty, her computer screen blank. She could smell tiger balm; Linda was always rubbing it on her temples to stop *heatiness*.

She rummaged through drawers, read faxes, letters and collected receipts. She came to a locked drawer in the bottom of his desk. Trying one key after another, watching the clock, she failed to open it. She was running out of time. Gathering up the evidence she had collected, she placed it in an envelope and left the office. Scurrying out onto the street, she saw Linda and Hallam's band of sycophants coming back from their long lunch.

All Saturday she was wretched. She took the children to ballet and soccer, gave them lunch at McDonalds and spent the afternoon at Amber's. The children played in the pool, oblivious to everything except the frenzied game they had invented. Lucy breathlessly told Amber what she had done and of the evidence she had gathered. The garden was peaceful and fragrant. Birds hopped about and squirrels ran up the coconut trees. The sound of the children's laughter was at odds with how she felt, her stomach lurching with nervous apprehension. Amber listened as a good friend would, but Lucy could see the pity on her face. She squared her shoulders and sat higher in the garden chair. She didn't want Amber's pity, she wouldn't allow herself to end up like Angel. Honeyko came, bearing drinks and a plate of canapés.

"Let the children stay with me tonight, it will give you a chance to hear Hal's side of the story without any interruption, send them over once he arrives."

They sipped their drinks in the fading light and then Lucy gathered her son and daughter, towelling them vigorously, as Amber watched.

She kissed the tops of their heads and Cameron said, "You seem sad today, Mummy."

Tears sprang to Lucy's eyes and she hugged the boy to her, hiding her face.

"Come on, you lot, go and get changed and say hello to your dad. Bring your P.J's and I'll order a pizza and a video."

"Hey, Cameron, bring your game gear over with you!" Tom called as they walked across the lawn to the hidden gate in the fence.

Holly called back to Andrea, "I'll bring my Barbie and Pictionary, okay?"

The night was balmy with the smell of frangipani and jasmine hanging heavy in the air. Esme cooked a banana cake, leaving the house with a delicious, fruity smell. The children went to take their showers while Lucy sat and waited for Hallam to arrive. She had another stiff drink and asked Esme to make seafood lasagne and salad for dinner. She nursed her drink on the patio, listening to the night sounds, and watched the geckos dart around the lights after mosquitoes, their little hearts beating as rapidly as hers. She scratched the rash on her hands nervously.

She heard the car at the same time as the children did, and they ran to Hallam before he had time to alight. He scooped them up and kissed their shining faces, he dropped his bags at the bottom of the stairs and distributed their expected haul of gifts.

Lucy stood watching, a coldness growing near her heart. "Off you go and let your Dad get changed, Andrea and Tom will be waiting for you."

Lucy fought to keep her voice calm. She avoided looking Hallam in the eye; he kissed her briefly and went to shower. She was waiting for him when he came down.

"How have you been, Luce, any more interviews with the papers?"

"No, but I have more commissions and my calendar for the Christmas fair is almost finished." She couldn't believe they could sit and have dinner in a civilised manner, with all the lies between them. It crossed her mind that they could probably go on like this forever, if she didn't say anything. Another drink convinced her that if she kept her mouth shut no one would get hurt; she could go on with her painting and her life as it was. Perhaps she would just let him get away with it. Many other women did. Why should she make waves and spoil her idyllic life?

Lucy forced down a few mouthfuls and then sat back taking gulps of gin as though it were fresh air. Silently she watched Hallam eat. She took a long swig and noted how he thoughtfully chewed each mouthful, his doughy, slabbed cheeks moving rhythmically. He looked at her with bovine concern when she reached for her glass again. She was seething inside. He wasn't even good looking. He was pale and fat, his lovemaking perfunctory and he snored like a pig. Suddenly she wondered what she had ever seen in him!

He finished his meal and went to the garden to have a cigar. Esme quietly cleared the table and asked Lucy if they would like some fruit. She had bought fresh mango from the grocer.

Lucy shook her head. "Maybe later."

Hallam poured another drink. Lucy could see he was on his guard; he avoided her and went to make a phone call in his office upstairs. She was waiting for him when he came out. She clutched the incriminating box of evidence to her chest with shaking hands.

"Oh shit, Lucy, what's all this! I knew the moment I got home something was going on. I don't get a moment's peace with you." He went into the bedroom and slammed the door.

Lucy, having had too much to drink, was past being rational. She threw open the door and dropped the box at his feet. The red shirt was the first thing he recognised and his face went white. He scooped up the contents before him and shook his head slowly.

"Can you explain any of this, Hallam? I want to know what's going on. Who gave you this shirt?" She picked up the shirt and threw it, hitting him in the face!

"Who have you been taking to resorts and on trains? Who is it that you're fucking? Because it's certainly not me, Hallam!" Lucinda's voice had risen an octave and she was fighting for breath.

He slowly sat on the edge of the bed and scrubbed at his face with his hands. Sadly he looked up at her. "I was going to tell you soon anyway, and I'm surprised it took you so long to work it out. I'm leaving, Lucy, I think you knew all along. I'm in love with Elvira."

A sob ripped through Lucy and she sprang at Hallam, slapping and clawing his face, spitting venomous accusations. He held her from him and waited calmly until her sobs subsided. She collapsed to the floor and lay motionless, feeling her tears pool beneath her. He went to the bathroom and returned, wiping her face with a wet cloth, and lifted her onto the bed. She was too drained to speak; she listened to the rise and fall of his voice, trying to take in his confession.

"We started an affair not long after I took over the position at the bank, but for the sake of you and the children I ended it the following Christmas and she left the office. It was hopeless. Neither of us wanted it to end. We couldn't stay apart, so after three months I started seeing her again. I didn't want to hurt you. I tried to be discreet and carry on with my life with you and the children, but I'm just so unhappy living like this. I want a divorce so I can be with her, Lucy. Elvira wants me to marry her."

His words fell about her, shattering on the floor where she lay with the blood rushing in her ears and nausea rising in her stomach. She lurched to her feet and stumbled, falling, towards the bathroom. "Fuck Elvira and fuck you to hell!" She choked, as she sprayed vomit all over the white tiles.

He left the room in disgust and went to the guest room; she could hear him late into the night on the phone, making his plans with Elvira. Finally, exhausted, she slept, waking to find him gone. Disorientated, she walked from room to room in nothing more than her nightdress; she picked up discarded clothes and tearfully pulled up the cover on the guest bed. Hallam's familiar scent filled her nostrils, causing her stomach to contract violently. She dry retched into the toilet continuously, getting unsteadily to her feet to answer the bleating phone in the bedroom. She could hear the children playing in the pool next door as she fumbled for the receiver.

"Hi, honey, have I called at a bad time? I hope you two have sorted everything out? We thought maybe you and Hallam would like to come over for a barbecue lunch."

Lucy cleared her seared throat and croaked, "Thanks, Amber, but Hallam had to leave on an urgent trip this morning. Some trouble in

Europe. He'll be away for a while. Just send the kids home when you're ready. We'll take a raincheck on the barbecue if that's okay."

"Hey, no problem. Poor Hallam, he only just got home. Listen, are you sure you're okay? Why don't I keep the kids here for lunch? My two will be unbearable if I tell them they can't stay. It will give you a chance to do some painting."

"Thanks, Amber, I'd really appreciate that. Send them home if they make nuisances of themselves."

The empty day opened up in front of her and she sank to her knees in self-pity and loathing. She got back into bed, shivering, and contracted her body into a foetal position and slept.

She woke to find the afternoon sun slanting across the wooden floor and her two small children pounding on her bedroom door. She ran the water and called to them.

"Mum's just having a shower. I'll be out in a minute. Why don't you decide what you would like for dinner? You can cook for me tonight, give me a surprise!"

She could hear them belt down the stairs two at a time, arguing what they should have. She studied her ravaged face in the bathroom mirror and brought her crudely disfigured hands to her swollen lids. She looked hideous. No wonder he had left her for Elvira! She tried not to start crying all over again.

The children accepted their father had left on another trip.

"Are you kidding? He's never here anyway!" said Holly. They were more concerned about her and how she looked.

"I think I have the flu. I haven't been well all day. If I have a good rest I should be okay tomorrow."

"You should have called us, Mum. We could have looked after you," Cameron said with a voice verging on tears.

He worried her. He was overly sensitive; how would he accept Hallam's betrayal? She pushed his hair back from his damp brow and kissed him.

They sat on the patio with a gentle breeze wafting about them as they ate macaroni cheese. Despite a violent headache, she managed to get through the meal, a video, and game of scrabble. Esme had returned earlier and cleared up the debris from dinner. She looked at Lucinda with concern, prescribing warm water and lemon juice. When they finally went to bed, she took a bottle of gin into the garden, and drank until she didn't care anymore.

Each morning at six, Esme unlocked the doors of the house and threw open the shutters, letting the warm, moist air invade the rooms. The fans purred, laboriously cutting through the humidity. She swept up the small black droppings left by the nocturnal wanderings of the cicaks, and unlocked the gates for the gardeners and yellow school bus.

She set the table on the patio for breakfast and went to wake the children; she didn't wake her ma'am. For the last four days, she had not risen from her bed until Esme and the children had retired for the night. She'd told Cameron and Holly their mother was unwell with influenza, but Esme had picked up the gin bottles each morning and deposited them in the garbage before they got up. There had been calls from ma'am Amber but Esme had kept her away; she knew her ma'am was not able to see anyone at the moment. Fortunately Amber was leaving for a three-week stint in Amsterdam.

Esme knew of Sir's infidelity. It had been coming for a long time. Esme had seen and heard things that her ma'am had not.

On Monday morning she found her madam's wedding china smashed and scattered in shards about the dining room, and the shredded red shirt and contents of the box of incriminating evidence strewn about the floor of her bedroom. She packed it away, placing it on the top shelf of the storeroom for when ma'am may need it again. Sir had called yesterday to speak to his wife, but she told him she was unwell; he vaguely left a local address where he could be contacted in case of emergency only.

The family of Indian gardeners sauntered through the gate, and started to rhythmically sweep the drive. She filled the plastic water bottles and rinsed the mugs she kept especially for their use, and placed them in the shade beneath the Tembusu tree. She collected the fallen rambutan before the gardeners could steal them, and put them in a tin plate on the patio to ripen. The children came down to breakfast. They were fractious and demanding, she knew they sensed something was wrong and were worried about their mother. She jollied them along and let them have a special treat kept normally for the weekend: a large plate of Coco Pops each. They brightened up enough to get ready for school, just in time for the bus as it pulled into the drive, full of shouting children.

Once they had left, she set about her daily chores. She had run out of gas and called for a replacement cylinder. She set a tray for her ma'am with tea, fresh fruit and raisin toast. When she entered the dimly lit room, the smell of alcohol overwhelmed her. Her ma'am lay face down, buried beneath the bedclothes. Esmirada tried in vain to wake her, but Lucy swatted her away irritably. Esme couldn't allow this to go on much longer. It was just like Rosa after the baby had died.

Lucinda woke to the insistent blaring of the scrap-paper man's horn. Where in the blazes was Esmirada? When she sat up, her head swam. She tried to focus but the objects in her view fluttered from her. Her brain sloshed heavily inside her skull, and the beams of dusty light from the shuttered windows hurt her eyes. She made her way unsteadily to the bathroom and vomited loudly into the toilet. She lay there, spent and empty, on the cool, tiled floor, where Esme found her hours later, jaundiced, sour smelling and bloated. Esme pulled the foul nightgown from her and put her bodily under the shower. She turned on the warm water full pelt and Lucy slumped to a sitting position, letting it pulse over her aching body.

Throwing open the shutters, Esme pulled the stained sheets from the bed, working quickly before the children returned from school. She didn't want them to see their mother in this state. She made the bed with fresh sheets, mopped the floors and sprayed the room. Fetching a clean cotton nightgown from the bureau, she entered the bathroom to find her madam dry, wrapped in a towel, sitting on the edge of the bath, weeping.

Esme tidied the room around her and said, "Ma'am, would you like me to call one of your friends? They have been very worried about you! You had the flu this time last year, remember?"

Lucy looked into the girl's sincere face. "Thank you, Esme, I think you and I can manage without anyone else for a while."

Esme helped her back to bed and fetched a fresh pot of lemon tea; she brought her aspirin and a cold compress for her head. She fussed about, plumping pillows. Lucy watched her movements, darting about the room, putting things in their rightful places, smoothing, dusting and clearing as she went. Finally she left her alone with Mozart gently playing in harmony with the ceiling fans. Lucy lay back, feeling the pulse in her temples subside. She listened to the late afternoon sounds, the laughing thrushes and sunbirds in the garden, the occasional car passing by the gate and distant dog barking. She suddenly felt safe with Esme looking after her.

The last thing she could remember was taking the scissors to Hallam's red shirt. She had read somewhere how a scorned woman in England had slashed all her husband's suits and demolished his prize sports car. She had thought about doing that but Hallam didn't have a sports car, and had taken all his suits with him. She did remember tearing open the door of her Chinese wedding cabinet and flipping the dinner set Hallam had given her as an engagement gift from the shelves. Her face burned with humiliation now, but it felt satisfyingly good at the time. She was drunk, of course, and had been ever since. She realised she didn't even know what day it was, and didn't care. Her wedding ring was missing; all that was left of its existence was a thin pale line on her tanned finger. She vaguely remembered flushing it down the toilet after a revolting vomiting episode.

Esme returned with chicken soup and crackers. She placed it on the bedside table and removed the towel Lucinda had wound around her hair. She gently teased the knotted mass with a comb and pulled it back into a braid.

Lucinda felt like a small child in the care of a loving mother. "How are the children? What did you tell them?"

Esme faced Lucinda, then looked at her bare feet. "I told them you had the influenza and that they couldn't see you until you were no longer contagious. They miss you and are very worried about their mother."

"I'm so grateful to you, Esme, and I'm sorry for all the trouble and worry I've caused."

Lucy's face burned when she learnt it was Thursday; she had been in a drunken coma for days. Without further discussion, Esme went downstairs to greet the school bus and bring the children to see their ailing mother. Two damp, sweaty faces pressed into hers, as they told her all that had been happening since she was ill. She learnt that Esme had taken them by taxi to their daily after-school activities, waiting in the car park of the club because maids were not allowed in, whilst they did their swimming lessons and karate. She had cooked all their favourite food, read to them each evening and told them stories from her own childhood.

They left her to rest while they did their homework. The magnitude of what had happened hit Lucy like a low blow to the stomach. Esme had been a better mother to them than she had. Esme had managed to run the house and keep everything going, while all she could do was grovel in self-pity and alcohol. She was ashamed and hated Hallam even more for the pain he had caused her and her children.

Esme arrived with a small dinner to tempt her; she placed the tray beside her and casually said, "Sir called two days ago with a contact address." She handed Lucy a scrap of paper.

"I haven't ordered any more gin from the grocer. I thought perhaps, having the flu, you may not want it."

Lucy held her head in her hands. "What would I do without you?"

Esme smiled at her and placed the tray in her lap. "You must eat, ma'am, you'll need your strength." She busied herself closing the shutters for the night, turning off the fans and putting on the air-conditioner.

"I'll send the children in to say goodnight. Do you feel well enough to read them their story?"

Lucy looked at her standing at the door, so small and so lovely. "Yes, I think I am well enough."

"My grandmother always told proverbs to me as a child. Sometimes I only half listened but she always spoke the truth. *Habang ang tao ay nasusugatan, ito ay tumatapang*. Hardship makes people stronger!"

Chapter Twenty
Life Goes On

With the support of Esmirada and the children, Lucinda managed to put some order back into her life. She completed the commissions that were outstanding, and had her calendar printed for later in the year. She started on a series of tropical flowers to have made into gift cards. Each afternoon after she had finished the ironing, Esmirada sat for her. It was Lucy's first attempt at a portrait in oil. Esme was a serene and lovely subject, but the painting, in Lucy's opinion, was one of the best she had ever done. She had started it as a kind of therapy, and then saw a new direction opening.

Amber returned from Amsterdam and pestered her to have lunch. When she felt strong enough, Lucy relented. They were alone having sushi at the Pacific Palms sitting on tatami matting in a small booth; the dainty kimono clad hostess slid the rice paper door aside and crept in. She bowed gracefully before them and placed a large platter of sashimi and a platter of hand rolled sushi in the centre of the lacquered table. Amber poured saki for Lucy and she in turn, as was the custom, poured some for Amber. Lucy tried not to laugh when Amber dropped a slippery piece of tuna.

Amber managed to manoeuvre it to her mouth, swallowed and said, "So when are you going to tell me what happened between you and Hallam?" She held up a perfectly manicured hand. "And before you tell me he's still away, you should know I saw him at Holland Village on Sunday."

Lucy took a sip of her warm saki and then pushed it away. Looking directly at Amber, she took a deep breath. "He left me a month ago, on the Sunday after he came home from Jakarta. I couldn't tell you at the time, I needed to get some control over my emotions. I was a complete mess for about a week, but with Esmirada's and the children's help, I managed to pull myself together."

Amber dropped her chopsticks, reached over, and took Lucy's hand. "Oh my God, Lucy, I knew all along something was wrong, why didn't you come to me, I thought I was your best friend, why didn't you tell me? Surely you knew I would be there for you!"

"You are a very dear friend, and I knew I could confide in you, but I needed to deal with it myself. I had to come to terms with the fact my husband had left me for another woman. A woman who is ten years younger, and his ex-secretary! The most humiliating fact was that the affair started a month after I arrived in Singapore and continued all this time right under my ridiculous nose!" Lucy took a deep breath and gulped her water.

"Oh, so that's who she is! One of the girls at mah-jong saw him having dinner with her at Da Godolfo's, the bastard, he's not exactly discreet!"

Lucy sighed. "He doesn't have to be. We have a judicial separation, and as of yesterday he has petitioned me for a divorce, siting irretrievable breakdown of marriage. Oh, Amber, I have been such a fool! He was sleeping with both of us during that time! I still can't bring myself to tell the kids. I'm worried about Cam."

"What about you, Lucy?"

Lucy raked back her hair and tucked it behind an ear. "When it first happened I was in a gin-induced coma for four days. Esmirada shielded the children from me and took over the complete running of the house. The following week I cried a lot when they were at school but stayed away from the gin. The week after that, I spoke to Hallam and knew with all certainty it was over. I had one last crying jag, pulled myself together and went to see a lawyer. This week … well, what can I say? Here I am, having lunch with you. I've completed my commissions and am halfway through a portrait, and now all I have to work out is what to do with the rest of my life!"

"Will you stay in Singapore?" Amber broke the rule and poured saki for herself.

Lucy tucked her hair once more behind her ears. "I probably could, with my business and work permit. Hallam, despite all that has happened, is being very generous with maintenance. He has carefully ruled up a division of property. The apartment in London will have to be sold, of course, and he has given me full custody of the children. I won't be able to stay at Bukit Lalang but he's allowed me an apartment in town. He wants me to stay so he can have free access to Cam and Holly, but once she has his child, I don't know how long that will last."

"Oh my God, don't tell me she's pregnant!"

Lucinda shook her head. "Not yet, but it's part of Elvira's ultimate plan."

The hostess came to clear the plates and set down steaming bowls of miso soup.

"I have spent a month of sleepless nights, Amber, thinking about what direction I should take. It's so tempting to stay. Can you imagine life in this small society, where everyone knows you, and knows your husband dumped you for his secretary? What will the kids have to go through at school, and what are the chances of meeting someone new? I can see it now, the number of friends I will lose as an available woman on the prowl. I'm young, I could start over, but all I've got to choose from are married men or the local Malay tennis coach!"

Amber smiled. "Hey, wait a minute. Ramly would be a great catch! But in all seriousness, I hear what you're saying, the girls are already talking and they had a feeding frenzy after Angel died."

"I've decided to pack up the house and leave with as much dignity as I can muster, and reluctantly go back to London. That brings me to my next point of discussion - my business."

Lucy mapped out her plan to continue accepting commissions, with Amber as her agent. She mostly worked from Polaroids, so even if the number of paintings fell off, she still wanted to keep it going until she found something new.

They finished lunch and walked through the Japanese ornamental garden, parting in the car park. Amber had been a good and entertaining friend to Lucy, but at the end of the day, she was, after all, a professional expat survivor.

Her parting words were: "Oh, by the way, have you got anyone to take the house, and what about Esme? She's a great maid, I know a couple of girls from tennis who are looking."

And so life goes on. She went home in a sombre mood to break the bad news to the children and Esmirada.

Chapter Twenty-One
The Gift

Alex slipped from beneath the cotton sheet and padded silently from the room. He filled the jug and measured coffee into a glass plunger. The piquant aroma made his nostrils twitch as he waited for the water to boil. He took the scalding mug, and as quietly as he could, unlocked the back door to the sprawling veranda beyond. It was not quite five; the sun had just risen over the hinterland, filling the valley with a golden glow. The undergrowth and forested areas were still dripping from the early morning shower. He spotted a koala with a baby cleaving to its belly as it picked tender eucalypt leaves. A sulphur crested cockatoo sat regarding him in a disinterested way from its perch high in a paper bark tree, as he filled a dish resting on the railing with seed for the rosellas.

His bare feet trod silently along the wide veranda, down the steps and along a camellia lined path to the waterlily pond. Alex had recently lined the pond with boulders from the nearby forest, and had bought a weathered old garden seat from a garage sale in Tewantin. Spanish Moss hung from a mango tree, glistening with dew in the early morning light. The sun warmed his naked body as he sat carefully on the bench and sipped the strong coffee.

He thought about the letter he had received weeks ago from Lucinda. The letter came after a long interlude in which neither had written. After reading the contents, he felt guilty. The whole timing could not have been worse. He slipped back up the path, carefully wiping the yellow clay from the soles of his feet, and went inside to see if she was still asleep. He looked in at the dishevelled bed. All he could see was a cobweb of dark hair threaded with touches of silver splayed upon the pillow. He could hear the even rhythm of her breathing and left her to sleep. An hour later, the smell of cooking roused her and she appeared, as naked as he, on the sun-warmed veranda for breakfast.

Alex had met Nicky at a Pilate's class she was conducting at the Hinterland Community Centre. He had gone at his doctor's suggestion because he was having trouble with his back. There were not many men in the class and Alex quickly became the centre of attention. Nicky was dark and attractive, in her early forties and divorced. She also happened to have a good sense of humour, and as Alex had found out on their second date, a very supple body. He was lonely and Nicky was the first woman since Lucinda to arouse his interest.

He never really thought about the sex side of things, but when she seemed to automatically expect it as an appropriate ending to their date, Alex thought, Well, why not? What the hell was he waiting for?

As it was, he acquitted himself quite well, considering the time lapse. If anything, it was like opening up the floodgates, and now that he had started again, he found he didn't want to stop.

◆ ◆ ◆ ◆ ◆ ◆

Two months had now passed and Alex had still not replied to Lucinda's letter. He knew by now she would be packing to leave for London and quite possibly would have left her Singapore address. This gave him an excuse to put off writing until she got to England. He wasn't sure what he was going to suggest.

The novelty had started to wane with Nicky. The sex was great but he found they didn't have that much in common. She was a passionate creature with a contagious zest for life, food, wine, travel, dancing and sexual exploits, but when she suggested 'swinging', as in swapping partners, he knew they were moving in different directions. She had, however, been highly therapeutic. Alex's back pain had completely disappeared, his paintings were more radiant and he was filled with a new confidence. He sat that afternoon, pen in hand and wrote a long letter to Lucinda.

◆ ◆ ◆ ◆ ◆ ◆

One of the hardest things Lucinda had ever had to do was tell the children that she and Hallam had separated. They knew about divorce from their friends in London but none of the children at school in Singapore were from broken families. The second hardest was to tell them that they were leaving and going back to England. As she had envisaged, Cameron took it

178

the hardest, retreating into his shell, clutching his baby pillow and keeping his own council. Holly became difficult, aggressive and demanding. She and Esmirada tried to compensate by overindulging and making promises that were hard to keep. Hallam took them on Sunday when he was in town but the children behaved so badly that eventually he neglected to call.

The divorce was made final after three months. She had her day in court, as did Hallam, but there was little to say and nothing to contest. She had hired a small, swarthy Indian lawyer, who was pleasant and efficient. He helped her prepare her legal documentation, advising her on custody, maintenance and division of the matrimonial assets, including the apartment in London. He generously calculated the extent of Lucinda's contribution to their assets and sorted out any debts owed. When her Decree Absolute was granted, the only emotion she could summon was a profound sadness.

Amber had been caring and supportive throughout the ordeal. She came with her to the intimidating cream and brown colonial building on the day, but it was all an anti-climax and was over within half an hour. She saw Hallam briefly in the lawyer's office when they were ironing out the division of assets. He had lost a lot of weight and looked pale and drawn, his complexion pasty. All she felt was revulsion. Elvira was waiting for him when they came out, wearing a short, tight skirt and skimpy top. Lucinda still thought she looked like a common prostitute; she averted her eyes when Lucy passed, tossing her thin hair over her shoulders. As they walked away, she thought how ridiculous they looked together.

She put off sorting out the house. The children finished the school term and they would return to London in the holidays. She worried about telling Esme, but when the time came, it was she who surprised Lucy.

Lucy was sitting on her patio listening to the night sounds, branding them into her memory, along with the smell of the garden, click and whir of the fan and chitchat of the geckos. She already missed it and she hadn't left yet. Esme came to her silently with a freshly baked plate of cheese biscuits.

"Sit down, Esme, we need to talk. With everything that has been happening, I haven't got around to asking you what you want to do. Do you want to transfer or perhaps you would prefer to go back home? I'll go along with whatever you decide. You've been so wonderful these last few months, more loyal and understanding than any of my friends have been. I don't know what I would have done without you; the children love you and will miss you so much. I only wish you could come to London with us."

Esme laughed at this suggestion. "It would be too cold for me, ma'am, and I would have to get used to wearing shoes all the time!"

Lucy smiled at the thought of Esme in sturdy shoes.

"I have my own plans, ma'am. I didn't want to tell you right away because you were so unhappy. I've met a wonderful man at church. An American named Timothy Waldon and he has asked me to marry him."

Lucinda was immediately on guard.

"He has met my family and spent time talking with my brothers, mother and grandmother. They like and approve of him and have given their consent. We can't marry right away because my brother Manny has to marry first, otherwise it's bad luck. With your permission, ma'am, I'd like you to meet Timothy. He's anxious that you know him as a honourable man. He's not like the men in the Philippines who marry and then have sex with other woman; it's common for them to have many mistresses. The other men are *hanga,* envied if one man can do it to many women. The wives, however, must remain faithful. A good wife is praised as virtuous if she suffers martyrdom and keeps her chastity for the unfaithful husband! Timothy is a deacon of the church and believes as I do in love, respect and trust."

Lucy didn't quite know what to say. This girl was more understanding of men and their weaknesses than she would ever be. She had obviously observed her society, as well as Lucinda's, with wisdom beyond her years. How tawdry her circumstances seemed.

"I would love to meet your fiancé." Esme deserved to be happy after all she had done for her in her hour of need.

At six in the evening, Lucy, Holly and Cameron were scrubbed and waiting for Esme's friend Timothy to arrive. Esmirada had spent the day polishing, dusting and arranging flowers. She had cooked a tantalising dinner and had changed into her best skirt and blouse with her hair piled on top of her head. They waited nervously as a taxicab pulled into the drive and a tall man stooped to get out. Esmirada clapped her hands together and demurely walked toward him. He held her in a warm embrace and then came to meet the family.

Timothy Waldon had a wide, clean-shaven face. He was attractive but slightly podgy. Lucy put his age at late thirties, early forties. Holly tried to captivate his attention immediately while Cam stood shyly next to Lucy.

"It's so wonderful to meet you. Esmirada talks about her Singapore family constantly. You've been very kind to her."

Lucy led him to the patio while Esme fussed with canapés. "Come and sit with us, Esme, the dinner can wait."

Esme did as she was told and sat quietly next to Timothy, her legs tucked beneath her.

"So, tell me about yourself, Timothy. Which part of the States are you from?"

He smiled at Esme. "Poor Esme has heard this all before. I come from Boston originally. My father died when I was quite young. He was a Methodist minister. After he died, my mother worked in real estate on Martha's Vineyard and I grew up there. It was a wonderful life for a young boy. I intend to take Esme there for a visit once we're married. I haven't been back since my mother died."

Holly, on her best behaviour, hung on his every word, reluctantly leaving to help Esme attend to dinner.

"I was sorry to hear of the breakdown of your marriage. If there is anything I can do for you, please don't hesitate to ask. Esme is so sad that you're going back to England. She prayed constantly that you would stay. She understands why you can't."

Lucy scratched at the back of her hands and then stopped when she saw the concern in his eyes. "It's been a devastating time for us all and I don't recommend it to anyone, but I am going to move on. I just hope I am doing what's best for Holly and Cameron. You know, you should be very proud. Esme is a remarkable woman."

He nodded. "I sense in Esme a deep understanding of human nature. She has suffered a lot in her young life and I intend to see that the rest of it is as happy as I can possibly make it."

Lucy felt a squeeze of envy. If only Hallam had loved her as much. How lucky Esme was.

Esme appeared, followed by Holly carrying the salad for the table. Timothy smiled at her.

"Are you going to stay in Singapore once you marry?" She helped Esme place the food on the table.

"Yes, I teach at a local primary school. I intend to carry on teaching and Esme and I are going to manage and run the foreign workers' refuge. Have you read about it?"

"Esme told me all about the counselling she does there. I was really impressed with the school you have set up. It's marvellous to think it's all run by volunteers."

"The sister who currently runs it is getting on in years. She wants to retire and has asked Esme to take her place."

Lucinda stood to serve the food. It seemed only fitting that Esme be treated the same as her guest. Timothy cleared the table after the meal and he and Esme washed up. The evening felt comfortable, like a family gathering. He played a game of Cluedo with the children and then they sat on the patio with coffee and spoke of the wedding plans to be held later in the Philippines.

Esme talked about the superstitions surrounding weddings in her culture. "You must never give knives or anything sharp as this leads to a broken marriage! Rain on the wedding day means happiness for the newlyweds but it also means the couple will have many, many cry-babies."

Timothy laughed good-naturedly. "I hope it pours buckets!"

Esme's face gradually coloured a rosy hue. "If a bride wants her husband to agree to everything she wants, she must step on his foot on the way to the altar."

"Oh, I get it. Remind the husband who is really the boss, eh!" Esme laughed with him and Lucinda felt somehow that she was intruding.

"Breaking something during the wedding brings good luck, but dropping something like the wedding ring will mean an unhappy marriage."

Esmirada looked sideways at Lucy. "Wearing pearls will mean your husband will be unfaithful."

Lucy's hand went instinctively to the creamy pearls around her throat, feeling them tighten like a noose.

"We have many superstitions. I don't believe in them all, but I know my mother and grandmother do. I have to keep them happy."

Timothy gently kissed her temple. "We'll do all that's necessary to keep everyone satisfied, and to ensure we have a long and blissful marriage."

The look that passed between them was so tender that Lucy had to look away. She went to bed that night in a melancholy mood. She couldn't sleep. Why did her marriage go wrong? Was it because they didn't respect each other like Timothy and Esme? After watching them tonight, her own marriage seemed sordid, her life effete. The only good thing to come out of it was Holly and Cameron. How much would they, the innocent, suffer as she tried to rebuild their lives? Lucy couldn't answer any of these questions. She missed having Alex to confide in. He hadn't written back. He probably didn't want to be burdened with her sorrows and now that he knew of her divorce, she had probably scared him off for good. She really believed they may have had a connection, that something could have come of it, but in reality not many men want to take on a divorcee and two small children. She envisaged the rest of her life spent alone in a cold, empty bed. Wallowing in self-pity and remorse, she finally cried herself into a restless sleep.

Amber organised a series of farewell parties for Lucy. She had one last boozy game of mah-jong, a tennis session that started at eight and ended at one in the morning at Devil's Bar in Holland Village, and a margarita lunch for the art class that finished when the children came home from school. There were, much to Lucy's relief, no couple's dinners or parties; Amber sensed it would be too painful. Amber didn't tell Lucy that she and Brian had had dinner at the British Ambassador's house, where Hallam and Elvira were also guests. She avoided them at first but Hallam carried on as if nothing had happened, and Elvira, Amber grudgingly admitted, acquitted herself well socially. There was a constant trill of laughter surrounding the men at her end of the table.

Just before the lease expired at Bukit Lalang, the agent brought around perspective tenants. It was painful for Lucy to watch another family discover with joy all the charms of the bungalow, as she had so long ago. They were an American couple with two teenage children and a dog, moving from an apartment that had become too small for their needs. They prowled from room to room, yelling to one another, "Hey, come take a look at this!"

As expected, they loved the house that she had so lovingly decorated, and didn't argue about the hike in rent. Cameron swam around the pool, sullenly ignoring their presence, like a wounded sea lion. Holly remained in the kitchen with Esmirada, making toffee apples to sell at the school fete. Lucy offered the tenants coffee and negotiated what furniture would remain, and how much it would cost. They beat her down on price in a friendly way but at the end of the meeting, she was left with an unpleasant taste in her mouth.

On the weekend she held a garage sale. Esmirada, Lucy and the children had painstakingly picked through their belongings, brutally culling what they could not take with them. She squared her shoulders and put stickers with price tags on the items they couldn't take back. An advertisement appeared in the paper for the following Saturday, naming place, time and date, with a brief description of sale items. Esmirada had inveigled the help of Timothy, and Amber, Brian and the kids were automatically lined up for the big day. On Friday night, a carload of locals arrived asking for old books, liquor or vinyl LPs, of which Lucy had none. It gave her a good idea what the following day would be like; they all went to bed early, ready for the onslaught.

As soon as she opened the gates at eight in the morning, in they poured. They swarmed over her belongings like starving jackals, offering her ridiculously low prices for her precious items. Some even tried to shoplift and were caught red-handed by Timothy. At times, they were three deep, swarming about the makeshift tables and prowling about the property. Brian kept them out of the house as best he could, but he did find one old couple sneaking about the upstairs bedrooms.

Tuppy scavenged through the boxes, leaving with her arms full, resembling a homeless bag lady. Amber and Lucy took money and made change as quickly as their rusty math would allow. Holly, Esmirada and Timothy did a brisk business, haggling over prices and swiftly closing a sale. Cameron manned the games and toy section, but Lucy could see by the dismal look on his face how disillusioned he was with the whole business. She went to him and ruffled his hair.

"Listen, honey bunch, why don't you go with Tom over to his place and watch a bit of tele? You've done enough for today. I don't know what I would have done without you."

Cameron looked at his mother with relief and ran to find Tom.

Timothy gave her a tin box overflowing with notes. "Best take this and put it somewhere safe. There are lots of sticky fingers about! I've kept enough aside to make change. How are you doing? You look a bit frazzled!"

"Oh, Timothy, I never thought it would be this busy!" Just as Lucy said that, a bus pulled into the driveway and a load of old aunties and uncles from the local nursing home piled out and painstakingly made their way up the drive to see what bargains they could find. Amber looked at Lucy in horror!

By nightfall, the last of their customers ambled out of the gates. Lucy shut and locked them before anyone else arrived. The garden was a scene of devastation: whole tables of goods had been denuded, empty boxes with a few discarded and unwanted items lay strewn about. Esmirada collected the remnants, and Timothy stacked and packed the tables they had borrowed from the church. Amber and Brian were exhausted and Lucy poured them both a drink. The children had given up hours ago and were happy playing in the pool next door. Timothy left with the tables in the church van and Esmirada set about preparing supper. Lucy was disillusioned. She had opened up her house but somehow all she felt was violation. People pawing over fragments of her life, and offering her next to nothing for it, was a final humiliation. Next week the packers would arrive and the final chapter in Singapore would end. She wasn't a very entertaining hostess that evening, but Brian and Amber were so tired they failed to notice.

During the packing procedure Cameron fell ill with a fever. Lucy moved the small child from room to room as they packed around him. By Friday the house echoed with emptiness, matching the feeling in Lucy's heart. She had put off saying goodbye to the two people who meant most to her until the bitter end. Amber and Lucy had a final lunch at the Marco Polo; it ended in tears with the two of them clutching each other in the car park, too emotionally drained to speak.

Esmirada remained at the house for the last container to leave, and then she cleaned it from top to bottom, scrubbing, polishing and finally locking it up. Timothy and she would pack her room after the family had left. She would move in with Sister Mary and live with her in her terrace until they married. She intended to go on with her studies at the school in Emerald Hill and continue counselling abused maids. The last afternoon at the house was distressing for everyone. Both children sobbed piteously, Esmirada held them to her, crying into their hair. Lucy waited and humbly said goodbye to the woman who had become her equal; she diffused the situation by promising to attend the wedding in the Philippines the following year.

She lifted Esme's chin and wiped away her tears. "Enough for now. We'll meet again at the wedding. I wish you all the happiness you deserve. You have been a true friend to me and I'll never forget you. One last thing … " Lucy retrieved a wrapped package from the storeroom and handed it to Esme. "A wedding gift from me to you!"

Esme stood, a small waiflike creature, dwarfed by the house, waving until they were out of sight. Lucinda slumped back into the seat, emotionally drained; she took a deep breath and drew the silent children to her, hoping with all her heart that she was doing the right thing. They had come full circle and found themselves back at the Pacific Palms Hotel. They stayed two nights, giving the children a chance to say goodbye to Hallam. It was not a joyous occasion but one of tears, bed-wetting and temper tantrums. Hallam was dismissive and offhand, promising gifts, holidays and exciting reunions to come. The children swallowed none of it, and when Elvira appeared, Cameron behaved so rudely to her that Hallam brought them back within an hour. Lucy and he exchanged forwarding addresses like distant acquaintances, rather than like people who had once been man and wife. She was glad to see the last of his pale, pathetic face and wished him and Elvira everything they deserved.

Lucy and two bedraggled children arrived into Heathrow after a horrendous flight. Cameron had vomited all over her not long after take-off; she spent the rest of the flight in a cramped window seat in economy, reeking of stale bile. The children were fractious and febrile with fatigue; they ate little and drank even less. By the time they retrieved their bags and joined the long refugee-like queue through customs, Lucy was close to tears. She sat in the back of the cab at a traffic-blighted intersection, watching the scowling commuters making their way to work. Her eyes felt raw, dry and scratchy; she ached for a hot bath. No one spoke as the driver, hurling abuse and expletives, negotiated the snarl. They literally fell from the taxi as they stopped in front of the small private hotel that was to be their home for the next few months. When Lucy wearily signed the hotel register, she found herself using her maiden name; it gave her a feeling of closure. She suddenly became Lucinda Glendenning, commissioned artist. She would have new cards printed and start all over again.

Chapter Twenty-Two
Breath of Hope

Esmirada had a room at the back of Sister Mary's terrace. She looked out onto a private courtyard tiled with terracotta and sheltered by a mature Neem tree. It was her favourite place within the house. The yard was cool and dimly lit, the sun penetrating in small patches throughout the day. The old tree protected it from the heat and the retaining brick wall, covered in creeper, kept out the rain. The terrace backed onto the Chinese Girls' School and throughout the day Esmirada listened to the laughter and bubbling young voices through the brick wall. She had a small hole that she could look through and see them sitting in the shade eating lunch. She remembered enviously her own school days and how they were disappointingly cut short.

The last few months were the happiest Esmirada had been in her life. Timothy courted her as a free woman. He took her to the movies and to the Botanical Gardens after church on Sundays, and came regularly to Mary's house in the evenings to visit. The diamond sparkled on her finger, and she would stop during the day to gaze unbelievingly at its beauty.

The Serenity Centre, as it was now officially called, had increased attendance with more than six hundred women participating. Besides learning new skills, the maids congregated there instead of hanging around the shopping malls, boosting their confidence. With help from the government, the facility had expanded into the building next door and now commandeered a sprawling colonial bungalow. The variety of classes had also improved with a dozen more on offer, ranging from business, counselling, cooking, hairdressing, dressmaking and basic accounting skills. Esmirada completed most of the courses, except dressmaking. She realised she did not have the patience or nimble enough fingers. She continued alongside Sister Mary, Sister Amelia and Nora, counselling runaway maids, and worked tirelessly with Timothy in the church. She had applied for a work permit through the refuge and was patiently waiting for a decision. She and Timothy knew it was going to be difficult, but when the envelope finally came, denying her a permit, she was bitterly disappointed.

She met with him that evening in the front living room. Sister Mary had made them iced tea as they sat and tried to decide what would be the next step.

"I know there's no point in approaching the work permit department. When they say no, they mean no, there's no recourse. We'll apply again, using another avenue. I said I didn't want you to work as a domestic maid ever again, Esme, but I think you will have to continue on your current permit through Sister Mary. At least that way you can stay until we're married."

Esme dutifully listened but she felt uneasy. It would put Timothy's permit in jeopardy. She wasn't working as a maid but as a counsellor at the refuge. If the truth was discovered, there would be trouble for all of them, and possibly risk the good name of the centre and refuge.

Esmirada traced the cracks in the walls of her room with tired eyes. She couldn't sleep. The wedding gift from Lucy was mounted proudly in the centre of the far wall. Her own luminous face looked back at her. She didn't want to start out this way: under a cloud, with dishonesty between them. She knew the only way she could come back to work as a counsellor was as Timothy's wife.

The service that morning seemed as though it would never end. Nervously she sat picking at her rice in the shade of a tree at the hawker stall. She watched the rise and fall of Timothy's throat as he drank his beer, wondering what it tasted like.

"Timothy, I have decided that we need to start our life with honesty. I don't want to apply for another work permit. I'm going back to the Philippines to my family, until I can return legally."

Timothy rubbed his tired face; he, too, had had a sleepless night and was feeling the effects after the long morning in church. He looked at her small, upturned face, her long lashes casting a shadow beneath her eyes.

He took a deep breath in frustration. "I can't bear to let you go, but yes, you are right. Surely this silly superstition about siblings marrying in the same year isn't strictly adhered to? When exactly is Manny getting married? The baby must be at least nine months old by now!"

Too late Timothy saw her hurt expression. He had to be more understanding of the foibles of her strange culture, but he had to admit he found it damned annoying at times.

"I'm sorry, forgive me for criticising Manny and your beliefs."

She was silent throughout the rest of the meal; Timothy wondered if this was the famed *tampo* that he had read so much about. He hadn't expected it from Esmirada. The day ended on a sour note with promises of seeing each other later in the week. He walked her to the now-so-familiar grubby bus stop, and waited until she was out of sight. He then turned miserably and strode along the uneven pavement in the relentless heat and humidity back to his lonely flat.

The following Tuesday Esmirada left for the Philippines. She had no choice, Timothy had been keeping her financially and she could not continue until a legitimate work permit materialised. She left the ring and her portrait with him for safekeeping, and took one suitcase with her. She knew she was testing their love; it had all been too good to be true. Suddenly she was unsure of her future. There had been tears and promises at the airport, but she also sensed a feeling of relief when she turned and walked through immigration. She ate a stale samosa and slept. When she awoke, she looked through the porthole and saw far below the rolling hills of the Philippines come into view.

Manny, grinning broadly, waited by his illegally parked, gaudy vehicle. With her return, he assumed the engagement had ended.

"I liked him, Esme, but he was not our kind. Too good for the likes of us. I'll find you someone. With your looks it won't be hard."

She said nothing, holding on tight as Manny carelessly cut a corner.

When she arrived at the cement house, her mother was at the *sari sari* window serving a small crowd of villagers. She looked up as Esme entered the compound. Esme could see she had lost even more teeth since her father had died. *Lola* was waiting, sitting on a straw mat, nursing a squirming Carlo. They were embarrassed, assuming, as Manny had, she had returned home because the engagement had ended.

As she and *Lola* prepared the evening meal, squatting in the courtyard, Esmirada tried to explain. "My work permit has expired. I'll go back once we're married." She described the size and shape of the beautiful *singsíng* he had given her.

Lola looked at her from the corner of her yellowing eye."*Walang matimtimang birhen sa matiyaging manalangin.* There is no firm virgin that a patient man cannot have!"

Her grandmother had a proverb for every occasion! Esmirada smiled; contented for the moment to be back with the old woman she loved so dearly. She took her thin, bony hand and kissed it, holding it to her cheek.

Esmirada couldn't quite get used to sleeping on a straw mat on the floor again. She had grown soft in Singapore and her aching body yearned for a yielding mattress. Late at night by the oil lamp, she composed a long letter to Timothy but did not post it. She was hoping his letter would come first, but so far nothing. Her days fell into a routine long forgotten: rising at dawn to prepare a simple meal, helping *Lola* with the chores and taking over the *sari sari* so Olina could look after the ever-growing Carlo, while Pinkie and Manny worked. The relationship with Pinkie was puzzling to Esme; the woman was in no hurry to marry, despite having shamed her family by having a child. Pinkie's gangster father and brothers had threatened to kill or at least disfigure Manny, but still the two resisted marrying. She missed Ricardo who had reluctantly moved his family to a remote fishing village. He had bought a boat and the fish were plentiful. His children were growing strong and healthy on lots of fruit, vegetables and all the fish they could eat.

The days in the *sari sari* were long and slow; she gossiped with the customers and swabbed the same green linoleum floor repeatedly. She fitted her pace to those around her and grew lethargic. After a month of mindless banter with the villagers, she decided to go back to church as a volunteer. The small Independent church she had always known had changed; it had suffered a great tragedy just after New Year when a fire completely destroyed the two-storey building. No one was hurt and thanks to God's intervention, the twenty small children in the orphanage attached to the church were saved. As usual in the Philippines, the insurance had been left unpaid, so replacement costs ran into the thousands. To replace the original structure, they were depending on God to meet their needs. Worship was now held in the orphanage.

A group of hard working Sisters ran the orphanage and gladly accepted Esmirada's services, much to the dissatisfaction of Olina, who had been only too willing to relinquish her duties in the *sari sari*, so she could sit and play with Carlo and eat prawn crackers all day long.

190

The Sisters shared a vision of a city without violence toward women. Manila was full of lurking danger, sexual abuse and many other potential threats. Life for most in the slums was brutal and all too brief. The Sisters filled Esmirada with hope and empowerment. She worked with poor resources alongside them for long hours without complaint.

Her day started early, feeding and bathing the babies. The older children helped dress and feed the younger. They had very little in the way of equipment or toys for the children. She taught them simple rhymes and naming games and gave them love in the name of Jesus. Finally, she sent her letter to Timothy along with a plea for donations to rebuild the church, and supplies essentials for the orphanage. His letters arrived one after the other, full of longing. He had taken up her cause and the generous donations from her church in Chinatown Point came flowing in.

In September the typhoons came. At dawn, Esmirada had left the compound along with many others going to work. A coal black cloud grew longer by the hour, filling the sky. She had seen the pointing finger of a typhoon many times before. Sheets of corrugated roofing were already flying about, swirled by the increasing rate of the wind. It had been moving across the country and already uprooted hundreds of coconut trees, devastating large areas of crops. Outlying islands had suffered the most damage with people missing, feared dead. Surging floods and fierce winds had destroyed shantytowns. Villagers had been hurled into trees or crushed by them when they fell, others died after being hit by flying debris.

The Sisters had readied the orphanage as best they could; they lit candles, prayed and prepared the small gas stove. Esmirada had brought in a supply of fresh vegetables, rice and meat. They stood by the caged window during the late afternoon as the storm gathered in intensity, watching branches of trees, sheets of iron, rubbish, chairs and a bicycle fly by. At midnight all the power, water and telephone lines had been disrupted. Even if she wanted to go back to the compound, she couldn't, as the road had cleaved open and split in two, and most of the bridges had collapsed. By early morning the following day, the residents of the shanties and slums had been roused from their beds by flash flooding. Two days later, the typhoon subsided and she returned to the family compound to help Olina and *Lola* start the inevitable cleaning, clearing and rebuilding. The number of dead stood at sixty-one, with over one hundred still missing. The weather bureau said the storm was moving west-northwest and was expected to pass by Thursday. It had been the fourteenth typhoon to hit the country since January.

The monsoon rains went on to cause more tragedy in Metro Manila. The poor trash-sifters who eked out a living amongst the garbage were buried in a monumental slide. The actual numbers were still unknown, but Esme knew that most would be children. She and the Sisters, along with many other churches in the area, provided basic items such as rice, sugar and drinking water. Once again, she appealed to Timothy and her church in Singapore to supply clothing and medicine. One week after she had spoken to him from the only working telephone, the church supplied one hundred bags of goods that were distributed by the 'Breath of Hope' Impact team, working at the dumpsite along with volunteer medical workers.

On Sunday, prayers for the families and relatives of the victims were held to relieve their burden in the name of Christ.

In Singapore, Timothy reminded his congregation: *"As we have therefore opportunity, let us do good unto all men, especially unto those who are of the household of faith. Galatians 6:10.* Thank you all for your donations, prayers and the compassionate mercy of Jesus Christ!"

Olina waited for Esme's return. Only then could she reopen the *sari sari* for the many who were in desperate need of supplies. Manny finally came to see his son. *Lola* and Olina had not heard from him or Pinkie for a whole week and had been worried about their safety. He casually picked up the baby with the curling eyelashes and kissed him as he slept.

"I have to go to San Fernando on business. Pinkie is there. I don't know how long I'll be. Can you take good care of him while I am gone?"

He shoved some dirty pesos into Olina's hand, looked once more at the child and abruptly left. The women of the house silently watched his retreating back, before sighing sadly and going once more about their work.

With no man in the house, Esmirada was the only one who could climb onto the roof and reattach the iron sheeting. She cleaned the courtyard of rubbish, pulled down the rotting, striped awning that flapped like a sail in the wind and replaced it with an iron sheet, which had fortuitously blown into their yard. After years of lying neglected in the dirt, she reaffixed the rusted San Miguel sign to hang below the *'4 Rosa Sari Sari'*.

The bamboo furniture in the courtyard had stood up well in the storm. She tied the bougainvillea that was trailing along the ground and trained it over the new iron awning, then trimmed the coconut palm's fallen branches. The *sari sari* had never looked better.

Later that afternoon, the old men gathered with their guitars and the children hung about the window after Pop Rice and Royal Orange. The few remaining chickens scratched contentedly in the dirt.

Manny returned two weeks later, looking thin and pale. He bought fresh fish for dinner and hung about the narrow doorway, holding the child while Esme cooked on the gas stove.

"So, when can we expect the *Pikot?*"

Esmirada's reference to a shotgun marriage caused Manny to colour profusely. She had never seen him so unnerved. His usual swaggering confidence had vanished as he held his son to him protectively. She saw the look that briefly passed between her mother and grandmother. She followed Manny out to the Jeepnee with Carlo's name on the back; she noticed Pinkie's had been removed.

"Where's Pinkie? Is she working in San Fernando? Doesn't she miss little Carlo?"

"No, *utol,* Pinkie is no longer my *syota.* She ran away and married some *promdi,* and she left me and little Carlo behind."

Esme studied her bare feet in the dust of the yard and looked up at her brother's pained face.

"I'm going to make sure she can't come back and take him, but it will cost!"

Esmirada looked at the sleeping baby. How could anyone possibly abandon something so perfect? A vision of the children that she and Timothy would have came to her; she almost doubled over with yearning.

"I'll help you, Manny, if you help me. Let me marry this year. I don't want to wait any longer!"

Manny smiled and kissed his sleeping son. "This *Amboy* must really be something. They get all the best girls! We better go and eat. You women have a lot of work ahead with a wedding to arrange."

She threw her thin arms about Manny's neck and nuzzled the fat baby as he crowed contentedly up at his father.

◆◆◆◆◆◆

Timothy had been depressed after Esme left; he walked down to Holland Village and consoled himself with four straight whiskeys in a row. Feeling even worse, he made his way to Mary's terrace and cried drunkenly on her shoulder, finally falling asleep in Esmirada's room, where he could still smell her on the pillow. The following morning he was chastened and humiliated by his behaviour, late for school and terribly hung over. All week he devised ways to get her back, but in the end knew that he would have to persevere with a long distance romance; in the meantime, he only hoped some Filipino Romeo would not move in and sweep her off her feet.

When Esmirada's phone call finally came, his throat contracted with nerves and he found it hard to speak. She told him that December was the most popular month for weddings. Her mother and *Lola* were busy organising the details. Stupidly he thought at first she was talking about Manny's wedding, but he recovered his senses and shouted with joy when he realised it was his own she was arranging!

Chapter Twenty-Three
Return to Sender

Over the following weeks Lucinda's emotions oscillated between hope and despair, one minute happy to be home, the next desperately missing Singapore. The rash on her hands mirrored her emotions, seeming to improve, only to return the following day with a vengeance. She briefly met with the girls for afternoon tea at Browns but she found the experience depressing. She had changed, but Emerald, Livvie and Hilary had not. Emerald's experience in Singapore was long behind her; she preferred not to talk about it, which hurt Lucinda. She had a new boyfriend, a dentist who had been widowed; her past was forgotten in lieu of the new relationship. The conversation over tea was stilted. She felt she had let them down somehow, gone away and failed to keep her man. They were no longer interested in the Lucy of old.

The private hotel was a sanctuary for the diminished family. It had a cosy Edwardian-style with heavy, framed art and airy suites. They ate baked beans on toast and treacle tart. She remembered now why British food had such a bad reputation: overcooked and grey, with tasteless sauces and watery vegetables that disintegrated into a slimy mush on your tongue. The puddings were not much better but she gave in and allowed the children whatever they wanted.

The summer was slow to start so they spent their days indoors, combing the musty museums and basement galleries. They went to the movies numerous times, taking the tube to Kings Road and Holland Park, and to stage shows and musicals. They ate at Hard Rock Café and in the small Italian restaurant next to the hotel. They were like wounded animals, clinging to each other for support. Lucy sighed frequently and Holly comforted her with soft kisses on the cheek, or brushed her hair until she became drowsy. Cam withdrew and started wetting the bed, which in the end severely tested Lucy's patience. At other times, he would sit, zombie-like, clutching his pillow and watching mindless programs on the television.

She left them with the hotel babysitter to look at apartments but she found nothing to inspire her. After the lofty colonial bungalow, they all seemed spare, cramped and dark. She decided that until the end of summer and the start of school, they would stay within the domesticated comfort of the hotel. She had to get them out of the depressing fug into which they had slipped. She bought a small car and planned a two-week touring holiday to Cornwall. For the first time since they arrived, Cameron's eyes lit up and he showed some interest in his surroundings. The weather improved and they packed the car and headed for the coast. The plan was to find all the places Cameron had ever read about in his many books. Lucinda had never driven so far on the island before but threw all caution to the wind, looked briefly at a map and set off. Once they had got out of the city and off the freeway, she started to relax and enjoy the drive.

Suddenly they were in a different country altogether. Fields of rape grew along a ridge, past a gentle valley. A string of grey-stone houses, bright with summer flowers, contrasted starkly against the medieval fences that divided overgrown gardens. This was postcard country in rural isolation. First stop was the four-thousand-year-old heritage of Stonehenge, about which Cameron had read avidly last summer. It seems everyone else had the same idea, as there were busloads of tourists dismounting as they pulled into the busy car park. Cameron was out of the car, camera in hand, racing toward the monolith. He paced the dark grey outcrop, taking photographs from all angles. When they paused, Lucy acted as tour guide and told them some of its history.

"The ancient Druids believed in the immortality of the soul and reincarnation."

Cameron's eyes, wide with wonder, added, "This was where they worshiped and had human sacrifices!"

Holly raised her eyebrows at Lucy. "Which book did he get that out of? Big words for a little boy!"

They spent a peaceful afternoon walking about the perimeter. An old gentleman took a photograph of the three of them, and then they found a dry wedge of grass to eat the packed lunch Lucy had brought. She gazed at the low hung clouds and consulted her map, wondering where to stop before nightfall. They drove on with the weather improving as they went; they passed picturesque hamlets with coppices and steeples. The villagers played croquet on the summer lawns and cricket in the village greens. At

196

dusk a darkening storm threatened. Cameron shouted in Lucy's ear, causing her to swerve violently.

"Look, a vixen, she must have babies close by!"

The children watched the small fox slink back from the lights and head into a roadside culvert.

Lucy pulled into the next village and looked for a bed and breakfast sign. She spotted a squat public house, which threw a warm yellow light onto the cobbled street.

A farmer with wind-burnt cheeks met them at the heavy oak door. She timidly asked for a room. Lucy recognised his lilting Midlands accent. He showed them to a room under the eaves at the top of a set of crooked stairs. The children loved it and ran to sprawl on the musty chenille counterpane, the iron bedstead creaking loudly as they did so. The room was all faded floral and dusty knick-knacks, the kind Lucy's mother once collected. A yellowed, nylon lace curtain parted to reveal a cobbled courtyard below and an overgrown rose garden. The farmer's meaty wife supplied them with a hearty meal of soup, fish pie, scones and clotted cream. They ate in the dining room beneath dark beams and walls the colour of café latte from the wood-burning stove. A gust of wind blew a smattering of raindrops against the window and Lucy shivered. The farmer and proprietor of the public house returned and threw more logs onto the fire. There was a brusque hardness about him but she complimented him on his wife's food. He sniffed without saying anything.

Lucy tried again. "I read in the London Times that we are in for some bad weather."

He chewed on his pipe reflectively. "Ahhhh, tis different for we. Us has our own climate, so dawn't listen t'they! T'woud the lad and lass loik some more b'uer for them scones?"

She smiled. "Yes, that would be lovely, thank you." He tipped his cap and went off to the kitchen to rouse the wife.

Lucy settled the children into bed after they had brushed their teeth in bitterly cold tap water. Holly was reading a book, the *Tales of King Arthur,* aloud to Cam who was already drowsing. She drew a bath in the ancient draughty bathroom with the hottest water she could stand, and immersed herself up to her neck. She closed her eyes and tried to relax. The steam coaxed a ripe mustiness from the old walls that was hard to ignore. Rain slanted against the window and the pane rattled as the wind moaned, distracting her. As she towelled off quickly she heard the bells ringing in the carillon in the square. Suddenly she felt profoundly lonely. Emptiness spread through her veins, chilling her soul. What was she doing, driving all this way in this cold, wet, dismal place? She crept into the lumpy, damp bed and held her children close, listening to the storm that lasted all night long.

By morning the storm was reduced to drizzle driven by a stiff wind. She sat in the wood panelled dining room, drinking Earl Grey tea in a dingy mood, while the children eagerly discussed how far they would drive today. Cameron clutched his *Tales of King Arthur* to his wheezy chest. She hoped he wouldn't be disappointed.

After leaving the small village, the country took on a depressing flatness until they climbed a hill and drove down the other side, catching a glimpse of shingled rooftops, and a verdant valley with rolling farmland, rich with deep red soil. The farmhouses had colourful gardens. Mellow cob walls made of mudstone and straw were handsomely thatched. Lucy stopped beside one such farmhouse where a rosy-cheeked woman welcomed them; she served them fresh strawberries, clotted cream and freshly baked scones on blue and white patterned china. It was a dairy farm, nestled in a lush dell. Cameron and Holly ran toward the fields to inspect all they could find. Fat brown and white cows grazed contentedly next to black woolly sheep. A wiry little Jack Russel belonging to the farmer's wife chased them, nipping savagely at their heels.

As they continued their journey the clouds were still turbulent but a pernicious sun crept through at intervals. They passed a muddy brown river that looked bereft of life until a flock of iridescent mallards lifted and flew away. The road they travelled had very few other vehicles; it was lined on either side with birch, holly, hazel and mountain ash. Lucy had gusts of panic until she spied the A 30 with a faded signpost pointing the way to 'Land's End'.

She drove westward, crossing the border near Plymouth. Suddenly the soft prettiness of Devon took on a much more menacing landscape, a little like the difference between France and Italy, thought Lucy. She ached to stop and get her sketchbook out of the trunk. They passed through towns with authentic Cornish pasty shops on every corner. It was odd to see exotic trees growing along the roadside. Stopping in a small village overlooking a peninsula, Lucy could see a white sickle of sandy beach. Small colourful craft sat becalmed on the water below. Lucy bought crab sandwiches from the corner shop, whose exterior was buried under a display of beach balls, floats, surfboards and fishing paraphernalia.

She eagerly drove to the wildly romantic coast of her girlhood novels, and the Cornish cliff tops of Arthurian legend and Tintagel Castle. They sat and ate their picnic in a sheltered cove above a lonely deserted beach and then walked the dizzying track to the ruins of Tintagel. Holly and Cameron were thrilled with all they found, but Lucy thought it was a tawdry tourist trap. The rugged cliffs and weathered stones held more magic for her; she longed to take a long walk alone, with the wind teasing her hair. She wanted to explore the lonely moors, sketching as she went, but her children's needs came first.

"Mum, can we have an ice-cream please?"

Holly and Cam stood before her, breathlessly pleading. She couldn't say no. The family spent the rest of the afternoon in the village taking photographs of each other in stocks, and then they drove on with Holly navigating, trying to find the farmhouse where Lucy had booked for the night. After last night, no more surprises. She did want a little comfort along the way!

The farmhouse turned out to be more of a manor house with a steep roof of Cornish slate, complete with tennis court and swimming pool. The interior, though, was faithfully decorated with heirloom tapestries, and gilt-edged paintings beautifully restored. After settling into a huge room with an open fireplace and two king-sized beds, they all took warming baths and changed for dinner. The chambermaid had stolen silently into their room, leaving tea, and freshly baked walnut cake.

Lucy and the children joined a communal table of holidaymakers. An American couple were entertained by Holly and Cameron's stories of local legends of smugglers and pirates. Lucy ate a delicious meal of fried Brie with cranberry sauce, game, poultry and a cider washed cheddar. She and the other guest sat in front of the open fire with their red wine and brandy; Holly and Cameron reluctantly went to bed.

The American couple quizzed her on her travels. "Where have you come from today?"

"We drove from Devon but we started out from London. Our aim is to reach Land's End later in the week."

The couple were beautifully groomed, silver-haired, and lavishly jewelled. Larry, as he wanted to be called, said, "I detect another accent, where are you from originally?"

"I grew up in Australia, moving to London as a young wife. Recently I left Singapore after living there for three years."

Larry raised a questioning grey eyebrow. "Now that's two places we just have to visit. And your husband, he's not travelling with you?"

Lucy sighed. "No, unfortunately we're no longer together."

Larry's silver-haired wife dug him in the ribs and looked at him as if warning him to say no more.

"I'm sorry, I didn't mean to pry. Bad habit of mine, or so my lovely wife tells me often enough."

Lucy waved it away with her hand. She would have to get used to such questions. It became a little easier each time she said it. The manor house receptionist entered the room with a bedraggled man, shiny with dampness.

"We have a walker today, all the way from Devon!"

All heads turned in appreciation; he was given the prime seat closest to the fire and entertained the guests with tales of his walk. After spending days with the children it was nice to have adult conversation once again. She stayed quite late, chatting until the fire died and the guests made their way to their respective rooms.

Holly and Cam were up early, breakfasting on freshly baked bread, eggs, bacon, sausages and mash. Afterward Cameron led them on a tour of the farm, where they came upon some mushroom-like sculptures.

"They're saddle stones, used to keep the rats out of the grain in the olden days."

Holly wrinkled her nose at him and spitefully said to Lucy, "I'm sick of him, he thinks he knows everything!"

"Well, you have to admit, Holly, all his reading has paid off. He does have an impressive general knowledge."

Cam's little face shone with pleasure, while Holly refused to listen and ran off toward the cow pasture.

"I didn't read about the stones, Mum. The farmer's wife told me about them this morning!"

They left after breakfast to make their way to Polkerris and Penzance. Once again the fickle weather turned and Lucy found herself driving through sheets of rain driven by an icy wind. They looked out upon vast windswept bays.

She told the children as they ploughed on through poor visibility, "This was the country of all my favourite writers when I was a young girl:

200

Thomas Hardy, the Brontes, D.H. Lawrence, Virginia Woolf, Dylan Thomas. But the one I loved most was Daphne Du Maurier. I read everything she ever wrote. I remember one summer reading *Rebecca* at least three times. I always wanted a house called *Manderley*."

She looked around to find she was talking to herself. Cameron was busy with 'Game Boy' and Holly was playing with her 'Polly Pocket.' She sighed deeply and drove on through the wind and rain. They reached Penzance under a lowering sky, the seawall was pounded by spumy foam that settled and blew away with the wind. Lucy parked the car and they got out, only to be driven sideways by the rain. They were wearing wet-weather gear but after only a half an hour of trying to traverse the steep cobbled streets, they gave up, drenched and soaked to the skin.

They found a pub still serving lunch that would satisfy Cameron's thirst for smugglers, pirates and sinking ships. The panelled walls were covered with paintings of shipwrecks, looters and drowning sailors. Holly and Cameron ate fish and chips while Lucy tucked into succulent oysters, mussels and crabs, cracking them heartily, sending shards of bright red shells spinning across the table in the direction of other diners, to the amusement of her children.

With the weather against them, she ventured forth and drove on to Enys for the night. Once again she had booked ahead to a farmhouse B&B. It was rapidly growing dark although the rain had turned to a miserable drizzle. She drove on, panicking when she found herself in a remote, overgrown lane. Just when she thought she might turn back, an old farmhouse came into view. As they alighted, the mist carded and she could see a wide, flowing river and cattle in the valley beyond. The children had fallen asleep in the back of the car. The owner of the establishment, a huge bear of a man with a crooked smile, lifted the sleeping children and carried them one by one into the surprisingly grand guest rooms, depositing them gently onto the antique four-poster bed. Lucy left them to sleep while she washed in the Laura Ashley style bathroom.

She joined the two other diners that evening, an elderly couple from Nottingham who said very little throughout the meal. Lucy wasn't concerned. She was just happy to be in a warm room, eating delicious home cooked food and drinking fine wine. The farmhouse hosts were very gracious and sent up soup and rolls for the children, in case they woke hungry. They woke briefly in a scratchy mood when Lucy entered the room. They ate the comfort food and immediately went back to sleep, leaving Lucy to luxuriate in a hot, soapy bath.

In the morning the weather broke fair. They packed the small car and headed off in the direction of Land's End. The farmer's wife gave Lucy a bunch of yellow daffodils to brighten their journey.

The three now had the touring down pat; Holly and Cam shared sitting up front navigating. As the days wore on she worried less about getting lost. Usually when they did they discovered something far more exciting than what they had set out to find, as was the case with Land's End. Like Tintagel, it proved to be a disappointment for Lucy. The drive there through overgrown country lanes was pleasant enough, with the children working on various projects in the back seat, but by the time they reached the southwestern-most part of the island, all they found were mobs of tourists milling about in the cold wind and dampness. There were buses full of complaining pensioners, wanting to take a photograph and then go on to the 'last pub in England' for a pint. She decided to give it a miss and drove along the brooding cliffs until she found a small public house for a ploughman's lunch before making their way back along the coast.

Confident now, she tackled the drive back to London in a matter of days, staying in Fowery in a small B&B along the way. She made good time using the freeway and avoiding the coast road. They arrived at Brighton by mid-morning and stopped off for lunch. It was blustery and cold, the sky leaden above a dirty grey sea. The threesome braved the winds and walked bent at the waist along the rubbish-strewn beach.

"Do you know they used to drink it for good health?" asked Lucy.

"Oh, yuck! I wouldn't even put my head under, if I swam in it!" a disgusted Holly said.

"Enough of the beach; not like the ones we're used to. Let's go see the Pier and the Royal Pavilion and be on our way."

The Pier was tatty and sad; teenagers abused the sightseers, and called each other obscene names. She steered the open-mouthed children in another direction. She took a sad little photograph behind a cardboard cutout of them skiing, but there was room for three people and one face remained poignantly empty.

The sky closed in as they returned to the car to drive the few miles to London. The rain splattered against the windscreen and the wind almost tore the door off as they hurriedly got into the welcome warmth. So this is summer, she thought. The drab, eternal sameness depressed her completely. Arriving back at the hotel, the doorman and receptionist greeted them enthusiastically.

"Welcome home, Ms. Glendenning. How was the trip? How are you, Miss Holly and Master Cameron?"

He relieved Lucy of her luggage. A fire was burning briskly in the grate, and a hamper of newly purchased food was waiting for them in the kitchen. She scrambled eggs and made toast and they sat watching the evening news before going to their respective rooms for the night. Lucy knew that later they would both make their way to her bed, which had been the custom since returning to London. She didn't mind. She needed the comfort of their warm bodies as much as they needed hers and while ever Cam slept with Lucy, he didn't wet the bed.

Downstairs on the receptionist's desk a buff envelope lay addressed to Mrs Lucy Leadbitter. The smartly dressed receptionist picked it up, looked at the return address in Queensland, Australia, sighed, wishing one day she could visit and promptly wrote in perfect copperplate: *'Not at this address. Return to sender'.*

Lucy lay listening to the gentle rise and fall of her children's breathing. The rain splayed sideways against the windowpane, and the magnolia tree creaked and bent in the wind. She imagined the warm night air against her bare skin, adhesive humidity as she ran down the textured sand to swim in the ocean. A spritzer of salty surf, and the water against her eyeballs as she rode the waves, pulling, crashing and ripping at her swimsuit, finally depositing her, spent, in the foamy shallows. She remembered too the yielding lips of a man with laughter in his eyes and the taste of the ocean on his mouth, a kiss that held so much promise. She turned over, an unbearable yearning rising in her belly, making it impossible to sleep.

◆ ◆ ◆ ◆ ◆ ◆ ◆

A pearly light played upon the windex blue water of the bay. Lithe surfers in slick wetsuits paddled furiously through the glassy swell to the point beyond. Alex pedalled his bike up the hill past the Pandanus Palms. He took a deep breath of syrupy air; he could feel the muscle in his thigh and calf flex cleanly, burning a little as he reached the top. He sat astride the bike to take in the view of the ocean and horizon beyond. Early morning joggers and power walkers wired to their walkmans, breathing without effort, passed him by.

He felt fantastic this morning! His exhibit had been a great success. Most of the paintings had sold and he had started working on a new series. Nicky and he, although no longer lovers, were still friends and he was still able to attend her classes, which his back appreciated! He squinted as the sun intensified and he spotted a pod of dolphins skimming the sparkling water.

He expected a reply from Lucy any day; he felt he had worded the letter well, making his feelings clear; it was up to her now to decide. He rode with the sun hot on the back of his neck. It was the winter months but the days had been warm and bright and the nights cool and mild, this was his favourite time of year. He stopped off at the deli and bought fresh bagels and coffee to have by the pond in the garden while he read the paper before starting work for the day.

Coming in by the back gate, he walked the bike up through the dense foliage. It was cool, the sun had not penetrated the undergrowth this early in the morning. He paused, listening to the native birds calling high in the stringy bark. Joanna was lying beside the pond, the white undersides of her belly splayed out beneath her. He quietly approached and she watched him sleepily from the scaly corner of her eye.

"I've been feeding you too much, old girl, you're getting fat!"

She closed her eyes, lazily dismissing him. He stashed the bike on the covered back veranda and padded into the cool interior of the house. The post had arrived! Geraldine, the postie, generally came around the back and left it on his outdoor table. If she was ahead of schedule, he'd offer her a cold drink in the shade before continuing her rounds. He fell upon the thick bundle expectantly, sorting the bills from the personal mail. He sat heavily in the old timber chair, when he saw his familiar hand and buff envelope. His so carefully rehearsed and worded letter had been returned without it ever reaching Lucy's hands! He felt foolish, each day waiting expectantly like a lovesick teenager. He took a sip of scalding coffee and slathered cream cheese on his bagel. After breakfast he would retrieve her letters and find the name of her neighbour. Maybe she would know of a new address. He berated himself for waiting so long, but he wasn't going to give up that easily.

Chapter Twenty-Four
Oriel Lodge

A month before school commenced, Lucinda decided to look for somewhere to live. She needed to make a home for the children and after the holiday in Cornwall, she knew in her heart that London didn't fit anymore. The pace, traffic and cost were too much for a woman on her own with two children. After months in the apartment, she thought nostalgically of the bungalow in Singapore. Realistically, she knew anything of that size and grandeur was out of the question, but a small cottage with a garden would be just what they needed. Surrey sounded like the right sort of place. She had checked out the schools' credentials and was more than pleased with what she'd found.

The real estate agent, a well-preserved woman in her mid-forties, with a pert little bottom clad in purple leather, collected Lucy and the children from the railway station in Cobham. She was taking them to see a small cottage in Manor Farm Lane.

"You'll love this little house. I'm like a sniffer dog when it comes to the right house for my clients. It's old but has been renovated by a French fashion designer for her son. The slate roof is new and all the windows have been replaced. It has a lovely courtyard that is virtually maintenance free. You'll find a lot of women in your circumstances living here!"

She patted Lucy's knee in a sisterly manner and Lucy noted the lack of a wedding ring on her finger.

The leafy streets were bordered by well kept cottages and gardens; the agent craned her sinewy neck looking for hidden house numbers and gave a small yelp of delight when she turned haphazardly into a narrow lane overhung with willow. Mulberry and hawthorn bushes enclosed a bed of scarlet-faced dahlias. An obvious recent addition was a Regency styled front porch.

They entered a predominately white, light-filled space. The kitchen, dining room and sitting areas were open and unfussy with 'tongue and groove' panelling, which was repeated in the bathroom in a soft green. Lucy sighed over the deep antique bath; the sink was large enough to bathe a small child. The cottage had only one bathroom but it was expansive with lofty ceilings and windows, which opened onto the courtyard below. The main bedroom could serve as a studio for Lucy with a good source of light. Doubled glazed doors opened onto the sandstone courtyard, surrounded by lace-cap hydrangeas, bowing in the last of the soft evening light. Cameron and Holly were upstairs investigating their rooms; she could hear the rebounding footsteps. Holly's gurgling laughter floated down to where she and the agent stood.

Lucy turned to the small, eager woman, took a great gulp of air and said, "It's perfect. I'll take it!"

The following month they moved into Oriel Lodge, but not without some sacrifice. Because of its size, most of the furniture from Bukit Lalang would not fit. Sadly, she sold the big black German piano and her beloved reclining Budda.

Holly begged her to keep the fat laughing Budda. "It's for good luck, Mamma. It can sit in the hallway!"

So Lucy furnished the house with her overstuffed sofas, Burmese lamps, Korean chests and Persian carpets.

She overheard the cockney removalist asking Cam, "Nice lot of stuff in' nit, Guv, very foreign like. Course it is, I know it!" He turned to Lucy, tipped his cap and gave her a cheeky smile. "It's come up nice, in' nit?" He stood rubbing his belly, admiring the furniture. "Lived abroad, ave you, luv?" Lucy had to admit the house exuded an exotic air.

They settled comfortably in their small oriental cottage, nurturing each other and falling into a routine of shared chores. She relished unpacking her paints and brushes, setting up her easel and looking forward to painting the many sketches she had done in Cornwall.

School started and after a bout of tears and first week nerves on Lucy's part, the children made friends and found they were well ahead of the others in their classes. They were objects of great interest in the playground, having lived in Singapore, and because they lived in the wonderful house with the fat Budda in the hallway!

Surprisingly, suburban life suited Lucy. The neighbourhood was friendly and she found a part-time job in an antique shop, run by a young couple on High Street. The shop was painted white with huge arched double doors, forming an entrance off a landing from the street. The windows were dressed gracefully with sweptback muslin, and the floors were covered in sea grass. The owners had led a gypsy lifestyle, living in Paris, New York and London, gathering a hotch-potch of jugs, umbrella stands, ceramic dogs and colourful artefacts. The walls were cluttered with sideboards, portraits, paintings and Venetian mirrors. Lucy loved the boldness of the collection, French crockery and bed heads, and on every surface stood lamps of all shapes and sizes.

The shop always drew a crowd, especially at the weekend. Cam and Holly would come and potter, helping Lucy dust and tag incoming artefacts. Laura and Hamish, the owners, became her friends, inviting her to dinner or long lunches with buckets of Alsatian wine, in their small glass conservatorium. After seeing her collection of artwork from Singapore, they enthusiastically displayed it in the shop. It sold well and Lucy soon became a solid business partner, painting in her spare time to meet the demand.

Laura liked to play matchmaker and Lucy indulged her, never taking it too seriously, until they introduced her to Sebastian. Seb, as he liked to be called, was younger by eight years; he was the owner of a small bookshop in High Street that specialised in photography, thick beautiful, arty tomes that were sought after as valued gifts. In his spare time he wrote novels, novels that were so far unpublished, but never-ending works in progress. He had a twin sister who was an Ambassador's wife, stationed in Geneva. He spent long hours on the phone with her and visited her often.

Lucy found him nerdy at first, but he grew on her. He had a schoolboy, slapstick sense of humour that appealed to Cam and Holly. His hair was thick and fell in unruly waves across his pale forehead. He was myopic and squinted with his dark-gold eyes through thick, wire-rimmed glasses. When she made an interesting statement, he reminded her of a huge puppy, over exuberant and easily excited. Awkward and clumsy, he constantly knocked into things, apologising profusely. Not Lucy's type at all, except for one outstanding feature. He was sexually adventurous, well endowed and inexhaustible in his endeavour to please her. She had discovered these redeeming features one Sunday evening in the small flat above his shop, when Holly and Cam were sleeping at a friend's house.

Seb, Lucy, and the kids had spent the day at a local agricultural show. The show was exhibiting cows, sheep and small animals, to which the children flocked. They wandered through the chickens, rabbits and lambs while a ruddy-faced farmer dispensed advice to the children on the joys of owning a hamster. Holly and Cam fed a lamb with a baby bottle, while Seb trolled about the horticulture tent admiring the forced bulbs. Lucy stood transfixed for a full hour at a stall watching elderly woman weave. As the sun set and the exhibiters started to pack, Sebastian came and breathed damply on the back of her neck, tipsy with apple cider, suggesting all sorts of ways they could spend the rest of the evening. She ignored him, watching her children disappear to buy coconut ice. In a sheltered corner of the green, warmed by the late afternoon sun, and a few more ciders, she finally agreed in principle to his suggestions. They dropped the happy siblings off at their friend's house, with the new hamster they had acquired, and laughingly climbed the wooden steps to Sebastian's flat.

Lucy was at first felt self-conscious as he slowly peeled away her clothes, flinging her greying underwear over the back of the sofa. She was suddenly aware of her dimpled thighs and soft belly. Her breasts, once full, now had a deflated balloon look about them; she hadn't shaved in days and had not had a bikini wax for two summers. Sebastian scolded her and gently removed her folded arms from her breasts, roving his hands over her body. He took hold of her tongue as he kissed her, and with half-closed eyes she fell back against the rough wool of the sofa. He nibbled playfully, teasing her nipples, moving slowly down her body with his tongue until he unsheathed the shy soft flesh, which had been neglected for so long. He lunged deeply into her, holding her hips high; she wound her legs about his waist and gripped him. She clasped the hair that curled at the back of his neck, biting down hard on his shoulder as she felt the familiar desire running through her blood. She shuddered, her body awakening as she studied his face above her. He let out a guttural moan and collapsed, panting on her breast in a forest of hair. A sense of complete happiness vibrated through her body, making her legs quiver weakly; he slept a small death, leaving her shoulder damp with his breath.

Ravenous, she sat naked at his table while he prepared a huge platter of pasta with fresh tomatoes. They drank red wine and then, sated, fell into bed, making love twice more. She reluctantly left the tangled, sweat-stained sheets to go home to her cottage in Manor Farm Lane.

◆ ◆ ◆ ◆ ◆ ◆

Before Alex could change his mind, he dialled the number and ignored the call-waiting signal. He had tried to make this call all morning, but had been harassed constantly by Rita, the wretched organiser of his latest exhibit.

A small voice answered, "Good afternoon, Van Engle residence."

"Hello, is Amber there?"

"No, I'm sorry, sir. My ma'am is out for the day. She will be back by six."

Alex could hear birdsong in the background and imagined the lush garden and the small woman on the phone. "Please tell her Alex Erindale called from Australia. I will call back later. It's with regard to her friend, Lucy Leadbitter."

"Thank you, sir. I have written it down. Goodbye!"

As he replaced the receiver, the phone immediately started to bleat once more.

Alex sighed and dutifully answered the call from Rita, the gallery organiser. Yesterday the woman had him dressed completely in black, crouching in a ridiculous position with a hand full of paintbrushes, for a promotional photograph. The preparation and shoot had taken up most of his day and tested his patience. Rita was quite predatory and made no secret of her availability. Unfortunately all he could think about was finding Lucinda. He was anxious to get out and do some plein-air work now this exhibition was established. In his mind's eye he could see the new series, which he had already labelled 'Beauty and the Beach'. Of course Rita was ecstatic and hounded him, wanting to accompany him on site. He had resisted, letting her down gently but the woman was persistent.

As the late spring shadows lengthened, Alex worked contentedly in his studio, mixing impasto and slapping it richly onto a freshly prepared canvas. The telephone rang repeatedly; he threw down his pallet knife and strode into the house.

A sultry voice with an unusual accent asked for, "Alex Erindale."

He cleared his throat and said, "Speaking."

"Alex, this is Amber Van Engle, how lovely to finally talk to you, Lucy has told me so much about you and your work, I feel I know you very well!"

Alex raised his brows and leant against the bench top, cradling the phone beneath his chin as he poured a drink. "It's good of you to call, Amber. Lucy told me all about you as well. I'm anxious to contact her. I've written but it seems that we have missed one another with her change of address."

In Singapore, the fans whirred overhead as Amber slipped off her sandals and reclined onto her silken four-poster. She took a quick sip of gin and said, "Alex, that's such good news, I know she was disappointed she hadn't heard from you earlier. Where did you send your letter to?"

Alex repeated the address of the hotel in London and the date he had sent it.

"Hmm, I think I know what may have happened, Lucy reverted to her maiden name. I received new business cards from her a month ago. She now goes by the name of Lucinda Glendenning and she's recently moved from London to Surrey. I'm waiting to hear from her any day now with her new contact number and address. You probably know better than I do that things can move very slowly once you get out of London, I lived there in another lifetime, Lucy told me you had as well. I'm waiting for the little minx to call; I have a whole list of commissions for her to get started on. You know, Alex, her work is selling really well here, and she's so talented. She's left me with a full-time job, stops me missing her so much but my two little ones, Andrea and Tom, miss the kids dreadfully, my new neighbours aren't nearly half as much fun!"

Amber seemed prepared to talk for hours and Alex was happy to sit in his darkening kitchen and listen. He was relieved. He was closer to finding Lucy and felt a certain pleasure that she had reverted to her single name. He wondered how much Lucy had confided in Amber. It didn't matter now she was divorced. He needed to finally talk to her and tell her how he felt; he had a feeling it wouldn't be long.

◆ ◆ ◆ ◆ ◆ ◆

Lucy's life was in sweet disorder. She spent her days inflamed with passion and her nights in great happiness. She had become as careless as a child. Sebastian returned secretly night after night to take her and then steal silently away before dawn like a thief. She wandered in a daze from one chore to another, forgetful and listless. Holly and Cameron were the first to notice her lassitude. Her paintings sat undisturbed in her bedroom-cum-studio, and her correspondence basket lay brimming with unanswered bills and letters. Laura and Hamish knew the reason why and were secretly pleased; they overlooked her preoccupation, happy that two lonely people had found each other.

Lucy's skin took on a luminous lustre and the disfiguring rash on her hands disappeared. After four months of constant lovemaking, her senses quickened, and she realised she couldn't remember the last time she had a period. She panicked, looking closely at her two growing children for the first time in weeks, realising how foolish she had been. Suddenly she couldn't think of Sebastian without feeling nauseous. She avoided him, ignoring his calls, and making feeble excuses to keep him away. The trauma she was going through was compounded by a call from Hallam. He had promised to take the children for a week in Singapore after Christmas, but he called to joyfully inform her that Elvira was pregnant and he felt it was unfair to expect her to look after two energetic children for a whole week!

Lucy sat in a state of shock, unable to speak; she had wanted to shout down the receiver, "Guess what, Hal, me too! I'm pregnant to a boy who is fantastic in bed, far better than you ever were. Sex with you, Hal, was flat and unsatisfying, and get this, he's hung like an elephant! We'll be just one big, happy family."

Fat chance! Instead, she sat, stunned, long after putting down the phone, scratching at her hands and yearning for the children to return so she could take them in her arms and hug them.

The weather had turned cold, and the sylvan lanes of Surrey were gauzy with frost the morning she left for London. The children were staying with friends for the night while she attended to business. She had lain awake night after night in her lonely bed, berating herself and making pacts with God if she could suddenly not be pregnant.

She ended the affair with Sebastian; he had looked at her with the expression of a bewildered child, his hair flopping over one eye.

"It's me, it's not you." She stammered the overused cliché, sitting on the rough woollen sofa that was so familiar to her touch. "You're too young to take on the responsibility of me and my children. I want more from a relationship: love, marriage and commitment. I don't think it is fair to expect that from you, Sebastian. You're a wonderful person and funny and smart, but I can't let this go on; I've been neglecting my work and family. You deserve a younger woman without incumbrance."

She looked at his eyes, soft with tears, and felt pathetic. He said very little, apart from that he understood her position. She was right; he wasn't ready for commitment, or a ready-made family, or any family for that matter. He had never imagined how strongly she felt. It was good she had told him now before he got really serious about her. He kissed her icily, and she walked down the stairs of his flat, relief flooding her belly as she tried to undo her mistakes one by one.

Chapter Twenty-Five
A Second Chance

Timothy fingered the carefully wrapped box that he had picked up from the corner post office. It was starting to rain as he and a handful of students, dressed in white tennis shoes, dashed across the road. The girls laughed and used their backpacks to shield their heads from the heavy monsoon. He sheltered beneath the M.R.T. station and bought a ticket from the dispenser on the wall. Today he was too impatient to wait for the bus. He reached his modest flat as the rain stopped, and waved to the old lady who owned the cane shop below. She was sweeping water from the entrance and winding up the chick blinds. Her hands were grotesquely swollen and disfigured with arthritis from years of weaving cane, but she never failed to open her shop seven days a week, from ten in the morning until nine each night. Her daughter and grandson helped from time to time but most days she manned it alone.

He opened his door and the stale smell of last night's curry hung in the muggy air. He flung open the barred windows and let a damp breeze enter the small flat. The overhead fan sounded like an oncoming train. It had become noisier lately, but with so much to do, he chose to ignore it. He poured himself some fresh lime juice and changed his cloying shirt.

The noise from the street drifted through the open window as he sat beneath the ceiling fan, and carefully removed the stiff brown paper and string from the package. With trepidation, he teased away a vast quantity of tissue and held the garment aloft. The fabric was diaphanous, the light from the window showed through with a translucent glow. He fingered the small pearl buttons, wondering how his cumbersome fingers would manage to fasten them. The workmanship was impeccable and his earlier doubts faded as he tried it on and stood proudly before the mirror. The *barong* was a gift from Esme for their wedding day. She was eager for him to wear the traditional dress of her countrymen. Timothy was hesitant at first, thinking, in keeping with his custom, he would marry in a tux, but soon realised that Esme had a small traditional ceremony in mind.

His salary was not grand but he knew he could afford to have a lavish wedding by Philippine standards. However Esme would not hear of any extravagance. Her family were simple people and he didn't want to embarrass them in any way, so he left all the planning to her, wanting only to fulfil her wishes. He stood admiring himself. The *barong* suited his large frame and flattered his bulk, and it was comfortable and elegant. He was pleased and wished he could call Esme and tell her how good he looked. His mother would have been stunned perhaps and proud to see her only son at this moment.

The school where Timothy taught would break for vacation in two weeks and not resume until January. By then they would be man and wife. He had already secured a large, airy apartment closer to Chinatown, within walking distance of the church and the training school in Emerald Hill. He planned to leave within days of school breaking up, tempering himself for the official paperwork, which he needed to complete in order to marry within the Philippines. He had to appear in person before a consular officer at the U.S. Embassy in Manila and complete an affidavit, and then he and Esmirada would apply for a marriage licence at the local Civil Registrar, where Esmirada lived. The licence would take ten days and would last for one hundred and twenty days. Having carefully read through all the requirements at least six times, he knew them off by heart!

Tonight he would have *laksa,* his favourite dish, for dinner with Harold and Joyner, the last before his wedding. Harold had been reticent when Timothy asked him to be his best man; he had shuffled about looking at his feet and then lunged at Timothy, grasping both his hands, pumping them vigorously with gratitude. Timothy, being an only child with deceased parents, had few living relations. A vague recollection of some cousins on his mother's side living in Canada came to mind, but otherwise he was alone. His college friends had all dispersed and gone separate ways, and he had failed to keep any contact since moving to Asia. Timothy had heard in the past that his best friend Joe had given up the priesthood and was working somewhere in the Far East as a missionary, but he had heard nothing since. Esmirada's vast, emotionally charged family was about to become his own, and at times he admitted to Harold that it kept him awake at night thinking about it. He was sure within his heart that this was God's plan, and he was only too willing to take on the extra responsibility.

◆◆◆◆◆◆

To get away from the squabbling at home, Esmirada spent her waking hours at the orphanage. Their numbers had increased since the tragedy at the dumpsite. The church in Singapore was still donating food and clothes, and she had taken charge of organising the distribution through the impact team and volunteers.

Rosa idly spent her days arguing with Olina over the wedding preparations. They both had a grand, expensive plan to which Esmirada refused to listen. Rosa wanted to exploit Timothy and his hard-earned money, while Olina, her ideas less elaborate, also wanted to milk him for all she could. Manny stayed out of it, knowing if he were to legally adopt Carlo, he would need Esme and Timothy onside. He didn't have the means to proceed and was relying on Timothy for that. To save them money he had volunteered his services at the reception, playing music with a group of buddies in exchange for food and drink. Olina wanted a full Mass in a Catholic church, but Esme had already spoken to the pastor of her church, "The Tabernacle of Hope", and the wedding service had been set for Saturday December eleventh.

Esmirada worked late into the night, returning to the cement bungalow to lie on a straw pallet, and listen to *Lola's* stertorous breathing. *Lola* convinced her to agree to have Rosa and Corky as her sponsors, only then would they leave her alone.

Through her work at the dumpsite, Esmirada found her old school friend, Angelika de la Cruz. She recognised her immediately, although Angelika had trouble recognising Esme from the small girl with the thick dark plait, from so long ago.

"You've grown very beautiful, my friend. I've stayed ugly, and no wonder I have never married."

They laughed together, remembering the all-too-brief time they shared. It was true Angelika was ugly, stout and thick with sturdy legs. Her wiry hair stood out from her head in a course halo. The small dark mole on her chin that had once fascinated Esme had grown and sprouted hair. A bad dentist had seen to Angelika's teeth, the amalgam flashing in the sunlight each time she smiled.

Angelika had realised her dream of becoming a teacher and helping the poor. She had been working daily at the dump, trying to set up a makeshift school for the scavengers' children. The parents were timid and did not feel their children had a right to attend school. The donations provided little, and trying to convince the scavengers, who made a small amount of money each day collecting plastics and cans for recycling, to journey out of the dumpsite was a long hard road. These people were so poor that they couldn't even afford enough rent for the worst slums of Manila.

The women sat alongside the road leading to the garbage dump, assaulted by the stench. They covered their faces with their T-shirts, trying to dampen the putrid smell, and to keep away the persistent flies. It was under these horrendous conditions that Esme proudly asked Angelika to be her bridesmaid. They then hatched a plan that would require the church and Timothy's help to ease the suffering of the squatters.

♦ ♦ ♦ ♦ ♦ ♦

Lucy sat in the front seat of her car, shivering uncontrollably as the rain coursed down the windscreen. Her tears ran unchecked, pooling beneath her chin as she looked out onto the deserted car park. It was half past three, but already it was dark. Small pools of yellow light shone on the slick street as the commuters, heads buried in their coats, rushed for the railway station. She sniffed and felt for her purse and box of tissues. She took a deep breath and blew her nose. Her cheeks burned and she mopped furiously at her face with the disintegrating wad. She looked in the mirror and brushed pieces of tissue from her cheeks. Swallowing hard, she tidied her hair and took one last look at the doctor's surgery, turned the windscreen wipers on full and swung the car out onto the street.

By the time she had reached the leafy avenues of Cobham, she was calm. She could see a welcoming light burning on the front portico, and knew Laura would have the fire built up and hot soup simmering on the Aga. She parked haphazardly, retrieved her overnight bag, and entered to the sounds of Gershwin in one room, and the television in the other. The children, warm and sweet smelling from their baths, ran to her. She scooped up their pyjama-clad bodies and buried her face in the soft folds of their necks. Laura was waiting in the sitting room with a glass of red wine. She fluffed the cushions, sat Lucy down, and wrapped a mohair throw about her shoulders. Silently she closed the door, and sat at Lucy's feet, her large eyes staring up at Lucy with concern. Lucy took a large swig of the wine and settled back into the soft warmth of the lounge. Laura took her hand.

"Was it really awful? I wish you had let me come with you. I can't believe you actually drove all the way from London!"

Lucy shook her head. "Nothing happened. It was a false alarm!"

Laura's hands flew to her face in disbelief.

"The doctor examined me when I got there, did some tests and told me in a very matter-of-fact way that I wasn't pregnant! I cried with relief and almost kissed the old fellow. He examined me fully and said I was suffering from anxiety. That's why my hands are in such a mess! He gave me a sedative and some cream and a course of birth control pills and sent me on my way, with some fatherly advice about using protection!"

Laura jumped to her feet and poured more wine, and together they sat in front of the fire, discussing Lucy's close shave, and deciding what to do about the suffering Sebastian.

"No more matchmaking, Laura. I've learnt my lesson. It's too soon for me. I just want to be a good mother and concentrate on my painting. I want to make a decent life for us. You'll find someone else for Sebastian!"

Laura's heart-shaped face glowed in the firelight. "He's gone off to Geneva to see his sister. He was miserable when he left, and frustrated because I wouldn't tell him where you had dashed off to."

Lucy took another sip of wine. "He's young, he'll get over it, but I don't know if I will. He was the best lover I've ever had!"

They sat in front of the dying fire with bowls of soup, finishing off the wine and then Laura left to go home to Hamish. Lucy spent a long time gazing at her sleeping children before finally going, exhausted and tipsy, with relief, to bed.

The following morning an icy wind blew as Lucy ferried the children to school, but it did not dampen her spirits. She felt as though she had been given a second chance. She rushed back to the warmth of Oriel lodge with a full day ahead of her to paint. She set herself up in the corner of her bedroom and looked out onto the bleak garden beyond. The skeletal trees were forlorn, as a pallid sun appeared from behind the heavy dark clouds. In contrast, she painted scenes of exotic palms, riotous tropical flowers and pastel street scenes of Singapore, and always, hidden in a corner or window of her paintings, her mascot, the little black cat.

She watched the clock, eager to call Amber in Singapore. With Sebastian as a distraction she had not advised her of her new address. At noon, she fixed soup and crackers and sat before the fire, which she banked up with sweet-smelling wood from the market. She heard the soft thud of the mail as the postman shot it through the space in the front door.

An envelope caught her eye amongst the bills; she picked up the coarse, heavy, white paper, and noted the foreign stamp. Inside was a wedding invitation, very simple, no velum lining or silver embossing, just a pale thin slip of flesh-coloured paper with a fine watermark of two entwined rings, a cross and candles. She read the details.

Esmirada and Timothy
Will marry at the Tabernacle of Hope Church
in Manila at three o'clock on the afternoon of
Saturday the eleventh of December 1993

Lucy's face suffused with warmth. Good on Esmirada! She had done it. She was marrying her quiet American. She sat for a long time in front of the fire, making and discarding plans. Finally, she called Amber to ask if she and the children could stay for Christmas after she had attended Esmirada's wedding in the Philippines.

Amber hung up the phone smugly. She loved playing matchmaker! Lucy had talked for over an hour, telling her about her cottage in Surrey, the success of her paintings and her job and the children's progress at school, but the most interesting detail was the affair with Sebastian, and the ensuing pain and distress. She told Amber that she'd sworn off men, so Amber cautiously said nothing of Alex's call! Instead she picked up the phone, dialled Australia, and before she could change her mind, invited Alex to share Christmas with them in Singapore, as a surprise for Lucy and the children.

Chapter Twenty-Six
Ninongs and Ninangs

Timothy smelt the dumpsite before he saw it. The stench permeated his senses and clung to his damp skin. A group of stunted children scampered about the road, piling cans for Timothy's jeep to crush. The malnourished crowd swarmed as he came to a halt. They shied away from him, trying to hide their filthy hands as he handed out sweets. Tears welled in their eyes and he questioned his motives. What could he hope to do for these wretched people?

Looking up, he saw Esme and Angelika walking toward him. Esme's beauty shone out of the smoking ruins. She had grown thin and her clavicles stood out at angles. Her eyes wide, she ran to him and threw her arms about his neck. Since his return to the Philippines, she had become more openly demonstrative. Now that the marriage licence had been issued, she was confident and sure of his love. Her family, too, had accepted him and the wedding was set to go ahead as planned.

Timothy had good news for Angelika. The church had raised enough money to erect a small concrete building that would serve as a schoolhouse. Attached to the school would be a fresh water supply and showers so the people of the dump could clean themselves at the end of the day. Through volunteers from the orphanage, the woman had set up a makeshift kitchen, enabling them to feed the children their daily ration of rice.

A huge truck, oozing with split garbage bags, rumbled to a stop. A young boy, riding on top wearing a torn singlet and T-shirt wrapped about his head commando-style, waved and flashed white teeth at the crowd who greeted him jubilantly. He hooked bags of garbage, spilling the fresh waste to the muddy ground. The scavengers swarmed, grabbing at tin cans, plastic and styrofoam and smashing glass in their wake. Pregnant woman and children as young as four sifted through the bounty. There were no fights or

218

squabbles, each worked their own patch, waving or raising an eyebrow in a common Filipino greeting.

Timothy looked to the lush horizons, trying to breathe in shallow bursts, fighting to keep the toxins out of his lungs. He was worried about Esme. She coughed consistently, and the fires burnt all day and night, spewing poison into the air. The hot sun cooked the topmost layer of garbage, creating a unique stench that clung to everything. The disease-carrying flies and mosquitoes gathered around a three-year-old in a pair of men's gum boots, as he triumphantly held up a handful of foreign coins that he had found in the waste. Esme left Timothy and went with Angelika to the makeshift kitchen. From beyond the huge mountain of trash, her laughter reached his ears as she traversed the muddy slopes. He knew the mounds were unstable, but it didn't stop the families from climbing them at the break of dawn each day.

In the late afternoon, when the heat of the sun gave them some respite, he met with the volunteers who would build the showers and cement block. Their enthusiasm and boundless energy inspired Timothy. Leading the group was a tall ginger-haired fellow who stood out from the rest. Timothy squinted his eyes against the lowering sun and looked more closely at the man as he approached with his hands outstretched.

"Timothy Waldon! I knew there could only be one!"

Timothy could not believe his eyes. It was Joe Miller, his friend from his college days! They had a loud and boisterous reunion, standing amongst the smoking debris, watched with amusement by the gathering crowd of children and scavengers. Timothy brought Esme and Angelika forward, introducing them to Joe and the other volunteers enthusiastically. Joe told the gathering crowd how he was convinced that out of a hellish inferno, Timothy's church would create a haven.

"A promised land for the families who live here!" It would give them hope for the future and some dignity.

Angelika taught the children the alphabet while Esme cooked the rice. At dusk when more children left the mountain to gather at the school, she taught them the rudimentary steps to traditional Filipino dances. They laughed and called to one another with Timothy and Joe looking on. A small group of three-year-olds ran off to fly a kite made out of a plastic bag. Timothy watched and his heart opened, thanking God for his generosity and allowing the smallest of scavengers a moment of lost childhood.

Each night they returned to the barrio, Timothy brought food for Olina to cook for the ever-growing family. Every night it seemed more chaotic, but at the same time there was harmony. He found himself lost with the names of nieces and nephews, *ninongs and ninangs*, and neighbours who were no blood relation but treated as such. The barrio was a very public affair; the dwelling doors and windows always open, washing hanging everywhere. The *sari sari* was the main meeting place, so Timothy's appearance and the coming nuptials involved the whole village. Esmirada was not ruffled with the ever-growing family each night for dinner, and they didn't seem to notice that most meals were the same: vegetables, chicken and noodles; if they did, nothing was said. He suspected by the joy on *Lola* and Rosa's face that they didn't have meat often.

Corky, Rosa's husband, sat and beamed at him throughout the meal, as thought he was the saviour himself. Timothy would sit in the courtyard watching the food preparation, trying to ignore the plastic buckets of dirty water and the flea bitten dogs hanging about the fringes of the corrugated iron. At times Esme and her mother would have words in Tagalog, which left Olina silent and tight-lipped in a corner, but generally the whole atmosphere was carnival-like.

Esmirada attended to the customers in the store, while Manny and the old men of the barrio entertained the masses with their guitars and folk songs. Olina set small tasks for Timothy to complete. He felt he was performing a sort of test set by the family. He guessed by the way Esmirada kissed him goodnight that he had passed. Reluctantly he returned to his hotel each evening, passing the prostitutes and glue sniffers, to lie awake restlessly in his damp room with the wheezing air-conditioner. He would think of his ever-growing love for Esmirada, and count down the hours and days until they could be together forever.

Esmirada, too, was growing impatient; her family's demands on Timothy's resources saddened her. Corky's latest catch was for Timothy to pay for new clothes for all the sponsors. She fought with Olina and won. Her mother could see Timothy was a good man, and not as rich as most Filipinos believed him to be. He had provided good food for most of the neighbourhood since he had arrived, and the cousins and nieces that she saw little of were suddenly present at every meal! She lay on her straw pallet each night, listening to the familiar sounds of the barrio, swatting mosquitoes and counting the moments until they could finally be together.

◆ ◆ ◆ ◆ ◆ ◆

Alex had had a series of happy accidents since Amber's call; Rita had proven to be quite an asset after all. The woman had deftly arranged a series of art fairs and group exhibitions in the U.K. that would tie in nicely with his trip to Singapore. Only yesterday, her pointy little face, pinched with pleasure, appeared at the studio door announcing that she had organised an exhibition of his work at the Australian Embassy in Singapore. Perhaps he would have to sleep with her after all, maybe just the once!

He had corresponded with his old mate Sol Colander in London. The old gay Jew's gallery was in its tenth year, and doing well representing emerging and established international artists. Last time he saw Sol he was recovering from a failed love affair with an artist's model. He never changed: small, rotund with a florid face and a combed forward Julius Caesar hairstyle. Sol was excited about Alex's work; he had connections with a gallery in Copenhagen where Inke once exhibited. It was double serendipity for Alex.

Recently, Rita had introduced him to a rather glamorous little number from Melbourne. They had a pleasant dinner at Ricky's on the river and discussed Dorté's new gallery in Swanston Street. Dorté or Dorrie as she laughingly called herself, had seen Rita's promo of him, and liked his work enough to want to do a solo exhibit in the new year. Alex had felt like a fucking rock star at the time, but he had certainly been in the limelight ever since the magazine had hit the stands. Suddenly his name was splashed across some weighty publications. *Who's Who of Australian Visual Arts,* described his work as 'A moving and explosive response to the Australian sea and sky.' *The Sydney Morning Herald* gushed equally, 'Alex Erindale's rich images evoke deep spirituality and insight using the most brilliant of hues.'

Recently he had been commissioned for a large work to hang in Customs House in Sydney, and a smaller piece for the International terminal of Brisbane Airport. His life was good and only Lucy could make it better. He counted the days until he boarded the plane that would bring them together once more in Singapore.

Chapter Twenty-Seven
A Humble Rice Stalk

Lunging from sleep, Timothy was momentarily disorientated. He kicked his way free of the tangled sheets, and looked down onto the chaotic street below. It was his wedding day! He wanted to open the windows and shout the good news, but the windows were sealed and he doubted if anyone would care. They were too busy haggling, stealing and begging to notice.

Last night Esmirada was the most radiant he had ever seen her. Angelika, in her role as bride's maid, organised a *Despedida de Soltera* or 'farewell to spinsterhood' but really it was just another excuse for a party in the barrio. All the neighbours, along with the whole family, celebrated. Included in the festivities was Joe, his long-lost friend, Ricardo the groomsman and Perpetua the matron of honour. Gigi, Mandy and Rose, the flower girls, and Enrique, the altar boy, were there, and of course the musical director, Manny. Carlo toddled about, eating things off the dirt floor and Rosa and Corky fought over who would be the Godparents and sponsors. Joey, Rodolfo, and Jose were nominated as cord and veil bearers. Torre, the youngest brother, was thrilled to have the job of ring bearer. In a very decent tenor, Harold took it upon himself to entertain the crowd, while Joyner helped Olina and *Lola* with the food. The neighbourhood women had been cooking for days; Manny had bought a *lechon*, which he spit-roasted over open coals in the courtyard, while drinking *tuba*, singing and playing his guitar. The festivities went on into the evening, finally coming to a boisterous end at midnight.

The vision of his *barong,* so carefully pressed and pristine in its humble surroundings, filled him with happiness. He stood under the green corroded showerhead and let the tepid stream of water wash over him, cooling his feverish brain. Carefully he shaved and dressed, fumbling over the tiny pearl buttons of his wedding shirt. All he could think of was Esmirada. Finally they would be together. He sang at the top of his voice as he tied his laces and brushed his hair, nothing could dim his anticipation and joy, not the faltering air-conditioner, or the lingering smell of the rat that had been caught in the shaft two days ago. Today was his wedding day!

Lucinda arrived in Manila late at night. She'd forgotten the unique Asian smell of open sewers, sweaty bodies and the acrid smoke from the open-air cooking. It all came rushing back as she pushed her way out of the crowded airport to a waiting car. The driver, who didn't smile, looked old and tired in his shiny threadbare suit and cap. He shoved her into the back seat and handed her a bottle of water and a plastic bag with a wet cloth. Taking the cloth, she wiped her face. It had a stale, musty smell. She balled it up and placed it on the seat beside her. Without a word he automatically locked the doors. The pockmarks on the back of his neck held her interest as she gathered her belongings about her protectively.

The streets were dimly lit with a halo of pollution around the street lamps. She could see the flare of open fires, and felt the beggars close in, pathetically pummelling against the darkened windows, leaving greasy marks with their desperate hands.

The hotel was neon lit and welcoming after the gruelling journey. The doorman, dressed in a naval uniform, kicked savagely at a mongrel dog as he ushered her into the foyer. A group of saffron-robed monks milled about as foreign businessmen openly herded underage prostitutes into the lift. A young girl took her through the formalities and pointed out the restaurants and pool area. She continued prattling on about the merits and facilities of the hotel, while Lucinda smiled, wearily nodding her head as if in understanding.

Alone in her room, she kicked off her shoes and prepared a bath, the sheets were flimsy but clean, and the air-conditioner over efficient and cold. Suddenly she longed for the children and the festive atmosphere of Bukit Lalang. Lying on her bed she thought of the last four days spent in Singapore, with Amber and the children.

Amber had given them a noisy welcome; Lucy at first felt lost but the children bloomed in the warmth and humidity. Discarding their clothes and heavy shoes, they ran, bounding like puppies down the grassy slopes to fall into the pool. Shouts and laughter, and remnants of forgotten games, drifted to where Amber and Lucy sat sipping cocktails, carelessly gossiping over old times. She made a pilgrimage back through the hidden gate in the fence to her old house. The neighbours had gone home for Christmas, leaving the dog and maid in residence. Esmirada's garden had flourished. The

223

passionfruit vine wound its way about the outhouses, abundant with fruit, and in the far corner of the garden where it flooded with each downpour, a coconut grove swayed in the breeze. Lucy remembered how she and the children laughed when Esmirada placed coconuts in a row, vowing they would grow into lofty palms. The house stood glowing in the afternoon sun as it had on the first day she saw it. It didn't feel like it belonged to her anymore. She walked away, not wishing to see it again.

Brian was travelling in Germany and Amber selfishly kept Lucy and the children to herself for four days.

"You'll see everyone at Christmas, I just want to spend time with you alone, I have a little surprise for you and I hope you won't be cross with me when I tell you!"

Lucy looked up from her drink and wiped the sweat from her top lip. Amber sat, grinning in that mischievous way that Lucy remembered so well.

"I've invited Alex Erindale for Christmas, he's exhibiting at the Australian Embassy!"

Amber watched carefully, gauging Lucy's reaction. She saw the colour rise in her throat.

Lucy took a sip of her drink and carefully placed it on the table. She raised her eyes to Amber, who could see the sudden excitement there.

"Alex! Oh Amber, it would be wonderful to see him again! Now tell me the truth, how did you engineer this?"

Amber threw back her head, exposing her white throat, and laughed. She topped up their drinks, as she told her the story.

◆ ◆ ◆ ◆ ◆ ◆

Esmirada and Timothy were the first to be married in the rebuilt Tabernacle of Hope. The church elders and sisters from the orphanage had spent long afternoons with the children, making crepe-paper flowers to garland the simple wooden pews. White plastic chairs lined the walls, hung with red banners adorned with passages from the bible. Rosa greeted the guests by pinning a flower to their lapel. Most were dressed simply in T-shirts and flip-flops. They assembled happily as Timothy arrived looking resplendent in his *Barong Tagalog*. Nervously he turned and looked at the gathering crowd, smiling with relief at Lucy who sat in a front pew, feeling overdressed in her mint-green silk suit. Corky and Rosa, official sponsors, formally walked up the aisle to join Timothy.

Angelika arrived, dressed in a simple *mestiza* in a *piña* fabric, hand-woven from pineapple leaves in natural ivory. On this day, she too, looked lovely, escorted solemnly by Ricardo, dressed in his transparent *jusi*. Harold, smiling broadly, escorted Perpetua, the maid of honour. She lowered her eyes discreetly and held tightly to Harold's arm. Torre and Joey, their hair slick and gleaming, came bearing the rings and *arrhae,* thirteen coins. Three serious little girls followed, marching slowly with great dignity, in simple dresses with butterfly sleeves. First Gigi, followed by her sisters, Mandy and Rose.

Lucinda craned her neck to see Esmirada's entrance. Timothy turned to look. His eyes suddenly filled as she appeared. The congregation audibly sucked in their breath; Esmirada was ethereal in her *mestiza* gown of white braided lace. Her luxurious hair was simply pulled back in a high bun set with a garland of small seeded pearls. At her throat, and accentuating the neckline of her dress, were more pearls. She walked serenely beside a broadly grinning Manny, handsome in his *barong*, his hair oiled and glistening. As she reached Timothy's side, he took her hand. She tightly clasped *Lola's* family rosary, the only heirloom they had, to her breast and kept her eyes lowered, which was the custom. Timothy could feel the warmth of her body, and feel the slight tremor that passed from her feet to the top of her sleek head as they knelt before the altar.

Corky dutifully lit the candles either side of the bride and groom. The flame from the candle, the icon of God's presence within the union, flared up brightly and burnt steadily as the ceremony progressed.

Rosa and Corky draped and pinned a long white tulle veil onto Timothy's shoulders and over Esmirada's head, as a symbolic union of two clothed as one. They then wound a rope in a figure of eight about them in the infinite bond of marriage. A joyful recessional played with great gusto suddenly resounded from the back of the church. Timothy and Esmirada were now man and wife. Olina held tightly to Manny and wiped away a single tear, *Lola* grinned toothlessly, as the congregation erupted, gleefully throwing handfuls of rice, a symbol of fertility as the newlyweds fled to Manny's flower bedecked jeepney.

Without a full Mass, the wedding ceremony was over within an hour. Lucy stood in the corner, feeling conspicuous, as the relatives, looking shyly at their feet, shuffled about. Joe broke the uncomfortable silence, introducing the *gwailo* to Esmirada's family before they all piled into various forms of transport to follow the happy couple to the reception. Jeepneys, borrowed bicycles and a horse and cart formed a ragged and noisy procession through the streets of the slums. The barrio came out to watch, the old men grinned with black teeth, swigging *tuba*, while the children ran after them, shouting until they reached the outskirts of the city.

Lucinda, her head thrown back to try and catch the breeze, watched as the corrugated iron and plywood gave way to open fields and palms. In the distance, silhouetted against the hazy blue of the mountains, she saw a large clearing with a simple open-air pavilion, surrounded by rough wooden benches. The wedding party dismounted and Manny ran to assist Lucy over the dry and rocky ground. She stumbled and at least four young men came to her assistance.

The barn was open on all sides and decorated with colourful paper chains. Lucy had not seen such simple decorations since her school days. Yellow orchids and red ginger grew wildly about the edges of the field, a small cement and iron-roofed structure stood in the distance, where Lucy could see a group of women in a frenzied preparation of food. The path leading from the makeshift kitchen to the reception area was lined with candles in brown paper bags. Timothy and his bride sat on a raised platform towards the end of the room.

Lucy and Joe joined the queue to offer their congratulations to the newlyweds. Manny ceremonially ushered them to the front. Esmirada threw her small brown hands into the air and covered her mouth when she saw Lucinda. Delicately she lifted the hem of her dress and scampered from the platform to fold Lucy into her lacy arms.

"Ma'am, you came! I am so honoured to have you at my wedding." Suddenly shy, she stood back from Lucinda, smoothing the lines of her gown with her small hands. "How are the little ones? I've missed you all so much!"

A glass of Californian wine that Timothy had ordered especially for the reception was shoved into Lucy's sweating hand and she gulped it gratefully, calming her nerves. Joe pumped Timothy's hand enthusiastically and chastely kissed the hand of Esmirada. Timothy motioned for them to sit beside them as they were introduced to an overwhelming array of relatives and neighbours. The aunties and uncles got confused and thought Lucy and Joe were husband and wife. Their names were odd to Lucinda's ears and she knew she would never remember them. She drank a second glass of wine and settled back onto the rough wooden bench, finally relaxing.

Joe was a good conversationalist and had led an interesting life. He told her all about Esme and Timothy's visionary plans for the people of the dumpsite. Dusk fell and a timid breeze stirred the scent of the ginger flowers and the tantalising aroma of roasted pork. A long table was set with proper plates and cutlery under the light-festooned trees. Timothy led his bride to sit at its centre with *Lola*, Manny, Lucy, Joe, Harold and Joyner, to one side. Olina, Corky, Rosa, Ricardo, Angelika and Perpetua on the other. The rest of the guests found their places amongst the wooden benches with plastic flat ware and paper plates perched on their knees. The local wine that Manny's friends had brewed in the barrio for the reception fuelled Timothy. At first it threatened to blow his head off. Made from strawberries, ginger and coconut, it had the consistency of molasses. After the second glass, it tasted less like kerosene and more like sweet rum.

A snaking line of Filipina's, bearing platters of food, formed in the yellow light of the kitchen and made their way along the candle-lit path into the centre of the hall. The old table groaned under its weight of delicacies. In the centre they placed the glistening roasted pig with baleful eyes glaring at the ravenous crowd. Surrounding the pork were plates of *lumpia*, Filipino egg rolls, *Pancit Canton*, sweet and sour *lapu-lapu* fillet, boiled rice, tossed salad, fruit, and a three-tiered coconut cream wedding cake!

Manny and Joey brought out more tubs of local wine, this time made with sugarcane and rice. Corky set up Ricardo's karaoke in the far corner and the guests continued to feast, dance and drink with traditional folk songs playing in the background. The moon came out from behind the clouds as Esmirada was led to the centre of the hall. Lucy watched in fascination as the men, one by one, asked for the privilege of a dance by pinning money to her dress. She watched the expression on Timothy's face. He glowed with pride and happiness as his bride delicately spun about the humble surroundings. Although she could understand little of what was said to her, Lucy felt the gratitude and acceptance of these gracious, fun-loving people of the Philippines. She danced with Timothy, pinning money to his *barong* and sat with Joe in the moonlight, listening and watching the folk dances late into the night.

The women never stopped working. By three in the morning the final clearing and cleaning was completed and the newlyweds left amidst tears, laughter and promises. Lucy watched the sad, gentle look pass between Esmirada and her grandmother. The old woman kept her dignity until the moment Esmirada disappeared from view in Manny's jeepney, then her wizened old face cracked and she slumped into the arms of her daughter.

Timothy had little time with his bride during the reception; she was in constant demand and, as always, was obliging. He kissed her briefly, breathing in the delicious scent of her warm body, and smiled from the corner of his eye each time she passed. When his arm or leg came in contact during the feasting, he felt a physical shock running through his veins, fuelling his desire for her.

Esmirada watched Timothy with great pride; he was wonderful with all her family and friends. She felt such a generosity fill her heart each time they touched. He tried so hard to please her and everyone else. He laughed, joked, and ate heartily, and she thanked God for the gift of this precious man. This was the happiest day of her life; the only sorrow she felt was leaving *Lola*. During the reception they had little time to exchange words, but when she was about to leave, the small woman gripped Esme and held tightly as though she would not let her go. She looked into her tired face and saw how clouded her eyes had become.

"*Kabang mikakalaman ya ing pale, duruku ya!*" As the rice stalk is being filled, it bows down! *Lola* reached up and smoothed Esmirada's lovely face with her coarse hand. "Stay as humble as the rice stalk, my little one."

The dry rumble of thunder competed with the wheeze of the air-conditioner as Timothy peeled back the crisp sheets and waited. His chest hurt with great happiness, each breath laboured with anticipation and passion. Esmirada stood in the faltering light of the bathroom. She wore a long, loose gown and her hair fell in abundant waves down her back as she came to him. With tightly closed eyes she kissed him, her mouth open and eager. She took him by surprise as curiously she explored with her tongue. He felt his blood draw back as he deftly removed her gown and looked for the first time at the amber skin of her naked body. He gently kissed her bare throat as his hands discovered the weight of her breasts and the soft skin beneath them.

He had expected tears and shyness but found instead a squirming, laughing Filipina in his bed, her eyes the colour of burnt toffee in the moonlight. She delighted him as she blossomed and opened to his touch, rising above him in a burst of fragrance from her loose hair as it cascaded over her shoulders and breasts.

Exhausted, they lay in the narrow bed, their bodies cupping one another. They both slept briefly, she holding his hand. He woke in the early hours of the morning and looked into the glassy darkness of her eyes. He whispered in low tones how he remembered the first day, and the first moment of their meeting. Esmirada lay pillowed on his arm, their feet touching. All night she held his hand as lazily the hours crept toward morning. Slowly she lifted the damp sheet to look at his body, the pattern of his body hair, the puckered nipples, his white arms and belly, her hands gently testing each surface until he smiled and she took the weight of his body on her once again.

Timothy and his bride disappeared to an island hideaway for their honeymoon. He needed to be free of the relatives, neighbours and friends that had filled every hour of their day leading up to the wedding. It was the first time since meeting her that they had really been alone. It was a long and arduous journey, but by the time they boarded the bamboo outrigger and passed the brooding black limestone cliffs that led to the island, he was restored. They leant into one another, watching the eagle's circle overhead, and forgetting for a short time the wretched souls who inhabited the slums and dumpsites of Manila.

The island was tranquil, set on a long arc of white, sandy beach, surrounded by dense orange, peach and red hibiscus. Each *bahay kubo*, native hut, was built from *nipa* and, for privacy, was rustically set amongst lush vegetation. Esmirada ran like a child up the fine white sand with Timothy in pursuit, discovering a tray of fresh pomelo, bananas and mangoes set inside the doorway on the terracotta tiled floor.

At sun-up, a crowing rooster roused them. The island, run by a small French man and his Filipina wife, was without electricity. A generator supplied enough power to operate a refrigerator and lights for the open-air restaurant. At dusk a houseboy placed kerosene lamps on each veranda. The bathrooms had cold water only. The Frenchman's wife raised poultry in an enclosure on the far side of the island, and they grew their own fruit and vegetables, going once a week by *banca* to the nearest town to buy provisions.

Esme and Timothy breakfasted on their veranda on fruit and rice each morning. Timothy then discarded his clothes to swim naked in the clear azure blue of the lagoon. Esme wore her sarong but lost it discreetly once she was submerged. Each day Timothy taught his wife to swim. She thrashed about, almost drowning them both, laughing and screaming like a child. The lessons inevitably ended in an energetic session of lovemaking beneath the lush palm trees. In the afternoon they slept or explored the more remote areas of the island, coming upon turtles, wild pigs and eagles' nests, while at the same time discovering each other.

They dined on simple meals by the glow of bamboo torches, and each night he would leave her a message on her pillow scrawled on palm leaves, telling her how much he loved her.

Esmirada listened with pleasure when Timothy engaged the owner in a conversation in French. She sat with his wife and watched her three brown babies romp naked in the shallows of the lagoon. Instead of joining in the traditional folk songs and dances performed by a nearby village, they would go back to their hut and sit in the dying light, talking in soft voices about their future.

"Do you want to go back to Singapore and continue with the shelter, or do you feel we would be more useful staying in the Philippines?"

Esmirada found it hard to think of her work in such an idyllic setting. Swimming naked in the blue lagoon each day with Timothy had washed all memories of the smell and wretchedness of the dump from her. Her cough had cleared and she'd gained weight.

"I feel so bad. I don't want to go back! Will God punish me for my selfishness?"

Timothy kissed her forehead. He noticed the change in his wife. She glowed with good health in these surroundings, and he was also reluctant to go back the pollution and filth. He sighed and looked up at the swaying palms, a full moon turning the lagoon to silver.

"Perhaps after all, Esme, we can do more good raising funds in Singapore. Angelika will carry on our work at the school. Mary is counting on us to take over the shelter. She's determined to devote her last remaining years to the church."

Satisfied, Esme bent her head to his shoulder. Timothy felt a spasm of guilt; he didn't mention that he wanted her to himself without the entire family. He intended to provide for all of them, but at a distance! He was sure God would allow him that much. After making love, they slept spooned together, lulled by the sound of waves and wind in the palm trees. By the time they left the island, she was already pregnant with his child.

Chapter Twenty-Eight
Memories of a Kiss

Lucy stepped in through the low cabin door and handed her boarding pass to a beautifully groomed hostess. She felt like she was home already. Thank God for luxury airlines. Leaving Manila airport was like leaving a zoo. She was shown to her seat, business class after being upgraded, and sat down, gratefully accepting a glass of champagne from the stewardess. She smiled at her companion, a young business-suited man. He too accepted a glass of champagne.

"What brings you to the Pearl of the Orient, business or pleasure?"

Lucy smiled and thought of the weekend, the wedding and the people. It had been simple but warm and full of spirituality. She remembered how radiant and lovely Esmirada had been as a bride. Adoration and pride had literally shone out of Timothy at the reception, leaving her with a warm residue of hope for her own situation. She turned to her travelling companion and admired his strong profile.

"All pleasure, how about you?"

He took a sip of his drink and set it down on the armrest between them. "Mostly business, but I managed to squeeze in a little pleasure as well!"

The conversation grew more familiar as they flew closer to Singapore. He told her about his job in the disposable paper industry. She talked about her painting, children and home in England, skirting briefly around her divorce and life in Singapore. By the time the aircraft had landed and come to a stop on the tarmac, they had exchanged phone numbers, promising to keep in touch. Lucy knew from experience it would be the last she would hear of him.

She searched the anxious faces on the other side of the window for Holly and Cameron and was disappointed not to see them. She retrieved her bag, her eyes following a Christmas tree wrapped in netting, as it went round the baggage belt. The airport was decorated in green and red with hanging stars and baubles. She made her way through the crowd, easily looking over the heads of the locals, and saw her travelling companion swept into the arms of a very attractive blonde. Discreetly, she looked the other way.

Brian rushed through the automatic doors, looking left and right, waving frantically.

"Sorry, love, just dropped the kids off at a party at McDonalds, I'm double parked!"

He grabbed her bag, manoeuvring her with his hand at the small of her back, through the doors into the thick, dripping heat of the late afternoon. He talked, she listened, as he drove through the heavy traffic, dodging motorbikes and pickup trucks.

"Amber's at home entertaining guests and preparing dinner."

Lucy knew that Alex would have arrived by now. Her heart raced at the thought of seeing him again. The lunchtime noodles lay heavy in her stomach.

Brian ducked his head, frantically looking for a car space, while Lucy walked up the drive to McDonalds. She threw open the doors and embraced the cool air. 'Jingle Bells' greeted her from the loudspeakers and the pimply young counter staff were all dressed in flashing Santa hats. Lucy looked through the glass windows of the party room and could see children deliriously stuffing their faces with cake. Others ran wild, bouncing off walls and dripping with sweat, their thin hair plastered to their heads. Holly saw her and flattened her small nose against the window.

"Uh oh, looks like we're in for a night of upset tummies and sugar highs," said Brian.

Too much of a coward to brave the mob inside, he knocked on the window, beckoning to the children. Holly, Cameron and Andrea left reluctantly. Brian had to go in a second time and drag Tom out, screaming and kicking. By the time they arrived back at Bukit Lalang, the streetlights were illuminated, and the children were dozing listlessly in the back seat. It gave Lucy time to compose herself, wishing it were light enough to reapply her lipstick.

They drove up the tree-lined drive and a welcoming light spilled out of the shuttered windows. She could hear the theme to 'Out of Africa' playing in the background. A six-foot high spangled Christmas tree stood just inside the entrance and fairy lights dripped from the trees outside, down the lawn to the pool and cabana beyond.

Amber and her guests sat at the bar in the fading light. When she saw the car headlights she put down her drink and ran up the lawn to meet them. She gave Brian a quick peck on the cheek and took Lucy by the shoulders, shooing the complaining children inside with Honeyko for a bath.

"Alex is just wonderful, he's an absolute doll! Why did you wait so long? Quick, go and change and come for a drink, I want you to meet my sister and her husband. Try not to make too much noise, we finally got the baby off to sleep." Amber rolled her lovely green eyes and hurried back down the lawn to the waiting party.

Lucy showered and changed into a cool linen shift. She brushed out her hair, longer now than when she had last seen Alex. Since her divorce she made more frequent trips to the hairdressers, the grey hair an unwanted legacy. She studied herself in the full-length mirror. She was pale and thinner than she had ever been, but her eyes still shone with vitality. A vitality that she didn't always feel! Quickly she applied blush and a slick coat of crimson lipstick.

His back was to her as she approached; it was broader than she remembered. He wore a loud Hawaiian shirt. His hair was slicked back in his usual ponytail and she noticed more grey at the temples. He turned, his eyes flashing as she came into the light of the cabana. He held out his arms and she calmly folded herself into them. Holding her close, she could smell the familiar clean scent of his body. Lucy stood back from him and he studied her in the light of the bamboo flair.

"It's so good to see you again! You look wonderful, thinner, but just as lovely as ever." He kissed her cheek and offered her a seat at the bar.

Sensing eyes upon her, she turned and with shaking hands was introduced to Amber's younger sister Lou, and her husband Wills. Lou was a smaller, less vivacious and less attractive version of her sister. Wills was tall and extremely serious, with dark-rimmed glasses and closely cropped hair. He was a genetic scientist and they lived in the Middle East with baby Tyrone, who was six months old. Wills asked her what she would like to drink, and she answered in a tremulous voice, knowing Alex was watching her closely.

Finally she turned to him and gave him her full attention while Amber fussed over the seating arrangements for dinner.

"It seems so long ago since Noosa. I've been reading good things about your paintings and I hear you have an exhibition this week!" She felt weak in the legs when he smiled at her. Wills had been heavy handed with the gin. It was going straight to her head! She faltered slightly on the decking as he took her by the elbow, steering her into dinner.

◆◆◆◆◆◆

Lucy hovered by Alex's side during the exhibition; the lofty ceilings and sombre grey slate of the walls of the High Commission had been transformed. The intense colour, light and lucidity of Alex's landscapes, and the bold shapes and form of his seascapes caught the attention of many local and overseas buyers. On the far wall above a raised stone platform used for two-up on Anzac Day, was another version of the pastel Alex had given to Lucy. Holly and Cameron were easily recognised as they played along the shoreline. She preferred the original, but this too was a magnificent work. The vast hall was full of interested buyers and critics; they drank huge quantities of champagne and greedily scoffed canapés. Their voices and laughter rose to the iron support beams, getting louder and more boisterous as the evening wore on.

Alex motioned for her hand as he conversed with potential buyers and reporters from various art publications. She was happy to make small talk, feeling the warmth of his body so close to hers as she calmly watched him network, winning his admirers over with his easy manner and sense of humour.

The evening before they had sat until dawn discussing the time spent apart: the hurt and pain she had suffered with her divorce, and her subsequent fleeing to England; the struggle to make a decent life for herself and the children; Inke's death and the undelivered letter. He kissed her, at first tenderly, and then with an urgency that surprised them both. Reluctantly they pulled apart when Honeyko discovered them cleaving to one another on the patio, as she opened up the house for the day.

She left his side to briefly chat to Amber and her sister. Amber raised her eyebrows menacingly and Lucy turned to see Hallam and Elvira enter. Lucy's stomach lurched and she felt her nerves tighten. Subconsciously she scratched at the backs of her hands. Elvira was obviously pregnant, but without the bovine, bloated appearance of her own pregnancies. Her brown arms and legs were still slender. She wore a full black dress, short and cut low, displaying her ripening breasts.

Hallam strode toward the pastel of the children, leaving Elvira speaking animatedly to a Chinese woman. He studied it briefly and then bounded down the platform to greet Alex. She watched as they shook hands. Hallam looked well, slim and tanned, his hair long at the back and cut on top in a stylish manner. Alex's assistant approached the pastel and firmly placed a red sticker next to it. It irritated Lucy that Hallam now had her painting's twin. She stood her ground and waited. Finally he turned and in three long strides was at her side, kissing her cold cheeks and greeting her as a long lost friend.

"Amber told me you were coming. I'm sorry about the change of plans with the children. I'm anxious to see them!" He looked away sheepishly and swiped a glass of champangne from a passing waiter, ignoring her empty glass. "It seems I can have them after all!" He turned to locate Elvira and saw she was deep in conversation with a group of locals. He lowered his voice and studied his drink. "Things are not going too well at the moment. The lack of a marriage certificate is causing some concern with her family." He still did not meet Lucy's eyes.

"Why haven't you married? I thought when she announced her pregnancy you would have gone off to Bali or somewhere."

Finally he looked at her. "Oh, we discussed it *ad nauseam,* but we had quite a bit of interference from her people. At the moment I am fed up to the teeth with the whole idea of marriage! You know, you are looking really well, Luce." She felt herself colouring and glanced across at Elvira. Some of her hatred dissipated and she actually felt sorry for the woman. "Anyway the latest plan is, Elvira is going home to Goa tomorrow. Can I have the children for a few days over Christmas before you go back to London? I won't upset Amber's plans. She has already threatened me with castration if I mess up or interfere in any way!"

Lucy laughed and saw Alex look in her direction his eyebrows raised. "I can't see any reason why not, I'll bring them over on Christmas night. They'll be thrilled. They are already starting to argue with Tom and Andrea. It'll do them good to have some time apart. They are getting spoilt rotten being back in Singapore!" Looking up, she saw Elvira advancing rapidly toward them. "Must go, what time do you want them to come around?"

Without waiting for a reply, Lucy turned and headed in the direction of the loo to compose herself before joining Alex.

◆◆◆◆◆◆

From the amount of preparation, Christmas at Amber's was going to be more elaborate than ever. On Christmas Eve she and Amber did some last

235

minute shopping in Orchard Road, amidst a throng of hot and tired tourists. As always the shopping malls were festively decorated with an assortment of tree lights, fake snow and moving parts. Late in the afternoon the heavens opened and they ran to a nearby bar for shelter. Amber caught the eye of the waiter and ordered two spritzers.

"Have you bought Alex anything yet?"

Lucy saw the look on Amber's face. She knew it well. She had been conspiring again.

"Not yet, I don't know what would be appropriate. I didn't want to buy anything too personal; I don't want to frighten him off. Since my chat with Hallam at the exhibit and his daily phone calls, Alex has backed off. Before that we were discussing the children and I moving back to Australia. Positive things were happening, passionate kisses and the tempting possibility of more to come. Hallam has managed to come between us!" She pushed her hair back from her face, and watched the rain in rivulets on the paned glass.

Amber drummed her long nails on the polished wood of the table. "He said as much, he's being cautious, he doesn't want to get hurt. He's very loyal and intense, you have to realise that Lucy! What is Hallam up to, do you think? Suddenly daily phone calls, and Elvira gone for months. You do know he called me yesterday to inveigle an invitation to Christmas dinner!"

"Oh, I'm sorry, Amber. I just didn't envisage any of these problems. I thought he was gone from my life for good!"

Amber flipped the straw from her glass into an ashtray. "He'll never be gone for good. Just because he was once a lover doesn't mean he can be a friend. Be careful, Lucy."

Later that afternoon, in frustration, Lucy bought Alex an antique set of jade instruments and a leather travel kit, avoiding anything too personal.

Amber organised a garden party on Christmas Eve catered for by the club. Tuppy and Major came; he disappeared halfway through, arriving back in a trishaw, dressed as Santa with gifts for the children. Then, all except Wills and baby Tyrone, they went to church for Midnight Mass. Alex held her hand during the service, and Holly claimed the other but Cameron she could see was confused.

On Christmas morning they sat around the pool drinking champagne and orange juice, while the children swam, waiting for the moment to come when they could open their gifts under the tree. Baby Tyrone gurgled happily in his bouncer in the shade of the cabana. With the smell of roasting turkey drifting from the kitchen, Alex and Lucy discussed their travel plans. He had wanted to travel with her and the children, but with Hallam's interference, it changed everything.

"I don't know if I can wait until next week. I need to get to London and meet with Sol and finalise my plans."

Lucy sipped her drink, watching the palms sway above her head. "I understand. You do what you have to. I can't disappoint Hallam or the kids. This is the first time they have seen him since we divorced."

Alex put his drink down hard on the table, slopping orange juice; abruptly he stood and started off toward the house. He called back over his shoulder to her, "You couldn't possibly think of disappointing Hallam. I can't imagine Hallam ever disappointing you! I'll go and see if Amber needs a hand."

A cloud passed, blotting out the sun and she suddenly felt very tired and depressed.

Brian played Father Christmas, handing out the gifts before they assembled at the long table for their Christmas feast. Alex had given Lucy a charm bracelet with twelve different little antique cats, her leitmotif! It was a lovely, carefully chosen and personal gift. He seemed pleased with her gift to him, but Lucy knew she could have made more of an effort to buy him something more meaningful. The situation had shifted between them, leaving her feeling helpless with disappointment.

The children, as usual, were swamped with toys. Despite Hallam not being invited, he made his presence felt by including a gift for both her and the children under the tree. She refused to open it in front of them, preferring the privacy of her room. Unfortunately Holly in her exuberance tore the paper from Lucy's gift by mistake, and held up a set of translucent, lacy underwear. Alex turned away and Amber's brow knitted in a disapproving frown.

"What a ridiculous gift for your ex-wife!" Brian blurted out.

He had had quite a few drinks and Amber dug him sharply in the ribs. Cameron came to Lucy's rescue.

"Mummy likes nice underwear, don't you?"

Lucy was embarrassed and wondered what Hallam's motives were. She pulled her son close, kissing the top of his head.

Christmas was too much for baby Tyrone who squalled throughout the afternoon. The children were fractious and fought over games and toys.

237

Lucy retreated to the kitchen to help Honeyko deal with the washing up. Alex, Brian and Wills tried to match each other schnapps for schnapps, followed by eating whole pickled herrings, a yearly tradition that excluded the women. Wills and Alex collapsed dead drunk in the cabana and Brian went to his room to sleep it off. Tyrone continued to scream all afternoon. Amber and Lou did all they could to comfort him without success. The four children were still argumentative and brittle by six, and Lucy was only too pleased to leave and take the children to their father's, promising Amber she would not stay long, she would be home for leftover turkey and ham by the pool.

Hallam and Elvira's apartment was on a shaded street in the centre of the island. The guard's house was festooned with fairy lights as they waved her through the boom gate. A foursome was playing tennis when they arrived and she could hear children in the nearby pool. The building had a central atrium open to the sky with a rocky waterfall that at intervals spumed water into the air.

Hallam greeted them at the large wood and brass door, which was decorated with a wreath of poinsettia. Plants and weathered statues from Bali stood guard over the tiled entrance. A huge balcony ran the length of the apartment, giving each room a spacious entertaining area. The balcony looked over a canopy of Rain trees and beyond to the islands of Malaysia. He led the children by the hand, showing them which rooms would be theirs for the next few days. A Norwegian Christmas tree stood in the corner, decorated entirely in white; more gifts lay under the tree. The décor was very Zen, all black, white and cream; Lucy could not see a baby being welcome here! She noticed the table beautifully set for four, a delicious aroma wafted from the kitchen. He smiled in the way that she remembered, the Hallam of old. She noticed there were no personal touches in the room, no photographs or anything individually out of place.

"Come and have a drink, Luce, I have some vintage champers on ice!"

She started to protest and then caught Cameron's anxious little face from the corner of her eye. "Well just the one, it is Christmas after all."

They sat on the balcony and Hallam ceremoniously poured the champagne. He offered her Russian caviar and blinis with sour cream and she couldn't resist. The children opened their gifts from beneath the tree, as though they were the first they had received that day. He ceremoniously presented her with a long green box. She was flustered, remembering the underwear. She wasn't sure what was going on. Amber's warning kept repeating in her brain. The champagne and caviar were delicious and she had more. The children were calm and relaxed, happy to be with their father. It was peaceful away from the boisterous atmosphere at Amber's. She had grown tired of the children's arguments, the baby's crying and the disappointment in Alex's eyes. She wondered if it had all been too much too soon. Hallam moved across the room in his bare feet to the stereo. He played her favourite Christmas music from past years discreetly in the background. He had thought of everything. The gifts for the children were obviously perfect. They were quietly absorbed in the family room. He urged her to open the mysterious box.

"Please, Lucy, go ahead. I bought them especially for you when I was in Japan last month."

She held up her hands in protest.

"I didn't think we would do gifts for each other. I have nothing for you."

He waved away the suggestion and poured her more champagne. His eyes were riveted on her and her palms began to sweat. The box sprung open, revealing a strand of luminous green baroque pearls. They were beautiful. He knew she had always lusted after pearls such as these. The gift was far too generous; once again she was confused by his motives and objected profusely. He took them from her.

"Look, I didn't mean to upset you. Let's put them aside. You can think about them later. If you don't want to accept them, I'll understand. They're meant to be a peace offering, nothing more. I've prepared a special dinner. Please stay and eat with us as a family for old time's sake. What harm can it possibly do to stay for supper?"

Cameron had overheard and came to plead with her. "Come on, Mummy, stay. You were only having leftovers at Amber's."

She looked at his little face and knew he couldn't possibly understand. Hallam, sensing all had been decided, went into the kitchen to check on the food.

"Stay, Mummy, please!"

She ruffled Cameron's hair and he came and kissed her on the cheek. Hallam returned, carrying a chilled bottle of wine.

"How was Christmas day? You haven't told me what I missed out on yet."

Cameron was walking about in his socks and sliding from foot to foot on the marble floor.

"It was okay. The food and presents were good, but Tom cheated at Uno and all the fathers got drunk!"

Hallam laughed and Lucy's face coloured. "Sounds like it was the usual Christmas at the Van Engles."

Lucy stayed for dinner and drank more wine. Hallam had prepared pork loin with apples, prunes and a mustard cream sauce and sautéed green beans, which the children didn't eat, and for desert a chocolate cream pie, which they did. Hallam's food, as always, was superb. She called Amber and told her not to wait dinner for her. Amber told her not to worry, the men were still out cold in the cabana, the baby was still crying, and she was going to bed!

After dinner they played a game of Monopoly and drank more wine. Hallam played his favourite music and danced around the room with Holly. Lucy, a little tipsy, danced with Cameron. At eleven the children fell asleep on the couch in the family room and Lucy helped Hallam put them to bed. She kissed them tenderly, realising she would be away from them for the next few days. They sat on the patio listening to the distant traffic. Hallam poured brandy and outlined his itinerary for the children. Lucy was impressed; he was trying very hard to please them. At twelve after another brandy, she knew he would have to call her a cab. There was no way she could drive. He agreed, but if she were to catch a cab, that would allow her one more nightcap and he fixed her his special Christmas Cocktail. Lucy knew this was his legendary leg opener! In the past, one of these and Lucy became insatiable, but she was a different person now. She was immune to all he had to offer: caviar, champagne, good food and wine; she was over him!

She drank the cocktail anyway and felt better for it. Unfortunately it loosened all the pent up rage, hurt and humiliation she had suffered at his hands! He went pale and seemed stunned as she blurted out all the indignities he had caused her. She told him in detail of her drunken binge that went on for days after he left. How, if it were not for Esmirada and the children, she probably would have taken her own life as Angel had done. The lonely nights in London, wondering what path to take next, the fear of starting over, the sleeplessness, hopelessness, anxiety, despair and blame. He had ruined her life; she would never be the same woman again. He had destroyed her trust and joy of living; he had taken away her future, all she had to look forward to was loneliness in her old age. She started to cry, holding her head in her hands.

She reached for the brandy and poured more, gulping it back, feeling it burn through her veins. Hallam sat white-faced, watching her, the debris of their meal, like their life, lying between them. Suddenly she was violently sick and rushed for his all-white bathroom. For the next half hour she clung to the toilet retching her soul down the drain. He came to her with a wet washcloth and helped her from the floor to the spare room. He put her gently onto the bed and removed her sandals. He brought her a bucket and wet towel and left her to sleep.

Alex called at eight the following morning.

"Alex, old boy, how are you? Seasons Greetings! Heard you tied one on yesterday. How are you feeling? I've felt the sting of Van Engle's schnapps before. Those bloody things are lethal!"

"I've got a shocking hangover, slept through until six this morning. I wondered if I could have a quick word with Lucy? I guess she stayed the night?"

"Hey, did she ever. Tied one on herself, just like old times, pretty big night for both of us. Sorry, old mate, she's still fast asleep. I'll tell her you called."

Alex dropped the phone, ending the call, and Hallam smugly went to the kitchen to prepare breakfast for the children.

Lucy didn't wake until midday. When she did she found the apartment empty. A note propped on the dining room table told her they had gone to the zoo and would not be back until supper. By the time she returned to Bukit Lalang Alex had left for London without leaving her even so much as a note. Amber walked about the house, picking up wrapping paper and sorting piles of gifts. A pale and nauseous Lucy followed in her wake.

"He must have said something. Did he leave details of where he's staying?"

Amber sat heavily on the sofa. "He told me he called you at Hallam's. Hallam told him you both had a big night, just like old times, I think his words were. You got drunk and were still asleep. After that he went upstairs, phoned the airlines, packed his bag and caught the midday flight to London. He was miserable! You're a bloody fool, Lucy. What in hell's name were you trying to prove? The best thing that has happened to you for a long time has just walked out the door because of your stupidity. I told you to be careful. Hallam's a snake!"

Lucy held her head in her hands. She was wretched. "The worst thing is, Hallam was right. It was like old times, me screaming abuse, getting drunk and throwing up in the toilet! He set me up, Amber. When will it ever end?"

A day later Hallam called, asking Lucy to come and pick up the children. Elvira had returned and decided they were too much to handle. He had found the pearls in the dining room and had assumed she didn't want them. He had given them to Elvira as a homecoming present!

◆◆◆◆◆◆

Lucy promised Amber she would stay until New Year's Eve, but her heart wasn't in it. She couldn't let her friend down; Amber had planned a special party for about eighty people. The theme was Bollywood Hollywood and the two had spent the week after Christmas combing the narrow lanes of Little India in search of costumes and traditional decorations. The fragrant aroma and bustling market place had taken her mind off Alex for a short time, as she and Amber haggled over garlands of jasmine, glass bracelets, bindii and tikis. She had found a lovely powder-blue sari and *lengka*, which she had altered to fit her tall frame. She felt sad that Alex wouldn't see her in it. Amber bought an emerald-green *Salwar Kameez* that matched the colour of her eyes.

The day before the party Lucy sat by the pool watching the children swim. The house swarmed with bare-chested men, erecting a silk-lined marquee for the event. They worked slowly and laboriously. It was still Ramadan, and as they were Muslim, they were fasting. Amber was not in the least sympathetic to their religious beliefs, and flitted about supervising and shouting orders.

On New Year's Eve, Lucy was in charge of the table settings and name cards. She and Amber had sat late into the evening deciding who would sit with whom. Lucy missed Alex and couldn't stop thinking about him. She had been such a fool with Hallam. She continually played out the scene in her tired brain, realising how badly she had handled everything. If only Alex would call, but as the days went by, she knew in her heart he wasn't going to.

Holly watched with great excitement as Lucy dressed in her sari. She sat swinging her legs on the bathroom vanity while Lucy applied kohl to her eyes, and deftly glued diamantes, following the curve of her eyebrows. She swept her dark hair onto her head and pinned the deep blue *tikka*, letting it fall into place on her forehead. Holly took her middle finger and carefully stuck the *bindi* between her eyes, and helped her with the large chandeliered earrings, necklace and bracelets. As she slipped her feet into her sandals, she stood back to admire the effect.

242

Holly clapped her hands together. "You look like an Indian princess, Mummy. You will be the most beautiful at the party!"

Lucy rushed downstairs to complete the table settings, while Amber, with the help of Honeyko, finished getting dressed. Brian greeted her with a namaste as she entered. He sensed her sadness.

"You look stunning! Come and I'll take a photograph. That colour suits you!"

She stood before the marquee feeling lonely, trying her best to smile convincingly as he snapped away. One of the waiters took a shot of them together. Brian was wearing a white embroidered *kurta* with a deep-blue silk scarf wound about his neck. On his head he had a turban hung with pearls and trimmed with gold. He too looked very handsome. She took a bag of rose petals and sprinkled them about the tables and entrance to the marquee. Holly and Cam pulled petals from yellow chrysanthemums and spread them about the walkway and garden. They lit the candles and bamboo torches and then placed the name cards on the tables. The finishing touch, a fragrant garland of jasmine as a centrepiece.

Amber looked magnificent in her emerald green; she had swept her bright hair into a high plait and decorated it with jewels. The three-piece band and sitar players arrived and Amber seated them on a raised platform beneath a tent she had brought back from Rhajastan. At the canopied entrance Indian dance music played out, while seated to the left was a lovely young Indian girl decorating her hands and feet with a tube of henna.

It was a magical night, balmy with no rain. As the guests arrived they were offered drinks and canapés. Everyone had dressed to theme; the marquee was a riot of colour, jewels and turbans. The noise intensified and Lucy was swept along with the euphoria of the evening. It was only at midnight when they kissed and sang Auld Lang Sine that she suddenly felt bereft, and perhaps the loneliest she had ever been.

◆ ◆ ◆ ◆ ◆ ◆

In the deserted London streets, snow began to fall in the late afternoon. At first heavy, it fell in deep drifts beside the curb, but by the time Alex had left his hotel it had turned to rain and slush. He wore a thick wool coat and cashmere scarf as he waited for a cab, pulling the collar close about his face. He watched as the rain turned once again to snow against the street lamp and thought of Lucy. He'd been invited to a New Year's Eve dinner at the Savoy with Sol and a group of friends. The exhibition was ready and

would start on the third of January; so far it had been well received in the arts publication, and quite a few of his favourite pieces had been pre-sold. He should have been happy, but all he felt was emptiness. Lucy wasn't over Hallam. She just wasn't ready. He'd been convinced of Hallam's scheming. He wouldn't put anything past him, but still she played into his hands willingly. He thought she would have been stronger; he was bitterly disappointed in her.

Christmas had been a disaster. Amber was a charming woman but acted like a cruise director, the house was like a zoo, constantly full of bloody people! He and Lucy had little time together. It had taken him two days to recover from the hangover, perhaps he had acted too hastily, but he wouldn't let Hallam make a fool of him! The children were really starting to warm to him, such a shame. Great little kids. Holly was a super child, fun, smart and the little chap was starting to get some confidence. He would have been proud to bring them up as his own. He sniffed in the cold air as he boarded the cab. All he could think of was how much he missed them all, that and Lucy's kisses.

◆◆◆◆◆◆

The sun rose high over Dubai, washing the clouds a salmon-pink as Singapore Airlines flew northwest on to London, carrying Lucy and the children home. Many miles southeast, flying in the opposite direction, a Qantas flight attendant was regaling Alex with the antics of his peers on New Year's Eve. Expertly he poured Alex another whisky and soda. Alex stretched out his long legs and pulled the window shade down, shielding his eyes from the blinding sun. It would be a long flight back home to Australia.

Chapter Twenty-Nine
Unsent Letters

Timothy carried a small Christmas tree home for the apartment in Singapore. After their honeymoon they had a brief farewell in Manila and a dinner for the whole family at Jollibee, all except *Lola,* whose failing eyesight had kept her in the village. Esmirada had bravely said goodbye to the old woman and left the barrio dry eyed. The rest of the family escorted them to the airport to see them off.

Timothy was secretly pleased to be back! The new apartment was spacious and breezy, high on the tenth floor overlooking the bustling streets of Emerald Hill. They placed the tree in the living room and went to Blanco Court to buy decorations. On Christmas day two small, carefully chosen gifts were placed under the tree. The couple were blissfully happy and welcomed back to the church by a joyful congregation. New Year's Eve was celebrated with Harold and Joyner, a simple dinner that Esmirada and Timothy prepared together.

On New Year's Day Lucy came with the children to visit their beloved *amah*, and to say goodbye as they were leaving soon for England. The children brought handmade gifts for Esme and Timothy, and he took them all to lunch in Emerald Hill.

On the second of January Timothy went back to school and Esme went to work at the shelter, now as a teacher as well as a counsellor, passing on the skills she had learnt at the Serenity Centre. Mary retired and Timothy converted the bungalow in the Serenity Centre, taking over the maze of servants' quarters to house the shelter. Although the status of maids had improved, there was still the occasional runaway and inevitable reports of cruelty.

Esme and Timothy continued working each Sunday at the church, and one month after their marriage Esmirada's work permit was granted, and Timothy applied for permanent residency. It was only then that Esmirada noticed her increase in appetite and the absence of her monthly period. She hugged the secret to her, waiting and wanting to make sure before she shared it with Timothy.

♦ ♦ ♦ ♦ ♦ ♦

The laughing Budda was the only one to welcome them home. Laura and Hamish were away in the south of France, and Sebastian had left for an extended holiday in Geneva. It was the bleakest January Lucinda could remember. They were severely jet-lagged; waking at three in the morning, they sat in Lucy's bed watching unsuitable television programs, trying to resume their former sleeping pattern. Holly and Cameron balked at rugging up after the freedom of running barefoot each day in Singapore. They were plump and brown from their holiday and miserable at the thought of going back to school. Each day it was dark at four and the sun, if it did shine, did so for only a few short hours. It was a chore to go to High Street each day to open the antique shop. The temporary manager brightened when Lucy arrived, handing over the keys and books and happily scurrying off for a week in Spain. Each day she stared into the deserted street with its wet and shining black road, and thought longingly of the gardens and palm trees of Singapore. When she really wanted to torment herself she visualised Alex in his studio, with the clear light of an Australian summer slanting across the floor, as he happily painted in the nude.

Business was slow after Christmas, so she spent time cataloguing, dusting and painting, completing commissions that she had taken on in Singapore and starting on a new series of tropical scenes for greeting cards. The children fell back into their routine of after-school activities, with ballet and music lessons starting once again. For something new, Cameron took up judo while Holly joined the gymnastics class. Laura and Hamish returned with more artefacts for the already burgeoned shop. She was once again invited to long lunches in their conservatorium, with a fresh batch of men for her to look over.

By Easter she had given up hearing from Alex. She had written scores of letters, only to put them in her bottom drawer, unsent. She went on a few dates but most of them were disastrous, or else ended in a frenetic unsatisfying grope on the living room sofa. Hamish and Laura were fast losing their patience and sympathy for her, but continued to bring in new blood each Sunday lunch.

Just after Easter she received a short note from Timothy and Esmirada, telling her of their blessed joy. They were expecting a baby in late August! She wrote back immediately with her congratulations. The children made cards for them one bitterly cold Sunday and she included them with her own. Amber called that evening to tell her that Elvira had given birth to a daughter in Goa. Hallam had visited briefly and then returned to Singapore, leaving Elvira and the baby with her mother in India. She waited for Hallam's call to tell her personally of the good news, but it never came. That miserable spring all that kept her going was the children, her art and Laura and Hamish.

♦ ♦ ♦ ♦ ♦ ♦

Rita met Alex at the airport and insisted on driving him the one-and-half hours home. Alex was buggered. He'd flown business class, but still the long flight had left him exhausted. He had a stopover in Singapore and was tempted to call Amber but in the end he went to the bar instead, and downed two stiff whisky and sodas. Rita practically jumped into his arms when he appeared, unshaved and stale smelling, through customs. She couldn't wait to tell him of the publicity his exhibits had generated, and the fact that he had been short-listed for three coveted art prizes. All Alex wanted to do was to get home and to bed, but not with Rita!

His old house in the rain forest was as he had left it; he entered the cool interior to find a stack of mail and a full refrigerator, courtesy of Rita. He ate and slept for twelve hours before resurfacing. The long days in the hinterland were much the same as Singapore, hot and humid. Slowly he got his head together and sorted out his coming commitments.

Padding through to the living room, he sat sadly at the piano. He opened it and pressed one sombre note, before closing it again. The basketball ring in the lower garden was also a mocking reminder of what hadn't eventuated. He'd been a fool. He would leave the piano and basketball ring there awhile, as a reminder of what he could have had with Lucy.

He went to the studio and opened it up; the dust motes flew about in the early morning light as he adjusted his materials. He wanted to start painting again; it was the only therapy he knew. His work had saved him after Inke's death and would be his salvation once more. His career was at its peak and he didn't intend to let it slide.

His next-door neighbour had been robbed while he was away, and after a week Alex realised Joanna had not been to visit. One morning when he came in from his bike ride, he noticed a stench from behind the lily pond and found her. She had been dead for a few days, bloated and covered in ants. He felt ridiculous wiping a tear from his eye, as he gently gathered up her body with a shovel for burial.

He continued to feel sorry for himself for another week, and didn't pick up a brush during that time. Nicky came round and bullied him out of the house for dinner at her favourite Thai restaurant. She was good for him and insisted he come back to Pilates the following day. It was all he needed to get himself going again.

A long Indian summer lasted well past Easter and Alex was painting furiously. He had a stack of commissions both public and private and he was playing tennis twice a week with a mixed group. A couple of the ladies had great possibility; their tennis was pretty good as well! Rita and he finally had an unsuccessful coupling, which left them both self-conscious but still good friends. They decided that the relationship would be better off on a professional level only. That part of his life at least was a great success. In June, summer finally came to an end, and Alex was awarded the major Sulman Art Prize. This boosted his professional profile and he was once more painting for an exhibition to be shown in Sydney in August.

He had composed numerous letters to Lucy both in his head and on paper but in the end none were posted.

He embarked on a sexually exhausting affair with Dorté, his Melbourne art director and burnt up his air miles flying to and from Melbourne. It was satisfying for both of them. His paintings were selling better than ever in that part of the country. He had grown used to seeing the piano in the corner. Dorté was somewhat of an entertainer and would spend hours after dinner playing Gershwin for him. He even shot the odd basket on his way out the back gate, when he went cycling on warm winter days around the beaches and waterways of the Sunshine Coast. Gradually the basketball ring and piano had become a part of his life.

Chapter Thirty
A Small Victory

Esmirada panted and strained with every fibre in her body, but still the baby did not come. Timothy, pale and haggard, sat at her side, praying for a safe delivery. Every now and then he wiped his wife's damp brow. She made no sound and had not complained once throughout the long labour.

Esmirada had glowed with good health and contentment during her pregnancy; she and Timothy walked each evening through the leafy streets of Singapore. As she grew larger with his child, the doctor had warned them a caesarean might be necessary. Together they had grown stouter each month, she with the baby and he with her cooking. In her seventh month Timothy made a wooden cradle, and they decorated the third bedroom in shades of green.

The midwife came and shooed Timothy away. She roughly examined Esme and tut-tutted under her breath.

"Baby too big for you, look what happens when Asian girl marries *Ang moh!*"

The nurse left her to prepare for surgery, saying nothing to Timothy as she passed him anxiously waiting in the corridor.

Left alone, Esmirada whimpered with each contraction. She had prayed to God repeatedly, but now the pain was too much of a distraction to concentrate on prayer. Timothy was comforting but she wished *Lola* were by her side. The old woman would know the right words to say to help her. *Lola* had wanted Esmirada to come home for the birth, but Timothy had insisted on a normal birth in a modern hospital with him in attendance. *Lola* and Olina were horrified; it would bring bad luck for the infant, already an easy target for the spirits. Next to her bed Esmirada kept the small pouch they had sent, filled with seeds, garlic, ginger and charcoal. They believed this would protect the baby from the evil work of the spirits, but Esme knew in her heart the only person who could protect her baby was Jesus!

249

A diminutive Chinese doctor breezed in and carried out a rudimentary examination.

She came to Timothy. "We are going to take her into surgery. The baby is large; she won't be able to deliver it naturally. Nothing to worry about, in fact it's better this way. The baby will be perfect, no marks, not like you get with a normal birth!"

She patted Timothy's hand and handed him her pen, instructing him to sign the forms and sit and wait. He felt powerless. All he could do to help was to continue praying. He stood as they wheeled Esme by and he took her cold hand in his. Her honey-coloured skin had turned chalky and she whimpered like a small dog.

Expectant fathers came and went. No one spoke, he felt alone. After what seemed like hours, the doctor returned. She took Timothy's hand limply and held it briefly.

"Congratulations, you are the father of a big, healthy girl."

She dismissed him abruptly, looking briefly over a chart that was proffered by the nurse. Her pager began buzzing and she turned her attention to other matters, leaving Timothy standing open-mouthed with shock.

Timidly he entered the dimly lit room. Esme looked so small lying on the gurney, covered in a thick cotton blanket. She was attached to an intravenous drip that ran continuously into the vein of her hand. He sat at the head of the bed close to her face, listening to her ragged breath. A nurse bustled in throwing open the blinds noisily, flooding the room with bright sunshine. Before her she steered a clear perspex crib. Inside was a tightly wrapped pink bundle. She settled the crib under the window next to Timothy. All he could see was a dark plume of soft black hair.

"Here she is, big strong girl just like her father!"

The nurse chuckled as Timothy stood cautiously and looked into the face of his daughter. He could feel the chambers of his heart open and fill with joy and gratitude as he studied her perfect features.

Timothy felt he had won a small victory. He had prayed for a daughter. The arguments over circumcision or *pagtutuli,* as it was known in the Philippines, had started with Manny as soon as Esme had announced her pregnancy. Timothy was unfortunate to have been present when the custom was carried out on little Carlo. It was a barbaric practice! The child was forced to sit astride a banana log and then a *manunuli* made an incision without removing any tissue, a traditional flower circumcision. Manny claimed it was a right of passage to manhood, and would allow the child to

250

grow taller! Timothy was of the impression that very little changed about these children's lives afterwards. He'd also seen the zinc-roofed medical clinics about town, advertising in bold red lettering: 'Circumcision, *Tuli* done here'.

The thought had haunted him throughout Esme's pregnancy, he had prayed to God he would be strong enough to go against their beliefs and traditions, but God had set him free and given him the gift of a daughter, who at all costs must be spared the life of superstition and fear.

Esmirada was a model patient, never asking for anything more than what she was entitled to. She had never been in a hospital before and was overwhelmed with the care she was given. She didn't complain and recovered quickly. She sat in bed breast-feeding her daughter who was propped on a pillow, listening to the whingeing and whining of the other patients, trundling heavily about the ward. From the corner of her eye she would glance at the other newborns. They looked like pink-skinned rabbits next to her baby. After four days she left to go home with Timothy, the baby as yet still unnamed.

The apartment was full of flowers from the church, Harold and Joyner and Timothy's class at school. On the day she returned home a huge bunch of roses arrived from Lucinda, Holly and Cameron.

Timothy had left the hospital on the night of the birth in a euphoric state. He had wanted to shout in the streets that he had a daughter, but instead he was pushed and shoved and pummelled as he tried to board the M.R.T. to go home to the empty apartment. With a permanent grin on his face and looking slightly simple, he made his way to Kentucky Fried Chicken and bought dinner. He had not eaten all day and was suddenly ravenous. Once back home he poured a stiff scotch and phoned everyone he knew to impart the good news!

On the second day after the birth, he had gone to the flower market and bought a large bunch of orchids. He made his way downtown on the crowded bus and stopped at the jeweller's where he purchased an eternity ring for his wife, and a gold charm bracelet for his daughter. Bearing his gifts, he made his way back to the hospital to see his family. He found Esmirada sitting in bed, radiant. The colour had returned to her cheeks and her hair shone in the sunlight that poured in through the glazed windows. Together they carefully unwrapped their child as though she were a precious gift, examining her from head to toe.

Timothy, with tears in his eyes, kissed Esme. "She's the most exquisite thing I have ever seen, angelic and as lovely as you! Thank you for making our life complete."

Esme gazed in wonder at her daughter. Because of her size - she weighed nine pounds at birth - and her extraordinary skin tone, the baby was the object of great curiosity within the hospital. Other mothers, fathers, staff and visitors would stop by the crib and gawk, making comments such as "*Alamak! So big lah*! This upset Esme. Timothy was pleased when she was finally able to come home.

The morning Timothy brought his wife and daughter back to their apartment the island was battered by wind and rain. Esme wrapped the baby in a thick white towel as they entered the taxi. Timothy tried to protect them both from the mercurial drops, and suddenly felt overwhelmed with responsibility. He prayed under his breath to God for strength and guidance.

◆◆◆◆◆◆

It was early morning; Lucy sat in her courtyard in a threadbare chenille dressing gown. The sun came slowly from behind the clouds and burnt off the dampness. Her feet, bare and cold, were propped on the chair opposite. She glanced at the paper. Splashed across the front page were the gory details of a recent serial killing. The house was quiet. The children were both staying with friends, and she had a blissful weekend of painting ahead. Timothy's call had come late last night. His deep broad accent had burst down the line with news of the birth of his and Esmirada's daughter. She would send flowers on Monday. She sipped her scalding coffee and thought in a slightly envious way of the odd couple back in Singapore, and how happy they must be at this moment. She brushed a shower of moisture from her hand as she picked a cobalt-blue hydrangea, planning to do a simple still life after breakfast.

Summer was already coming to a close; they'd had a short jubilant burst of glorious weather after a long, bitterly cold winter and spring. She longed for the endless sun of her own country or the balmy nights of Singapore. She wasn't sure how many more winters she could endure in England. The summer holidays had been long and tedious and the inclement weather didn't help. The children spent their days helping her in the shop, playing on the new computer or staying with friends. Cameron went camping in Cornwall but they were washed out on the first night. Holly went on a horse riding camp in Ireland and came back with a heavy cold and tonsillitis. The weekend before last, it rained continuously. They were all bad tempered and argumentative and she couldn't stand it any longer. Impulsively she booked them on a flight to Madrid for a long weekend of sunshine, food and culture.

They checked in to a rather fancy pastel hotel, with soft buttery walls just off the Plaza Mayor surrounded by outdoor cafes and bars. Lucy and Hallam had been to Madrid many years ago, but that was a very different holiday to what she and the children had planned. Fondly she remembered long afternoons eating ham in sardine-packed tapas bars, drinking cognac and smoking cigars at four in the afternoon, and talking, talking, talking! Throughout the holiday she and Hallam averaged about five hours sleep, and then at midnight, after a delicious bout of lovemaking, they would eat at one of the outdoor restaurants, and then crawl from one bar to the next, only stopping when the sun came up. Late at night they milled with the crowd at marble topped tables, dipping churrios into cups of dark rich chocolate.

The service at the pastel hotel was breezy. Their first meal was fried aubergine and fish. Cameron was eager to eat. He had grown plump over the winter, and she was a little concerned about his fascination with food. Holly, as usual, ate like a bird, distracted by the oily waiters and the out-of-place, themed music. Their room was smallish but had a lovely view looking across the Royal Palace.

The first day was scorching. Lucy could feel her bones thawing, and they eagerly set off for the Museo del Prado. The Art Museum was crowded with locals and tourists all flocking to Goya and Rubens. They stopped briefly and then ventured through the vast rooms to view other works. It was a feast for Lucy's jaded eyes and she gorged herself for the better part of the day, ignoring Cameron's pleas for an early lunch. Later they walked to the crowded Plaza De Mayor and took a table under a blinding-white awning. Platters of deep fried baby squid and prawns with potato tortilla arrived. They sat in the drowsy heat eating the delicious food, watching groups promenading, gathering at the slightest excuse to stop, talk, eat and drink. Lucy ordered a plate of empanada pastries for the children and drank her Sangria, feeling slightly sad at the sight of couples strolling arm in arm.

Late on Sunday afternoon an incident took place that left them shaken. Lucy had taken them to see the gardens of the Royal Palace and then they walked back along the narrow streets and jam-packed bars to the Plaza De Mayor to listen to the street performers. Along the way two bedraggled woman approached, one young with a sad face, the other older and heavily lined. They both gave off a sour, unwashed smell; she knew they were begging gypsies.

After living in Asia, Lucy made it a practice not to give to beggars. She held up her hands to them to say no, briefly letting go of the children. The older woman spat at her feet and gave her a heinous stare. They walked swiftly on and she could see in the plate glass of the window that the gypsies were following closely. She pushed the children before her and tried to enter a packed tapas bar. As she did so, the women jumped on her back, riding her like some carnival animal. The children stood silently, watching in horror the unravelling drama. The foul-smelling women clung on, grappling with the folds of her clothing, trying to find her wallet; she spun around, searching the startled eyes of the onlookers for help. The crescendo of voices in the bar was suddenly muted, all eyes on Lucy!

A burly man came from behind the bar and yelled at the women in Spanish, loosening their grip. Lucy threw them off and breathlessly reeled away from her attackers, but not before they spat at her a stream of abuse in an unknown language. The patrons in the bar sucked in their breath in unison, and the two foul predators ran from the room. Lucy looked wildly about but they avoided her eyes, going back to their conversations as though nothing had happened! She took the stunned children, and went to the washroom to try and clean the stench of the women from her hands. On the way out she once again tried to catch the eye of the bartender but he, too, chose to look the other way.

They walked back in silence, the day clouding and taking on a menacing feel. The children clung to her and made walking difficult. She wanted to comfort them in some way, but she too was in shock. The menacing abuse rang in her ears and she wondered if it was some kind of curse they had spat upon her, so bad that the customers in the bar would not dare to look at her!

That evening they stayed close to the hotel, without appetite, going early to the sanctuary and safety of their room. She distracted the children with an English cartoon channel until they finally slept. Lucy, however, could not sleep. Her nostrils were full of the gypsies' filthy smell and her ears rang with their evil words. She drank wine and sat at the open window, watching the pre-dawn streets, listening to the faint echo of flamenco music emanating from the back rooms of the bars.

The sun came up like a red ball and the streets returned to normal. The oily waiters warmly greeted them in the sunny dining room, and rock music blared throughout the hotel. Hungrily they ordered hot chocolate and churrios. Yesterday suddenly seemed like a bad dream, one Lucy was happy to put behind her. They all laughed at a lame joke of Holly's and ordered more hot chocolate and churrios.

Chapter Thirty-One
The Gypsies' Curse

After ten days of chaotic trial and error, the Waldon household settled down to a routine of sorts. Angela Joy ruled! When she cried, she was fed. When she slept, they slept. When she wanted to play, no matter what time of day or night, Esmirada and Timothy complied. She was a happy and contented baby, but only because things were done her way. Timothy was besotted with his daughter, and spent all his free time playing music and talking to her.

Each day he returned from the school with a gift. Esme, despite all her promises to Timothy, did revert to her superstitious ways. Angela Joy was far too precious to tempt fate, so secretly she relied on both the Lord and *Lola's* herbal bags for protection. She was a lovely child and grew fat and sleek with all the attention that was bestowed upon her. She was baptised at the Chinatown Church when she was one month old, and Esme held a small gathering at the apartment to celebrate.

When Angela Joy was three months old, Esme went back to teaching and counselling at the Serenity Centre. She took the baby with her, carrying her close to her chest in a sling as she rode the bus downtown. Once there, she placed her in a cot next to the newly acquired computer, where the child was doted over by a stream of aunties. She was nursed and petted and responded daily to the sights, sounds, and stimulation of the centre.

As a family they were very happy. The only thorn in Timothy's side was Esmirada's family and the constant drain on his patience and finances. *Lola* was sick again and needed medicine, which he didn't deny but Rosa and Corky were constantly in need of funds, mainly because Corky gambled most of what they had. Manny had won custody of Carlo when Pinkie couldn't be located, but only after considerable expense to Timothy. Gigi, Mandy and Rose where still at school thanks to his generosity, and the *sari*

sari had added another room and running water to make life easier for *Lola* and Olina.

The letters came weekly, pleading that they bring the child 'home'. He reluctantly promised that in the New Year he and Esme would visit, bringing the six-month-old Angela Joy back to the Philippines. He prayed to God his little girl would have built up enough resistance by then to deal with whatever disease and pestilence came her way. Esmirada secretly sent a letter off to *Lola* asking for more special herbs to ward off the evil spirits.

◆ ◆ ◆ ◆ ◆ ◆

The new school year was unsettling for Cameron and Lucy. While Holly flourished with her studies and collection of new friends, Cameron floundered, falling behind, inventing vague illnesses so he could stay at home to play on the computer or watch Disney movies. He was at times listless, without appetite. He lost weight, which at first didn't bother Lucy. She'd cut down his food portions, but the reoccurring ear infections and colds started to worry her. She finally took him to a paediatrician to have him thoroughly checked. The doctor could find nothing wrong and gave her a prescription for a tonic, asking her to follow up in a few months. By the end of October, Cam seemed his old self, bouncing off walls, and tormenting his sister.

November came and went with snow flurries and increasingly bad weather. In early December, after another long, boozy Sunday lunch in Laura's conservatorium, Lucy was introduced to a doctor who managed to capture her imagination. His name was Angus McInroy and he would change Lucy's life from that first meeting!

The bad weather continued, but Lucy failed to notice. Angus was wooing her, taking her to dinners and concerts and introducing her to his own group of friends, whom she found funny, stimulating and inspiring. Most of them were in the medical profession and kept odd hours. She tried to be spontaneous and not too disappointed if he cancelled a date at the last minute. Lucy was a shade taller than Angus so she started wearing lower heels. He was of Scottish ancestry and claimed he had a family pile back in Scotland, which he would take her to visit when the weather improved.

He had a shock of greying hair that stood up in all directions on his well-shaped head. His eyes were a piercing blue and his skin pale and flawless. When she talked he had a way of listening so quietly and directly that at times it unnerved her. Angus had never married. His job was too exacting, but in the last few years he had gone into private practice and was at last keeping more civilised hours. He was a paediatrician in a practice with an oncologist at Bathgate Hospital just outside of London. His small apartment in a renovated mews sat in a tree-lined street within walking distance of Bathgate.

Christmas was upon them once again, and Laura and Lucy were busy cataloguing a new shipment. The heat in the shop had malfunctioned and the place was freezing. Snow gusted against the muslin-draped windows and Lucy stamped her feet to keep warm. Laura looked up from the ticket she was writing.

"I've everything organised for Christmas! I'll do the turkey and ham, and you do the pudding, Ness is bringing a stilton soup to start and Fie is doing something marvellous with smoked salmon. All the other little bits I'll take care of. Oh and Angus, the little darling is doing the wine and bubbly. He and Hamish are going down to London on Wednesday to fetch it all."

The phone rang and Lucy could hear Laura's sharp little voice admonishing the repairman over the lack of heat. She came back with a pencil stuck behind her one protruding ear. Lucy idly wondered if her ear stuck out because of her habit. The other one was perfectly normal.

"Now, where was I? Oh yes, Angus. How are things going between you two? He's such a catch, Lucy, I quite fancy him myself! What do the children think of him?"

Lucy rubbed her hands to get some circulation going. She hated these third degrees. Laura was just like Amber in that respect.

"We're taking it slowly, just dinner, dancing and a few shows. I'm not rushing into anything and neither is Angus. The kids have only met him once or twice so it's a little too soon to tell, but he is extremely good with them. He's taking us all to the Panto in London next week. A girl I knew in Singapore has a son appearing as Dick Whittington. We're all looking forward to it! We are going to have high tea at Browns before we go. I just hope the weather improves; Cam hasn't been well again, same old ear infection. Poor kid has lived on antibiotics these last few months. Angus wants me to bring him in. He's going to do some blood work and a complete check-up."

Two days before their trip to London, Cameron became very sick. Lucy fed him Tylenol and continuously tepid-sponged him, but the fever persisted. He lay on the lounge, listlessly watching television. He requested 'cold' things to eat and complained of a stomach ache. Holly tried to interest him in one of her games, but he couldn't be bothered. Angus called later that night and Lucy repeated Cameron's symptoms.

"I'm going to drive down and see him. I've finished for the day, and only had a tedious farewell dinner to attend. I'd much rather come and see you and the children. Have a glass of red waiting!"

Lucy was flooded with relief; to be able to share her fears with another adult after so long was comforting. She banked up the fire and busied herself decanting a bottle of red wine while she waited. Cameron had a few spoonfuls of ice cream and then dozed in front of the television.

Angus arrived, bringing a bitterly cold draught through the front door. His pallid cheeks were frozen and she rubbed them with her hands before pouring him a glass of wine.

"Where is the little man?"

Cameron smiled weakly as Angus began to gently examine him. "Your hands are cold!" he said as Angus pulled down his eyelids and looked inside his mouth.

"He's too pale, Lucy!" he said, shaking his head. "Let's take a look at your tummy, old chum."

He raised Cameron's pyjama jacket and palpated beneath his rib cage. He then turned him onto his stomach, and it was then that Lucy saw the bruising along his spine and pinprick rash. He turned his face toward her and she could see the alarm in his eyes.

"Pack him a bag, I'm going to take him into Bathgate. I want you to come with me. Can you get Holly over to Laura's for the night?"

He picked up Cameron with ease and wrapped him in a tartan blanket. All Lucy could see was his pale frightened face above Angus's broad shoulder.

"What's wrong, Mummy? Where is Doctor McInroy taking me?"

Angus kissed the boy's forehead and reassured him. "Listen, old man, you're not well and your Mum's very worried, so we're going to take you back to my hospital and do a few tests. You're going to have to be very brave for her. Do you think you can do it?"

"I don't know. Will I have to have a needle?"

"Yes, I would say most definitely, old chap, but I know how strong you really are!"

Cameron looked unconvinced but was too sick to protest. By the time Angus placed him in the back seat of the car, he was asleep.

Lucy watched Angus, his profile illuminated with each passing car. She could see the set of his jaw and the vein pulsating in his temple. Her neck and shoulders ached as she twisted her body, trying to keep one hand protectively on Cameron's back.

She suddenly felt as though she was falling apart; her eyes burnt with unshed tears. All she wanted to do was to lie down with Cam, hold him and go to sleep.

A needling, icy rain hit them in the face as they alighted into the fluorescent-lit entrance to the Accident and Emergency. Angus wrapped Cameron tightly and lifted him to his chest, hurrying in out of the cold. Lucy stumbled after him, wiping the damp hair from her face.

A softly spoken young woman greeted them in the harsh glare of the corridor. Angus introduced her as Doctor Petra Ross, his partner and oncologist. She held out her hand to Lucy. Lucy took it and looked into Petra Ross's wide blue eyes. Lucy knew at that moment what she was asking. She wanted Lucy to trust her with the future of her son!

During the night Lucy's life stopped and then somehow started again. Cam's blood test confirmed Angus's worst fears. Her son had an extremely elevated white blood cell count with some blasts. She couldn't breathe when they told her.

She kept thinking, 'Blasts? What the hell are blasts, and isn't it a good thing to have a lot of white cells? They fight disease, don't they?'

Petra Ross carried out an emergency bone marrow aspiration and lumbar puncture on her uncomplaining son as the bitterly cold night turned into a bleak day.

Lucy remained huddled in the corner of the cold waiting room as Angus came to tell her Cam had leukaemia. She couldn't look him in the eye; she didn't want to know the worst!

He stilled her shaking hands in the warmth of his. He spoke calmly and clearly but she couldn't take in what he said. He had to repeat himself several times before she understood.

"Childhood Leukaemia is the common cold of the oncology world, nothing you or Cameron did has caused it. It's not contagious or generally genetic. The leukaemia that Cam has is called acute lymphoblastic leukaemia or A.L.L."

A good risk, he told her, eighty percent cure rate. Her exhausted brain kept repeating his words as he went to get her coffee from the cafeteria. A good risk! What the hell was a good risk and eighty percent, what about the other twenty! She felt an uncontrolled anger toward Angus for telling her these things, all she wanted to do was pick Cameron up and go home.

He returned, bringing with him a tray with coffee and muffins. Her head ached and her stomach roiled. She pressed the palms of her hands against her aching eyeballs, and then she started to cry.

Angus held her until her sobs subsided. She blew her nose noisily on the handkerchief he offered her. She sat wretchedly in the bleak waiting room while he mapped out Cameron's treatment.

"We're going to start him on chemotherapy immediately. To do that we need to insert a catheter just under his collar bone. The catheter is semi-permanent and it's called a Port-a-Cath. That means we can introduce the chemotherapeutic drugs and take regular blood samples without constantly sticking him with needles. What we aim to do is to destroy all the cancer cells as quickly as possible. Cameron's a lucky boy in that he was diagnosed early, and here at Bathgate we have state-of-the-art treatment. In my opinion Petra Ross is the best oncologist in the business."

Lucy swallowed hard and she tried to take a sip of coffee. She felt heartened at what he was saying.

"This induction phase is the most intensive part. Cam will be given four different drugs, and although the chemo causes a lot of very unpleasant side effects, most of our kids come out of here with ninety-five percent complete remission, sometimes after just one week."

Lucy's hands flew out of her lap and she stood and clutched at the lapels of his white coat.

"Are you saying he will be cured after only a week of chemotherapy?"

He took her hands from his jacket and sat her down gently.

"Lucy, induction is the first phase. Once we achieve remission, Cam will probably go home, but he will be in post-remission consolidation. He'll be given drugs orally to kill any remaining cancer cells. Lucy, you and Cameron have to prepare yourself for months, or possibly years, of treatment to ensure his best chance of cure for the disease. You're going to be his major caregiver. You have to prepare yourself for what lies ahead!"

Lucy stood unsteadily and paced the small room, wringing her hands. She turned to Angus, tears streaming down her face.

"I don't know if I can do this, Angus, I don't think I am strong enough!"

Angus came to her and held her by the shoulders.

"Listen to me, Lucy. You don't have to do this alone. Petra and I will be with you all the way. We have a support group right here, a clinical social worker and a psychologist on staff to help families. We also have a parent

261

support group but most of all you'll gain strength from Cameron. You have to be strong for him! Have faith, Lucy. Look at Cameron. What he's going through at the moment, it's the worst thing that will ever happen to him. He'll be your inspiration to do what you have to do!"

Chapter Thirty-Two
God's Will

Laughter, and the occasional high-pitched squeal, burst forth from the open windows of the Serenity Centre. The maids were preparing for their Christmas party. Esmirada had taken up a collection from the church and business houses. They had been very generous this year. She spent the morning at Prosperity Plaza buying gifts and filling out vouchers for prizes. She supervised the decorating of the tree before she boarded the bus to collect Angela Joy from Sister Mary.

This was their first Christmas as a family, and Timothy had been as excited as a small boy when they went to choose a tree. He dragged out the dusty box from beneath the bed with the decorations, and they spent the evening transforming the apartment, while the baby slept peacefully beneath the lazily turning fan. When Angela Joy finally stirred Esme fed her and placed her in her sling. Hand in hand they walked the short distance in the warm night to the hawker centre. They found their favourite table beneath the mango tree and ordered chicken rice and cold beer for their supper.

Timothy watched with pride as the aunties and uncles from the stalls gathered to admire the baby, who slept on, oblivious to the chaos and hungry customers about her. She was a beautiful child and grew lovelier by the day. Timothy's heart ached with happiness every time he looked at his girls. A breeze cooled the sweat on the back of his shirt and he took a long swig of cold beer.

"I'll distribute the canned food on Christmas Eve to the various old folks' homes. Angelika and Joe will be pleased. I have a nice fat cheque from the church to give them for the school; it has been a good year!

Esme looked up from the sleeping baby. Timothy had not lost his weight after the birth! He looked more prosperous than ever, and with the year of the pig fast approaching, she laughed as he shovelled chicken rice into his lusty face. Tomorrow she would thank God for the joy that the child and Timothy had brought into her life at their special midnight service. She ate some chicken rice and took a small sip of his beer. She played with him and brandished the daily paper in front of his face. He grabbed at it and snatched it away from her.

"Oh, what do we have here? A not-so-subtle hint for a Christmas gift?" Timothy was looking at the page advertising watches and jewellery.

In fact, what she had wanted to show him was the cheap airfares advertised to Manila in the New Year. She laughed and let it go. She knew he would take her and the baby back when the time was right. He knew how much her family meant to her. Timothy grinned with pleasure, watching her eat. He thought of his gift under the tree. He had chosen with great care a delicate gold cross for Esmirada. He watched her slender brown throat as she stole a sip of his beer and thought how fine the cross would look around her lovely neck.

◆◆◆◆◆◆

Margie won first prize for her sexy rendition of Madonna in the playback competition. She had the loudest applause by far and was a clear winner. The women were playing musical chairs before starting the buffet that had been laid out in the computer room. Esme was supervising the dance music with Sister Mary and Joyner. They were getting more boisterous and excited by the minute. Esme decided a bit of Philippines folk dancing would calm them down before they had to go home to their families. Timothy was looking after Angela Joy; at six she would relieve him so he could do his charity round before joining them at church.

When she arrived home she found the baby gurgling happily in her bouncer, while Timothy wrapped gifts to go under the tree. This year there was more than ever. He had lit the candles near to the nativity scene and poured each of them a small glass of wine.

"A little celebration before we join our extended family!" He held up his glass. "To my beautiful bride, I love you more and more each day, and to our perfect little girl."

They took a sip of wine and Timothy picked up the baby and held her to his chest, kissing her tiny brown fingers. She crowed at him, showing her pink clean gums. Esme watched them together; she planned another child as soon as possible, perhaps tonight!

"Must go, my two beauties. Now don't go snooping about the tree. Tonight after the service we'll open our gifts together, promise!" Esme laughed. He knew she couldn't stand secrets or surprises. She was too impatient. He kissed the top of her head and was gone. Esme stood with the baby at the window watching him cross the street.

"Say bye to Papa, Angela Joy." She turned and a draught from the fan suddenly blew out the candles.

Esmirada dressed the baby in her finest clothes and walked the short distance to the church. It had rained late in the afternoon and now the night air was cool and fresh. She admired the lights and decorated trees as she walked. The streets were busy with last minute shoppers and young revellers.

It was a long service, with carols by candlelight, and a special service for the girls' and boys' brigade before midnight worship. She knew that Timothy could quite possibly be late, as he and the other elders had most of the island to cover, visiting hospices and homes. When he had not arrived by ten, she started to worry. She had a queer feeling in the pit of her stomach as she drew the baby closer to her. Suddenly she saw the ashen face of Harold making his way roughly through the worshipers.

The twenty-minute journey to the hospital was the longest of Esmirada's life. She held tight to Angela Joy and Harold's hand. She continuously prayed that he would be alright, just some minor scratches. He was big and strong, but then why didn't he call her to tell her himself? She prayed again. Nothing bad must happen to him, she loved him too much.

All Harold could tell her was that a car outside of the Seventh Day Adventist Hospice had hit Timothy. The staff had given him first aid and sent him to the National Hospital. He had been conscious and asking for her.

"He's probably hurt his head. Perhaps it is serious but he's strong, Harold. God will watch over him!" She looked at Harold hopefully, but he stared straight ahead, his face white in the glare of the headlights. Angela Joy slept blissfully in her arms.

They reached the hospital and found it chaotic, the emergency room full of glum looking people waiting to see a doctor. Harold went to reception and gave them Timothy's name. They were asked to wait in a small room off Accident and Emergency. Esmirada's breath was coming shallow and fast. She found it hard to concentrate on her prayers. After at least two hours a grim young doctor approached and quietly closed the door behind him. Angela Joy started to fret and Esmirada held her close to her breast. The doctor couldn't look her in the eye but instead addressed the top of her head.

"I'm sorry, Mrs Waldon, but your husband has gone. We took him to surgery, but he didn't survive the operation. He suffered a cardiac arrest on the operating table."

Her brain was in a state of confusion, and she started to shake uncontrollably. Gone! What did he mean 'gone'? Timothy would never leave them like this! The baby started to cry but no words came from Esme's mouth. Harold, with tears flowing freely, led her from the room. Nausea washed over her as they waited for a taxi. Angela Joy continued to scream as if in disbelief. Was this some kind of cruel joke of God's, she asked herself, as she started her lonely journey home.

Chapter Thirty-Three
Comfort

The Childhood Leukaemia Centre at Bathgate was decorated in full Christmas regalia. Cameron's saline drip had a Santa dangling from it, and Holly had wound his bed with tinsel. For Holly it was a novelty to spend Christmas at the hospital. Those children who were well enough stood on I.V. poles and raced around the wards, enjoying the celebrations. Daily visits from soccer stars and various television celebrities, bearing gifts and handing out autographs, kept Holly bubbling over with enthusiasm. She didn't seem to miss Christmas this year. Cameron was too sick to care, his body in chaos from the leukaemia.

Each day Lucy heaved her exhausted body from the lumpy couch, and faced another day of nerves, inner trembling and feelings of loss of control. She had tried to make the nauseous-green room pleasant for Cam. Laura and Hamish had brought in his favourite posters and soft toys, she had pinned all the 'get well' and 'thinking of you' cards up on the wall. A bouquet of deflated balloons wafted sadly above his bed, sent in by Amber and the children. His teacher sent in a large box containing games, drawings from his classmates and colouring books. Hallam had given him a tape recorder, with tapes of favourite children's stories. Holly tried to distract him by blowing bubbles and squirting water from a used syringe at the nurses who came to take his blood! Lucy confiscated it the first chance she got.

Lucy spent her days trying not to lose her mind with the inevitable waiting. At other times she helped the nurses and Cam by making his bed and cleaning up his vomit and diarrhoea. She was getting better at this. The first week, every time he vomited, so did she, but now she had grown accustomed to her gut churning nervously. She managed only a small amount to eat; the occasional sandwich and coffee that Angus brought for her kept her going.

Cameron was well into his induction period and nearly all of his hair had fallen out, leaving him looking like a wispy old man. Lucy placed a receiving blanket on his pillow to collect his hair each night, saving it religiously in a small velvet box. The anti-cancer drugs had made him violently ill but seemed to vary from child to child. Lucy came to learn that his protocol would have to be tailor made to suit his needs. Petra adjusted his drugs and dosages constantly according to his blood results. He had a C.B.C. or complete blood count twice a week and Lucy learnt to live in terms of white cell, platelets and haemoglobin counts, religiously recording his blood chart. Cameron's immune system was greatly compromised, so she and Holly wore masks, washed their hands constantly and used antibacterial wipes.

The little old man lying in the bed was no longer Cam; she felt in her heart she'd lost him. Each day she put on a happy face, her heart rending painfully as she tried to distract him from painful procedures. Each night she would lie on the couch next to him, and let the tears silently run unchecked, pooling in her ears. She was exhausted, but as Angus had said she would, she gained strength from Cameron. His little white face when he had a bone marrow aspiration became pinched, but still he didn't complain. On occasions he'd whimper like a small animal, but all he said was "Mummy, I don't want people looking at me all the time, and I don't want any more needles, they make me sick!"

The vincristine made him constipated and the saline drip made him want to pee constantly. He hated bedpans and urinals, but the worst was the nausea and ulcerated mouth. He ate little and had no appetite. He didn't care about his loss of hair; all the other kids were bald as well. It bothered Lucy more than it did Cameron.

Hallam kept his word and arrived Christmas Day. As soon as he walked into the ward, Lucy knew it was a mistake. He broke down, blubbing pathetically at the sight of his son. Lucy didn't have the energy to comfort him as well!

"Don't cry, Daddy, it makes me sad. Why don't you go home? You can sleep in my bed," said Cameron, clutching his ever-faithful baby pillow to him.

Hallam wanted to go. He was awkward and uncomfortable and got in the way. He couldn't stand seeing all the sick children. Thankfully he and Holly left to spend Christmas back at Oriel Lodge. It was a relief for Cameron once they had left.

Amber came to visit, offering Lucy a shoulder to cry on. At Cameron's request, she didn't bring Andrea and Tom. He didn't want them to see him like this. Once again Lucy gained inspiration from her son. Lucy lent heavily on Angus throughout Cameron's induction phase, constantly bombarding him with questions. With Petra she built a trustful relationship. She had a warm and caring manner with Cameron, and was easy to talk to. Lucy read everything she could get her hands on about A.L.L., and talked to the other mothers in a unique medical terminology that only they would understand. She put her life on hold until finally, after five weeks, Cameron entered remission and she gradually got her child back!

♦♦♦♦♦♦

After the funeral and cremation, which Harold Seng Loh and Joe Miller organised, Sister Mary came to get Esmirada and the baby. She found them lying in bed together, asleep, in the middle of the day in a darkened room. A dead Christmas tree, complete with decorations and gifts, sat forlornly in the corner. She decided to take the child and her mother and deal with the apartment later. A sour mustiness filled her nostrils as she roused Esmirada, gently taking the infant from her. Esmirada was unwashed and disorientated but the baby appeared well fed and clean. She packed their belongings and took them to the waiting taxi and home to Emerald Hill.

She prepared Esme's old room at the back of the house and borrowed a cot for the child. She bullied Esme into showering, and took the infant and placed it in a deep chair, where it looked at her curiously with enormous brown eyes. Esme returned, her wet hair flowing down her back to her knees. Mary could see the suffering in Esmirada's face. Her eyes were puffy and darkly ringed, her usual bright complexion pale. She forced her to eat a bowl of herbal soup she had made that morning with a black chicken and two pieces of kaya toast.

As Esme fed the baby, Mary spoke gently, "Have you let your family know?"

Esme flinched. "How can I tell them? They'll blame me; I'm bad luck! My uncle Buboy always said I was bad luck!"

Esme put the baby down in the cot and watched over her sadly as she fussed briefly and then settled. Mary started to plait Esme's long hair.

"He was such a good man, Mary, the best husband and father a woman could ever want. I miss him so much. Brides should never wear pearls on their wedding day. It causes heartache and tears. I wore pearls, Mary!"

Mary took the girl by the hand and led her out to the courtyard. They could hear the laughter of the children in the adjoining school. She left Esme in the dappled shade of the old tree and went to make tea. She came back to find her quietly weeping.

"It's all my fault he died, something bad happens wherever I go. Buboy died after touching me, and Rosa's baby girl died before it had a chance to live. Poor Uncle died only six months after I went to work for Madam Wei Ling Leng, and then look what happened with Madam Yi Feng. She saw the bad spirit and tried to beat it out of me. It was poor Timothy who saved me from her! My little friend Laani, so young but she too died. With me around, my ma'am Lucy's husband divorced her, and just before Christmas I received a letter telling me that little Cameron is sick with cancer. My father knew I was bad. That's why he sent me away, and he too is in his grave!"

Mary had had enough. She grabbed at Esme's hands, sending the teacup flying. "Stop this talk, it's poisonous superstition! You are a good Christian girl; Timothy would be ashamed to hear this talk! Buboy died at the hands of one of his debtors, your father died after having a kidney removed. Uncle was an old man who had had a stroke and Madam Yi Feng was a cruel and evil woman! People get divorced and children get sick and unfortunately accidents happen. It's Gods will!"

Esme turned away from God after Timothy's sudden death; she was full of anger and confusion. It was easier to revert to the superstitious beliefs of her childhood. Olina always taught her that protecting the home from evil spirits and curses was women's work. She had failed!

A month after Timothy's death she went back to the apartment. She had sat day after day in Mary's courtyard, brooding, and had finally decided what she must do. Esmirada made a call to the Philippines. Rosa, the only one with a phone, had to fetch Olina. The wait was endless; after the news was delivered she was met with a stony silence. Finally her mother spoke, demanding she come home at once with the baby. Rosa came back on line, wanting to know if Timothy had insurance and if so, how much? The call home convinced her she was making the right decision!

◆ ◆ ◆ ◆ ◆ ◆

A hard, snow-chilled wind threatened to blow Cameron over as Lucy helped him from the car. Holly and Hallam had erected a banner that flapped wildly across the portico, 'welcoming him home'. Everyone except Cameron was nervous and over-bright. His wispy baldness was covered by a red beanie, which made his face seem even pastier in the cold light.

With Lucy home, Hallam stayed for the weekend and then headed back to London before flying to Singapore. He had taken leave but couldn't afford to take any more. Lucy found the house unwelcoming and despite a roaring fire in the living room, she was constantly cold. She wandered about, starting a task only to lose her train of thought midway, and then wonder what she was doing. After being in the hospital so long and becoming used to its daily routine, she found she had none of her own.

Her first priority was to clean and sterilise the house and set up a neutropenic diet for Cameron. She felt as though she had brought home a new baby and didn't quite know where to start. The weekend was tense and never ending. Cameron was taking Prednisone orally and it made him moody and hungry all of the time. She could already see a new pudginess emerging in his pale face. He only had mild nausea and a little vomiting but Lucy gave him zofran and that took care of that, but then he developed constipation so she gave him a laxative.

During the balancing act with Cameron, Hallam decided to share his problems. His marriage was failing and Elvira had refused him access to the baby. He was having difficulties with his job and was tired of travelling all the time. He was considering returning to London but then that meant a loss of revenue and no contact with his daughter, who now resided in India with her mother.

Lucy wanted to shout at him, "Stiff shit, Hallam, I have a few problems of my own, and not to mention your poor heroic son and what he's going through!" But instead she listened, too exhausted to speak.

On top of Hallam's problems, she was also dealing with Holly and her resentment towards Cam's cancer. Lucy knew she'd neglected her, but didn't expect such hostility. She went to bed that night, her heart heavy and cold with fear. She couldn't sleep, she'd been so used to sleeping on the couch next to Cameron. Halfway through the night she crept into his room and lay down on the sofa at the end of his bed.

Sunday afternoon Hallam finally left, she was glad to see the back of him!

Angus said that if Cameron remained well throughout the following weeks, he could go back to school. Lucy wasn't so sure; she was worried about infection and how the other kids would respond to him. What she didn't count on was Cameron's eagerness; she couldn't deny his wishes. He had been through so much, and in hospital for such a long time. Two weeks later on a rainy Tuesday, he went back to school. The teachers were marvellous; the school nurse went to the classroom and addressed the children, explaining to them all about leukaemia, and the side effects of the drugs and why Cam had lost his hair. They knew he wouldn't participate in all activities, and that they all must be very vigilant in washing their hands and covering their mouths when they sneezed. They wanted to shave their heads to be like Cameron but the nurse told them it wasn't necessary. Much to Lucy's relief, Cameron came home happy and little like his old self, only stronger!

The special diet was turning out to be a real challenge. Cam wasn't allowed any fresh fruit or vegetables, raw meat or sushi, which was his favourite. Much to Holly's chagrin, going out to eat held too many hazards, another reason for her growing resentment. Lucy's cooking had become very much like her mother's, overcooked meat bordering on grey, canned fruit and vegetables and everything pasteurised to within an inch of its life. Her kitchen was like an operating room and her hands were raw from constantly washing them with antibacterial soap. Gradually she established a rough routine, she didn't know when she would be able to paint again, and had given up her business in Singapore, the commissions having all but dried up. She did go in occasionally to the Antique Shop to help Laura, who'd been a rock but Lucy knew it was more to preserve her sanity, than to actually be of any use.

When Cameron was well, he and Holly quarrelled constantly. He was exempt from his usual chores because of his illness. The extra workload fell on Holly's shoulders. Holly wasn't allowed to hit Cam, but Lucy suspected he took advantage of this, and pinched and kicked out at her in his anger and frustration. Lucy chose to ignore it. How was she supposed to discipline a child so ill?

Angus visited regularly but the relationship had changed. She no longer looked at him romantically. He was the man who had saved her son's life, and she needed his full focus on his ongoing care. She had no time for romance. Cameron had good days and bad. His Port-a-Cath became infected and his temperature skyrocketed, meaning another week in hospital. He missed school for regular C.B.C. and lumbar punctures and a change in his daily oral chemo saw him vomiting continuously. That was when the self-recriminations started. What had she done to cause this? Was she careful enough during pregnancy? Did she expose him to radiation or some sort of poisonous substance in Singapore? They were always having

272

the house fogged for mosquitoes and the walls pumped with arsenic for termites. Could it have been that? These bouts of self-doubt left her crying hysterically in the toilet, hunched in the corner of the cubicle in frustration.

She never lied to Cameron; she was always as positive and truthful as she could be, as were Petra and Angus. He trusted them with his life, constantly amazing her. After the last bout of chemo, Cameron's bone marrow was slow in recovering and he fell behind his protocol. Angus assured her that was perfectly normal. She took to doing her own research late at night, poring over books she had borrowed from the library. She would sit in the eerie glow of the lamp with a cup of coffee or glass of wine, browsing, looking for information or new treatments. She found more and more for parents living with leukaemia. She started writing to a woman called Sally in the States who also had a son, Vincent, a little older than Cam, who was going through exactly the same thing. She found her details on the hospital notice board, under the International Parent Support Group. It caught her eye, mirroring her feelings exactly.

Sally wrote:

"Just the other day a well meaning friend asked me how was I coping with my son's life threatening disease? How do I answer that? Aside from crying in the shower and pounding the walls in frustration, before falling into bed each night numb with exhaustion, only to lay awake helplessly. Followed by days of depression, unsocial and anti-social behaviour; I am coping beautifully, thank you!"

They became pen friends and Lucy came to depend on her replies, and any scrap of information she could give her. At the same time, she sent a letter to Amber asking for news of Alex. Amber had done some research and sent her back pages of bio data about his latest exhibition, art prizes and rising success. She felt she had found him again, and took great comfort in reading about his latest achievements.

In April, Holly turned nine. It coincided with a week when Cameron's port was playing up, causing his platelets to drop dramatically. He was hospitalised for five days and given a platelet transfusion. Lucy stayed with him throughout, but things got worse. His blood pressure dropped and he complained of an aching head. Petra did a blood culture, discovering he had a bacterial infection. She found herself sitting in his room, waiting out the long hours, thinking about what she would do for his funeral. She was so ashamed and thought perhaps she was having a nervous breakdown!

He finally came home on I.V. antibiotics to a sister who would not speak to him because they had missed her birthday. Lucy promised her a party the following week, and although she was exhausted, she went ahead and organised a disco for twenty little girls.

The party was not a complete success. Only sixteen children came, the others, fearing leukaemia, stayed away. Holly took her disappointment out on Cameron and Lucy. She became recalcitrant and moody. More that once Lucy had been called up to the school because of Holly's behaviour. Angus urged her to talk to Holly and try to understand the depth of her pain and fear.

Over breakfast she cornered her daughter. "You seem scared, honey. I am too!"

Holly turned to her sulkily. "This was the worst Christmas and birthday I've ever had! I hate cancer! People are always sorry for us. At school all the time, it's 'poor little Cameron, poor little boy'. What about me? Nobody cares about me anymore. Cam gets all the cards, presents and games. We can't go to restaurants or have friends over to play. The boys in my class tease me about Cameron because he has no hair. Once, another big kid said he was nothing but a spastic. I feel sad all the time, Cam and I can't wrestle like we used to, and I can't hit him when he makes me mad, but he can hit and pinch me all he wants! I want things to be like they were, why can't we go back and live in Singapore with Daddy and Andrea and Tom. I miss Esmirada, I wish she was still my *amah*; at least she had time to read to me at night!"

Lucy watched as Holly left for school, rugged up against the cold in a red pea jacket, blonde hair flying out from her small head as she slammed the door in Lucy's face. She felt as though she had been winded, she had to sit and catch her breath. Cameron stayed in bed, too sick to even come downstairs.

Her writing table was awash with sunlight, beckoning her.

To Sally:

"How is Vincent getting on? Things have been a bit difficult here lately with poor little Cam; he has been in hospital for five days with a bacterial infection in his port. He's still very unwell and sleeping all the time. It was Holly's birthday yesterday, quite exhausting for all of us. It has been very hard on her; she's been left with other people quite a bit, friends but still not the same. Keep in touch, I'll say a prayer for you all, Love, Lucy".

The mail thudded through the front door onto the mat and she picked it up. She sifted through, discarding the bills and hospital paraphernalia. A pale-blue airmail letter in a familiar hand caught her attention and she went to sit at her desk, carefully opening the thin envelope.

At the top of the page in Esmirada's neat scrip was a passage from the bible:

"Let your hope keep you joyful, pray at all times and be patient in your troubles" Romans 12:12

She read further:

"I lost my precious Timothy at Christmas, a tragic accident. At the time he was doing what he loved most, helping other people. Angela Joy and I are not alone. I'm living with my dearest friend Mary, and I am continuing Timothy's work with the church and the Serenity Centre. He's provided well for both of us and we want for nothing. I have my residency and work permit so I'm able to stay in Singapore indefinitely. I get great comfort from the church and helping those less fortunate than me. Later this month I will visit my home in the Philippines. My mother and grandmother are both unwell. I want them to meet Angela Joy.

The school and amenities block that Timothy worked so hard to build at the Manila dumpsite will be dedicated to his memory. When his daughter grows into a woman, I know how proud she'll be of her father!"

The letter finished with prayers and comforting words for Cameron's recovery.

"Cancer cannot destroy your soul or conquer your spirit! Have faith in God, ma'am, he will not let you suffer alone!"

She let the letter drift to the floor. She thought sadly of the quiet American and of Esmirada's loss. Suddenly she was overcome with sorrow, so disheartened she found it hard to stand. She practically crawled up the stairs to Cameron's room, and got into bed with him, folding her arms about his spare little body.

Late that afternoon, Laura dropped Holly off after ballet. Her mother had failed to pick her up. Holly looked in and found them both asleep. She closed the door and went to the kitchen to eat bread and jam. She then sat in front of the television until her mother woke and remembered she had two children to care for. It wasn't the first time this had happened. Holly was slowly getting used to living with Cameron's cancer.

Chapter Thirty-Four
Strength

Alex lay curled in the warmth of Dorté's bed, reluctant to move. He could hear her padding about the small kitchen of the South Yarra apartment. He liked this apartment. It was compact but well appointed, so different from his sprawling bungalow in Noosa. She'd decorated it in soft charcoals and almond. Lots of suede and crushed velvet, everything was warm and soft underfoot.

Last night they had a long bout of lovemaking that seduced him into making promises he was now not so sure he could keep. Did he really mention a more permanent arrangement? He shouldn't have drunk so much red at dinner but that too proved to be a delicious seduction. They had eaten with a group of art collectors and gallery owners at Vue De Monde, a chic little restaurant in Carlton, to celebrate the success of Alex's latest exhibit. The menu rambled on for twelve courses with wines to compliment each dish. The food was superb, creative and colourful, each dish better than the one before. He found the guests stimulating and entertaining. Dorté shone, sitting at the head of the table, holding forth on up-and-coming exhibits, tossing her tawny head as she spoke, and licking her voluptuous lips in between courses. She was friends with the chef and bantered with him, inveigling an invitation for her guests to view the kitchen. He was young and talented and looked like a model or rock star, with his streaked blonde hair wildly sticking out at angles. One of the guests was an avid collector of art, and had four of Alex's large canvases hanging in his beautiful home. He was also an avid collector of women. They seemed to get younger and leggier each time Alex met him!

He could smell coffee, eggs and bacon but still he did not attempt to get up. He buried himself deeper into the soft warmth of her bed. They planned a trip to Prague and London; he was exhibiting in both cities and would leave early tomorrow morning. He had an enormous amount of work ahead of him, but this morning all he could think of was Lucy. Last night he had dreamt of making love to her on a beach, her presence was so real he was surprised to wake and find Dorté lying next to him.

♦♦♦♦♦♦

Prague had always been one of Alex's favourite cities but for Dorté it was her first visit. She immediately fell in love with the strange onion-roofed buildings, which looked down on the changing face of the city, and the ancient stone, black with pollution. On Sunday they strolled with the hordes on Charles Bridge, listening to the European accents and the loud shouts of the Americans, while heavily pierced teenagers necked below sombre tributes to Mary Magdalene and Jesus. They listened to a jazz band playing old favourites and had tea in a Russian tearoom. With a band of tourists they stood in the wind waiting for the astronomical clock to expose its wooden depictions of greed, vanity and death as the pale sun picked out the twelve signs of the zodiac.

The weather had turned cold, and the exhibit was disappointing, with a smaller turnout than expected. Perhaps they all had tickets for the opera because Alex sold only a few paintings to an English expat couple, who had moved from Singapore. They chatted over cocktails and promised to take him to the markets to buy inexpensive caviar before he left for London. During a mediocre dinner of onion soup and grilled trout, he discovered that they knew Hallam Leadbitter and Elvira. Unfortunately they had never met Lucy. He was disappointed and changed the subject when he saw how bored Dorté had become with the conversation. All four retired to an empty red-velvet bar to drink cognac and smoke cigars.

It was when they were saying their goodbyes that the woman turned to Alex. "You know, this has been bothering me all night. I have heard of Lucy Leadbitter, only now she goes by the name of Lucinda Glendenning. She's good friends with Amber Van Engle. Unfortunately I also heard her small son has leukaemia and is very sick."

Alex's heart jerked painfully and sour bile filled his mouth. He swallowed and steadied himself against a wing chair as he watched the couple leave the warmth of the bar and venture out into the cold night.

♦ ♦ ♦ ♦ ♦ ♦

Anyone passing by Oriel Lodge would have been forgiven for calling the police. In the early hours of a late July morning, frantic screams were coming from the upstairs bedroom. Holly was running a temperature and had a sore throat. She sat in bed, hysterical, thinking she too would have to go to hospital and have a blood transfusion and maybe even die. Lucy tried to calm her while Cameron threw up repeatedly in the next room. He was in his consolidation phase and the chemo was very harsh on him. Cameron had not been to school for weeks, he was bloated and irritable, and his limbs had given up. The chemo had completely cleaned out his bone marrow.

Lucy administered zofran to Cam and sat nursing him until it took effect. The codeine was slowly working on Holly who had quietened down and was now dozing.

Earlier that day she had found the hamster dead in its cage. She didn't have the heart to tell the children. She had hurriedly wrapped it in newspaper and put it in the garbage bin before Holly found it. With no time for a proper burial, she was consumed with an irrational guilt. She watched from Cameron's bedroom window as the sky lightened. It would be summer school holidays in another ten days. She wouldn't bother to send Holly back. It was easier to keep her home and have some one-on-one time together. She wasn't sure how much more she could cope with; she wasn't sleeping and was drinking too much red wine each night.

Sally's letters kept her sane, but it was Laura's encouragement and Esmirada's prayers and spiritual guidance, in light of her own tragedy, that kept her going long after she had exhausted her resources. She wondered each day if she would have the strength to endure yet another trial, but then she'd look at Cam, and realise he didn't have a choice, he just had to tough it out. Just to look at his face gave her the courage she needed to take on one more day. Earlier this evening she had written another letter to Sally in Pittsburgh, Pennsylvania. Vincent had not been doing too well lately, and she hadn't heard from her in a while.

At five in the afternoon that same day, Cameron and Lucy were back in Bathgate. He was on I.V. antibiotics for an infection and would require another blood transfusion. Holly had thrown a tantrum when they left and Lucy threw one of her own, slapping the child. She was wretched and stood sobbing in the hallway as Laura gathered her things together.

"Just exactly what do you think you are doing, Lucy?" Laura demanded, pushing her hard against the wall.

"I don't know anymore!" Lucy sniffled and wiped her nose with the back of her hand.

"Lucy, even though Cam is very sick and Holly is full of resentment, you must set some limits. At the moment neither of them respect what you or anyone else is doing for them! When this is all over, you're going to have two overindulged brats on your hands!"

Laura's words rang in her ears as she watched her son sleeping. Lucy was grateful Laura wasn't afraid to tell her what she needed to hear. The room was filled with a yellow glow as the sun set over the chimneys of Bathgate. She could hear the murmur of the nurses' voices and the quiet sounds of the hospital as it wound down for the day. Picking up the phone silently, so as not to wake Cam, she dialled Laura to say goodnight to Holly.

"I feel a lot better tonight, Mamma. How is Cam? I'm sorry for being naughty today. Laura said I shouldn't be so naughty when you are so worried about Cam!"

With a lump in her throat, Lucy spoke to her small daughter. "I'm sorry too, honey. Cam's sleeping right now. Be good for Laura and Hamish and don't forget to say your prayers! Love you, sweetie. Bye."

She settled back and picked up a book on clinical trials and the mail she had collected as she was leaving. She tore open a letter with a U.S. postmark.

Sally's reply was chilling, putting her own life in perspective.

"Eight months into therapy my poor little Vincent lost his heroic battle, and died early on Saturday morning. He was my little soldier; he gave me strength when I had none to give. We have to keep our chins up as we have another child, a two-year-old. It has been very hard on him. I really hope your little boy carries on the fight. Never lose hope. Our little angel will not have to suffer any longer! Keep in touch and God bless you all, Sally."

Lucy let the tears fall unchecked for the little boy in Pennsylvania, and his family. How could God let this happen to innocent children? She stood over Cam's bed, watching the rise and fall of his chest, wondering how much longer he could keep fighting.

She was dozing when Petra and Angus came to check on Cam. Angus had brought her a meal from home - lasagne - his specialty.

"You've lost more weight, Lucy. You won't be much good to Cam if you get sick!"

279

She was grateful for his attention; she knew she looked a mess. She hadn't been to a hairdresser in eight months. Her hair had grown long and streaked with grey. Make-up was a thing of the past. Petra looked up from Cameron's bedside and scrutinised Lucy.

"Cam will be having another lumbar puncture in the morning to determine if he is neutropenic. If all goes well and his bloods have recovered, I'll discharge him on Thursday."

They left her to eat her dinner in peace and she settled back with her book. She heard familiar footsteps coming along the corridor and looked up, expecting to see Angus.

Alex, his face reddened from the cold night air, filled the doorway, blocking out the fluorescent light from the hall. Lucy felt her heart drain and then fill rapidly again, suffusing her body with warmth. Her eyes filled with tears and he pulled her to her feet, holding her against him tightly. She could feel the rough wool of his jacket and smell his lovely familiar scent. She went limp in his arms and let the tears flow, releasing all the pent up fear, anger, sadness, grief and guilt she had suffered alone over the last eight months.

"You're here! I can't believe you're here!" She put her arms around him, feeling the hard muscle of his back beneath the palms of her hands.

He tilted her face and wiped her tears with his thumb. He smiled and kissed the top of her head, sighing heavily as he looked toward the sleeping boy.

Alex stayed the night, dozing restlessly in the chair next to Cameron. Lucy slept, from time to time waking to watch his profile in the dimly lit room, praying silently that this time he would stay. Bright sunlight was slanting across the floor by the time Lucy woke. She found Alex helping the nurse make Cameron's bed. She felt awkward over a lukewarm breakfast, their knees touching at a small table in the cafeteria.

"I can only stay until lunchtime, then I must get back to the hotel. I have a dinner and a showing tonight."

She reached over and took his hand. "Oh Alex, I'm just so grateful you came, it means so much to me, and you've made Cameron very happy seeing you again. Things ended badly that Christmas in Singapore. I just wanted to say how sorry I was how everything turned out."

He put his finger to her lips and shushed her.

Petra stuck her head around the door and said, "Sorry to interrupt, but I need to see you Lucy?"

Lucy's hand automatically flew to her face.

"Don't panic, it's nothing serious, just some paperwork I need your signature on."

She introduced Alex to Petra and then he stood and pulled out her chair for her. "You go and do whatever you have to. I have some calls to make. I'll be there when Cam comes back to the ward."

Alex and Cameron were laughing over some private joke when she entered. Alex let out a low whistle and winked at Cam.

"Guess what, Mamma, my counts have recovered and I can go home Thursday."

Lucy clapped her hands together. "Well done, Cam!"

Alex kissed the top of his fuzzy head and said, "I have to go, matey. Now you remember what I told you! Stay positive and I'll see you again as soon as I can."

Lucy walked with him to the car park. They kissed chastely and she watched as he bent his large frame into the driver's seat. He waved and drove out of the gates into the midday traffic. She walked back slowly, giving herself time to recover. She wasn't going to let this get her down, but by the time she reached the children's wing her tears were flowing, and she dashed into the toilets to clean herself up before Cam saw her.

Alex drove like a maniac through the middle of London, missing his exit twice. He'd tried to be brave in front of Lucy, but seeing the little fellow brought back all the memories of Inke when she was going through chemo. His thoughts were in turmoil. Facing Dorté was going to be a nightmare, but there was no way he could have left Lucy and Cameron last night. He had to think fast and make some major decisions before he left for Australia next week. The sight of Lucy had shocked him. She was so thin, and he could see the suffering in her face. He had been exactly the same with Inke; he knew what she was going through. He wasn't quite sure, though, how he could help her. In the meantime he had to focus on the exhibition and all the work Dorté had put into this show. He drove into the entrance of the hotel, trying to pull himself together before he confronted her.

Chapter Thirty-Five
Fulfilling A Vision

The afternoon Esmirada arrived back at the barrio there was a brownout. The sullen taxi driver dropped her off under a busted neon sign. The burnt out shells of houses hung listlessly with tattered banners of laundry, welcoming her home. She walked purposefully, eyes straight ahead, sniffing the familiar smell of kerosene in the sultry air. She held the growing Angela Joy close; she was a large baby and at twelve months of age was walking.

The haemorrhaging corrugated iron of the *sari sari* had not changed. A few old uncles sat about the courtyard drinking beer, idly betting on the outcome of a half-hearted cockfight.

Lola had become increasingly decrepit, her spine painfully deformed and her chest cage visible. Her eyesight was all but faded but she had lost none of her spark. As she spied Esmirada and the baby walking into the courtyard, she clapped her hands together and called to Olina to come. Her mother, smelling of fried fish, came, holding out her dirty hands to take the child. She had lost all of her teeth and her jaws had caved in over her shrunken gums.

They were all there to meet her, Manny and a much grown Carlo, Rosa, Corky and Ricardo in from the coast. Perpetua was due to have her fifth child and couldn't make the journey. The girls and Enrique were all at school, due to Timothy's never-ending generosity. Her family were excited by the baby, dismissing her presence, never once mentioning Timothy's name or the tragic circumstances of his death. The money they had poured into improving the cement bungalow and *sari sari* had been squandered on more pigs and lime trees for Corky.

Esmirada spent her first day home cleaning the dwelling before it was fit for the baby. She cooked the evening meal, after scurrying down the narrow, muddy alleyways of the markets for some fresh ingredients. She tossed and turned all night. The sounds of the barrio that she once found comforting now disturbed her. She slapped at mosquitoes and fashioned a makeshift protective covering for the baby out of an old sarong. Angela Joy slept soundly at *Lola's* side. She hadn't had the heart to say no to the old lady, and Angela Joy was quite contented after being petted and rocked to sleep by her great-grandmother.

They broke their fast in the courtyard, eating fried eggs and sticky rice. Esme and Olina did the laundry while *Lola* played a dandling rhyme with the child. She watched while the old woman bounced Angela's feet up and down in time to the beat. The baby crowed and gurgled happily.

Corky came to hang about the bamboo bench in the courtyard, drinking San Miguel and gossiping with the women of the barrio who gathered to see the child.

"She's a beauty, just like her mother, and big like the father!"

Esmirada watched as the oldest of the women massaged the baby with vinegar to reduce the heat. The ancient customs irritated her, as did the flies, smell and filth of the barrio. She felt ashamed, seeing it now, imagining what it would have been like through Timothy's eyes.

She spent the day seeing to her grandmother's medical needs, replenishing supplies, cleaning and cooking. Late in the afternoon she took the baby to the church under the old mango tree to visit the Sisters and children at the orphanage. They welcomed her back warmly, cooing over the child, and extending their deepest condolences on Timothy's demise. *Lola* had begged her not to take the baby to the rubbish dump, but Esme figured it could be no worse than the disease in the barrio. She desperately wanted Angelika and Joe to see Timothy's child.

As she took the winding road, Esme could see the changes that had taken place. The road had been ploughed and cemented over, leaving a drain either side to prevent flooding. Timothy's vision, with the aid of the church, had taken on a life of its own. The school was much larger than she had imagined, and within the playground, attached to the rear, was a small wading pool full of happy and laughing children. Besides the school there was also a day care run by church volunteers and mothers.

Angelika ran the school and a Sister of the Church ran the day care. Joe Miller, along with the local activists, had taken on the task to fulfil and improve on the original plan after Timothy's death. Esmirada tried to control her tears when Joe and Angelika approached. She passed the baby into Angelika's arms and Joe hugged her to him. She had not seen him since Timothy's funeral. He took her by the arm and led her down to the cement school; above the door on a wooden plaque with gold lettering were the words 'Waldon Oasis' and then a smaller plaque dedicating the school and day care to 'Timothy and the Tabernacle of Hope Church'.

♦♦♦♦♦♦

It was as though *Lola* had waited, waited for Esmirada and her child's return. On the fifth night after they had come home, *Lola* enjoyed a meal of noodles and fried pork rinds, held the child in her arms, gave Esmirada some superstitious advice about bringing up children and then went to bed and died.

No one, not even her daughter Olina, knew how old the woman was. Esmirada found it hard to cry. After Timothy's death, *Lola's* seemed a blessing. Olina cried for both of them, keening night and day, hunkered in the corner like an abandoned child.

Manny and Esmirada were left to arrange *Lola's* final farewell. It was all done quickly as she decayed rapidly once she had gone. Her ancient face, collapsed and waxen, peeked out from her coffin. The yellow and black banner was hung in the window of the *sari sari*, and the old men and women came. They piled into the small room two by two, praying and paying their last respects to the woman most had known all their lives. They sat jabbering in the courtyard, playing cards, eating and drinking faster than Rosa and Esmirada could keep the food coming. Olina was useless. She continued her weeping in the corner. Manny tried to take her to Rosa's house to allow *Lola's* soul to find some peace.

Esmirada took Angela Joy from the wake to stay with the Sisters at the orphanage until after the funeral. She remembered her promise to Timothy and didn't want the child involved in the ritual. She did, however, remember to cut the rosary to break the cycle of death and allowed Manny to pass Angelina Joy once over the body. Finally, after a respectful number of days mourning, they laid her to rest in a decent grave next to Boboy.

The courtyard gradually emptied with a few old women and men remaining to play cards and gossip. Esmirada reopened the store and Olina took to her straw pallet. Manny did some repair work about the house before taking off to the coast with Ricardo to celebrate the birth of his fifth child, a boy!

During the following month, Esme drew great comfort from Joe. He was solicitous and sympathetic, and told her long, colourful stories of his and

284

Timothy's time at College. He was playful and loving with Angela Joy and Esmirada was grateful for his care and attention, but when she saw the greedy glint in Corky's eyes and the knowing smirk on Rosa's face, she put an end to it. She wouldn't allow them to exploit Joe as they had done Timothy.

She was able to care financially for Olina and was only too happy to help Manny with Carlo. Timothy had made provisions in his will for the education of Ricardo and Perpetua's family, but from now on no more handouts for Rosa and Corky. They had their pigs and lime trees and were still collecting exorbitant rent from the dwellers in the slum. They had done well enough out of her marriage to Timothy, and should be grateful.

As her visit came to an end, she found them sulky and resentful. She was eager to get back to her life in Singapore. She was satisfied that she had broken the cycle of poverty she had been born into. She wanted nothing more than to carry on the work she and Timothy had started. Her plans for Angela Joy were quite grandiose compared with her humble beginnings. She'd promised Timothy she would be educated as a Christian without the suffocating caul of superstition she had been born into. One day she planned to take her home to Timothy's birthplace. She was, after all, part American.

As the month came to a close and the monsoon season approached, she said goodbye to her mother. She didn't linger in case she weakened and changed her mind. She visited Angelika, taking one last look at the wording above the door to the schoolhouse. Timothy would have been pleased! She went back to Boboy and *Lola's* grave and said goodbye.

Joe came to see them off at the airport. Angela Joy held out her arms to him and he took her and kissed her tenderly on top of her glossy head. Their eyes met and he held her hand longer than necessary. Esme knew once his work was finished here, he would come to take up a position at the church in Singapore. Joe wouldn't push her, he knew she wasn't ready; it was too soon. She was still very much in love with Timothy and his memory, but then Joe was a patient man and Esmirada was worth waiting for.

Chapter Thirty-Six
Hope

Summer came suddenly to the British Isles. Lucy's small garden had become overgrown and leggy and Cameron was finally into delayed intensification treatment! She didn't want to get her hopes up, but it seemed the bad days were long past him. He had finished another course of Vincristine and Decadron and all he suffered with was constipation.

He and Holly were content to play in the garden each day and carry on with their ongoing project, a cubby house in the old hawthorn tree. Most of their friends had gone abroad for summer, but they were happy just to be together at home. They still had the inevitable trips to London for blood tests and follow up visits with Petra. Lucy tried to inject a bit of fun into the trips by visiting gardens, museums and even a show, with dinner at Hard Rock Café afterward. She spent more time with Holly, cooking, reading and teaching her to knit and crochet. She was knitting a multi-coloured scarf for Cam, which kept shrinking and stretching, depending on the dropped stitches, as the days went on.

A bird had built its nest in the geraniums that were blooming on the windowsill, and the children watched their progress from afar. They were delighted to find, at first, two eggs, and then two naked pink birds one morning. Since then they had watched as the mother returned each day with food to fill the ever-demanding beaks. It had been ten days now and the chicks were covered with feathers and growing rapidly.

Her little garden had flourished despite being neglected for so long. It had a wonderful riotous feel with flowers tumbling from walls and pots. The lavender along the borders had attracted all kinds of butterflies, and the fruity fragrance of her rambling rose was home to numerous gnats and bees. Sebastian had given Cam a book on birds and he spent the early mornings and late evenings bird watching. So far he had identified quails, cuckoos, larks and the little thrush that was nesting in the geraniums.

Laura and Hamish had left for summer in the south of France. The antique shop was closed for a week until Sebastian returned from Geneva. He had agreed to run things while overseeing the refurbishment of his own shop during the summer months. Lucy saw him from time to time, mostly in town or at Sunday lunch. He was always polite but guarded and cold; she knew she had hurt him badly.

The sky remained a milky blue late into the evening. Lucy had cooked chicken on the small barbecue in the courtyard and they sat at the trestle table beneath the hawthorn tree to eat. She'd started reading 'The Lion The Witch and The Wardrobe' in instalments each night until they fell asleep, and then she would take her wine and sit in the courtyard thinking of Alex. She'd heard nothing from him since seeing him at the hospital. The children had received cards and gifts, but nothing came for her. She knew from reading the latest Art News that his exhibition was a sell out, and that he had returned triumphantly to Australia with numerous coveted prizes.

The fickle weather changed and they had a week of slate-grey storm clouds hanging low on the horizon, finally evolving into rain and fog. Cam was sick again and didn't eat for days. The weather affected his progress. Everything was grey, nothing but grey, including Lucy's state of mind.

The first fine day after weeks of bad weather, Lucy took them down to the meadow to hunt bugs. A family of ducks lived in a dark pond near a copse of beeches. The three sat beneath the trees, lifting their faces to the filtered sun while they ate their sandwiches. Holly went pond dipping, and disappeared to eat blackberries from the hedgerows while Cam fed the ducks the leftover crusts from their sandwiches. They took the long way home through a woodland, the crushed camomile beneath their feet giving off a delicious scent.

As they approached the house, Lucy noticed a strange car in the drive. They rounded the corner and there, sitting in the late afternoon sunshine, was Alex! Holly and Cam ran to him, giving Lucy time to slow her racing heart.

Alex had rented a bed and breakfast not far from Manor Farm for the summer.

"I need a change of scene, I plan to do some sketching around Devon and Cornwall. I've just about exhausted my inspiration for the moment in Australia. You remember I told you about Liam and his girlfriend Spanky?" He said this with a hint of mischief in his eyes, and watched her closely for her reaction.

"Yes, of course!"

"Well, they are going to look after my place for the winter."

Lucy couldn't stop smiling. She felt idiotic, but having him here now and for the summer was just too unbelievable. Cam and Holly started talking at once, telling him about their day, and the thrush that was nesting in the garden. Holly had her knitting out, and Cam was showing him a kite he'd made yesterday. Lucy held up her hands.

"One at a time. Let poor Alex catch his breath! There'll be plenty of time for 'show and tell' over dinner. You will stay for dinner, won't you? I'm poaching a whole salmon with garlic mayonnaise."

The warm night air was scented with the heady aroma of profusely blooming stocks as they ate at the trestle table. Lucy had made a salad of lettuce, tomatoes and cucumber to go with the salmon. Earlier in the afternoon Alex had sat at her kitchen bench and watched her as she made a blackberry pie, meticulously plaiting the pastry. Holly went to bed early with a tummy ache from all the blackberries she had eaten in the fields. Cam had taken his medication and was running around the garden trying to catch fireflies, while she and Alex lingered over white wine.

"He looks good, Lucy. All his hair has grown back and it's a different colour!"

It was true. After the last bout of chemotherapy, Cam's hair had grown back rapidly, darker and thicker than before. He had lost the pudginess from the steroids after not eating for a week, and had some colour in his face from his days in the sun. Alex cleared the table and washed up while she read the latest instalment of the happenings in 'Narnia' to the children.

As she came back downstairs, she paused on the landing and listened. She could hear him in the kitchen. Leaning forward, she watched him. A soft yellow glow illuminated his silver-threaded hair. He opened a bottle of red wine and poured two glasses, placing them carefully on a tray. He turned out the light and made his way out of the French doors into the courtyard. She gave herself a cursory glance in the hall mirror, smoothed back her hair and went to join him in the garden. They sat silently, savouring the cool night air. She glanced at his strong profile and his hand brushed against hers. She could feel the warmth radiating from his body.

She put down her wine and turned toward him. "Stay, Alex, don't leave us again. I want you to stay for the summer!"

He traced her cheek with his fingers. "Are you sure, Lucy?"

She swallowed hard and took his face in her hands, kissing him, searching for his tongue, tasting the ripe sweetness of his mouth. She pulled away, breathless. He smiled and then left the soft imprint of his mouth at the notch of her throat, his fingers in her hair.

"I'm sure, Alex!"

Lucy's body trembled as his hands brushed over her damp skin, removing her clothes. The moonlight streamed through the window, turning her breasts milky-white as he bent to kiss them. Her hands swam over his body. His chest and back were strong and well defined. She straddled him, easing herself down; she was soft and moist as he took hold of her hips, clasping her to him. She could feel his breath on her face as he whispered to her. All through the night his arm lay lightly across her soft plump belly, his body cupping hers, their fingers entwined.

She woke in the morning with the sun on her face. Alex had gone. A tangle of sheets where he had slept was damp with his sweat. She took her chenille gown and covered herself. Looking down into the garden, she could see the children in the hawthorn tree. She descended the stairs and could hear him in the kitchen preparing breakfast. She paused on the last step and sat down hard. An unfamiliar feeling washed over her, leaving her helpless. Then she remembered what it was - happiness!

The temperature continued to climb, and the children took to cavorting in the garden under the hose. The cubby house was finally finished and the birds left their nest. Alex spent his days sketching, and taking long field trips into the woods, creating treasure hunts for the children. Lucy dusted off her sketchbook and was blissfully painting landscapes and flowers. They ate outdoors every day. Lucy would do lunch and Alex dinner. He loved to barbecue, and surprised Lucy with the purchase of a full-sized gas model, which took up a great deal of her small courtyard. After dinner each evening the children ran wild about the garden, while he and Lucy sipped wine in the fading light.

They took day trips, never straying too far; Cam was still going regularly to London for blood work and adjustments to his protocol. Petra was pleased with his progress. If his counts continued to do well, she planned to start him on maintenance therapy, which would consist of daily low-dose chemo for another two to three years, killing any remaining cancer cells. Cam would tolerate this medication much better, as it was less toxic than the consolidation therapy. Lucy dared not hope; she took one day at a time. After being buffeted by his illness for so long, hope was a thing of the past. Now that Alex was here, she had a renewed appreciation for life, and considered each day precious. She wouldn't allow herself to think beyond summer!

Alex took them to Cornwall for a mini holiday. He booked a charming hotel in Fowey, a graceful old mansion that looked out to sea. He and Lucy made exhausting love in a huge wooden bed, facing a picture window with views across the estuary. Each day the children packed their buckets and spades, and took a picnic lunch to spend the day lazing about on the creamy sands of the beaches. Alex and Cam decorated a wine bottle and put a message inside, casting it out to sea.

Lucy loved the rambling garden walks. On one occasion she stopped to sketch a bank of phlox. She looked up to find Alex watching her with a look of pure longing on his face. She took his hand in hers and reached up and kissed him, aware that the children were watching. Afterward they picnicked with a ploughman's lunch and prawn sandwiches in the shade of a huge rhododendron. She and Alex dozed side-by-side, touching, while Holly and Cam discovered the children's maze.

On the last day Lucy drove them all south to the cliff tops of Porthcurno. She had brought her favourite crab and mayonnaise salad and a bottle of wine for lunch. They feasted with the vast blue sea before them, and then walked around the headland to Minack after a siesta. Alex bought tickets to the open-air theatre, while Lucy headed to the ice-cream shop. With vanilla ice cream dripping down their hands, they sat on the rock wall, taking in the matinee of Romeo and Juliet, the cliff face, blue sky and ocean as a backdrop.

By the end of summer they had become a family. Holly and Cameron had grown used to the displays of affection between Alex and Lucy. They accepted without comment that Alex slept in their mother's bed, and didn't come down until late in the mornings. Holly took on the task of making breakfast, having finally reverted to her sunny disposition.

Cameron continued to do well. His blood and lumbar aspirations showed he was in remission; both Petra and Angus were thrilled to start him on his maintenance therapy. Lucy called Alex from the hospital, giving him the good news.

"Oh, Alex, there is reason to hope after all!" she sobbed over the phone to him.

Alex organised a party for their homecoming, with all of Cam's favourite food. Holly made a banner saying, 'Cameron Leadbitter, Our Hero!' That night they laughed and danced, and the children put on a show for them, staying up well past their bedtime.

Lucy could feel the welcome weight of Alex's body upon her breast. His thick hair hung down, creating a curtain about his face. Lazily they made love for the second time that night. They lay together, brow to brow, whispering. He kissed her fingers one by one as she pushed back his hair.

"Should I cut it? Your friends look at me strangely. That long-haired artist from Australia!"

She laughed and playfully licked the shell of his ear, sucking noisily on his lobe.

"Don't you dare, it's so sexy. You're beautiful, Alex. I love you! Promise you'll never change!"

Suddenly he held her from him, gazing at her in the wavering candlelight. What had she done? She was too impulsive! Oh fuck; too late, she had said it! It felt so good to say it at last. She had wanted to tell him how much she loved him for so long, but was waiting for him to say it first.

He sat back on his haunches and took her hands in his. "Lucy, I have wanted to hear you say you love me ever since that very first kiss! I want to marry you; I want us to be a family. Come home with me, you don't belong here."

Lucy leant into his hard body and started to cry. He kissed her wet lips, waiting for her to stop sniffling and catch her breath.

"I want to marry you. Yes, yes I do, Alex! But Cameron, what about his treatment? Angus and Petra have saved his life."

She started to shiver; he closed the open window, and went to get her wrap, placing it about her bare shoulders.

"Listen to me, Lucy. I've looked into this carefully, knowing that Cameron must come before anything else. There's a very good children's hospital in Brisbane with excellent doctors. In fact I have spoken to Petra and she's recommended a colleague of hers. She even went so far as to say that the winters here are too harsh on Cameron and she's worried he might regress."

Lucy bit the inside of her cheek, thinking about the bitterly cold months ahead.

"We can marry in Singapore, in Amber's garden! Would September be too soon?"

She laughed and kissed him. His eyes were bright with unshed tears.

"Yes. A marriage in Singapore, Amber would love that! But I need a bit of time. I'll have to talk to Cameron and Holly and there's the house, and oh God, a thousand and one things to think of!"

She fell back on the pillows.

291

"Let's sleep. We can talk it over in the morning. I should have waited, but I am running out of time."

They lay entwined, Lucy's mind racing as fast as Alex's heart.

Chapter Thirty-Seven
Moving On

The persistent ringing of the phone in the early hours of the morning roused Esmirada from a sound sleep. She dreaded answering it, fearing bad news. As she picked up the receiver, she prepared for the worst, expecting it to be Rosa. Instead it was a Filipina named Ventura Binay, whose family were away. Ventura was alone in the house with two ageing cats and had just had word that her mother had died. She was having trouble locating her ma'am and needed Esme's comfort and help.

Esme felt guilty when she realised it wasn't Rosa. She spoke quietly so as not to wake Mary and Angela Joy. The baby was sleeping with Mary in the adjoining room, a habit that had started when Esme returned from the Philippines, after letting her sleep with *Lola*. The child was running about now, and a handful to watch. Mary needed her rest.

Esme padded to the kitchen and made a cup of cocoa and some kaya toast. She sat silently, waiting for the dawn, thinking of her mother, passing the time until Mary woke. The family Ventura worked for had two children who attended the German School. Esme called and found they were staying with friends while their parents were in Europe. Ventura had been told none of this, nor had she been given any emergency numbers. Ventura's mother had died of a stroke after a fall; she was only forty years old with five small children. Ventura's father had left and gone to sea after the last child was born and she had not seen or heard from him since. Ventura, the eldest, was the sole breadwinner. Her mother brought in a few pesos from the sewing she did for the more affluent of the village, but that all went toward food for the children.

Esme located the maid's employer and called Italy in the early hours of the morning. She got a frosty reception.

293

"How can that be? Ventura's mother is a young woman. She spoke to her only ten days ago. Are you sure this is not a ruse for a quick holiday home?"

Esme tightened her grip on the phone. "No, ma'am, I spoke with Ventura's aunty myself. Ventura's mother died of a stroke after a fall. The family want her home to organise the funeral. You need to buy her a ticket to the Philippines so she can lay her mother to rest."

The woman was still unconvinced but agreed to remit some money and make the call to organise the flight.

Esme loved her work at the Serenity Centre but she missed having Timothy to share her frustrations. She thought about Ventura and the dashed dreams of her family, and the homecoming she would receive after a three-hour flight and another four by bus to her village. She thought too about the thousands of maids who work endlessly to look after the elderly, and take care of everything from feeding the children to clearing the garbage. Invisible, menial workers, why couldn't they be treated with a little compassion and respect? She only wished Timothy was here to answer her questions. Ventura Binay had not seen her mother in four years and now they would never see each other again.

After a long day at the Centre, Esmirada caught the bus home, bringing with her fresh meat and chicken from the markets. Mary deserved a good dinner. Joe was coming to visit and she was looking forward to holding her child after so many hours apart. She decided she would call Rosa and see how Olina was. Before she reached home she went to the church and knelt before the statue of the Virgin. Fingering the gold cross at her throat, she sent up a silent prayer to Timothy for watching over her and guiding her through each day. She asked him for inspiration to find the right words of comfort and hope for Lucy.

Timothy's favourite Chinese proverb came to mind. *If you keep a green bough in your heart, the singing bird will come.* Timothy was always right.

◆ ◆ ◆ ◆ ◆ ◆

The echo of Lucy's footsteps through the empty house reverberated in her heart. The last of the furniture had gone. The laughing Budda had been wrapped in bubble wrap and then in corrugated cardboard, wiping the smile from his face. It broke her heart but she couldn't take everything. It seemed with each move her life was pared down even more. She stood in the kitchen, looking out of the French doors to the small patio beyond. The hydrangeas were in bloom, and the last of the scarlet dahlias dipped their heads as if to say goodbye. The cubby stood forlorn, empty, too, of its occupants. She walked through to her bedroom-cum-studio. It was, as always, suffused with light.

Lucy thought after what she had been through this last year she could deal with anything, but saying goodbye to Hamish and Laura had torn her apart. They had given her a farewell party in the infamous conservatory with buckets of champagne, red wine and a groaning board of delicious things to eat. All her friends had been invited. Some were easier to say goodbye to than others. She had shared a lot of raw moments and had depended on them heavily in the last year. The outpouring of love and support had been overwhelming. Her friends had provided her comfort and sustenance. Would she find that in her new home? It didn't matter as long as she had Alex and the children. Hamish had been a saint, sharing Laura with her at all times of the night and day; they promised to come to visit, unable to make the wedding. Still she didn't know when she would be back again.

Alex had been very understanding, giving her more time to sort herself out. It had taken longer than she had anticipated establishing Cam's routine, and transferring his notes and treatment to the doctor in Brisbane. Summer and autumn had come and gone before she was ready to make the move. Instead of a September wedding, it would now be a November wedding.

She wandered out into the garden and looked up at the house full of memories. The late afternoon sun burnished the windows. In this house her strengths and weakness had been exposed. She had suffered the pain, depression and fear of Cam's illness as well as the fragility and beauty of life. After finding Alex once more and discovering a summer full of love, they had become a family. Alex offered them a new beginning. It was time to move on.

◆◆◆◆◆◆

To dilute the emptiness he felt back home without Lucy and the children, Alex threw himself into his work. He was a finalist in the Archibald Portrait Prize, but didn't win. He picked up the paper that morning while he sipped his coffee on his back deck, and read with interest about the controversy that embroiled the winner and runner up. Nit-picking about the chosen media, some people were bad-losers! He turned the pages listlessly as the sun rose higher over his shoulder, warming his bare skin. It was going to be another scorcher. The phone rang and he picked it up, knowing it would be Dorté. She'd handled their break up badly at first, throwing things, yelling, screaming and calling with abuse at all times of the day and night. Eventually she had settled. She knew he was a money-spinner for her gallery, and she couldn't do without him. They had an exhibit organised for October in New York at the Ward gallery, and he was appearing in the Singapore Art Expo early next year. He also had a commission on the go for the Legends Hotel in Shanghai.

Apart from painting, he had pulled the house apart, cleaning and culling, getting rid of old furniture and having it painted and redecorated. He personally chose the décor for Cameron and Holly's room, and had transformed the guest room into a sunny studio for Lucy. The room at the end of the hall he had left empty. He planned perhaps a study or a baby's room. He would wait and talk to Lucy about that!

He walked down the end of the garden to the basketball ring and threw a few baskets, just to keep in practice for when his son arrived. Yesterday he had the piano tuner in and later today the new car would be delivered. A Land Cruiser big enough to take a growing family and perhaps a small dog!

The only habit he may have to curb was walking around the house naked. That he could do, but the kids would have to get used to him painting in the nude, some things never change. He whistled as he took the steps two at a time, and went inside to his office to complete the paperwork for their wedding in Singapore.

Chapter Thirty-Eight
Tempus Fugit

Lucy was so nervous that she had been on and off the toilet five times in the last hour. Amber helped her with the flowers for her hair. Her hands shook as she poured two glasses of champagne. She was hung over from last night. Amber had organised a girls' night out and they had gone pub crawling, ending up at 'Anywhere' Bar at five in the morning, dancing with Julian, the transvestite singer. The last two weeks had been full of parties by the pool, dinner out, and late nights, but Lucy had never looked or felt better.

The weekend she arrived, Amber whisked her off for a spa experience on a nearby island where they spent hours being draped in seaweed, scrubbed with mud, pummelled and polished. It had paid off. Lucy shone with an inner glow. She had spent all afternoon yesterday at the hairdressers and had a pedicure and manicure. Brian and the boys had given Alex the pre-wedding treatment. They played golf and had a buck's night that ended with Alex walking home naked, dragging a ball and chain. In the early hours of the morning, the police picked him up, covered him and brought him home, dropping him off outside the front gate. He was so drunk that he tried to pay them for their services!

Amber stood back and took a deep breath. "You look stunning!"

Lucy wore a long ivory lace skirt with a plain silk camisole and jacket. Her newly darkened hair was piled on top of her head with a spray of stephanotis. She looked at herself in the mirror, and Amber, who was dressed in Thai-silk in a soft shade of lavender, came and stood by her side. Lucy kissed her with gratitude, not trusting herself to speak.

Footsteps thundered down the wooden hallway, and Holly burst through the doors in a flourish of diaphanous white tulle, a halo of pale roses and baby breath crowning her blonde curls.

"Mamma, come quick and see Cam, Alex bought him a real dinner jacket!"

Cameron came into the room shyly; he was immaculate in a black tie and jacket that Alex had bought for him in New York. He knew how handsome he looked; he couldn't stop admiring himself in the mirror.

Lucy gazed out onto the broad expanse of garden from the louvered windows; wooden flooring and a silk marquee concealed the lawn. Ten tables were in place, decorated in white silk, the centrepieces were pots of pale pink and white peonies with trailing ivy. The guests, dressed in summery jewel colours, gathered at the cabana for canapés and champagne, waiting for the bride. More champagne cooled in ice buckets and the caterers were swarming out the back in the kitchen under Honeyko's supervision.

Lucy had asked Amber and Esmirada to be her witnesses. She had gone to visit Esme at Mary's terrace, finding a beautiful toddler, tall for her age, riding about the small courtyard on a trike. Esmirada had blossomed into a very handsome woman. Proudly she took Lucy on a tour of the Serenity Centre where the maids were at work on computers, cutting each other's hair, dressmaking, cooking or improving their English. Lucy was impressed with all that Esmirada had achieved, and the refuge Lucy and Timothy had created for the girls.

Esmirada talked quickly, outlining new plans, "Joe and I have been given a grant by the government to include foreign workers in our scheme. They can come here if they have a problem, but mainly we want them to come to better themselves! We're always looking for volunteers, we never seem to have enough; although the church elders are wonderful, and spend many hours working here, as well as giving their precious time to the church."

She confided in Lucy that Joe had asked her to marry him when her mourning period was over.

"He'll never replace Timothy in my heart, but he's a good man and he loves Angela Joy and me very much. Mary has given her blessing and so have Joyner and Harold. It was important to me that they approve of Joe. I think Harold thinks it's too soon, but having spoken to Joe, he agreed next April would be decent. Timothy will be gone a year next month."

Tears sprang to Esmirada's heavily lashed eyes, and Lucy took the small woman by the shoulders and held her close, comforting her.

During all Lucy's tumultuous emotional journey, Esmirada too was suffering, but she never had a word of self-pity. All her prayers and letters of encouragement were for Lucy and Cameron. Lucy wanted in some way to help her with the Serenity Centre, as a way of saying thank you for her support and comfort.

Over dinner that evening she spoke to Alex, "I want to raise some money for Esmirada, how about we auction some of my paintings?"

Alex agreed, "We could have a cocktail reception and I'll donate some of my works as well. Amber will know the 'A' list of Singapore. All the proceeds will go to the Centre. We should do one for the Children's Leukaemia Foundation as well. What do you think?"

Lucy gazed across the table at him; he had the look of an eager child. He was a gift and she thanked God for letting him back into her life when she despaired she had lost him forever!

It had rained heavily the morning of the wedding, leaving the vegetation spangled and fresh. A soft breeze wafted in and around the clusters of bamboo and travellers' palms. Alex was already standing under the creeper-covered arbour waiting for her, resplendent in his black evening jacket and bow tie. They hadn't slept together last night and she had missed him. This morning over breakfast he had presented her with a diamond ring. She'd protested saying she hadn't wanted a engagement ring, but when he placed it on her finger, she gave in and started to cry, throwing her arms about his neck, kissing his face repeatedly.

Amber, Brian, Esme and Joe joined her at the bottom of the staircase. Esmirada was wearing her Filipino national dress and she and Joe together made a very handsome couple. He was different to Timothy, less portly, with a thick thatch of reddish hair and good strong square jaw. Lucy thought of the lovely babies they would make.

The music started, giving the guests time to take their places. Lucy drew the children to her and knelt in front of them, taking their hands.

"I want to tell you both how much Alex and I love you! You've made me so proud, I promise we are going to be a really happy family." Her tears threatened and she sniffed noisily.

"We know, Mum, Alex has already told us how much we'll love Australia. Did you know he has a piano for me, and a basketball ring for Cam? And our very own rooms."

Lucy looked at them, standing there, trying not to fidget in their hot clothes. They deserved to be happy; they'd been through so much already in their young lives.

She composed herself, listening for the bridal march, and together they walked down the dappled jungle path, past the grinning guests to Alex, standing with the Justice of Peace under the arbour in the shade of the Tembusu tree.

Lucy stood, trembling, by his side. He mouthed the words, 'I love you' and she picked up his hand and kissed it. The Justice of Peace, an elderly Chinese gentlemen with thick glasses, was very solemn during the ceremony, but as soon as he announced them 'man and wife' the assembled guests erupted and cheered, whistling and clapping their hands. The little gentleman was stunned, and even more so when the music suddenly burst in with a loud 'Congratulations' sung by Cliff Richard. Everyone, including Lucy and Alex, burst into laughter. She threw her arms about his neck and kissed him passionately, to more cheers. The ceremony over, the celebrations began!

In the late afternoon as the guests began to disperse, she walked with Esmirada through the hidden garden fence into the compound of their old home. The garden was lush with overgrown creepers and swaying sealing wax palms. The Balinese stone lanterns were covered in moss and the Japanese urns had taken on a patina of verdigris. The kitchen and maid's quarters were shaded by a cascading passionfruit vine, which Esmirada had planted years before. She disappeared around the back to see if her lime tree had flourished. Lucy gazed up at the white stucco of the house, blinding in the late afternoon sun, remembering the first time she had seen it. The pool had been enlarged and was surrounded by waxy pink ginger flowers. She remembered, too, the sunset cocktail parties, the clink of ice and the sound of the children's laughter as they played in the pool. Picturing her small studio in the shade of the bamboo blinds on the veranda, she could close her eyes now and smell the paints and the texture of the heavy paper under her fingers.

A kingfisher startled her as it swooped from the frangipani tree into the pool. She watched Esme as she picked her way across the grass, carrying a bounty of limes.

"I don't think they'll mind if I pick a few."

Lucy sat on the bench and told Esme of her and Alex's plan to raise money for the Centre. He had an exhibit in Singapore in the New Year, and the timing would be perfect for them to return.

"Amber is already planning lists and preparing invitations. It should be a huge success."

"Oh thank you, ma'am Lucy. How can Joe and I ever repay you for your kindness!"

"You don't have to, Esme. You've done so much for me over the years, I don't think you realise how much. In your own quiet way you have helped me more than any close friend or family ever could. It's I who could never repay you!"

The laughing thrushes grew excited in the Tembusu tree as the sun set in the west. She could hear Alex calling her to say goodbye to their guests. She passed by the sundial she had placed there the year she arrived. It, too, was covered in a layer of verdant moss: *Tempus Fugit*. Time flies. She would never forget. Once she had a house on the edge of the jungle and there she met a woman called Esmirada who enriched her life in so many ways.

"Ang Hindi marunong lumingon sa pinanggalingan ay hindi makakarating sa pinaroroonan."

"Those who don't know how to look back will not arrive at the place they want to go."